The Magic Fairy Rose from Scotland to America then Vermont

BOOK III

A.E. Fortin

THE MAGIC FAIRY ROSE FROM SCOTLAND TO AMERICA THEN VERMONT

ISBN (Paperback): 979-8-89672-231-1
ISBN (Hardback): 979-8-89672-232-8
ISBN (Ebook): 979-8-89672-233-5

PROMINENT
BOOKS
EDGE

5830 E 2nd St, Ste 7000 #9983
Casper, WY 82609
USA

CONTENTS

A Hundred Years Have Passed

MARCOS HAD IT with everything, time was going too slowly. He knew that two hundred years had to pass, before his father let him on earth. Lucifer had let his son watch what was happening there in Scotland. Marcos had men in Scotland trying to stir up trouble. How he laughed when he heard the people of Scotland couldn't worship their own religion. "There always crying about their own religion or this is my land. My men have been working overtime, it's about time they get these crybabies out of here. Hasn't it been long enough that they have been fighting these wars over religion or land? Here it is the 18th century. I had to wait until two hundred years went by. I see the MacGregor's are still in the Highlands."

The Head Demon

Then he had a report from the head demon on earth. "Sire, here on earth the year is 1850. Currently there are 600,000 Scotsmen who have left their homes. Sire, the Scots spoke out. Here is what they had said."

Marcos laughed when he heard the voices of the people. *"The Episcopal Religion is not Ours. Our land and way of life ye have wiped out."*

It had taken a long time to get them to leave Scotland. "Sire, we found a way to do property transactions, it made it easier to take the clergyman land from them. Those farmers didn't bring in enough money to pay our rich landowners. They decided to remove the farmers. They replace farms with cattle or sheep. We had to bring in soldiers, they had ordered to remove any recognition of Christian denominations. As well as handicapping, non-Anglicans. The English liquefy the Catholics and Calvinists religion, by revoked religious liberties. The Treaty of Limerick forbade public worshipping. To be able to worship the Scots had to belong to an Episcopal church of England. Sire, you should have seen them.

Marcos laughed when he heard about the Scots. "Sire, they whined about the greedy landlords forcing them off their land. Soldiers follow the letter of the law; the orders were to put the Scots on ships. They forced them to immigrate to North America and Australasia. The Commonwealth and elsewhere in the UK. The Scots who left had skills we needed. They were the educated ones who had left, that was over half of the people of Scotland."

Note: "Without true guidance and history of the pass. How would anyone not make the same mistakes? Without knowledge, our ye not led like sheep?

Before leaving their homeland, they spoke these words. *"Us Scots they bought and sold us for English gold. No more…we Scotts will live the way we see fit. They took our land from us and forced us to leave our country. It's time to find another place to live."*

"Sire, Neil Heart's parents had just died. Before they did, they used white fire to destroy the land. We can see now that they used their blood, along with white fire.

"Sire, nothing will be able to grow from here on out. It will take someone of their blood line to get the land to grow again. They must have magic to do this. Besides that, as you can see the moon light is from the Magic Fairy Rose. The prophecy states: that a MacGregor will be taking the Magic Fairy Rose to America. If this is true Thomas and Eleanor will be meeting with Alex and Neil tonight."

Then Marcos yelled. *"Damn those, Hearts. Neil's parents were poison. It was you're knew man that did the deed. Tell him to try to kill Neil. The Hearts use magic on the land, even though we could get Neils blood. I have a feeling his blood won't work.*

"You are right Thomas and Eleanor will be coming to see Neil and Alex. If ye can kill Neil tonight. Be Aware his grandfather trained Neil. Let the new guy try to kill him. When he dies, I will give him to my father. I can't have men not listening to orders. Neil has taken demons down in the pass."

Marcos was angry. "The head of the Heart's knew he was poisoning them. Did he tell ye what he had done?

Sire, no he didn't tell me, one of the other men saw him coming back. He told him that he just took down the old man and wife it was the Heart's. That man came to me about this. It was too late for me to stop them. They did it right under our nose.

Marcos slammed his hand down. *"Who was watching the heart family? Tell me was it that knew guy. Keep an eye on him, I know he will mess up soon, I'll take care of him when he gets here. Leave the boy and his sister alone, let them go, I will be heading to the new world before long. I don't think you could manage the two men. They would take you down before you could even get close to them. Don't tell any of the men yet, that Neil knows when demons are around. Specially don't let the new guy know that. The Heart's and MacGregor men has strong magic. Ye must beware of the magic roses. Those roses protect the MacGregor's land. If the new man can take Neil down, that's a win in my book. I don't think he can.*

"After the new man is dead. Let them go. Now don't even try to take them down with taxes. The roses, make sure they have money to pay the taxes on the land. Do what you can, let me know what you find out. You can try ones there in the new world to stop them. Not now."

A Great Amount left Scotland

Throughout time men went to war over religion. In the 17th century, 400,000 Scotts started leaving Scotland. It had carryover until 1850. Over 600,000 Scotsmen left their homes. They told the Scots Ye could not worship their own religion. These days felt as if darkness had fallen over Scotland. Our land and way of life are wiped out. The English liquefy the Catholics and Calvinists religion, by revoked religious liberties. The Treaty of Limerick forbade public worshipping. To be able to worship, Scots had to belong to the Episcopal church of England.

CHAPTER ONE

A Visit from Thomas and Eleanor

HIGH IN THE heavens Thomas and Eleanor watched over their family. *"My love it's beginning again. Do ye think it's time, to pay our family a visit."*

Thomas looked at his wife and spoke. *"Aye…, ye take Alex. I don't think Neil will be good company after he gets a visit from his mother."*

Eleanor nodded her head. *"That poor boy he loves his father and mother. If I know Alex, he will be at the roses. I know he is waiting for Neil. Dear do ye know who poison the Heart's."*

Thomas looked at his wife. *"Aye…, it's a new man. He took it upon himself to do so. The poison works slowly. After it happen, they knew he was a want to be a demon."*

With the soldiers overrunning the Highland's. Alex's father thought to remind his younger son, of the story passed down from father to son. "Son, ye know the story that Meghalaya told Thomas?"

Alex looked at his father then spoke. "Aye, dad she said that a MacGregor will take the roses to America. Thomas believed in what

Meghalaya had told him. I was talking to Neil about this. I know that I'm the one to leave Scotland, Ginger is now in America. The rose dropped into my hand for her. Dad, I remember a story about a door that went to the land of the Fairies. Eleanor found out that the door in the castle can take us to the new world. We can use our magic to change the place where we can go."

His father smiled at his son. "So ye been looking for other ways to get to America. Does Neil want to go?"

Alex shook his head yes. "Aye…, Dad there is one thing is holding him back. He will not leave his parents. The soldiers will be here next week. If there not gone, they would throw Neil's parents off the land with nothing.

His father bent his head. Then he spoke. "Aye, I know all about this son. I have asked the Hearts to stay with us; we would build a place for them. Neil's father told me that they had made other plans. Son for a long time the Hearts family and MacGregor family have had magic. Marcos had his men to try to kill all the roses. He was hoping to kill both magics. After that had happened, they thought best not to use their magic. The demons here on earth has been trying to change Scotland."

His father then looked at his son. He spoke. "It's time ye leave before the soldiers get to the SHearts land. I believe, the Hearts are going to do something to their land tonight."

Alex looked at his father. "That makes sense, that's why his parents didn't go with them."

His father rested his hand on his shoulder. "Aye, I thought the same thing. The cross and rose they wear, gives them their magic. The fairy magic knows when they should and shouldn't use their powers. For a long time, I haven't seen our mark or the Heart birth mark. Son our mark we can see it in the moonlight. If we were in trouble our magic is there to help us. That one book Marcos had messed up with, he didn't want ye to know about your grate grandfather. He made a mess of that book; there is nothing about the magic that the roses have.

"Your grandfather was a powerful Wizard the best swordsmen around. Men came to try to take his magic. They weren't as good in a sword fight; they were the ones to die. Their magic came to your grandfather, after all those fights were getting excessive. When his son created these roses, the power from all those men went to the roses.

"Marcos had mess with the history of Thomas and Eleanor. One day I found the doorway in the castle to a hidden lab. Your story starts tonight; this book can write itself it has magic. It was a spell that Thomas placed on this book. I see ye must have found that book to know of that door. Marcos rewrote the first book, but Eleanor found the book Thomas wrote. She had also found one of his grate grandfather's books.

"The story goes Thomas asked Father if he could bless them. Father had placed a cross around their necks. Eleanor was the one who convinced Father that the roses were good, not evil. On the day when all the vests had to get recharged. Father had the chance to pour holy water on the roses. It was our heavenly Father who sent a bright light to let him know the roses came from him. After those two rose petals placed over the cross. Thomas and his brother fought with The Lord's help.

"In the Highlands everyone had to wear a cross. In the battle Father Sinclair had placed a cross on Garret's chest with two rose petals. When Marcos was inside the locket, The Lord sent a beam of light to burn the body of Garret. It was the Lord who gave Garret a birth mark on his chest. All evil went to The Lord to be judge. Once again, Lucifer, Marcos's father pulled him down to hell."

Alex looked at his father. "Wait The Lord burn Garret's body. If The Lord burn his body what did Garret use."

His father had a big smile on his face. "Remember Garret was a teenager. When Thomas killed the demon after the three demons were gone there was two bodies. One was evil and the other was good. They used the evil body to trap Marcos.

Eleanor had produced a spell to protect Ronald and the men he fought with. She given him a heavenly light, inside one hole rose. Anyone he touched had that heavenly light. Those demons with Marcos couldn't get into their bodies. He always knows when a demon is around.

"The Lord imprinted them on every MacGregor, ye can only see it in the moon light. Every child was born with this mark on their chest. The day the Heart's adopted Garret; he made a spell that his children will wear the same birth mark as his.

"Garret had married a McGowan; her aunt was Eleanor's mother. Our great grandfather from the 15th century was a Wizard. He had married a Fairy; his wife gave him two sons. When the first born married the Fairy Princess, when she gave him two twin boys. He was the one to make Magic Roses. The two sons pledge their magic to the roses. That way all the MacGregors will have magic when they need it. When Garret came into the picture, he pledged his and his father's magic. His magic is in his birth mark. Just like the MacGregors, that's how Heart's gets their magic. These magic roses came from the valley of the Fairy's."

Alex looked at his father. "So, it was the son of the Wizard who married the Princess. He became King of the Fairies."

His father had stopped and scratched his head. "As ye know both boys had their mother and father's magic, they were born with it. Their father had fought men with strong magic.

"Marcos had heard the young men, and their father had magic. Power was always the reason he fought anyone with magic. That's why he challenges both men. They had to fight Marcos in the valley of the dead. Back then he had black magic and the demon that fought with him. Ronald had the two twins to fight with him in the valley of the dead.

"When the men died by their hands their magic goes to the one who killed them. Remember Marcos didn't have his magic anymore, he lost it to MacGregor's, he tried to get Garret's father's. Ye can't stab him in the back, Garret's magic he was born with it. When his father died the magic went to his son. Because his son had gone over to his father and took hold of his hand. Garret was a young man of ten. Marcos had a demon to take over his body.

*   *   *

"The Fairy's from the valley planted three rose bushes outside the waterfall. That's where Thomas had found them. In the next two hundred years the roses will travel to the new world. The castle door in the basement will take ye to your new home. Ye and Neil must take the roses to that place.

"Ye don't have to buy the land, Thomas took care of that. Before Garret died, he wanted everyone to forget about their magic. Even MacGregor's forgotten, the two families have strong magic from Garret's family also from our own. When ye go away ye will need your magic. Three more roses will go with ye.

"Ye must tell the story about Marcos that he was once a fairy. His father is Satan himself. In the 15th century he fought the two MacGregor twins. In the 17th century he fought Thomas's brother in the heavens with the two twins. I don't know when Marcos can come back to earth. So far, it's every two hundred years. But he has demons watching our family. There will be another Eleanor and Thomas. They will be name Ellen and Tom; Thomas had a dream about them. Ellen's magic is stronger than the first Eleanor. Tom will have all the skills that Thomas had, even more.

"Remember evil will be watching ye, your cross will tell ye when they are around. Ye do know when Garret gave his magic to the roses. There are three kinds of magic that protects our land and keeps us safe from evil. When ye were born, I knew ye were the ones to leave Scotland. The day ye told me that the rose dropped in your hand. I knew it was Ginger Ye, had gave the rose to. Ye told me that ye were all happy and scared at the same time. When she breathed in the scent of the rose did ye know what it meant?"

Alex smiled at his father. "Aye…, as I held her in my arms, I understood that she became my soul mate. Dad, don't worry, I will find Ginger once we get to America. Right now, I'm worried about Neil. He keeps having these feelings there is something wrong with his parents."

His father's face changed right off. "Neil has the right to be worried."

Alex looked into his father's eyes. "What's wrong with them?"

His father looked incredibly sad. "Now that Neil's sister is on her way to America. His father told me that his wife and he were dying."

Alex shook his head no. "Dad, dying from what?"

His father closed his eyes. "He didn't tell me. I believe they don't have time left. They used their magic to hide their sickness. What he did say, he was going to put a spell on the land. It will make the land useless to grow grass for sheep. No one will be able to use their land."

Alex took a breath to clear his mind. "Neil said he was going to come here to sleep. I think I'll sleep outside near the pond. There is magic in the air tonight. Do ye mine if I get a bottle of scotch?"

His father smiled and waved his hand. "I don't mine, I can feel the magic in the air. It could be coming from the roses. Neil will need more than one drink tonight. It's going to be a full moon with no clouds around. Aye, staying outside is a clever idea, it's warm in the house. What Neil's parents told me, ye better get the roses tonight. If they put a spell on the land, Neil should leave the Highland soon. The soldiers will think he was the one to put a spell on the land. They will say he killed his parents. Alex, I think ye should put a bubble around ye tonight. Make it so evil can't see what ye are doing."

Alex looked around. "I believe ye are right about that. Good night, dad."

His father went over to his son and gave the bottle to him. "May The Lord be with you tonight. Good night, my boy."

The ride to the ship

Neil Heart rode with his sister and newlywed husband. His sister was leaving Scotland for good. There wasn't anything there for her husband to make a living on. That's why her older brother rode with them. The soldiers are everywhere. Neil needed to know his sister made it to their ship. Aboard the ship her husband can keep her safe. His fighting skills were right up there with his own. Besides his sister has her magic, now that she has turned twenty-one. When she married, she gave her husband her cross and rose now he has her magic. At last, the three of them had found the location of the ship.

Tonight, would be a full moon, the temperature of the air was cool. The moonlight will make it much colder on the water. In town, there were soldiers everywhere. When the moon comes out, it will be high tide. Neil watched the ship as it sailed out of sight. He noticed that the moon was extra bright tonight. It made it safe to ride home late at night. As Neil rode, he noticed the trail of light was getting smaller and brighter than before. Why was the moonlight shining on him?

Neil spoke. "This can't be all moonlight; no this has to be magic."

*   *   *

Quickly he stopped his horse, the brilliant bright light made it extremely hard to see the trail. Suddenly, he heard his mother's voice. *"Neil, my only son. I hope ye know that your father and I love ye. Forgive us! Our health has been failing us. We should have told Ye what was happening. We used our magic to keep it from Ye and your sister. Your father has put a spell on our land. No one... Will be able to use this land. It will not support any animals after we are gone. Don't be sad for us, go on with your life my boy. I hope ye will have children of your own.*

"If one of your children's comes back here. Tell them to come to the land that belongs to the Hearts. Use a drop of their blood at all four corners of the land. On the first Sunday go to the middle of the property. With a drop of their blood, do it one more time. Come back at the end of the month. Ye will see the grass is growing again. Take the deed that I gave ye, pay the back taxes on the land. Tell them nothing, of how ye brought the land back. If they ask what ye are going to do with the land. Tell them ye are going to raise horses. Son, ye have your magic from Garret. The birth mark of the cross and rose will give ye your magic. Go to America with Alex. Teach your sons how to help Thomas. Your father and I love ye, my son, always remember that."

*   *   *

In his mind's eye! Neil found himself standing at the corner of his father's land. He watched his father place one drop of blood at each corner. He lit the blood with white magic, with all four corners done. He waved his hands as he drew out the box with white fire. The fire ran around the shape of the box. Neil never saw that kind of magic.

In the blink of an eye, he found himself inside the house. He watched his father drew out another drop of blood. He cried out. "Dad…!" His father turned and looked right at him. "My Lord tell me this isn't my father."

Through the window, moonlight shone on the mark of his father's chest. How could his sister and he be so blind? His father's face was all drawn in. The man looked as if he was already dead. He saw his father drop, as he took his last breath. Neil shook his head. "No this can't be happening."

Then his mother came into the picture. She looked at her son, then he felt the tender touch of her hand on his cheek. In his mine he heard, *"My boy I'm sorry it had to be this way. Your father is now at peace. Son could ye place us in our bed? I'm not strong enough to do this myself."*

With the wave of his hands, he slipped them under both and picked them up. In their room he placed them in bed. White fire went red hot; flames danced around their bed. Neil helped his mother to lay her head on her husband's arm.

With the last of her strength, her arm went over his chest. Neil heard. *"We love ye son. Thank ye."* He knew then she was gone.

A red eagle

When he opened his eyes, out of nowhere came a red eagle. It swooped down in front of him; it flew right past him landing on a stump. There was a bright flash of light. Neil blinked two times, his eyes cleared.

The eagle was gone, sitting on the stump was Thomas MacGregor. *"Neil, do ye feel the mark that your grandfather gave to all his children's children?"*

Neil placed a hand on his chest. *"No, should I? Ye are Thomas the keeper of the magic roses. I know ye are no demon."*

Thomas smiled at the young man. *"Aye, that's who I was. It's time to take the roses to America. This is yours and Alex's destiny. We didn't know what Marcos would do. If at any time ye feel your mark get hot, ye must be on guard for a demon is nearby. In the new world, ye will be able to find your mates. Your children's children will help the next Thomas. Ye have heard the stories about our great grandfather. That he was part Fairy and Wizard. Ye also knows about your grandfather Garret. Neil, ye have strong magic from the birth mark on your chest. Ye can see your mark, but Alex can only see his in the moonlight. The two of Ye have strong magic from the roses. As I speak to ye, my wife is with Alex. Everything ye will need is with the roses.*

"Neil, Marcos will do anything to stay on earth. Lucifer has given him only five times that he sent to hell. Right now, he can only be a spirit on earth. The next Thomas will save his love from dyeing before she is born. Marcos can send demons to be his eyes. He must wait until two hundred years have passed. Teach your children to fight and use their magic. Now that your father has killed the land. The soldiers will think ye are a demon with black magic, who has killed the land. Don't blame your parents for keeping their illness from Ye and your sister. Do ye understand why they used their magic?"

Neil nodded his head yes. "Aye, I know now, don't worry about us. The time we had with our parents, those were happy memories for us. I will make sure that Alex will get to America. My children will know about the demons. They will also know what the cross and rose can do for them. Thank ye for telling me about my parents."

The spirit of Thomas said his goodbyes. *"Neil when I leave ye, be careful of the demons will try to take ye down. Alex will send a vest to Ye to keep Ye safe. Don't take it off, it will save ye from a dagger in ye back. Ye have a safe trip."*

As soon as Thomas left, his mark went hot. He knew there were demons coming quickly behind him. Right then a vest was on him. Neil took off down the road, he felt something bounce off his back. He waved his hand, and a dagger appeared, Neil through it taken one of the demons down.

** A foolish demon**

Marcos had been watching. He yelled. "Damn it, I knew he couldn't wait to take Neil down. What a fool he is."

Then there was a demon that appeared in front of him. He heard a voice calling for him. "Sire, I told him don't try to take Neil. He is a demon hunter. This man thinks he can do anything. He doesn't like to take orders from me. I'm sorry Sire."

Marcos looked at the boy. He had a look on his face that scared the young man. "I'm sorry Sire."

Marcos shook his head he then called his father. "My lord I have a boy here that don't like to take orders. Do to him what ye see fit, I know ye will have better luck with him. This boy needs to change." Then the boy was gone from his sight.

White Fire

Alex was building a fire for him and Neil. Then he saw a flash of the brightest white light. There were four corners of this light. The light moved to connect all four corners as a box. The smoke of this white fire came to a point; he saw that it burned red hot. As quickly as it came the smoke past. That white light came from magic; the location was Neil's parent's land. His father needs to know about this fire.

He went to run to the house but stopped quickly. In his mind's eye, he saw Neil and himself walking through a covered bridge. Alex thought he heard two lassies speaking, it was in his native tongue. Once they were out of the covered bridge, he noticed the lassies were close to their age.

He spoke. *"Hello, could one of ye lassies tell us where we are?"*

The young women were very pretty. *"Aye, Ye are in Vermont, this is the town of Pittsford."*

Alex wondered. "What the hell was that all about."

When his eyes cleared, there before him was his grategrandmother Eleanor. At that moment of time, he didn't know she was there. "Are my eyes deceiving me? Are ye my grate grandmother Eleanor? If ye are, I'm sorry for that outburst."

Eleanor just laughed. *"Aye, that I am. Ye may call me granny."*

Alex smiled at her. Then spoke. "Granny, are ye here to tell me about the roses?"

He could see that it made her smile. Then she spoke. *"Aye, I know that ye have heard about the roses. Just let us sit and go over everything again."*

Alex knew about the pouches. He also knew how to get to the new world.

She could see that he had information about what he needed to do. She spoke. *"Alex, if ye let me tell ye about all of this, then ye will know."*

He bent his head. "I'm sorry Granny, I saw a cloud of smoke shaped as a box. That's near Neil's parents' land."

Eleanor looked at him. She spoke. *"Neil's parents are with their mother and father. There is much to talk about, Neil will be here in a while."*

The spirit of Eleanor floated over to him. She then sat on the grass near the fire and patted the ground. *"Alex will ye come over here and sit with me."*

He was watching the bright light but turned and walked over to her. "Granny I just had a vision. Two young women told us that we were in Vermont."

She turned to touch his face. *"Aye…, so ye understand the vision ye had?"*

Alex took a stick to poke the fire with. He was a little up tight being around her. He spoke. "I believe we will be heading to Vermont. To a place that will remind us of home."

Eleanor nodded her head yes. *"That is right. Your vision was to show ye the way. Ye know about the door in the castle. What ye don't know, ye must make a person that looks like ye and Neil. There are demons that will be watching the two of ye. They don't know about that door. Your ghostly match of yourself, will do everything ye would have done. It will show them that ye were riding toward the ship. They will watch them saying goodbye to your parents and getting on that ship to America. Ye don't have to build your two homes. William and Thomas had built the homes. They went there to get away from the highlands. Once ye are on your land, go and pay the taxes for the money will be running out. Thomas had gone through that door and bought the land. He had a trust fund to pay for the taxes. Ye can set up that trust fund to keep paying for the taxes.*

Alex nodded his head. "All right I will make sure that is done Granny."

She nodded; Eleanor was pleased with him. He knew it was time to find his love. *"Alex I'm pleased with ye, I know ye would like to find Ginger. When the two of ye find them, marry them before ye kiss them. For the heat to have sex with her, will run through your mind and loins. It will be too much for ye to stop yourself. The two of ye can use your magic now. I'm pleased that ye saw the need for the vest. The roses told you how to do everything.*

Alex was looking at his grandmother. "Granny we were told to forget about our magic."

She nodded yes. *"It was to throw the demons off. The mark of the cross and rose ye both wears. It can give ye both the magic and can take it away. Ye see the demons thought the roses were gone; a spell placed on the roses to make it look like a different rose bush. The two of ye can make everything ye need smaller, even your horses. This way ye could keep it in your sporran or in a box for the horses.*

*   *   *

"As ye know Thomas always wrote in his journal. In that time Marcos had change things. He wanted Ye to find the people so ye could buy the land from them. How could ye when the land already belongs to ye? Ye would be looking for yourself. In one of the bags, ye will have the money ye need for the taxes on the hundred and fifty acres. Once ye are on your land. Ye know the story of how Thomas had retrieved the roses."

Alex nodded his head yes. "Aye… I read this story a long time ago. My family try to figure out who would take the roses to America."

She laughed when she said. *"Did ye figure it out?"*

One eyebrow went up; he had made her laugh. "Aye… Neil and I will take the roses to America. I will tell Neil we have to make a ghostly person of are self. If we make our horses as wooden, we can keep everything safe."

She was still smiling as she told him what else they must do. *"When ye find your love bring her to your home. About the roses. Ye will bring only the tablet and the deer skins. When ye remove the tablet? Everything will get larger. Ye will have two small pouches. One for the soil. Ye can use your magic to fill the pouch. The soil keeps everything hidden. Ye must make yourself two vests. Ye must wear the vests while you're traveling. When there is a full moon. Place everything in the moonlight. The moonlight gives everything its power. For the last pouch. Ye said, "Ye need to pay your way. This pouch can help. Don't worry about the pouch. It will only work for a MacGregor. This pouch will always go back to the magic roses. Give money for your ghostly people to get on the ship, ye must make them a vest also. About the locket, give Ginger. Do ye remember when Thomas had Garret make two lockets for him?"*

He smiled and remembered that his brother got the first locket, and he got the other one. "Aye, my mother had one of the lockets, it was your locket. My brother has it, the other locket Ginger has with my hair in it."

She smiled at him; she was pleased to hear the young man knows what he must do. *"Aye… Ye gave that locket to her before she left for America. That locket will help ye find her. After ye bed her, give her your cross and rose. Your children won't need the locket. They can use their cross and rose. As time goes on sex for couples will find the need to be one with their love."*

Alex was pleased to know that he had done the right things. "Thank ye Granny. It's good to know. I heard that her family was going to New York. The vision told me the name of the town in Vermont. It was the town of Pittsford. Granny, my brother had a rose drop in his hand first. I tried it with Ginger. It also happened to Ginger and I. My father had said, she is my soulmate."

Eleanor then spoke. *"Alex, did ye ask her for some of her hair?"*

He nodded his head yes. "Aye, I put rose petals on the braid she gave me. She has a locket with petals inside it. Along with my hair."

She smiled at that answer. *"Then ye will fine her, she is your mate ye can call to her. Be careful, Marcos will have demons watching ye. Use that door and make those ghostly people of yourself. Alex, when ye have your home remember this. Only your mate will find the right rose bush. She must work the soil with her bare hands. If she gets her finger picked on a thorn. That drop of blood will stay on the thorn. The rose bush will show itself to her. Ye must take the rose bush and plant it in your rose garden. Alex, this is important, don't let your youth cloud your mind. Ye can use the locket and her hair to marry her.*

"In the basement of the castle there is a door. When the door is open, wave your hand and tell the vortex to take ye to Vermont. It will take ye to where my husband found the land for ye. Read the journal. It will tell ye everything ye must know. It's time for me to leave ye, my husband is waiting for me. Be safe, remember who ye are. We will keep an eye on the four of ye."

There was a flash of light, and she was gone.

*   *   *

Alex sat down; he had everything they needed from the roses. He made the vest out of deer hide and Neil has his. Now he was going over everything she told him. In his mind he heard Neil calling to him. Alex called back. *"Neil is that ye?"*

He knew that demons were hot on his heels. "Aye! We need to cover, make a bubble to hide us. *"There are unwanted company just behind me. There trying to kill me, I don't think they want us to find the girls. Alex did ye make that vest?"*

He then heard the horses riding hard in the distance. There were a substantial number of horses coming closer toward him. He stood up with his hands together he made the bubble. He drew it out until it covered all his father's land. *"Neil come to the pond I made us cover. Aye, I made that vest for the two of us."*

Neil smiled that Alex had decided to send the first vest to him. *"I'm glad you send it to me, when ye did, that unwanted company thought to try to kill me."*

Alex then felt his mark burning his chest. He knew they were close. He spoke. *"I saw when I touched the roses. I all so saw ye throw a dagger back at them. Marcos must not like that demon trying to kill us."*

Then he saw Neil coming toward him. Quickly Neil got off his horse, the two of them were ready to fight. When the demons were gone, he spoke. "What a hell of a night. Those demons were hot on my heels. I need a drink, make it two fingers."

He poured Neil two fingers of Scotch. He watched him toss it back. "Alex my parents are dead. But my mother had called me. She had pulled me on to the land. I saw my father and he didn't look like himself. I watch him take his blood, and light it with white fire. I didn't know he could do that."

Alex found it hard to see his friend this sad. He spoke. "Neil, I saw four corners of white fire, then it came together as one. Dad told me he had seen them when they were not using their magic. Here I have another drink. I also know that the two of us had a visit from Thomas and Eleanor. It looks like we are going to America. Your parents brought over all the things ye may need. Thomas and Eleanor had bought us land. We will have to pay this year's taxes when we get there."

He then poured him some more scotch. Neil took the drink and tossed it back just as fast. He took his saddle off his horse to let him go to graze. "I hope your grandmother had more to tell ye."

Alex spoke. "Just before my visit with her, I had a vision of where we are heading. Eleanor is quite a woman. When the next Eleanor is born, she must be just as strong and witty as the first Eleanor. Those demons needed to stop us. We are the ones that will get the two parents ready to train the next Thomas and Eleanor. Ye and I will not be the ones to bring them into this world."

Neil smiled then spoke. "I knew that it hasn't been two hundred years yet. Where about in America are we heading?"

Alex sat down and he had Scotch in a cup for himself. "Ye do know that we are not going to be sailing across the ocean to America. We are going to have our doubles do that for us, they will be landing in New York. We will have them change are names for us. They will do everything that we have done. The two of us will know if something happens. They will have everything we have, right down to are birth marks.

"While they are doing that, we will be already in Vermont. William and Thomas had made us homes. I will make two drawings to change anything that we would like in our new homes. We will bring are horses with us. They will be change into wood, it will be easier to keep them safe. I have a horse for Ginger, my horse and her horse mated. We have a horse for our child. Everything we are going to take with us; we will make everything smaller. Aye, we are going to use are magic, it feels strange to say we have magic.

"Do ye remember that your horse mated with Ginger's friend's horse. The one that her father had sold to my father. I remembered that the two of ye had hit it off, ye had kissed her goodbye. Tell me have ye ever thought of her?"

*   *   *

Neil went for the bottle of Scotch; he found that it hadn't hit him yet. "Aye, there were times I had dreams of her. That one lit my blood on fire. She left with Ginger's family; with any luck I will find her when we find Ginger. Alex, the Scotch isn't numbing my pain, mama pulled me right into that moment as they dyed. I can still see them, as the white fire dance around them. Whatever illness they had, made him look like someone else. I saw the birth mark of the cross and rose."

Alex knew his friend would find out what killed them. He spoke. "Tell me what killed them."

Neil smiled and drank the last of his Scotch. "Wow Alex. I know ye are not my mate, we spend too much time together. But here it is ye knew I would do a spell to see what killed them. It was one of the landlords. He brought over a bottle of Scotch. There was poison in the bottle. The landlord knew that at night his parents had a drink in their room.

He looked at his best friend, as Neil told him what he saw. He could feel his pain; Alex's parents made him one of their children. "Ye saw them in your mines eye. I saw a cloud of smoke shaped like a box. The roses are with me and everything we will need. I see ye have the vest I made ye. I'm glad I had sent ye that vest when I did. Tell me did ye feel the knife that the demon through at ye?"

Neil just looked at his friend. He took off the vest and looked at the back of it. He ran his hand over the spot that had a mark on the vest. "That was a knife that I felt."

Alex smiled at him. "The moment I touched the roses, which was just what I saw. I made the vest Eleanor told me to make tonight. Tomorrow I will get our horses. When we get our doubles done. We will take and go to the castle; there is a door we will take to Vermont. The two of us will sleep in our new homes tomorrow night. For tonight, we drink to the memory of your parents."

Neil nodded yes. "Aye, let us do just that, after we have drunk all the Scotch. I hope I can dream of the young woman who could light a fire in me."

The two men drank and talk of what they had learned. Alex knew the next ship would be leaving in four days. The two doubles we are going to make will help my father with anything he needs done.

He told Neil that he has the money to cover the trip to America for are doubles. We will be able to feel what are doubles feel. Eleanor said we can see things to a point, at least we will know of it. When they land in New York, they will head to Vermont. They will tell people about the bridge that I saw in my vision. But I will send them to our land. They will make changes too our homes. We will be on are way to the bridge that I saw in my vision. It will lead us into a town of Pittsford, Vermont."

Neil looked at the bottle that was empty. "Alex do ye want any more Scotch? I can get us another bottle if ye like."

He looked at his old friend. "Hell no…! I've had enough to drink, I think I'm going to stay outside tonight. I'm too fox to walk to my room. This has been a hell of a night; I'm going to go to sleep and dream of Ginger. Tomorrow we will take and make the clay and put four drops of our blood in the clay. Then we will take are hair and cut a bit. Will also take round glass and place the color of our eyes. They place rose petals in the clay. They will have the same clothes that we have on. We will say the spell that Granny gave me."

With a wave of his hand, the bottle of scotch disappeared. Alex spoke. "Is there anything I can get ye before we go to sleep."

Neil then burped; the Scotch then hit him. He spoke. "No, old friend that meat was enough for me. The Scotch just hit me, I think I can sleep now. I have my best friend with me tonight. This will be our last time getting foxed in Scotland. I want to dream of her; the last dream I had, she wasn't married. If she has me, I'm going to enjoy taking off her clothes. She wanted me back then, but we were too young. I will see ye in the morning old friend. Thanks for being there when I needed ye the most.

Alex watch Neil's eyes close. He had a big smile on his face and was fast asleep. As he closed his eyes he thought of Ginger. That night will be wonderful to be one with his love. He saw he was out cold.

CHAPTER TWO

Their Doubles go to New York

IT WAS A beautiful day in the Highland. On Wednesday, they walked to the castle. One last look at the home the two had played and fought with wooden swords. Alex met the young woman that he would make her his wife. She was the one for him, at the magic roses. He thought of Ginger, that's when a rose drops into his hand. When he breathes in the sweet aroma of the rose, he found that it made him pass out. His love was next to him; she smiled at her man. She took the rose and breathed in the sweet aroma. There Alex caught her and broth her to the bench.

On that same day Neil met his soulmate. He never thought a young lass could light him on fire. From that day when their ship sailed, he would dream of her. The two of them were always together, they grew up in their dreams. Now it was time to find them and start their family. Neil knew it would be his son that might bring the next Eleanor into this world.

It was time to leave and head to Vermont. His mother sent food with them, for their trip through Vermont. Once they step onto their land. They felt right at home. Tonight, the young men will sleep in their new home. The next day Alex had to pay the taxes on the land. That night Neil and Alex went swimming. They lay on the rocks and looked at the stars.

*   *   *

On the ship the two doubles watch dolphins run with the ship. Occasionally they saw whales and on other days it rained and rough seas. The had to deal with the demons that watched every move they made. Neil and Alex took time to see what their doubles saw.

They took the doubles to take the trip by ship. The two doubles said goodbye to Alex's parents and boarded the ship. He and Neil were already in America.

They head to find the women they loved. On the ship their doubles had felt two demons. In Vermont as they road down the path, they had felt the demons on the ship. At night they were able to see everything the double saw. Now they had knowledge of what happened on the ship.

The days were long; there was nothing to do. All they saw was water for miles, then at last land. In front of them the Statue of Liberty. Neil and Alex felt pride from their doubles, Freedom that's what lady Liberty stands for.

The men watched as they pulled up to the docks. They were now in New York. Slowly they made their way to fill out papers some change their name. After all the paperwork done. Neil spoke to an old man who knew all about the covered bridges. The man told them to take the train to Castleton. In Castleton, buy yourselves two horses. You will be heading to West Rutland. In Rutland. There you can take a trail. This will lead you to the covered bridge called Gorhan. On the other side, there will be the town of Proctor, Vermont.

Alex knew this place was where Ginger lived. They had the directions to follow now. It was great to see what their doubles had gone through. In Castleton they bought their horses. But they weren't going anywhere but to their new home. They would take care of all the horses that they had brought.

* * *

The trail to Proctor wasn't hard to fine. They had arrived at the covered bridge. The two of them dismounted their horses. It was good to walk after being in the saddle for a long time. Neil went over to read the sign that said Gorham Bridge, built in 1842. The bridge was Proctor's town line. They walked through the bridge with their horses. Alex was hoping to hear the voices of women talking. Disappointed, he got back on his horse and rode into town. Neil stopped in front of a barn. The sign had read, MacKay's blacksmith we also bed horses.

Alex looked at Neil. "Stop looking at me, you're the one that needs to fine Ginger. See if it's her father. It was your vision that had gotten us here."

He nodded his head. He knew he was right. Ginger was the key to all of this. "Hello, Mr. MacKay are ye here? I'm looking for a place to bed down my horse."

John replied, but that voice sounded familiar to him. "Aye, I'm out back, and we have two places left."

Alex went through the door that led outside. There was a man working on metal. His back was facing him, that voice sounded the same. The man was still as big as he was back then. But was he the same man he knew as a child. "Are ye John, sir."

23

The man was still hammering out the metal. "Aye, that's what my friends calls me.

Alex smiled when he saw him. "Hello sir, I would take your two last spots. We haven't been here in America for long. I used to know a family of MacKay's. I been looking for a young lass name Ginger MacKay, could she be your daughter."

John put down his hammer and slowly turned around. "Aye, which is my daughter's name. Who is asking about her."

He smiled and took a deep breath. "My name is Alex MacGregor. I have come to ask for your daughter's hand in marriage, that's if she is not married yet."

John smiled at the young man; he made the sign of the cross. "Thank heaven ye came for her at last. No, she is not married yet. Her heart is still yours, come here and let me look at ye. Ye are a fine-looking young man, ye have filled out quite nicely. So ye couldn't get my daughter out of your head."

Alex smiled at the man. "Thank ye sir, ye have done well here in America. How is your wife and son?"

Right… then a young man came into the shop with wood. He was so happy that he almost took off his head. Neil yelled. "Alex duck before the wood hit ye."

John had caught the wood from hitting Alex. "Ben ye almost hit your sister's future husband."

He stopped and put down the wood near the wagon. "I'm sorry Alex. It's good to see Ye and Neil. May be now those men will leave the girls alone."

Neil came in behind Ben. "What men are ye talking about, are the girls in trouble."

John just glared at his son. "Ye haven't said hello to Alex. Ye couldn't wait to get that information out. At least say hello to him before ye say anything else."

Ben knew that he had spoken out of line. "Hello Alex, what do ye think of America?"

He had a feeling there was more he would like to have said. "It's a beautiful place."

Without missing a beat, he was back on the subject. "Tell me Neil are ye married yet? If not the lass ye was smitten on is living with my parents."

Neil smiled and wondered what she looked like now. "No… I'm not married yet. Ye took all the young women with ye. Alex ye were right both women are together."

John went over to the young men; he had to give them each a big bear hug. He was hoping to distract them for what Ben had said. At the same time, the two men asked now what men are ye talking about.

John closed his eyes and tried to think of what to tell them. It was Ben who spoke up. "Dad stops tiptoeing around the subject. There are these men wanting to marry Ginger. She keeps telling them no, I don't love ye. I want ye to leave me alone. That didn't work he has two men watching over them. There will be another man who will be here soon."

Alex had noticed that Ben didn't live with them. "Ben so ye had moved out of the house. Does that mean ye got married."

Ben smiled; he was glad to take a break from telling them anything else. "I met her on the ship; we are going to have our first child. Tell me, do ye remember Father Paul? He is visiting with my wife and me. When he met my sister and her friend Caroline. He had said something I didn't understand until now. What he said to them so ye two women are the once who the young men are looking for. Ye are there soulmates, Father Paul went to see your father before he left the Highlands. Your father showed him the painting of Thomas and Eleanor. Father Paul thought he heard a voice; it was coming from the painting of Thomas. The voice told him to go to America. Visit John MacKay and his wife Sue, they are living in Vermont. When the men come to Vermont, ye must marry them to their soulmates Caroline and Ginger.

Caroline what a pretty name for a beautiful woman. When we met, she didn't tell me her name. We were too busy kissing each other, all this time I've been dreaming about her. "So Caroline is living with Ginger and your parents. Why isn't she living with her own parents?"

John had gone back to work, but the fire had dyed out. "Ben the fire has gone out again, we're going to have to buy that part. I know it's going to cost. Where not going to get these wagon's out on time without that part."

Alex looked at Neil, it was as if he asked if they should pay for that part. He then took out the pouch that had the money. "John, here take this money and buy that part ye need."

He just looked at the two men. "I can't do that, ye need to buy yourself some land."

Alex just smiled at them. "We have land and two homes to take our brides to. Just take the money and get what ye need."

Ben then went on with his story about Caroline. "I don't know why things went wrong for her parents. She was only going to stay until school was out. The ship they were on hit high seas. They assumed the ship had sunk and they never found them. They had thought they were dead and declared them to be so. That's when those men started to come around. They believe those men had them killed.

John looked at the money that Alex had given to him. This money could fix all the things that are broken. Everything was working fine until those men came into town. He thought. "All right thanks ye for this gift ye gave me. Ben let us get that part now, Alex we will be right back."

He watched them go down the street. "Neil those men that Ben was talking about. I have a feeling they are demons. Marcos thinks if they can take us out of the picture, the next Thomas and Eleanor won't be born. They tried to kill ye and fail to do so. How about ye cut the wood and I will make the spikes."

Neil also watched them. "Alex, I don't think we will have Thomas and Eleanor. Marcos can't come back to earth for a hundred years. Ye are right, if we were out of the way, it would mess with the timeline. These men think with us out of the way the roses here in America won't have the chance to come about. "Alex, I don't think we have enough wood. But we will see."

He thought before he started, he would put a barrier up. This way no one will see what we are doing. I have a feeling these men were the once to brake things. With a wave of his hand, he put a bubble outback. He had to do ten spikes; first he needed to get the fire hot. With that done he made the spikes, magic had help.

Neil had all the wood cut; he went right to work. The wagon went together quicker. The first wagon was now finish. Alex was working on the next ten spikes. It took Ben and John longer than they thought. They had to go to the next town over for that part.

In two hours, they had both wagons done. When John and Ben got back, there wagons were done. They had found them sleeping in the hay. Their horses brushed down and fed. Ben and John took the part out back and saw all the wagons done. "This is some fine work that they have done for us."

*　*　*

Ben knew now the four of them should head to the house. At nighttime, the man next-door watched over the horses. "Neil and Alex Ye done those two wagons."

John looked the wagons over carefully. "Ye two do nice work, thank ye for helping us. I think it's time to head home, ye two would like to see the girls now."

Alex opened his eyes he was tired. "Did I hear we are going to head for your place. Neil wakeup where going to head out to John's place."

The men got their saddles back on their horses. Alex had a bad feeling. There was trouble at John's home, then he felt that Ginger was scared. That was the first time he felt her. "John how did all those thinks get broken, does those men who's after the girls have something to do with it."

John wished he didn't have to go into that. "It started out these men came around bringing things for the girls. They were working at this place making young women dresses for their coming out party. Every day the men came, and the girls wasn't there. But the gifts were there, to give them back to the men. It made us look like we didn't want them to marry. The shop equipment broke, one every day. The girl's told them it came from them not my parents. Two weeks ago, a letter came to the house. One part was for us; the other part was for the demon hunter. The letter was from Caroline's parents."

Alex had a feeling, this is why she was scared. "John has Ginger been getting scared when they come around."

John turned quickly and looked at him. "How did ye know, she told him she was promised to someone else. These men were also threatening her; it's your parents that don't let ye marry me.

"Neil, Caroline was only to stay with us until she was out of school. Her parents were killed not long after they sailed away. They gave us this letter for the demon hunter who will save her. I didn't understand what they were telling us until now. On the envelope, the day her parents died. May 10, 1850, appeared on the envelope.

Today is May 10, 1850. Neil, could this letter be talking about ye? Your grate grandfather always knew when demons was around."

Neil didn't look at them. "Aye, the men in my family sense when demon's is around. That is one of my gifts."

John made the sign of the cross. "Neil ye are the one her parents were talking about. They had come over one day. What they told us when Caroline is twenty-one. She will receive her magic. If anyone other than the demon hunter mates with her. She will lose her gifts. Her birthday is tomorrow. That means she must be married tonight."

Neil then had a vision of a young woman walking down to him. She had long golden-brown hair. Her eyes were sea blue. Her lips were in the shape of a rosy-red heart. He knew he wanted to have someone with him. His dreams were always of her; he knew that Caroline was the one he'd always wanted to find. "Tell me could the four of us get married tonight."

Neil had looked at Alex to see if he liked that idea. "Aye, will it take us long to get to your home John."

John was smiling now. "Son it's time to head home, we must get the girls ready to be married tonight. Let's clean up, ye tell Sam where going to head home. He can keep an eye on the horses."

Ben knew this would take a big worry off his father's shoulders. "Alex and Neil thank ye for helping us this much. I know Father Paul, we'll be happy to marry ye tonight."

He kept having these feelings about Ginger. "Will it take long to get there."

John looked at him. "Alex what's going on."

Neil then felt the need to get to John's home. "Alex and I are going to your house now, point us which road to take?"

He told them to take the road to the left. We are the third house on the left.

The barn doors close, without saying a word they had meant right now. With a wave of his hand, the two men were at Ginger's home.

John's wife came running out of the house. "John, Caroline had another vision. She didn't want Ginger to go out today. I'm sorry, you're not John. My I ask who ye two are and what I can do for you."

Alex looked at Neil. He wanted to ask what did ye feel. "Hello Mrs. MacKay. Do ye remember Neil and me? May I ask if Ginger and Caroline are around, I know we haven't seen each other for a long time. It was time to bring the roses to America. I'm Alex MacGregor and my best friend Neil Angel-Heart."

*　　*　　*

John's wife looked at the two of them. "Thank heavens, my daughter's savior is here at last. Caroline had a vision; it was about Ginger and her. Whatever it was it scared her, she didn't want my daughter to go outside. But Ginger wanted to make a blue berry pie. Whatever she saw she knew she had to try to stop her. When Caroline stepped outside, she then agreed with Ginger. It was as if the two of them were under a spell. It was over an hour a go; I'm worried about them."

Then she looked at Neil. "Caroline talked about ye. She said that Alex and Neil would save Ginger and me. Mamma was right, the demon hunter will save us. I have a letter here for ye."

Neil looked at her. "Save the letter for me when I get back. Now which way did they go."

She was now pointing out the way they should go. "Take the path on the side of the barn. It will lead ye to the rock wall. They should be nearby, when we get back, we are going to marry the girls. Your husband and Ben will be here very soon. Will take care of those men, tell John not to follow us. He needs to help ye get the house ready for a wedding."

She cried with happy tears. "I was hoping for this day, I will fix something for the wedding."

Both smiled at her. "If there are any demons, will find them and take care of them. Don't worry."

After they passed the barn, they use their magic to get to the berry patch. Once they looked around, Ginger or Caroline was nowhere. "Alex sees if ye can call to Ginger."

He cleared his mine then called her. "Ginger my love can ye hear me. Please hear me sweetheart, where trying to fine ye."

In the cave the two women sat close to each other. Ginger was looking around, she thought she had heard Alex. Caroline had asked her what's wrong. "I hear Alex, he's calling me. But how can that be when he's in Scotland."

Caroline looked at Ginger. "Alex is calling to ye. He may be here, call back."

He kept trying to call her. *"Damn it… Why can't she hear me."*

Then he heard her say *"Stop swearing, I hear ye. I wish ye were in America."*

He took a deep breath and let it out. "Neil, she hears me."

He hit his forehead. "Alex get your head out of the clouds, asks her if she knows where there at."

Alex shrugged his shoulders. He was happy she could hear his voice. *"Honey where are ye, we're not far. Witch way did ye go from the rock wall."*

Neil was wondering how Marcos would know about Caroline. "Alex ask's her if there are demons with them. Marcos had to know all about what we been doing. He knew about are girls when we were younger. That means he's been watching anyone from our pass. I've been thinking about all of this. Marcos did things with all those women. I remember that Thomas and William had to keep their marriage a secret. What if one of the girls is from the women that he raped and killed. Could of the children be involve in this."

Neil the women back then the babies went inside the women's body. The babies had the women's mind. If ye think that they will help him, I don't think so.

Then Alex heard Ginger. *"We're near to the berry patch. On the other side of the rock wall. There is a path to a cave, it's more in the woods. There are two men outside watching over us. Their waiting for another man to come here. Alex the two of us are scared."*

He put up a hand. *"All right we will be there soon. The two of us won't let anyone hurt ye two."* Neil the girls are scared. She told me there is a path on the other side of the rock wall. It leads to a cave; there is two men guarding the entrance."

*　*　*

Caroline looked at Ginger. "What did he say, are they here? Tell me this isn't a dream. Does Neil remember me."

Ginger had patted her hand. "Why don't ye call to him and see if he can hear ye."

She nodded her head and went to clear her mine. *"Neil can ye hear me, it's Caroline, do ye remember me."*

Neil had waved his hand, and the rocks disappeared. He stopped and looked at Alex. Caroline was calling him. "Alex, she just called me, what should I tell her."

He smiled at him. "Ye can say I hear ye, I'll be there soon. Caroline will ye marry me."

Neil looked at him. "Did ye ask Ginger if she marry ye tonight."

He gives him a big smile. "No not yet, I'll do it right now."

Both men called to the one they love. "Now the girls have hope, we better get there before the other man does."

The two of them went quickly down the path. They didn't want those two men to hear them. Getting off their horses they made their way to the cave. It was right where she said it would be. They hid behind a fallen tree. Both men knew these two men were not demons.

Alex had turned around and leaned against the fallen tree. "I know what Marcos is up to, like we thought this other man is a demon. He's sent to rape them, so we won't marry them. Do ye remember the color of her hair."

Neil thought about it. "She had goldened brown hair and bluest green eyes. She looks like Eleanor. Ye looks like Thomas, if ye think about it. All through time, the women our family marries look like Eleanor or close to her. Ginger's mother said the letter is for the demon hunter. Neil ye know that is ye. Your always the first one to feel if demons are around us."

Neil felt everything come at him. "Damn it all. First, he takes my parents now he wants to stop both of us. I've been waiting for a long time to get back to Caroline. She's in my dreams, I can almost feel her body next to me whenever I dream. No way, are they going to take her from me."

Alex knew how he felt. "One thing we can't see them until it's time to marry them."

Neil shook his head. "I know it will be bad luck; our demon is here. It's time we take them down."

Alex wonders if the two of them will have sons. "Neil do ye think our son's will have Eleanor and Thomas. May be it will be their sons who will have them. Time will tell; now shell we take care of these men."

Neil thought about how to do that. "We been using a great amount of magic. The people who came to America, don't like magic. They kill people who they think has black magic, they believe all magic is evil. Remember our doubles we saw and heard what anyone said to them. Salem Massachusetts, there we be careful. The laws here are different then back home. Do ye think he knows about the cross and rose? I know that it was burn into Garret skin. We can see ours but not yours. Thomas doesn't want demons sneaking up on Garret. He went so far to asked Father Sinclair to bless Garret."

Alex smiled. "Ye can see mine on the full moon. Shall we take them down."

Neil smile thinking back on how Caroline made him feel. "The two of us will be marrying those two women in the cave. Alex, ye are right. It will be my son or his son that will give Eleanor life. Marcos doesn't want Eleanor to have magic. She must come from Garret sister to have magic. He doesn't want her to give him any trouble ones he's back on earth. Neil, that letter could be from Garret sister. Marcos doesn't want ye to marry Caroline. Ye are my best friend. Remember Caroline's lost her parents; her mother could be the one who has the powers. The demons will be after both girls. Marcos didn't know about the locket that Thomas gave Eleanor. He may think if he has Ginger virginity. I may not want her to be my wife. What he doesn't know is I can give her the cross and rose. At the time, my family didn't have magic.

"We can't use our magic yet. These men don't look as if they could even fight. They are going to be demons, after they die. It's time we made a move. The demon is heading for the cave. He may have a time limit; he must leave both girls not a virgin."

Alex was getting anxious to be with Ginger. "Neil before we fight, remember we don't know the laws around here. I can only hope these men are going to be demons. Then it will be a quick cleanup for us."

One by one they took down the two men. The men disappeared right before they even hit the ground. Now they must deal with the demon.

Alex yelled. "I don't know your name, but I do know you're a demon. We know that Marcos sent Ye to stop us from marrying Ginger and Caroline. Your men are dead; they disappeared before they hit the ground. Come out here and face me if ye dare."

The demon walked out of the cave. "So ye are hear in America. My men didn't know how to use their magic. They were and easy mark, I won't be that easy to get rid of."

Neil had stepped out into the clearing. "Ye underestimate us." He through his dirk that carried his small cross and rose. The dirk landed deep into the demon's chest. Like the others, he disappeared. Only Neil's dirk and cross were left behind.

CHAPTER THREE

Together at last

A LEX WANTED TO see Ginger; he forgot that it's bad luck if he sees her before the wedding. "Neil, ye stay here."

Neil wanted to do the same, but he was willing to wait. "No… ye not going in there. If ye go in their Ginger will not stay a virgin for long. It's bad luck to see your wife to be."

Alex stopped and closed his eyes. "Damn its Neil… Why must ye be always right."

Neil just laughed. "Alex, think about it. We know that Father Paul is visiting Ben and his wife. I now know what Father Paul was talking about. All we need is two marriage licenses. Then the four of us can get married.

He knew he would love to just kiss her. But he knew if he did, he wouldn't stop making love to her. "All right we must tell them were sending them home. It's time for us to get ready for are wedding tonight."

Neil closed his eyes and called Caroline. *"My love are ye ready to get married to me. I know I'm ready to be with ye and start our lives together. I'm sorry but I was told I have a deadline for me to take your maiden head. I think the two of us will simply do fine together. The name ye will take is Angel-Heart."*

He could almost see the big smile on her face. *"Neil, I love ye. Those dreams I had about us, made me feel that I was there with ye. When we say I do. Ye will have to do what ye must."*

Neil waved his hand and sent his bride to get ready for her wedding. Then he thought about what they need to get married. First the marriage licenses for the two of them. Next a place to have their night together. Then new kilts to get married in.

Alex came out of the cave. "Neil come over here. Look at this cave. We can have the first night with our brides. All we must do is cut the cave in half. It's big enough for a bed and a tub on both sides for the two of us.

He went over and slapped him on the back. "Let us make the walls. Then the floor with a rug to walk on. Now a big bed to enjoy are brides. Next a hot tub to lay in. Wooden walls to make it look like a place we would have taken them. Then a fireplace to warm themself."

Neil thought about what else we need. "Alex how about we make four rings for us to wear."

Alex smiled. "To show we married them."

Then he waved his hand and flowers to the brides. The two had their new clothes on. They waved their hands, and the horses were taken care of. Now they were at the house and knocking at the door. "Neil that idea for a fireplace, made it cozy for us."

He then handed Alex flowers to their bride. "Neil ye remember that she loved roses. The flowers that I had picked out for Caroline was a flower from every place she had lived."

There was laughter upstairs. Ginger's mother and sister-in-law were helping the girls get dressed. When the door opened. They handed the flowers to Ginger's brother. He took them upstairs to his wife. There was one red rose for his wife to carry. Neil was handed the letter from Caroline's mother. A scotch to drink was at the table.

He opened the envelope. When his fingers touch the letter. Neil felt the magic pour into him.

*　　*　　*

Hello Demon Hunter.

My name is Leslie; I am Garret sister. I know that ye come from my brother's children. Marcos was the one who killed my family. At first, I thought Garret had died. It was hard to see my brother standing there. Marcos had brought Garret into the room. He wanted to make sure Garret was dead. I screamed when he ripped my clothes off me.

Then Marcos had me tied to the bed. I heard my brother's voice in my head. He was speaking a spell as he tied my hands. Only our father would know this spell. Garret had used both magics. His own and our father's. He took my spirit from my body. I didn't have any pain or knowledge when Marcos raped me. He had no idea that Garret took my spirit. I stayed with my brother until I was with a child. When Garret put my spirit back. He had switched my baby spirit with me. He given me a second chance to live. He had helped me see into the future.

I'm sorry, no one knew what happened to me or my child. Marcos had demons that could have overheard. My father and mother before they died. They gave all their magic to my brother. At the age of twenty-one, my magic came to me along with my mother's powers. Thomas understood what was happening to Garret. When he killed the demon, Garret who had died when the demon took over his body. There was one good, and one evil bodies Thomas freed. Marcos doesn't want ye to mate with my granddaughter. For she will have strong magic. When Tom and Ellen's born, they will have strong magic together.

He found out that she was my great, great, granddaughter. My brother knew he had to keep his magic hidden from Marcos. Remember, Marcos thought Garret's body had magic. He only had a piece of the boy's magic. With our father's power, he was able to keep hidden from Marcos. Along with his knowledge of how to use magic. When his body died, both magic's went with Garret spirit. When he was in with the demon. A wall of magic and prayers kept him safe. The demon didn't fine Garret anywhere inside his mine. When I was born, the evil died with my body. I lived once again, through my daughter. To keep me safe he forgot about me and what he had done for me.

*   *   *

This letter is for anyone that needs information. The one who holds the letter. Ye can ask about the past or things to come. Beware of this timeline, Salem kills witches. Stay away from there. Only use your magic when ye must. I know now that the roses that Thomas brought back with him. He found out that the roses holed the magic from the human fairies. His grandfather was a wizard with strong magic of his own. Thomas thought of the cross and rose to keep them safe. At the time he didn't know he had fairy magic. This magic from the fairies will not let ye use your magic if it put ye in danger.

*   *   *

There is a place in Dorset, Vermont. A hundred and fifty acres. Thomas and William went there to make two homes. This was a place where they went to just enjoy life with each other. Exactly right for two families to live on. I know there is more ye need to know. It was Garret who set this in motion. He made it possible for Ye and Caroline to dream about each other. When ye see her for the first time. It will be as if ye grew up together. Your dreams started when ye were fifteen and she was thirteen. After your wedding ye will have just two hours to bed her. Your seed must spill into her. Marcos will still try to stop ye from marrying her. Go now and be quick about it. Keep this with the magic roses when it's not needed. The power those roses have is strong. Give your wife the mark ye ware. Love her with all your heart. I know Caroline will love ye deeply.

Be safe demon hunter.
Love Leslie.

*   *   *

Neil went outside to where their wedding was going to take place. Father Paul was waiting for the two grooms.

He asked them. "Are ye going to do both weddings together?"

Both men were happy to say. "Aye… Father."

The men were in place. Ginger and Caroline came downstairs. John step between both women. When Neil first saw his bride. It felt like he knew her for a long time. The wedding was over before they knew it. Neil kissed his bride. The papers signed and there was a toast given to the two couples.

After the toast. He had told Alex don't forget about the spell for the door. We must go now. My time is running out; Caroline must be mine before midnight. That's the only way to guarantee she will have her magic on her birthday tomorrow.

Then he pulled Caroline away from everyone, he took her to the bathroom. There behind closed doors he kissed her, as his hands found her pussy. Caroline went very still as his finger moved inside her. Neil's tongue made love to her mouth. He found out that his wife wanted him now. Her hands ran over his back and under his kilt. He drew in the air when she taken hole of his shaft.

His eyes showed Caroline the hunger to have her. There was so much love for her. "We're going to do simply fine together. We made a place to make love to ye. With our magic we turn the cave into a getaway place."

He saw in her eyes fear. "Why are ye scared of that place. They didn't touch ye did they?"

Caroline bent her head. "I don't know why it scares me of that place. But I will be all right. Ye took care of those men."

He looked at his bride. "There is a picture of our knew home above the fireplace."

Neil pulled her into him. He kissed her and waved his hand. In the blink of an eye, they were inside their room. He put a strong spell on their door. There was food and two glasses. Niel saw her go for the food, she took the glass and drank the liquid. He ate food and drank his Scotch. As she ate, she looked at everything in the room. He had a fire going and above the fireplace was the picture of their new home.

She was so pleased with the home that will be ours. "Neil, It's beautiful and that's our home."

She went and placed a hand on the picture. When she did the picture change. There were three bedrooms and a kitchen that she wanted for a long time. When she saw their bedroom and a big bed to make love on. "I can't believe everything I had dreamt about is coming true. "Neil, I feel a little tipsy."

He smiled at his wife. "Forgive me, I must have ye now. Drink all of it. Your body will relax more with it."

Caroline giggled. "I know we have a time limit. Do what ye must do. We will have time to enjoy each other later."

She made it easy for him. Slowly she took off her dress a piece at a time. Caroline giggled, as she moved sexily in front of him. It was making Neil hot. She went and sat on their bed naked. Her finger wiggled for him to come over to her.

*   *   *

On the bed she sat with her legs a part. With a wave of his hand. His clothes were gone. Caroline could see he wanted her. She smiled and ran her tongue over her lips and giggled. She quickly put her hand over her mouth. Neil walked toward her, as his heat bounds with every step he took.

She couldn't believe he was that big. "Did I do that... so ye like what I did."

Neil knew that she was wondering if she could take all of him. "My love aye, that ye did. Honey, your body will adapt to me. Ye do know where our child will come from. My job is to get ye to come as much as possible. I will have it open more to me, ye will see."

When he sat down Caroline ran a finger over his heat. It moved when she touched it. She giggled and placed a hand over her mouth and giggled again.

Neil took her hand down he kissed the inside of her hand all the way up to her lips. With the other hand, he cupped his hand around her neck as he laid her back. It was time to prepare her heat for him. He moved slowly down her leg then up the inside. She giggled and gave a little shiver. Neil had put a spell on his finger. When he pushed into her heat she came. Each time he moved in her his finger got bigger around. Now he was between one of her legs, as his heat moved over her leg.

His tongue made love to her mouth. He was bringing out the butterflies in her heat. His tongue played with her nipple once it was hard, he sucked on it and pumped his finger in her heat. "Neil I can't come any more."

It was time, his finger was out of her. He had cleaned his finger with his mouth. "Damn it… ye are sweet to me. The next time, I will drink your pussy after ye come. I like your nectar. Aye… this I will do."

She looked at him. He could see there was a question. "Neil why does my heat Ake here inside me."

He smiled. "The story about this if it was your first time, and my heat was close to your pussy. Then I sucked on one of your nipples, would bring out the butterflies. Ye want me inside ye, not my finger. Ye see on my Twentieth first birthday. We went to the pub to make me into a man. She had shown me how to please a woman. She was one of the ladies of the night. Ye pussy is ready for my heat. I'm going to make ye into a woman. After this when we make loved one of those times, we could have a baby inside ye.

Neil had felt the opening was bigger. He made it bigger each time she came. When his finger was as big as his heat it was time to take her. Caroline remembered watching him put his finger in his mouth. She didn't know what he meant when he told her your sweet. The next time I will drink your sweetness.

He had moved quickly between her legs. His shaft now in his hand, he guyed it inside her. Laying on top of her, he started to move. The pleasure was wonderful; he took her maidenhead quickly. He had to give her his seed before midnight. He lifted her bottom as he pumped his seed into her. She watched as he came just after her. It was just like her dreams. But the pleasure was much more.

He then turned her over on top of him. She looked into his eyes. "Ye didn't hurt me. Women say why did ye hurt me. I liked the pleasure ye gave me. I felt when ye pump your seed in me. I can't believe we our one. I know ye are inside me I feel him. The way ye claimed me was over the top. What's wrong, ye had to move quickly to make me yours. It pleased me that ye didn't hurt me when ye came inside me. I like being your wife, the best part is having Ye inside me. Those dreams made me hunger to have ye friend inside me like this."

Now he was smiling, he brought her mouth down to him. "I like what I see, do ye want to know how deep I went inside ye."

She looked shy with him. "Honey, I see all ye body, my heat is inside ye. He is safe and warm in ye. I want to have ye as ye let me. Aye… I could get ye with our child. That is the chance we take each time I pump my seed in ye. I want to fuck ye even now."

Caroline watched as the hunger poured in him. She was going to make him come again. As she wanted to sit up with him inside her. She started to do just that. He tried to slow her down. When her eyes went wide. "That is one of the ways I can go deeper inside ye. Doing that, ye must go slow. Ye could grind yourself on me now. That's if ye want to come more. All ye must do is move your hips.

That's it now she watched him as if his hands helped to move her. He came up to her and kissed her.

Neil, I'm not worried about getting pregnant yet. My mother had given me something to stop that from happening. I have one year to enjoy ye fucking me. So let us play around, she gave Ginger the same thing."

Neil had the biggest smile. "Thank heaven… I like feeling ye come. When ye get to that last climax then and only then I follow ye, to see the pleasure in your eyes." Then he laid her back a bit to suck on her nipple. She braced herself with her arms as he ran his hands over her body. "Ye are everything I want in a woman."

Caroline pushed him back as she came again. She saw his eyes as he got ready to come. He made her sit up straight as he pumped his seed in her again. She took hold of him with her pussy and felt as he came. I want more of this she thought.

She was now on top of him fully. "Ye our mine I didn't think ye wanted this again. I filled ye with my seed, way before midnight. Your body holds a bit of me inside ye. I like doing this with ye."

Neil was rubbing her back; it wasn't a dream this time. He likes being inside her pussy, to feel the little quakes as she reacts to them. Aye… he thought, she is my wife. Her body holes a part of him inside her. We will pass our magic down to Ellen. He waved his hand and covered them up. Her face nuzzled between his face and neck. She was fast asleep on top of him. This time, his seed went inside her. Not on his bed when he dreamt of her.

As the two of them woke up, she knew he wasn't inside her anymore. "I need to wash up."

With a wave of his hand, they were in the hot tub. Neil went to touch her heat. "Are ye sore here."

She looked at him suspiciously, then gave him a big smile. "No… Why do ye ask."

She knew right off that he wanted her. "I like fucking ye, our dreams were enough for me at the time. Now I have the real pussy, and I want more of her. I haven't been with anyone. The woman gave me a blowjob she had swallowed my seed. I told ye I will make love to ye as often as ye let me."

Neil grabbed her around the waist and pulled her on to him. "I know it's getting a little too much. The dreams I had of Ye. I can't get enough of ye, forgive me. I want this and need ye. Sit on me let me go inside your sweet pussy."

Caroline then had an idea what he wanted from her. She knew if she were someone else, that woman would have said no. But she liked having him inside her. He kissed her lips, and his hand moved over her body. When she came, he lifted her off him and into the air. He had parted her legs and brought her pussy to his mouth. There his tongue moved in and out of her pussy as he swallowed her nectar. Her bottom tried to move her. But couldn't all she had air to push against.

He enjoyed her sweetness, as a horse would when he was going to mate. It made him feel drunk and horny. This was new to him as enjoyed moving his tongue in her pussy until she came. Neil's finger with magic he made it like his loin. Now he pumped his finger in her to get more of her nectar. She didn't know how he could get her to come so much. He stood up and his heat found her wet pussy. Then she was in his arms, and she was tasting what he had done to her. She found that he was right, she was sweet.

She was sitting on him. "Neil when we are going to our new home. For I know ye will fuck me all those days. There ye can have me as much as ye like."

He pulled her head to him and framed her face with is hands. "Tell me did ye like what I did to ye."

She looked at him and realized what he had done had been going on for a long time. We humans are from the animal kingdom.

"I know one thing my body wanted to move away from ye. I felt that I couldn't claw anything but air. Aye, I enjoyed that. I fine there are different kinds of ways to make love to ye. I want to try before we can leave this cave."

He thought a bit more. "There are other ways to make love to ye. Damn it… a horse fucks, a filly until she had enough of him. Tell me have ye had enough of me."

Caroline thought about that. "No… can we eat and drink a cup of coffee. After ye can do what ye like to me. Just remember when we are home, ye will have me any time ye like. Do ye know I felt the twitching when ye had come, it made me come again. No…I haven't had enough of ye. I like finding out things that makes your eyes go wide."

He had food set up for them. "Do ye know it will be easy to have ye in the woods."

She thought he was trying everything we did in are dreams. "Honey the two of us had a place to go to make love. Marcos will come on strong with our granddaughter. Ye had shown me a waterfall. I want that to be their safe, haven for Tom and Ellen."

Caroline had finished her coffee and food. Neil done also. With a wave of his hand, she was in a skirt and a low-cut blouse. He was in his kilt and had no shirt. He had come over to her and put her up against the wall. "Ye have this blouse I can pull down. Look at those beautiful breasts. Your nipples like me, my heat likes ye."

Neil took the hard nub and suck on it. Then he pulled up her skirt and his kilt. He pulled her legs up and braced her back to the wall. "Slide my heat in ye, do ye like what I'm doing? How I love the feeling of your pussy when ye slide him in ye."

Each time he tried something new it was part of their dreams. She had moaned, now her back was arch. He could play with her breast and pumped his heat in her pussy. Then they were on the bed, and they were naked and, on her knees, and hands. "This is another way to go deep in ye."

He moved slowly within her. "Now put your arms down, I will go slow at first. Play with your click to get ye to come, that's it.

She had all different; he could have her. When her body let her come, she wanted him to go faster and deeper. "Give me more, oh aye…"

She had come hard; it was an explosion between her and him. Now she was flat on the bed, and he was on top of her. His hands were cupping her breasts. He had turned them over with him on his back. "I love all your toys. Ye matched my hunger. I love feeling ye come. When it's time to have our child, we will enjoy doing this again. Ye have enough of my sperm in Ye. They say my little fish swam to your eggs and tried to get inside one. But this time they will have to wait tell the time is right for us. Do ye know I had given ye the cross and rose. It will tell ye when demons are around ye. Also, we have all the magic from the roses. Now I want ye to try this last way."

She had found herself face down and looking at his heat trying to stand up straight. "I want ye to give me a blow job. That will be the last time we will make love. Tomorrow we will send your things to your home. Then we can ride home, what do ye think of that."

She thought about it. "I will try but if I don't like it, I'm not doing it. I don't care if it's the last thing we do.

He moved her legs apart and brought her heat to his mouth. His tongue went between her moist lips. Caroline cried out as she came again. His tongue played with her click; she grabbed his legs and came again. Neil enjoyed everything he was doing. "I want more of ye. Take a hole of my heat, put your mouth around it. Honey don't bite or we won't have children."

Caroline had found that she had enough. "Neil please stopped; this way is not for me right now. I want ye inside me."

Without thinking Caroline waved her hand and spun him around. Neil was floating over her. He could see in her eyes she didn't know what was happening.

He gave a little laugh. "I see ye have your magic. Happy Birthday my love. So ye don't want me to come in your mouth. There will be other times ye can try. Come up here and let me come into ye."

She smiled from ear to ear. "I have my magic. This means our granddaughter will have her magic. I'm so happy ye save me. Now when we make our son. He will be the one to give life to Ellen. That mean Ginger son will have Tom."

Before we leave this room ye have this letter from your grandmother. Take your time and read it.

*   *   *

Hello Granddaughter,

I feel ye have found out that ye have your magic. My parents died because they didn't want to hurt anyone. They couldn't use their powers to even save themselves. Evil uses power to control people. Because men like Marcos needs to be powerful. They use religion to control people that are weak.

I remember when I grew into my magic. Before my birthday, the woman who saved me. Gave me a book that was my mother's. Inside was this letter. When my father gave Garret his powers. The letter came to him. Aye… this letter that ye are holding. Everyone gets different information from this letter.

Ye see Garret made it so anyone who picks this letter up. Will have their question answered. This happens even before ye speak it. Your powers will not let ye hurt anyone of your family. The mark Neil gave Ye, has the magic fairy rose on the cross. Ye can only see the mark on the full moon. If there is danger that someone will know ye have magic. The fairy magic will not let ye use your powers. Remember, your powers can be given to your children. Their magic could be strong in mine and the body. Ye and Neil have all these things. With your thoughts call Neil. I know ye can hear him. He was able to hear ye. These powers Eleanor will need. Make them stronger for her. She will need that kind of magic. The stronger ye get in anything ye do. Will make your children stronger and grandchildren.

Ye would like to know if your child will give Eleanor life. Your child will not be the one to bring Eleanor into the world. It will be the third generation, around 1900 or the middle of that year. I can't tell ye when it will happen. I can tell ye this. When Eleanor is thirteen years old Marcos will try to rape her. I have a feeling that he will lose interest in her. He may give the two of ye to others. There is something in the wind, he may find what he's been looking for. Take care of each other. Time will tell. If Marcos wins or we will beat him.

With Love,
Leslie

CHAPTER FOUR

Their new home

T HE NEXT DAY the girls got everything ready to go to their new home. Neil and Alex sent the things by magic. Then the boys got the horses ready for them. When the girls went outside, they saw the horses they had in the Highlands. Ginger spoke. "Are these horses the ones we use in the Highlands?

Alex was pleased she remembered her horse. He spoke. "Ye remembered aye. She remembers ye, that's good."

While the men got their horses ready. Ginger wondered if Neil was kind to Caroline, on her first time with him.

She smiled and gave a giggle. "Even though we had a time limit, he didn't hurt me. I can't ask for, anyone better. He's a wonderful lover."

Caroline knew what kind of man she had. "Ginger are ye happy with your husband?"

She bit her lips trying not to giggle. "If your mother didn't give us that medicine. I know for sure I would be pregnant; we were hungry for each other. I'm glad that we had our dreams until we met again."

She had looked to see if anyone was listening. "Did ye have a dream about Marcos."

Caroline had a bad feeling somehow; Marcos was able to get into their dreams. "Aye, did ye have a dream of him?"

She looked at her and shook her head yes. "In the dream Ellen had felt Tom was in trouble. He was trying to kill him in his sleep. Could we see what he is trying to do? We must pass that on to Ellen when she is older."

Ginger had done the math for when he came back. "If I'm right we will have to live close to the age of ninety. There will be three generations, maybe more or less. We will have to be ready. We will make sure our sons will know, and their wife also. Sometime men forget."

Caroline thought about it. "We can't live in fear; Marcos has that vendetta for the MacGregor's and Heart's. Now Neil said that we can go skinny dipping at the waterfall. Both of our men had a nice built, would we be strong enough to not look."

Ginger looked at her friend. "What about them, we both our built. Ginger, do you have feeling for my husband?"

She looked at Caroline. "No, I guess I was wondering but you."

She smiled at Ginger. "No, I think the men and us will be too busy, to even care about our friend's mates.

The ride home

It was time to take their brides to their new home. "Mamma don't cry will see ye again."

Caroline went over to them. "Thank ye for helping me."

She gave them a kiss on their cheek. The men place the girls on their horses. Both girls couldn't believe they were married. Everything was in bloom; the air smelled sweet. The ride home was beautiful; it was interrupted by the dark rain clouds heading their way. Softly the rain was coming down, little black flies were coming out.

Neil rode up to Alex. "I think the rain will be coming down hard. I can see over there at the dark clouds there is lightning. I'm going to take Caroline home now; this storm looks like it has helped.

Alex then felt his cross go hot, their women also felt it. "Damn it, Marcos don't let up, he's coming fast we got to put a bubble around us, I'm glad that we had place one around the hundred fifty acres. I don't want him to know where we are living. I'm glad there are ten acres on the side of ye, and twenty acres between us. What do ye think about us using a bubble around us to transport the girls and us? That bubble we had added, they can't see into our land. The rain can come through I would like to keep out the snow, but we need it. That black cloud is coming fast."

With the women beside them each man made their bubble. Together they disappear and reappeared on Neils land. Caroline then spoke. "Us women have are magic. The bubble will be stronger with the four of us."

Neil thought about it, Thomas and William had placed one back them. When we got here, we placed one, now we will add another that evil can't see in.

The men agreed they went quickly to get the women off their horses. They join hands in a circle together, and they start to say the spell for the bubble. They thought of the hundred and fifty acres. With their hands in the air, they turn into a circle. Now to draw the bubble out they all spoke. "We draw out the bubble to cover the hundred and fifty acres. Rain and snow can come through; no magic or demons will be able to get through. We four seal this in Jesus's name Amen."

White light filled the outside of the bubble it had come down and round to the bottom of the land.

Neil shook his head. "Good he can't find us yet. Before long, the rain will be coming this way. Ye two better get going enjoy your new home."

Ginger then thought. "Neil you and Alex must stop saying ye. The word is you and Aye is yes. Off and on it's okay to say, not all the time. Caroline, you must help him with it."

Caroline wanted to give her it right back. "Aye mother or should I say yes mother. Get going and enjoy your man, I know I am."

Ginger shook her finger at her. She thought she was right I been like a mother hen; that will have to stop. "Alex where lucky to have all this beauty to look at. What beautiful flowers it looks like it goes a long way."

Ginger started to laugh. "Leave it to you to do that. See you two later in the following week."

*　*　*

The two rode down the road. Then Neil got her off her horse. She couldn't believe that she had a new home. Caroline took her horse and led her to the barn. Inside they took off their saddle and Neil put them away. He had waved his hand, and each horse was brush down, Neil took Carolines hand and ran to the house. The rain was starting to come down. On the porch Neil took her in his arms and kissed her. Then she waved her hand, and the door opened. He carried her over the threshold. He kissed her again before putting her down. "This week I will make love to ye…I mean you in every room in this house of ours."

After that kiss she touched his face. "When the rain stops, I like to see the outside of our home."

She couldn't believe how big it was. "Our we going to have three children."

He smiled all he wanted was her in their home. "If that is what you want then we will try for them."

Caroline looked around, everything was so beautiful, the living room had a fireplace. There was a walkway to get to the other rooms. There were four bedrooms, there room had a big bed. Two doors going on to a porch, everything was beautiful, they could see the waterfall from the porch. It was a good walk to the waterfall, but they had a pond that turned into a lake down aways.

Neil watch Caroline face when she saw the lake in front of their home. "My grate grandfather and grandmother built our home. They use this place to get away from what was going on back home. Thomas wanted to be in the back. We have a long driveway. Neil was happy their home was private. Even Alex home was away from them."

Then the rain stopped, he waved his hand, and they were five miles down the road. They took a walk to see part of the road to their home. There were trees on both sides. When it cleared, she saw water, then a beautiful ranch house. The barn was larger with fencing for the horses. When the cabin came into sight all she could see was her home. The barn was off in the distance and there was grass all around. Neil told her William Heart built this place. Each family that lived in it, updated this place. It was a place to get away from whatever was going on in the Highlands. Before we left here, I had to put a new deck and stairs on the front. The roof needed work, but I got everything done."

Caroline looked at her husband. "It's time I try out my kitchen."

Ginger's new home

Ginger watched Neil take down Caroline. She was so please that both of our men found them in time. As the two of them rode up the road. Beautiful trees just started to bloom; each tree had lovely colors of flowers. There was a small hill that they could slide down in the winter. A fence that went all the way up the road on both sides. In the trees they could hear birds singing. There were horses in the fields. Alex and Neil's father gave them horses.

The water had ripples on the pond as the wind blew across. That storm followed them all the way here at their new home. Each house had two men that look after the ranch. Alex got off his horse and came over to Ginger. She couldn't believe all of this was their homes, both homes had two floors. In the background she could see the mountains. She could hear the waterfall that was outback. Now they can start their life together.

War

The time in Vermont was getting a little scary. In 1860 there was talk about a war breaking out. As things heated up Neil and Alex thought of sending the children to the Highlands. The two men had their first son a year after they were married.

At the time they didn't think Dorset wouldn't hit. Alex had given money to help their men in the war effort. Scots help during the American Civil War. The Scots were no stranger to war. Freedom, they knew the cost of being free. America was a young country, from which it had things like the country they came to. Vermont was the first to abolish slavery. Neil and Alex were firm believers in fighting for what they believe in. Vermont gave support to the union war effort. They went out of their way to help raise troops and money. There was a woman who kept track of how Vermont was doing. She had told everyone, by the spring of 1865 Vermont will be devastated. We had sent one tenth of our entire population to the war. We have lost over 5,000 lives to the battle and their wounds a long with disease. Vermont did their full duty to our country. After the war Vermont put monuments of heroes in their towns.

They put up a statue of General William Wells. In Battery Park in Burlington, Vermont.

The Battle of Big Bethel they fought on June 10, 1861. This was the first military action Vermonters seen. The battalion, who was the 1ˢᵗ Infantry of Vermont had engaged in this battle of Big Bethel.

*   *   *

When the fighting was over it was time to have another child. Their next child was another son, both women wanted a girl. Every two years they planned to have another child. At last Alex and Neil had given the girls a daughter for themself. Like in the Highland it was a longways to your neighbor. The two oldest, Scott MacGregor and Rory Angel Heart hung around each other.

Now there brothers had it harder being the youngest boys of the two families, having to watch their sister. Keith always fought with his little sister. Fiona had two brothers, the oldest showed her how to defend herself.

Keith always teased Fiona, sometimes he would laugh at her. She was a little heavy, so he called her fatty. At school on the playgrounds, he pushed her and laughed at her when she fell. "You're a bully, stop pushing me. You don't watch yourself; you're going to be like my friend's father. He hit his daughter and her mother. That's why she doesn't come to school sometimes. Keith don't push me, or you will be sorry."

Then he did it again and she hit Keith in the nose. That was it for him. "Damn it if you were a boy, I could give it back to you. It's not fair I can't hit you. Just because you're a girl."

The teacher had seen what he had done. She also saw what Fiona did. She came running then came over to them. She had grabbed Keith, one of the girls had a tissue. She was trying to take the little rock out of her knee.

Logan had come over to her. "Fiona let the nurse take it out. Keith from now on you can look after my sister. I will take care of Fiona, just stay away from her. If you hurt my sister, you will deal with my brother and I."

Logan was a strong boy and scooped her up, before the teacher got to them. Her brother always found a way to get her back. The battle was on, one time when it was winter he got his sister with a snowball. It hit her hard, it made her fall on the ice. Logan was there and hit Keith and knocked him out. "Sis take care of him; I've had it the way he treats her."

Alex saw what was happening with the two of them. "Take her to Ginger I will take care of him."

He threw him over his shoulder and brought him to the house. He flopped onto his bed. "I don't know what got into you."

Neil had seen what happened and followed him upstairs. "Alex this is getting out of hand. Then he gave him a cross and rose petals. "You have tried everything and nothing works."

Alex nodded his head. The moment the cross touches his skin. The demon howled; he came out quickly as Neil sent him back to hell. Alex put three rose petals on his chest. Everything seeped into his skin. "Thanks, old friend, I just didn't see it at the time."

Neil shook his head. "You were too close, to see it. Marcos has been quiet too long. Logan had told me what was going on, this is what I saw. There was a demon making him do things too his sister. Each time he did something the demon got bigger. There with that done, all the kids are going to get the cross and rose. Marcos sends demons to make are children fight with each other. Why didn't his cross go hot. Unless he found a way to get around the cross and rose we been born with.

Logan Angel Heart wasn't as bad as Keith was with his sister. Elsie always complained that he didn't like her around him. He shot back and she didn't listen to me. He found Fiona listening to him, even when they were little. He took care of her, even played with her. One day Keith and Fiona were getting in it again.

Logan then yelled. "Enough you two, remember I'm watching Fiona. Your taking care of Elsie."

A pact between the two boys. What happened in the past, will come around in the future. There was always a MacGregor with an Angel Heart. It didn't matter if it was a boy or girl.

The boys took on another sister, Neil looked at Alex. "Where did I hear that from."

Alex laughed. "It was Thomas and William. They started switching sisters and they found out they liked being with them. There still young, anything to stop Keith from killing his sister."

As time went on the youngest wasn't fighting with their sisters. Even at toddler's fight siblings, but when friends swap sisters, the fighting slows down.

* * *

Elsie loved history; every twenty-one years she would write down one thing that happened in that year. This was the year her brother Rory Angel Heart fell in love with Olivia. She came from the Lowland of Scotland. Her parents came to Vermont when she was eighteen. He met her at a football game. Her best friend was Mhairi. The boys had been set near them; it was Elsie and Fiona who introduced them. After that day they were always together. It was the girls last year. Two years later Rory and Scott married Olivia and Mhairi.

Olivia and Mhairi had their first child, which both was a boy. Elise thought it would be an idea to keep track of the timeline for the two families. Marcos wouldn't come back until Tom and Ellen were born. They didn't know who would give life to them. But when their sons were born it was close to the right timeline. Both families agreed that Logan and Fergus, were the ones. It will be their sons will give life to Tom and Ellen.

Scott MacGregor and Rory Angel Heart got married on May 10, 1885.

Olivia MacGregor had her first child, a boy born on December 15, 1890.

Mhairi Angel Heart had her first child a boy born on October 20, 1890.

Olivia MacGregor had her second child was a girl she was born April 9, 1893.

Mhairi Angel Heart had her child a girl born on July 10, 1892.

Olivia MacGregor had her son Logan who was born on February 27, 1896.

Mhairi Angel Heart had her son Fergus was born on August 10, 1895.

*   *   *

After Logan and Fergus were old enough, they join the Navy on June 6, 1917. They had heard that the Navy had called it Winds of War, Winds of Change. The U.S. Naval Academy during the World War II Era. Fergus Angel Heart heard about the Naval Academy. They could earn ranks through ROTC. ROTC plan was to find officers to go to the Naval Academy. But the boys didn't want to be officers. Four years was enough to find themselves a wife. But they did ROTC and got themselves two ranks up. After school they sign up for the Navy.

When they were in port, they went to see Dean Martin. He was at the USO he was singing and entertaining the service men and women.

Logan went to the bar to get two beers, while Fergus looked for a table. There was two beautiful women setting by themselves. Fergus went up to them and asked if they would like company.

Right then Logan came with four beers. Fergus looked at him, "Ladies this is my best friend, Logan MacGregor."

He smiled at the young women. "Ladies would you like a beer. I thought if we wanted another beer, I better get four beers right off."

Allison looked at the two men. "I would like a beer, but it was hard to get up to the bar for any service. You said your name was Logan.

This is my best friend, Mackenzie. "Hello Fergus. I would love a beer, I see you got Scottish beer. Is it just because it's made in Scotland or is it because ye are Scottish."

Logan and Fergus spoke at the same time. "Aye, that we are. Do ye come from Scotland."

Allison and Mackenzie also spoke at the same time. "Aye, that we do. So, what part of Scotland does ye come from? I would take it ye family comes from the Highlands."

Allison was looking at Logan. "With the name MacGregor I heard about your family from my parents. Tell me how long are ye in the service for."

Logan looked at Allison. "This is our last year. My father needs me to take over the ranch for him. We live in Vermont, how about yourselves? The same with us, but where not in Vermont we live in Bosten. This might sound strange to you, do ye believe in spirits."

Fergus looked at the two girls. He spoke. "Are you talking about family spirits."

Mackenzie looked at Fergus. "Allison, we been in the service about three years. We were nurses, one day we were setting in are apartment when a spirits from Logan side of the family. He told us to go to USO sitting in the back. There will be two young men looking to meet women. He even told us their names. It was you two."

Fergus smiled and he looked at Logan. All he did was nod his head. "Mackenzie, was his name Thomas MacGregor."

The two girls looked at each other. "Aye, he said that we would find our soulmates tonight."

Both men had down their beer. "I was wondering if you like to go somewhere, where we can hear us talking. I could get us a bottle of Scotch to take with us."

Both women did the same with their beer. "Aye, so ye believe us."

Then a woman came to pick up the Empty bottles. She asked if there was anything else she could get them. Logan replied. "Yes, we like a bottle of Scotch to go."

She smiled at him. "I will be right back."

When the woman came back, she had it in a paper bag. She took the money and left. "I could get us two rooms so we could talk."

The girls laughed. "We have a car and apartment also. There is much to talk about."

The four of them left together. At the girl's apartment they made something to eat. The girls had put four small glasses on the table. They had steak and everything to go with it. Logan poured them Scotch. Allison spoke. "When my family came to America, I was fifteen at the time. Our father loves to talk about the Highlands. Every Friday, we would have Scotch. Now tell me, do you believe us."

Logan smiled at Allison. She spoke. "Yes... I'm from the MacGregor side. Alex niece married a young man from Florida. Mackenzie side was from Neil niece; she married a man from Texas. You two are from Neil and Alex side. There are children in between the bloodline it's spread out."

After eating the boys helped them to clean up. The boys asked them when they were out of the navy. The two girls replied. They had six months left.

The two men looked at each other. They replied that they had six months. Virginia is their home port. Logan spoke. "Now we can get to know each other, if the two of ye would like."

The girls looked at each other. "Logan in our family the women had a rough time. The bloodline is well mixed up. The women married more of them ones."

Mackenzie looked at Fergus. "Allison, and I was wondering if ye like to stay the night with us. We never have men stay over if you two do we are not virgins. I know that they said us girls are our soulmates. If we are, I would like to see what kind of lover you're. The reason the women had married more the ones is because of sex and the men hit them. That's why the bloodline mixed up. We would like to know about you two. We have six months to know if you're the one."

Logan and Fergus liked the idea. The girls were near the base and liked the idea of having sex. They played games and talked while playing. Allison went to get more snacks; Logan went with her. Ones in the kitchen he had spun her around. He had enough games. If she was his soulmate Logan wanted to know now. He looked at her deep in her eyes his little friend liked her.

He wanted to know how she kissed. "You want to find out what kind of a man I am. I want to know how you kiss me. I need to know if you like the way I get you hot. I want to know how sweet your nectar is when you come."

Allison looked at him. "What do you mean my nectar."

He smiled. "You don't know about your own nectar; it comes from your flower. It will be new to you; I like this idea."

Logan made his moves on her and he pulled her into him. His hand cupped her breast they were firm, and he wanted skin. Allison had on a blouse he could take down. When he found skin, he made her nipple hard. He had one leg rubbing her heat."

She was digging her nails into his back. "No fair, I can't get to you."

Allison pushed him away and fixed her top. She took his hand and led him to her room. Mackenzie and Fergus were nowhere.

Logan put her up against the wall, he kissed her and went for her pussy. She came long and hard now he tasted her nectar. "You're sweet I want more of that."

She couldn't think. "Hold on I need this uniform for Monday."

Logan thought about it. "I need mine also, where is your room."

Allison opened the door and pulled him inside, the door closed behind them. She took off her uniform and put it aside, he took his uniform off also. When they saw each other, he went for her. She was up against the wall kissing her. He noticed she had no panties. His was also gone. He pulled her legs up and sucked her nipple. She wanted him as much as he did. "Do I need to cover him before taking you."

Allison smiled at him. "I'm on something if you think we could get married, then your good. I always ask for the man to cover him."

Logan thought about it, Eleanor had told them these women was their soulmate. He took hold of his heat and slide it into her pussy. He had pumped her heat until she came. A little more and she came again. "Allison, hang on to me."

He took her to her bed and laid her across the side of the bed. Logan had one thing on his mind that was having more of her nectar. Allison didn't know what he was up to. The other men just did straight sex, until he came out of her. She watched him go to his knees. Her legs went over his shoulders; she wasn't prepared for what came next. She couldn't help herself he got her to come until she couldn't do it anymore. She dug her nails into the blanket; sweet cries of pleasure came from her.

Then he placed her on her pillow, and he was back inside her. He kissed her and let her taste what he had done to her. Then he brought her up again, each thrust drove her to another climax. The last thrust he came with her, her body never felt this relax after sex.

Logan came down on top of her, he buried his face into her neck. She never felt the power of a man's climax inside her. He kissed her neck, cheek then her lips, she felt little quakes inside her. He had watched her eyes as he shot his seed inside her pussy. Then he turned her over on top of him.

He felt when she tried to get off him. He thought the other men never gave her that kind of pleasure. "Allison where are you going, have you had enough. Is this too much for you for I'm not done with you."

She looked at him, the other men didn't want her to stay on them. He smiled and told her to sit up slowly on him. She did what he had said. This was new to her as he went deeper inside her. "I never done this before."

Logan liked the idea that this was all new to her. He watched her eyes as she noticed his heat going deeper inside her. He sat up and made her ben backwards having her arms hold herself up. He went for her nipple and made the butterflies come out. Then she took hold of his heat, he laid backdown, "I want you to grind yourself on me."

He helped her as he got her to come. He had to work hard for his next climax; that's it. Yes… that's it."

Logan made her set up straight as he filled her again. He pulled her to his mouth; she came down on top of him straightening her legs. They were both breathing hard. Her head was on the pillow with him; there she fell asleep.

Logan waved his hand; he had covered them. He had closed his eyes, and at last he found his soulmate. She woke up and looked at him.

His eyes open. "Sit up a bit. When we find are mate, we give them the cross and rose. I have magic and you will also have magic. It will also tell you if demons are around you. The cross and rose will stop you from using your magic. Only if it would put you in danger, of someone finding out that you have magic.

Allison had never used any magic. Her parents said she does have magic. "I was told that I have magic but never used it."

He looked at her. "Allison my family depends on Eleanor MacGregor. Her spirit comes to us when we need help. She had told me you're my mate; I haven't enjoyed sex until I met you. We have been looking for three years. I will tell you this, the women I had sex with didn't let me do anything but strait sex. When you let me pump my seed in you two times. That was a first time someone matched my hunger for sex. Tell me this, did you enjoy the way I made love to you?"

He put his hand on her chest. Logan was thinking about when to marry her. He had given her the cross and rose to keep her safe from demons. He knew that they would come after her.

Allison heard what he had said. "Did you just say that the demons could come after me."

Logan looked at her. "Did you hear that," I was thinking. My family always says if you hear each other thinking that means you are my soulmate. Down the road would you like to become my wife? We have three months to explore the idea.

Allison could now hear his thoughts. She was so happy to know he was the one for her. She knew it was getting close for Tom and Ellen to be born. "Logan, I can hear you. I heard you talking over to yourself, when to marry me. Do you think the demons will come after me? It is getting close for Marcos to come back to earth. Then we could be the ones to give Tom life. Then again it could be our son. I love the way you made love to me. This was the first time; you enjoy sex with a woman. It was the same for me with other men it was wham bam thank you mam. I could tell, Am I right… because this was my first time to have this much pleasure. Thank you. In three months, you will be away from me. Tell me you want a child right off."

He didn't realize she could hear his thoughts. "I'm sorry about that. For the past three years Fergus and I have been looking for a mate. The men in my family like sex. I was twenty-one when we came into the service. The Navy sent us to various places. Every time I got to make love to a woman. She wanted it wham band thank you mam. I didn't realize I was that hungry. For someone I could love, who would love me back. How about this, we have three months to see if this is what we want. It will be our son to bring Tom into this world. My Aunt likes history, so she keeps records on the two families.

Fergus and I are the youngest, I thought the pill should be out of your system before I take you with my child. When I'm out of the Navy I will be Twenty-five."

Logan noticed he was sticky; he waved his hand to clean them. "Thank you but I have to go some where's."

He watched her run to the bathroom. She had a beautiful body, yes, she's the one. If she lets him, he will make love to her again. "You do know I'm two years younger than you. What... you want sex again. Thank heaven I found a man who like sex."

He laughed. "You heard that. Did you also hear that you have a nice bottom? I will tell you this my little friend like your girlfriend."

She walked out and started to laugh. "No... I must work tomorrow; I know how to make him go to sleep quickly."

He chuckled. "You have to work on a Sunday."

Allison hit her head. "That's right it's Saturday. I don't know if I have it in me to do it again."

She looked at him. She found herself walking over to him. He was sitting up when she came over. He had put his hands around her waist and picked her up and laid her on top of him. She thought, why do I want him inside me again. He kissed her. "Damn it... my little friend has a mind of his own. Don't move, just let him have her. No sex involved."

Allison laid her head next to him; she was asleep before her head hit the pillow. With her soft breathing he found he couldn't keep his eyes open and went right to sleep.

The next morning, she woke as she always did at 7:00. She found herself in the creak of his arm. Her hand was on his chest; she could feel his heart beating. Her body felt so relaxed, for a long time she never felt this way with a man. The men she went with wound her up. Then her thoughts change, it felt like a whisper reminding her of what she thought he said.

Did Logan say he will marry me? Allison didn't know what to think. She remembered her mother telling the story of MacGregor's. After Thomas and Eleanor passed away, their spirits stayed close to earth. Hardship was heading for her child if she marries a MacGregor. Her mother told her that Marcos would try to stop the ones who would give Thomas and Eleanor life. It will take the parents to get them ready to fight Marcos. She wondered if she was strong enough to do just that. Being in the service she managed patients that were fighting to stay alive. There were even ones that wanted to die.

This will be different; her son will be confused. Then she thought, how would I even know this. She thought about it; Thomas didn't tell her that her son could have troubles. Do I have the insight like my mother?

She went and turned away from Logan. Then he turned towards her, his arm went around her waist. His hand found her breast as he pulled her close to him. In her mind she heard *"don't worry about it. There will be four of us taking care of the two boys. All he heard was okay."*

CHAPTER FIVE

Getting to know each other

ONE MONTH WENT by the two couples found they were falling in Love. The girl's love their time with their men. Being with each other, any stress from work, melted away. The two women talked as they waited for their men to come out. What was it with a Scottish man, looking at them walking over to them. Both men were hot looking and all muscle, with strong arms to hold them. Just looking at them made their heart skip a beat. When they took them into their arms, they felt safe.

Their kisses could light them on fire. Fergus spoke. "Are you two women hungry. Logan and I would like to take you girls out to eat."

Mackenzie looked at Allison and the two started to giggle. They looked at their men and lick their lips. Logan looked at Fergus, his face was red. He spoke. "Will now it seem that were going home."

Both women laughed they got their point across. When they got into the car the boy saw two baskets with a bottle of wine. There were two blankets their women found a place that was quiet. They knew today was the day their men were going to propose to them. They had heard them talking about where to take them when they proposed. The women didn't say a word to them; they made plans of their own. With two baskets of food and blankets they found the perfect place. With soft music they propose to their women. They had told them that they were taking them back home to Vermont this weekend. They looked at their man. They had the same thought once there they would have to turn around and come back.

Both men had the biggest smile on their face. That day they found out; they could use a closet to be able to call the vortex. It was a week before the men had to go out to sea, they took their future brides to the two ranches. By magic the men made a door going to Vermont. With their arms around their brides to be. They walked into the vortex, then out in front of them was a waterfall.

The four of them walked down the path to a beautiful log cabin. Allison knew this one was going to be theirs. Both parents of the men along with the women's parents. This was the time to make plans for their wedding. Logan's father had looked into the water to see what was a goodtime to marry. He saw that their sons, were going to stay out to sea not for three months but six months. At the time they were in the month of February that would bring them to August.

Logan couldn't believe it. "Dad, are you sure about that. Damn it… Why now, are we going to do the work ups? Our ship was going back to shore to get everything we missed. We could have left then; every plan went up in smoke."

Fergus looked at Logan. He spoke. "Logan, I heard the guys talking. They knew the rumors were true. They had stop talking when they saw me."

His father came over to him. "Son as I was checking the dates. Thomas came to me and told me that Marcos mess with the timeline."

Logan wanted to hit something, but Allison walked over to him. She didn't say anything aloud. But in her mind as she framed his face with her hands. *"Honey don't worry about it. That month you are heading back home; I will go off my pill."* Then she put her arms around his neck. She heard him say, *all right. I guess we will see what happens. I'm so glad I have you."* The kiss made him feel much better.

*   *   *

During that time, the women moved their things to their new home. The two families had all their things out. They didn't want to have that big place. A small home on three acres. There was a house already there, for each parent just took over for the other parent's home. They had people to take care of them.

Their men were home at last. Their things were out of the barracks a month before they left. Everything was in motion; the wedding was down by the water. It was a beautiful day; the two couples were married together.

Elsie had made a timeline of things that happen after they were born. She thought it would be nice to see what had happened during that timeline that their parents went through.

Logan MacGregor and Fergus Angel Heart got married on August 20, 1921.

The year the men was born Logan was born on February 27, 1896.

The history of their time: February 27, 1896. The Birth defeated Zanzibar in a 38-minute war (9:02 Am 9:40) Am Shortest record war in history.

Fergus was born on August 10, 1895. He was older then Logan.

Scott MacGregor and Rory Angel Heart got married May 12, 1885.

A bit of history

On August 26-27, 1883… eruption of Krakatoa. The volcanic island of Krakatoa erupts at 10:02 AM. Local time…163 villages destroyed, 36,417 killed by tsunami.

May 1, 1893… The World's Fair, also known as the World's Columbian Exposition, opens to the public in Chicago, Illinois.

June 28,1914 there was a man assassinated it was Archduke Franz Ferdinand, and just five weeks later the Great Powers of Europe were at war.

The 1935 act, passed by Congress on August 31, 1935, imposed a general embargo on trading in arms and war materials with all parties in war.

Logan MacGregor married Allison on August 20, 1921.

Fergus Angel Heart married Mackenzie on August 20, 1921.

Logan and Fergus history

After their wedding, the two couples were enjoying each other. This was the time they were planning to have children. Nighttime the waterfall was a beautiful place to make love to their wife. The men only had eyes for their wife. The women all so had blinders on. Magic made it possible to walk out of the water and lay on the rock naked. This was the time to be like teenagers,' They had sex whenever the urge hit them. In the hayloft there was another place. Their wife was always ready for them. In that timeline women wear dresses. One time Logan had her go up the ladder and stop her on the first step. He then turned her around and lifted her dress. He had her put her legs around him, this time he used his kilt. A quick way to get his heat in her pussy. Allison was always wet for him. He knew what she liked and didn't like.

They didn't think if a month went by, she wasn't with a child. Six months and they found out Allison was pregnant. The year was February 10, 1922. Mackenzie got pregnant three months before Allison. On November 30, 1921.

The history of the world: After winning the civil war in Russia, the Bolsheviks established the Soviet Union in 1922.

The history of the world: In November there was an ice storm in 1921. They say history repeats itself in Massachusetts to New England. It hit on April 19, 1925

Two more years past Mackenzie was on August 12, 1924, she had a son Stuart. Allison had her daughter on November 20, 1924. Her name was Emily.

The history of the world: 1923 was a memorable year. Among the events was the Tokyo, Japan earthquake.

Five years went by the two women had their next children. Mackenzie had a little boy on May 19, 1927; they called him Daniel Angel-Heart. Allison had a little boy on September 10, 1926; his name was Michael MacGregor.

Two more years went by. Allison had a son on May 18, 1929. They called him James MacGregor.

Two more years went by. Mackenzie had her son on August 16, 1928. His name was Joseph Angel-Heart.

The history of the world: The stock market crash on October 1929. It had led directly to the great depression in Europe.

*   *   *

Two years went by the year was 1931 a man came over to them. It was a demon who had confronted Allison and Mackenzie. This demon told them that the babies you are caring. Something will happen and you two will miscarry your child. After that day, the two of you will not conceive, a child. He then resided with a spell a gray cloud enveloped them. After that when the cloud and demon were gone, they didn't remember anything. That night they were in great pain. Logan and Fergus took them to the hospital. In the hospital two young girls of the age of seventeen gave birth.

By magic, Thomas had the four babies change places. The young teenagers had received Allison and Mackenzie, still-born babies. It had been hard for these young girls for what they had gone through. It was a blessing that the child didn't live.

It would be a long-time later Joesph and James would find out that Desiree and Malaya weren't their sister. By Lesley letter will tell the boys. Their parents found out what happened to their child. Thomas and Eleanor told them.

World History

The history of the world: In 1931, Japan invaded and conquered in northeast China, Manchuria.

The history of the World: 1945 was a year in the 20th century that saw the end of World War II.

CHAPTER SIX

Joseph and James were born

THE YEAR IS 1945, the boys were now sixteen. Both boys played football Joseph was the captain of the team. James was the second captain when they were practicing against each other. They also were in ROTC; they worked hard to go up in the ranks.

The girls were two years younger. But they love being around their brothers. Desiree and Malaya didn't want to hang around their brother, but each other's brother. It was like the time with Thomas, Eleanor, William, and Catherin. They took on each other's sister, at the time they didn't know the girls weren't their sister either one. The two of them always hung around them. Both girls were very smart, they didn't act their age. The boys were tall and so were the girls. Every day, they ran with the boys, they kept up with them. In school they were a year behind the boys, even though they were almost fifteen. While the girls ran on track the boys practiced football. The four of them were good at what they did.

Desiree looked at Joseph as if she wanted him to notice her. As children, he would played school with her, he was always the teacher. He showed her how to ride a horse and learn how to swim. She could feel something more than pretending he was her brother.

Malaya also looked at James. She loved being with him; he showed her how to ride and learn how to swim.

*　　*　　*

Joseph was lying on the rock looking at the clouds. Desiree swam over to the other side of the waterfall. She went over to him. "What are you doing tonight? I saw Jane swimming off; I thought that you two was going to the drive in."

Joseph shaded his eyes and looked at her. She thought, "Could he be looking over my body? Then she heard him in her mind. *"Damn it… she has a nice shape, what the hell am I doing."*

Then he got up and went over to that big rock. "Desiree what do you think of me going into the Navy. I like to become a Navy Seal."

She looked at him and thought he was running away. *"Becoming a Navy Seal is dangerous, has he forgotten that he is the one to give life to Ellen."*

She didn't know what to tell him. "Have you asked every girl you went out with that question. Joseph, you've gone through too many girls; do you think you will find the one somewhere else? You would have to tell her about Marcos."

Joseph had been thinking the same thing. "Why haven't you gone out with anyone. The same thing with my sister. Desiree what do you think of me going into the Navy."

She turned away from him. In her mind she cried out. *"It scares me to hi heaven. But I'm not the one to give birth to Ellen. You don't think of me that way."*

She knew she had to ask him why he was asking her that question. "Joseph why are you asking me about this. I'm not your girlfriend; you haven't thought of me in that way. I'm just your little sister."

He was having a hard time at that moment, he couldn't think. Then he had a thought. *"Would she want to be my girlfriend? I haven't had feelings like I'm having right now. She's my best friend and I've always had her near me. I know she's not my sister, damn it. I've haven't made love to anyone. Damn it, why am I thinking this way? Does Desiree love me to become my mate? Would she follow me as my wife?"*

As far back as he could remember, he wanted to go out running. He would always ask her to come with him. One time when they were playing around. They rolled down the hill and he landed on top of her. Did he see hunger for him to kiss her? He heard the answer, when she cried out, it scared me. Would he be strong enough to do that kind of work?"

He thought take it slow. "Would you like to go to the drive in with me. If you like we could call it a date."

Did he ask me to go on a date with him? "Joseph, are you thinking of not calling me your little sister anymore."

He looked at her. "Do you want me to spell it out for you."

She looked at him and nodded her head. "Yes… that is what I need you to say. That you want to start dating me."

Joseph smiled at her. She has always been with me. He wondered if she would let him kiss her. "Desiree, would you like to be my girlfriend and go out tonight on a date."

How long has she wanted to hear those words? She turned and ran into his arms she looked into his eyes. "What took you so long to ask me to be your girlfriend. Yes… I will be your girlfriend."

He couldn't think she was in his arms. She was so close all he had to do was bend his head and kiss her. Then he felt her lips on his, he ran his tongue over those lips. She opens; he didn't stop, he took and deepened that kiss. So sweet, he pulled her into him. The kiss lasted longer than any other kiss from any of the girls he dated. Joseph found they lit each other on fire. She was digging her fingernails into his skin. "Desiree, slow down my god woman you must help me. I want you, damn it woman. I can't do this right now, please honey help me to get control over myself.

Then she looked at him. "Joseph did you say you want me in that way."

She felt his little friend pushing against her swimsuit. He had pulled her legs up and put her against the rock. I want to touch you and give you some pleasure.

She was trying to get him to put her legs down. In her mind she told him *"Let go of my legs."* Something was wrong, he had never acted this way before. "Joseph let go of my legs."

She pushed him back and yelled at him. "What do you think you're doing. Let go of me now. Is that how you treat your girlfriends? You're not going to use me… I'm not your plaything."

Then she heard a deep voice telling him to get up and get her now. She heard Joseph telling him *"No…"* the demon spoke. *"You will do what I say."*

Right then Joseph dropped her legs and went to his knees. His hands went over his ears. He yelled. "Get out of my mind."

She felt the cross and rose on her chest go hot. There was a demon trying to mess with his mind. "Desiree, get the hell out of here, I can't hold him back."

Then she remembered what her mother told her. If a demon is around to call for holy water. With her magic she called for the cross and rose. She then brought holy water; how did the demon get into his mind. Jane was the only one with him who could have placed a demon. What happened to his cross and rose. In her mind she called out for him. *"Begone Saten… I am his mate."*

All she heard was him laughing. With the holy water she put a cross on the top of his head. Then on the back of his neck. Joseph raised his head, and she quickly put a cross on his forehead. Then on his ears and last the cross on his chest. She poured over the cross the holy water. It burned and Joseph cried out.

Desiree didn't understand how it was burning him. Then Joseph spoke. "Pour the rest over my head. She did what he had asked her. His back was strata his hands were in a fist. As the holy water ran down his body. She waved her hand again and the bottle of holy water appeared. Desiree poured the last of the holy water and heard the demon scream. A black smoke came out of him. Joseph pulled her to him he was shaking and couldn't stop.

She held him, his breathing slowed. She had rubbed the holy water into his skin. "I got you… just hold on to me, the demon is gone."

That is how her brother found them. "What the hell is going on here."

She knew he didn't understand why Joseph had her that close to him. "James shut up and let him be. There was a demon that took over his mind."

James and Joseph's sister came over to him. "What can I do for him."

Then he raised his head and looked into her eyes. *"Thank you… are you still going to be my girlfriend."*

She smiled at him; she would love to kiss him right now. *"Yes… we have some explaining to do."*

Joseph sat back on his legs. "I believe, Jane was a witch. The spell blocked the cross and rose. She let the demon become a cover over my skin. When the cross and rose with the holy water, had touch the demon's body first. He was the one that screamed, I had no control over my body. The demon wasn't touching me; it was Jane's body who touched me. There had to be a shell over the cross and rose."

James was wondering how long the demon was with him. "I been seeing her for a week, each time the demon joined with my mind. She was letting him go in slowly. They didn't think that Desiree had powers, James that pack we have. I don't want it anymore. From this moment I'm starting to date Desiree. She can now hear my thoughts; the demon feared her. She told him she was my mate. At the time, they knew she wasn't your blood sister James. Malaya you're not my blood sister either. When the demon thought he had control over me he had told me this. A demon killed our real sister. That's why our mothers had to go to the hospital, there were two young girls giving birth. When both sets of babies before they were born, the angels had switch them. Thomas had asked The Lord if the angels could do this. For a demon had killed the two babies. The young girls had a rough time; they were always sick. It was a blessing that their children died."

Then Malaya looked at Desiree. "Yes… I remember that Thomas came to us. But he told us we wouldn't remember until now. He had said that our real grate grandmothers were the ones saved by Garret. Marcos's child went to heaven. The young women parent, and the boys who got them with child had magic."

Joseph then decided to tell James what he was feeling. "Right now, I like to talk with Desiree. I'm going to date your sister; you must find out if you have feelings for my sister. We can show then the letter from Emile. You also must tell her what job you're going after."

*　　*　　*

James and Malaya left; it was time to find out what each other felt for the other. Joseph felt weak and lay down on the grass. He had his eyes closed and didn't see what Desiree was doing. She had laid down next to him, his arms were up over his head. For a long time, she wanted to feel his body against hers. She was a strong woman; she was able to hold herself up. Until her lips touched his, he then felt her body above him. His arms went around her as he pulled her down on top of him.

That kiss lasted for a long time; he worked his legs between hers so she could feel his heat. Joseph placed his hands directly on her bottom. He pushed her into his little friend. When the kiss ended, he spoke. "Desiree, do you know what you're doing to me."

*　　*　　*

She knew what she was doing, many times his eyes were on hers. She took his mouth again, Joseph let her rub her breast over his chest. They went after each other's mouth. She raced her head and looked at him. "What else will you do to me."

He smiled at her. "I like to suck your nipple; that will bring out the butterflies deep in your pussy."

Joseph watched her eyes close as she thought about it. "What if I ask you to do something. What would you do then."

His eyes stayed on hers. "You ever heard about finger fucking."

She remembered hearing the girls talking. "Yes, would you put a finger in my pussy?"

He didn't smile but kept his eyes on hers. "Yes, when I do. I know you will come; the pleasure will drive you to push my finger deeper. I know myself, the dreams I had of you, I want to make you come again. To help myself I will rub my heat on your leg. I'll go after your nipple. Then back to your mouth, my tongue will make love to your mouth."

He wanted to touch her to get her hot. Both hands were on her bottom, he lifted her a bit. When he started to rub his heat over her pussy. Her head went back as she pushed down on him. Her breathing was coming quicker. "All right… I give in. Joseph, please touch me. I love you, from here on no one will touch me this way only you."

He took her mouth and turned her over until he was on top of her. He went under her top, to play with her nipple. When her nipple was hard, he went for it. The feelings he brought out in her, it drove him to give her more. She grabbed his hand and pushed it in her panties. When she felt his finger go over where the butterflies were coming from. She pushed his finger inside that spot; her head went back as the pleasure washed over her. He waited for her; with his magic he made his finger bigger around. He knew she was small there. She was his mate, and he wanted her ready to take his heat inside her.

All this time she was the one he was looking for. Does his parents know that the babies were switch on them. His thoughts were portraying him.

She is still young I can't have her this soon. "Joseph, have I done something wrong."

He took out his hand and put his finger in his mouth. His eyes closed, she sweet he thought. "Joseph, I know I'm still young. Eleanor was my age, I love you. Why did you touch me and make me want you."

She felt hurt the moment he left her. She fixed her top but still felt his finger inside her pussy. Desiree knew he was still hard; he looked into her eyes. He saw the hurt in them, then he got angry with himself. He walked over to the boulder and slammed his fist down.

Then she knew he wanted to be one with her. "What do you think you're doing. I know you want me, as much as I want you. I got you hot, this young girl who doesn't know much. I know more than you think."

She grabbed his arm and spun him around. She pulled his swimsuit down and took hold of him. Her mouth went around his heat. She had control over him. Joseph didn't think, he went after her breast and started to play with her nipple. His other hand on her shoulder to steady himself. Quickly he left her breast for he was about to come. His fingers titer on her shoulders. Joseph watched her swallow; he pulled her up to him. She brought his swimsuit with her. "You didn't have to do that. What am I going to do? I love your toys; your pussy is sweet. I would love to have more."

Her eyes dared him to do so. He took her were her brother wouldn't see them. There was a rock with a tree growing out of it. A part where he laid her down on. He took off her bottoms of her swimsuit, that's when he went for her pussy. His finger pumped her heat, as his tongue played with her clit. With his magic he made his tongue go deeper in her. He was able to get her to come until she couldn't anymore.

He pulled her into him and kissed her lips, as his tongue made love to her. She tasted what he had done to her. "Joseph, I want you to take my maidenhead. I want to be yours only yours."

Joseph ran a hand through his hair. She knew what she was doing. Tomorrow she will be fifteen. Her magic was strong, they were naked, and he was on the ground. Now she was on top of him as she slipped him inside her. She came down on his little friend and took him deep inside her. She didn't feel it when his heat took her maidenhead. His eyes were big and there was a panic look in them. "What are you doing, you're not ready for this."

When she took hold of him and started to move, he lost it. Damn it woman you want this, okay will do it. She was down on the ground, and he started to pump her pussy. He drove his little friend to her repeatedly. She came until she couldn't anymore. That's when he sat up straight in bed. It was a dream, a hell of a dream.

Joseph wondered if it was a warning. The part where she wasn't James's sister. Then he thought what about Jane could she be a witch. She could be an older woman who knew a thing or two.

Then it was Desiree is she my mate or is this just a dream. Tonight was the full moon; a swim would help. He waved his hand and was in the water naked. When he came up for air there was Desiree. She liked to swim naked also. He stayed where he was and watched her. How he would like to know how she felt about him. The things she did to him, and he did to her. That stuck in his mind, then he wondered if she had the same dream. You're here…, and she's here…, either call to her or go back to bed.

What was it with him? He always could talk to her. Damn it, he thought. "Desiree, I see you also couldn't sleep tonight."

She turned quickly and saw it was Joseph. "A dream woke me up, how about you."

He swam over to her. "Why do I have a feeling we are both naked. My dream woke me up; it was about you and me. I don't know what to think about it. One part was about Jane, she a witch who got a demon in my head."

She looked at him, this was not funny. What is going on, she thought. "What else happen in your dream."

What could this mean, is she telling me she had the same dream. "You saved me, but I was doing things to you at the time."

Oh no she thought he had the same dream. "Then the demon told you I wasn't James's sister. The same with your sister."

He thought I need to keep my cool, then stop going closer to her. "That is what I heard. After you saved me, you told the demon that you were my soulmate. Tell me what you think about that."

Desiree thought about it but didn't know how to deal with it. She always had feelings for him. These feelings were strong, and she didn't know how to tell him. She closed her eyes and just spoke what was in her heart. "Joseph yes, I have feelings for you. The kind of feelings that a man and woman have. But you think of me as your sister, I want to be with you. Yes Joseph, when you go into the Navy, I will follow you. The Navy Seals do scare me; I want you to be mine. To love me while were teenagers. I don't want to be your little sister. I want to go out with you and become your girlfriend."

How can this be that a dream could tell us; what we been feeling right along? She loves me, here we are naked and getting closer to each other. "How in Sam hell can I keep my hands off you. If the dream is right, you made me take your maidenhead by sitting on me. You use your magic on me. If this comes about, I want to take you myself and make you mine.

The two of them were behind the rock. She was close to him. "Are you telling me that you want me."

They were just shy of the rock to stand on. He had pulled her the rest of the way. "Jane don't love me, and I don't like being with her. She noticed I look at you when you walk by me in school. I didn't give her anything of mine. Do you think I will give you Ellen."

He had her against the rock she could touch his heat if she likes. "Yes…, that is just what I think. Were the once that will give life to Ellen. But we will have a son first."

Joseph found he wanted this. He liked that idea about having a son with her. I can get her with our child. "Desiree, do we have time to get to know each other."

She looked into his eyes. One hand on the rock and the other hand on the back of her neck. "It will take time to get you ready for me. I guess we have been going down this path for a while. Don't rush this I will have you soon enough."

He wanted to do the things in their dream. "Joseph your body is strong, not overdone in muscles."

How could we stay this way knowing we are naked? "You are a beautiful woman, if the girls knew you were younger and have a body like you do. They couldn't look at you."

She laughed at that. "They don't like to see me looking like I do. They think I stayed back a year in school. Why do you think I don't ask for a cake with candles."

Joseph started slowly, he bent his head and kissed her. He looked at her as her eyes open after the kiss. This time when he bent his head he ran his tongue over her lips. She knew what to do as she parted her lips. He should have been ready for this, but he wasn't. There was a tase of cherry on her lip.

He's been so blind, the woman for him was always with him. "I want to go slow with you. Damn it, my little friend and mind are both together on this. You have toys; any man would love to have these toys to play with."

He wanted to touch her breast; they were full and wanted to be touch. Her hand took his hand and laid it on her breast. Right off his thumb started to rub her nipple. His tongue made love to her mouth as if it was her pussy. He had to put something over their bottom, her hands like squeezing his bottom. Then his lips touched her nipple until she couldn't take any more. She took his hand and ran it into her swimsuit that he put on her. He had big hands, and his finger was right for the job. She shook her head. "Were going too fast for right now."

He saw her wave her hand and she was gone. She was dry and in bed but not asleep, it took her a bit to fall asleep.

That morning, Joseph called Jane and told her he had enough. He's not going to date her anymore; she is not the one for him. He told her he had a dream that she was a witch that was helping a demon get into his mine.

When she hung up. She spoke. "Eleanor sent him a dream. He knows I'm a witch, and a demon was going after him. It's over with."

Joseph was outside waiting for her to come by. She was so pretty this morning. It was Saturday, and the two of them ran together. James came by just after they left, and Malaya was waiting for him. They ran without talking to each other. The four of them ran five miles on Saturday and Sunday. After school they ran before they ate, after the run he asked Desiree if she would like to go to the movies with him. She said yes.

CHAPTER SEVEN

Emile's letter

Hello Joseph,

I've been thinking about you and James. It's a big step volunteering to become a Navy Seal. You boys wanted to be just like me. I've heard this also from your fathers. I made those stories glamorous. I'll tell you a little bit about how I became a Navy Seal. As you know I joined the Navy in 1943.

After the attack on Pearl Harbor. They started an Amphibious Training Base. This base was adapted for both land and water. The units UDT-1 and UDT-2. The Birthplace for UDT-Seal teams: was Waimanalo, Hawaii. The service took men from the Air Force the Navy, Army, and Marine Corps. I became a diver for the UDT that they called a frogman. They were the first Airborne Frogmen. Not only went under water. These men took on difficult assignments. They would jump from a plane landing in water with full diving gear. In 1948, a team of three men in a small submersible. Made the first docking with a submerged submarine on the USS Quillback's. These men work on the Sea. In the Air, and on Land. These men go wherever needed, their history from the elite frogmen of World War 11. Special Operations missions in all operational environments took special men. "Amphibious Roger." Trained for at the Scout and Ranger school at Ft. Pierce, Florida.

In 1962, President Kennedy. He had set up SEALS Teams ONE and TWO from the existing UDT Team. To develop a Navy Unconventional Warfare Capability. The Navy Seal Teams, designed as the maritime counterpart to the Army Special Forces *"Green Berets."* They deployed act at once to Vietnam. They work in the deltas and thousands of rivers and canals in Vietnam. These teams effectively disrupted the enemy's maritime lines of communication. The SEAL was so effective that the enemy named them, *"the men with the green faces."*

*　　*　　*

Emile tries to let the boys know what they were going up against. "Joseph, this job is one of the dangerous jobs to get into. Your mind must always be on your job. One slips up and a man could die, or it could be you. Two months ago, I sent both father's letters. I told them everything you will be going through. If you think High school was hard, think again. I asked your ROTC teacher to tell me your grades. I'm impressed by what he sent me. Both you and James are right at the top. I also told him to add more on your running and other things. Remember this isn't a game. For twenty-five years I have been a Navy Seal.

There is a six-month training course, called BUD/Seal, which is a 6-month SEAL training course. It's held at the Naval Special Warfare Training Center in Coronado, CA. You'll start with five weeks' Indoctrination and Pre-Training as part of a Navy Seal class. Then you will go through the Three Phases of BUD/Seal. Called Basic Underwater Demolition/Seal.

Joseph, you wanted me to tell the two of you what the test is like. The way we would describe to anyone who would want to volunteer for the Navy Seal. This is all true what I'm telling you. It may change your mind about volunteering. This part I'm not going to sugar coat it. I'll tell it like it is.

First, Phase is the toughest. It consists of 8 weeks of Basic Conditioning. It peaks with a grueling segment called *"Hell Week."* This is a midway point where the two of you will be tested to your limits.

Hell Week: Is a test of physical endurance and mental, tenacity.

Tenacity: to see if you can stick to a goal. If you have staying power to keep going.

Teamwork: Efficiency of the whole team, and courage. There can be two-ninths of your classmates that call it quits or *ring the bell.*

To ring the bell some men, have its others don't. Physical discomfort and pain will cause you to decide it isn't worth it. The miserable wet-cold approaching hypothermia will make others quit. Sheer fatigue and sleep deprivation. Will cause every candidate. To question his core values, motivations, limits, and everything he's made of and stands for. Those who grit it out to the finish will hear their instructors yell the longed-for words,

Hell Week, secured

There will be an exceptional few. With burning desire, they will persevere. Were their bodies are screaming to quit yet continue. These men experience a tremendous sense of pride, achievement, brotherhood, and a new self-awareness.

I can do anything I put my mine to!

The most outstanding among them. The man whose sheer force of will becomes their example. He inspires his classmates to keep going. When they're ready to quit, he Will become the *"Honor Man"* of the Class. These determined men will continue.

Second Phase: 8 weeks of Diving.

Third Phase: 9 weeks of Land Warfare.

Most men who have succeeded in Hell Week make it through these phases. If not, it's usually due to academic issues.

For example, diving physics. In the Dive Phase, or weapons and demolitions safety/ competency issues. In the Land Warfare, weapons, and tactics Phase. When you complete BUD/Seal, trainees go through 3 weeks of Basic Parachute Training.

At this point, training shifts from testing. This part will see how you react in a high stress moment, called *Gut check."*

Environment: The circumstances, objects, or conditions one surrounded as a life-or-death moment. To make sure the trainees are competent in their core tasks.

The men go through a final 8 weeks of focused
Seal Qualification Training.

In mission planning operations, and tactic, techniques. Upon completion they may wear the coveted Navy Seal Trident Insignia on their uniform.

Seal training ends with the formal BUD/
Seal Class Graduation Training.

In mission planning operations, and tactic, techniques. Upon completion, they may wear the coveted Navy SEAL Trident insignia on their uniform. SEAL training ends with the formal BUD/s Class Graduation.

Here are the proud few in their Navy uniforms. They our recognized for their achievement in the presence of family and senior SEAL leaders.

The Commanding Officers and senior enlisted advisors of the Naval Special Warfare Groups and SEAL Teams attend. The BUD/ Seal graduates, as their newest Teammates. These men if they make it, this elite group that they have entered. To be worthy of the sacrifices of the courageous Frogmen who came before them. This is a great honor it is to serve as a U.S. Navy SEAL.

*   *   *

Joseph, this part is for the woman that you would like to marry or go out with. My wife said I need to tell you everything about Navy Seal. Women will have to be able to deal with this if they get out. It takes a strong woman, to deal having their man gone all the time. This is also any part of the Air Force. The Navy, Army, and Marine Corps. It takes a special kind of woman, to be able to deal with this.

"As my wife said, she will deal with it when it happens. To think about what he is going through is too much. He has a job to do; she also has her job. Her job is to take care of their children and their home. If the children are all in school, she may have a job or she volunteer."

A SEAL must devote 100% of himself to his job and having a family needs 100% of a man's attention! One element in his life is going to suffer, it will be his family. His family can take more than a job as a SEAL.

If you don't show up to your child's game nothing happens. Your child could adjust to it, or he will start to resent you! A relationship with a Navy Seal is a tough one! A SEAL is on call about every moment that he stays a Navy Seal! If you and your Seal boyfriend are having a wedding ceremony. He could deploy right in the middle of it if it were necessary! They are constantly in war zones that are extremely dangerous, and unforgiving.

In these zones. His mind must be on what he is doing. It could cost him is life. If he is thinking about the fight with is child, or his wife. Which means you are constantly worrying about them coming back home safely! Their training is dangerous. If you ask the men, they will say that he has almost died more times in training than in actual combat! Seals are always training. This means, even if there isn't a war, they could die in training! Navy SEALs can't even tell you when they will be deploying! It's also hard to get a Navy SEAL to quit his job! Imagine being the best of the best at everything. Surrounded by amazing people from all over the world. Doing everything, shooting, blowing stuff up. Going on adventures. Taking risk. Jumping out of planes. Occasionally you get a shot of adrenaline throughout your body. It's hard for them to retire.

The woman who holds the family together. If your man gets out remember P.T.S.D all men have this. Post traumatic stress disorder, even you may have it. As his wife you are the one who deals with everything. Like with your children, bills, things that break. If you are a woman that is needy and has to me the center attraction. I will tell you this don't marry a service man.

My wife told me about what a Navy wife had done to her husband. Her husband was on an Aircraft carrier. He got a letter saying she was pregnant, then told him it wasn't his. That young man had dove, off the top of the carrier. The aircraft stands twenty stories high.

The service life can be hard; some men don't truss their wife with money. If you marry and don't like to be alone don't marry a service man. The Army and Marine men and women can't keep a promise to come back a live. When the good book opens and your name is on that page. That means your time here on earth is over. If your man makes it through his time in the service. After a while he will remember all the things he had done. Then it will hit him. How could he top all of this? He wonders what to do next! For the past years, all he has known is grind, grind, GRIND, and now there is nothing! Let the girls know about this.

Good Luck, Joseph.
Your Uncle Emile

CHAPTER EIGHT

Getting to know each other

THAT NIGHT JOSEPH took Desiree to the drive-in. "Tonight, they have pizza; I can get us some along with popcorn. How about soda I'm getting root beer, would you like that or a different kind."

She smiled. "That will be find, I think I'm take this opportunity to go to the ladies room."

He looked at her. "You may see Malaya in that line. If the pizza is gone would hot dogs or hamburger do?"

She knew that this was awkward for them. "I'll take a hot dog if no pizza."

The two got out of the car. Then they saw James and Malaya. They were doing the same thing. "Hay you two. Ones we got inside and after where done. We will come and help the two of you."

Both girls got in line. "How is it going with the two of you."

She thought about that. "It's going slow, I feel lost. How about you two."

Desiree wanted to laugh. "We want too, but one of us always chicken outs."

Malaya shook her head. "I know just what you're saying. Do you know Joseph called her and told her it was over with. That he doesn't loves her."

The line was going fast. "Joesph didn't say anything about that."

Malaya thought about that call he made to Jane. "You know, she's going to give us grief about this."

Desiree shook her head. "No, she's not, her and I have tangle before. I'll meet you out at the snack bar."

She walked right up to Joseph and kissed him on the lips. Malaya was just behind her when she gave James a kiss on the lips. The two girls saw their classmates, they grabbed the sodas and went off in different directions. Both boys had big smiles on their faces. That will do it, one of the girls likes to gossip. With the food and drinks, Joseph put the pizza and popcorn on the roof of the car. He took the drinks from Desiree so she could get inside. They had drink holders on the door. He held the soda until she closed the door. Then he passed the pizza to her. "This pizza smells good."

*   *   *

At her door Joseph pulled her away from the light. "I had a good time with you; you know that kiss will be going around school."

Desiree's back was against the wall. "I know that, why do you think, I did that."

He was close to her, as he touched her face. "Once Jane finds out that I'm with you. She is going to give you some trouble."

She put a finger over his lips. "Don't worry about it, Jane and I have gone around before. Now are you going to kiss me before my brother gets here."

Joseph had one arm around her waist and the other behind her neck. The kiss was hot. "You may be younger then I, but damn it's woman. I don't know how you did it, no one before you could light me on fire. What am I going to do? My little friend wants your girlfriend."

Desiree felt the heat between them. She had also felt his little friend, she touched him. "Don't do that stop encouraging him. Damn it woman I want you."

She smiled at him. "I think you should take a swim to cool off. Good night."

James was coming up the stairs. "Tell me why it took us this long."

Joseph through up his hands. "I don't know. What I do know, Jane finds out that I'm dating Desiree. She will make trouble for her.

He smiled at his best friend. "Desiree can take care of herself; I think we should put a bubble around the girls. It would be just like Jane to do a sneak attack on her, that's what she did to you."

Joseph closed his eyes. "James, I want you to have Malaya help you with the roses. That way your father will be pleased with you. The roses will find out if she's your mate. It's time we get to know them."

James closed his eyes and shook his head. "I know I must take her to the magic rose. To see if a rose will drop into my hand. I think we should give the girls Emile's letter. They must know what there up against."

He looked at his old friend. "Malaya has seen the letter, our mothers gave the girls the letter Emile sent them. We got to talk to them about this. Tell me have you had that dream about Marcos?"

He looked at Joseph. "It's as if I have it once a week. I wish I knew who's pushing us to become Navy Seals. I have a bad feeling, Tom and Ellen will have it rougher then Thomas and Eleanor. Damn it, I see children in this big place, it looks like a jail. It's all fence in; there is a boy side and girl side."

Joseph remembered every part of that dream. "I don't know what to think about it. It's in Scotland, I don't know what to do about the dream, see you tomorrow.

*   *   *

In bed Joseph couldn't sleep. He waved his hand; Joseph dropped into the water. When he came up, he saw Desiree. "Desiree you couldn't sleep either."

She waved to him and swam over. "Hi, I had a dream that has me confuse."

She went into his arms. The two of them felt each other skin. "Your naked again, Desiree this is getting to much for me to deal with. I never had these feelings for any of the other girls. That's why I dated so many of them. But you get my little friend hot without trying, it gets to the point I want to take and make love to you. I want to be one with you. I want you to have my cross and rose. The only way I can do that is to become one with you and give you, my seed."

She went over to him and wrapped her arms around his neck. "Honey, could you show me Leslie letter to me."

He looked at her. "How did you know I knew where the letter was."

She wrapped her legs around him. His little friend, was between the two of them. He took her mouth in a hungry kiss. They went under the water when she waved her hand to bring them to the big rock. Desiree was under him; he needed to touch her. He kissed her all the way to her breast; were he suck on her nipple. She was moving her hips. "Joseph what is these feelings I'm having in my pussy."

98

His head popped up, he thought I need protection for her. "Desiree to give you my cross and rose, I must spill my seed inside you. I could get you pregnant, are you on the pill?

She had told him yes. "Tell me, what are these feeling? There is an ache in my pussy."

Joseph knew it wouldn't be long before he took her. "I call them butterflies; your pussy knows that my little friend is near her. She knows that he wants to mate with you. You have control over her. My little friend and my brain are fighting a battle for control. He wants to take you now; I want to get your pussy ready for him. He's quite strong, there is a battle between my brain and him. Tell me now to stop or let me finger fuck you. With my magic I can make my finger get bigger each time you come."

Desiree wanted him, he said that she was his mate. "Joseph, tell me when will we marry? I know it will be after your done with bootcamp am I right?"

Joseph looked at her, she been always around him. He would go out of his way to be with her. All the girls he dated never got his little friend to wake up before. There scent never tempted him, but when Desiree was around him. Something was happening to him, he waved his hand and called Leslie.

Hello Desiree, Joseph.

If the two of you want to mate. There is no chance of her getting pregnant, she is on the pill.

Desiree for a long time Joseph tried to get his feelings for you out of his head. At first, he didn't know that you and Malaya weren't James or Joseph's sister by blood.

Let's get to the heart of all this. Desiree yes, you will have Ellen, and Joseph will be her father. How did that happen? A demon had killed his real sister; there were two teenagers that were sick there whole pregnancy. The demon killed James and Joseph's sister, it was

Eleanor who saw the demon. She went to The Lord and asked if her cousin's daughter was one of the girls. Before the babies were born, an angel had switched them.

Your real mother is a distant cousin of Eleanor's. When she was sixteen her cousin's mother was giving a coming out party. Eleanor's cousin had been missing for nine months. They found her dead, with a cut in her neck. After she gave birth to a little girl, Marcos had killed her.

The day her and her baby were found, her brother had held the baby. He heard his sister's voice; she had asked him to raise her child. What he didn't know, he was going to raise his sister. Garret switched her mind and soul with the baby.

The baby went to The Lord, Marcos found out went he saw his father. Albert Huascaran met Eleanor's cousin. They lived near each other, the young men who like the girls dated them. Marcos bided his time until they were teenagers. He sent demons to possess the young men. These men raped the two girls, once the demons were out of them. The young men went to war and died from his wounds. It was a blessing that the girls' babies were dead.

The girls left and came to America, after the boys had raped the girls. When their church found out that demons had possessed the boys. They were shunning the girls and putting them down, they tried to get away from the past. It was the child blood line; they found out that Marcos had rape their mother. Once again, it was the blood from Marcos's that had kept coming up. It was also what had happen to the girls. They were shun because of the demons that had possess the boys. The girls tried to fight them off but couldn't.

Desiree your mother was grate-grate-grate granddaughter of Albert Huascaran. Marcos thought that Albert was his son. Malaya mother was Eleanor's cousin. The past came to haunt the girls. The letter told James he was going to mate with Malaya. He didn't want a letter telling him what was going to happen. He was thirteen and Malaya was ten. She didn't know about Leslie's letter. James wanted to burn the magic letter. Joseph understood that Lesley letter was hidden from James. Then he put a spell on him and James. Only the girls could break the spell. A kiss of love had broken the spell, the feelings for the girls would come back. You are at that point. Remember the girls cannot be with child until you two men are in the Navy. Malaya, Joseph, and James will be fine with the Navy Seal. You will make a fine Navy wife for him. He will not die in the Navy. Good Luck.

The letter came to his hand, and he read everything that Desiree had asked her about was true. He sent the letter to the magic roses. "You were right about everything."

Do you want me, Desiree? For here and now, I will give you my seed so you can have my cross and rose. When I get out of bootcamp we will get married. For I don't want anyone else to have my seed."

Desiree looked at him and, in her mind, she said "*Yes.*" "Tonight, I will make you a woman, as you will make me a man. For this is our first time together, hold on to me because I'm going to take your maidenhead. She didn't feel it when he went pass it. All she knew he was hers, now she was going to take his seed. It didn't take much, all she did was take hold of his friend. Joseph was under her and his little friend's control. When she came, he came right after. Joseph dropped on top of her; he kissed her neck then her lips. He turned her over on top of him. "Left up a bit so you can receive my cross and rose."

At the same time, she gave him her cross and rose. At last Joseph felt hold. "There was one thing she told me. If you got sick and had antibiotic don't have sex for you would get pregnant."

She looked at him. "Good to know. That mean he must have a rubber on him."

The two of them were getting to sleep. She was falling asleep on him; he cleaned her up and put her nightgown on her. He had his bottoms on now; he kissed her and sent them to their rooms. That was the best sleep the two of them had in a long time.

*　*　*

The next day was school; it was Joseph turn to drive to school. Before they got out of the car the girls kissed them. Three of their classmates saw them kissing, two of the girls who had dated the boys. Their teammates couldn't believe they were kissing. The boys had their arms around the girl's waist. "Joseph do you two have football practice?"

He was on cloud nine. He knew he would give Ellen life. "Do you have track today?"

Desiree saw everyone was watching them. "Yes, we do have practice, there is a track competition this week before your game."

The guys were surprised to see three of their teammates. "Joseph, we heard about Jane, so we came out to make sure she keeps away from you and James. Hay Desiree, will about time. I had a feeling that you had a crush on Joseph. That's why you didn't want to go out with me. You two Malaya, had a crush on James. Will now that open the field up, maybe I can get a girlfriend.

Malaya and Desiree started to laugh. "What did I tell you, I knew the word would get around. John, will you go and ask Lindsey out, she does have a crush for you."

John eyes open with surprise, he turned and saw Lindsey looking at him. Slowly she walked over to him. He looked to be frozen in place. Her hands went and framed his face. She had place a kiss on his lips. Quickly his arms went around her waist and pulled her to him. "Wow, boy I've been blind to all of this. Would you like to go out and get an ice cream with me after school?

Lindsey had a big smile. "I would love that."

Desiree smiled at Lindsey. "It's about time you two."

Then they saw Jane coming over to them. Desiree had brought up the cross and rose. She had sent it at her chest. Then place a bubble around her she had sent her away from them. No one saw what happened to her.

Joseph felt good free at last. "It was hard not to be with her. "For a long time, she has been there if I needed help, she runs with me. We have been together, just not in that way. Until Jane tried to put a spell on me with black magic. Desiree was able to stop her."

James's smile. "Don't feel bad John, we had blinders on. I'm glad there off, we been together. We ran and swam together, I always enjoyed being with her. I guess we been going down this path for a while."

Their teammates walked with them; Malaya and Desiree teams came around them. Three of the girls that were on Desiree track team, were dating the football players. "Is it true? Did Joseph and James also John find out that they were smitten on girls."

To hide their red faces, James, Joseph, and John kissed Desiree, Malaya, and Lindsey. "Go on with your teammates, will you have lunch with us."

Their eyes met; she smiled at him. "That sound like a plan."

Joseph and James were worried that Jane would give them trouble. Desiree went over to Joseph. "Stop worrying about us we have are friends around us, we will see you at lunch."

*　　*　　*

The two of them went to the bathroom and they saw Jane. Desiree shows Malaya her hand that had three rose petals, Malaya did the same. They walked up to her and placed their hands directly on her shoulder. "I'm sorry it didn't work out for you and Joseph. Don't worry, we have their backs, and they have are backs. You're not free from them yet here is the cross and rose for your heart, mind, and soul. You're going to be sick, I hope you make it. Desiree sent a note that a girl is very sick."

Jane looked at Desiree. "That demon you locked me into a bubble. He always kept to my back of me; I couldn't get to him. Thank you, I'm free of him. I then got sick and threw up the black stuff, I feel free at last. Malaya and Desiree, he told me that other demons will be coming after you. Take care their very mad at you Desiree."

They smiled at her then were into two of the stalls. The other teammates came into the bathroom. The girls saw Jane getting sick then went out of the bathroom quickly. Desiree and Malaya had popped into class without anyone seeing them. One of the girls that saw Jane, came over to Desiree, she told her about Jane was sick in the girl's bathroom.

* * *

At lunch, the girls were in line for food. Today, there was fried chicken. Joseph and James came over to them. "Good fried chicken for vegetables green beans."

At the table, the girls who saw it told them about it. "I heard that they had to call an ambulance for her, she couldn't stop throwing up. They said it look like black stuff."

Joseph looked at Desiree. He spoke to her in his mind. *"What did you do to her?"*

She looked at Joseph. *"Okay, you caught me. Malaya and I give her the cross and rose on her shoulders. Evil didn't like it one bit they must have called for other demons to help him take her back. I didn't want a fight, let her fight evil not us."*

* * *

One of Janes friend was in track. She came over to Desiree and Malaya. "I heard what you did to Jane she is sick. What spell did you put on her."

Desiree looked at her. "I put no spell on her, leave me alone I know your evil."

The girl staired at her. "Know I'm not, take it back."

She had pushed Desiree. "Okay you say you're not evil, then your just starting out to become a witch. Magic that you do is evil, it's black magic. Jane is an evil witch. There are good witches you just must find the right one."

Then the teacher came over to them. "What is going on with the two of you. I can't have you two fighting with each other. We have a big competition coming up. Now shake hands then the two of you take a lap."

Desiree had three rose petals in her hand. She said a prayer hoping she wasn't into deep with black magic. "Boy your hand is hot, I'm sorry that I pushed you. You may be right about Jane; she was showing me something about magic. thanks for telling me."

*　　*　　*

Of course, James and Joseph heard about what happened at practice. The girls reported it to their boyfriends; who then told James, and he told Joseph. He had seen Desiree come out of the girl's locker room. "Desiree are you all right, I heard you had a tiff with one of Janes friend."

She had seen Malaya with James. "I'm okay and that girl she as okay. I just told her that Jane is evil, and she dabbles in black magic. I used the rose petals on her; Jane was doing what she had done to you."

She had seen him let out the breath he was holding. "I had to find out if you were all right. It's something about how far we came. I don't remember being this worried about you."

Desiree touched his cheek. "I know how you feel, but you must get yourself in the game of football. They need you now, go on, get going."

The girls had one more class. Afterwards, they went looking for the boys. Practice must have gone into overtime. They headed down to the football field and the boys were just coming out of the locker room. James came over to them with Malaya. How about we get food and ice cream before going home? I'll call mom to let them know we will be eating out."

*   *   *

This year was going fast for them. The boys took the girls to their Junior Prom then it would be the Senior Prom. Time was going too fast for them. Summer is about to be over. James and Joseph were talking about the Navy Seals. Who was it pushing them into becoming Navy Seals?

At the waterfall someone came out of the cave behind the waterfall. The boys saw a man and quickly they got out of the water. James and Joseph were quick to protect the girls. "Who are you, how do you know about this place."

The man came down to them. "Hello Cousin. I come from the valley of the Fairies. I have news for ye two. Oh, I know you two lass your Desiree and Malaya. Ye are the once to give Tom and Ellen life. It's nice to meet ye two."

The girls grabbed the towels and gave one to each of the boys. Joseph spoke. "All right you know us, but we don't know you. Could you tell us your name and why you are here."

The young man had looked at the four of them. "I'm sorry, it's a great honor to meet the four of you. They call me Laughlin; I'm here because of Marcos. We have heard that he found one of are fairies who wants to be with him. There is a demon woman who also wants to be with the two of them. It's said that Lucifer is going to give him a country to run. He will be able to have many women to bear his children.

Joseph went up to him, he shook the young man hand. He had done what Desiree, had done to her teammate. "They call me Joseph it's nice to meet you."

Laughlin smiled at them. "Your hand was extremely hot. The King told me that your women us the magic rose petal on two of the girls. The King saw that in the water, he thought it was to see if they were evil, one of the girls was evil. Did that young woman died or was she saved."

Desiree looked at him. "Why would the king want to know?"

James came up behind him and placed his hand on his shoulder. Joseph still had the rose petals in his hand; he put the petals on his chest. The man wasn't a fairy he was a demon and got sick. Joseph sent him back to where he came from. "What the hell is going on."

Malaya and Desiree had been watching. They had seen the demon having a rubber glove on his hand. The girls had told their man what they saw. It was good that James was behind him.

Then Malaya knew what was happening. She waved her hand over the water; she called the queen of the fairies. "Your majesty I'm sorry to bother you. But a demon came from the portal, we needed to place a spell on the doorway. That demon didn't know how close he was to the roses. He couldn't get to them if he tried to. Eleanor had placed a cover over all magic roses."

*   *   *

James had a dream of things that were in the future, he saw a country where their people were gassed with poison.

Joseph saw a bomb had sabotaged the twin towers. Then the girls also saw them in one of the countries. People were doing experiments to see if they could control their minds. They saw their man leading teams to take down what was happening. At eighteen James and Joseph went into the Navy. They had married the girls right out of boot camp. After they got back from their honeymoon they got the girls their ID's. A year went by; they became Navy Seal.

At that time Desiree had her son at nineteen. Malaya got herself a job, the girls got apartment near the base. Desiree had work for a childcare where she could take her son with her. At five years old she got a part-time job, until he went to school all day.

CHAPTER NINE

When the Children were born

MALAYA WAS TWENTY-TWO when she had her daughter, evil tried everything to stop her pregnancy. Marcos thought she was going to have Tom. That didn't happen until she was twenty-four. For a while it was quite busy, Malaya came to see James off. With a wave of his hand, he had a quickie with Malaya. That's when she conceived Tom.

Nine months later, the day she was going to have her baby. A tornado was coming up along the coast. It was too bad to drive. James and Joseph had their children in their arms, and their wives in there other arms. The six of them were able to get Malaya to the hospital, in time for her to have Tom. The baby came into the world when the lights went out. When his head cleared, he screamed. Ones his arms were out there a flash of light from his fingers. Then the lights were back on, the tornado tried to take the roof of the hospital. Joseph used his magic to keep the roof on. When Tom was born, the scream was as if he was telling Marcos to leave my family alone. For the high winds stopped at that moment and Tom went quiet.

When he was two years-old Desiree got pregnant with Ellen. She babysits Tom while Malaya worked. They were living on base at the time. The two men had come home after doing some training.

At that time Desiree was in her ninth month, Tom would take nappes with her. But he would talk with his Angel to let her mamma sleep. They would talk for a long time, that's when he found out that Marcos was scaring her to the point that she could die. With her twisting the umbilical cord was working its way around her neck.

That night in his bed Eleanor came to him. *"Hello Tom, I'm your great grandmother Eleanor. I know you're scared for your Angel. My grandson, you have strong magic; you can tell Joseph what Marcos is doing to Angel. Wave your hand and talk as an eight-year-old would. That's it my boy now talked to me."*

When the men came home Tom had come out of the room. "Uncle Joseph the beautiful Eleanor came to me last night. She told me to tell you that Marcos is scaring my Angel. She is very close to having the umbilical cord going around her neck. You must put a protection spell, around the apartment and the hospital delivery room."

James went over to his son. "How are you talking like this son."

Joseph and James were surprised to hear this toddler speak like this. "Uncle the beautiful lady Eleanor. She told me how to change my voice. I can use my magic when I remember that I have magic. Eleanor has been coming to see me these past two months. Marcos has been upsetting Ellen. When the two of us talked, she told me someone was scaring her. I told her I was going to talk to her daddy. He will know that evil is after you. Don't get scared any more, I would fight him to save you. You must rest for soon you will come out to meet me and your brother."

*　*　*

That day the sky was dark the rain was coming down hard. Desiree was having contractions, and they were getting closer. Joseph had just got home; there was a small window so that the rain wasn't coming down hard. They took her into the delivery room.

Tom told his father Ellen is going to be born. "We must go to the hospital, I want to see my little Angel." It was slow going and the rain came down hard. It felt like they wouldn't get there. Tom was looking at the black clouds. He saw the face of Marcos, and knew he wanted him and his little Angel dead.

In the waiting room Tom went to the window. He watched the cloud turn into a man. The man started to jump on the limb, he saw it was going to brake. He felt the man's power trying to keep him there at the window.

Right then James heard a man's voice yelling. *"Get the boy away from the window. Do it now!"*

James felt two cold hands pushing him forward. He grabbed his son and went quickly to the other side of the room. He sat his son down on his wife's lap. There was a loud crash a tree limb broke through the window. The limb would have pushed the broken glass into his chest killing him.

This made Tom angary, they didn't see his little fist ball up. He jumped off his mother's lap and ran to pick up the pointed piece of glass. The young toddler waved his hand, there was a bright light, and the piece of glass shot out from Tom's fingertips. When the glass hit its mark, they saw a spirit with a piece of glass covered in blood. Everyone heard a cry of pain in the wind, it was Marcos.

Then they heard the toddler's voice. He was talking to me older than a two-year-old. "You tried to kill my little angel. You couldn't do it, so you tried for me and lost. I'm sending this piece of glass back to you."

Then they saw a spirit who spoke. *"Marcos this time you will stay gone from this earth. You will see that Tom is stronger than Thomas. His magic comes from the ones before him."*

Then Tom spoke. "Baby Ellen is here. She is safe, she doesn't like to be cold. Marcos had scared her. Ellen gave her momma a rough time. I told her everything will be all right. Mommy, can you hear her crying?"

Raymond knew it was time to get this place cleaned up. He spoke "Be Gone Satan! You can't have my sister or my friend. Be careful Marcos when Tom's older you will be no match for him."

One of the spirits spoke. *"Be gone Marcos! Ye can't have her or the boy. Go back to your master. Tell your father Marcos, you were taken down by a two-year-old. He beat ye Marcos, a baby boy beat ye."*

He had waved his hand, and Raymond had fixed the window. As a young boy he had strong magic. He then put a protection spell around the room. James then checked his son's hand; there were no cuts anywhere. In the blink of an eye the glass was gone. The door open and standing in the doorway was Joseph. In his arms wrapped in a pink blanket was a baby girl, he looked at everyone.

He knew that something had happened. "Is it safe to bring her into the room?"

Joseph had seen his son wave his hand. He had made a circle as he opened the door. "Raymond, what are you doing?"

He looked at his father. "I just made the room safe. Tom took care of Marcos; he would think twice before taking him on again. Can we all see my little sister?"

Joseph sat down in a chair. He then opened the blanket to reveal his daughter. Raymond and Tom looked at her with loving eyes. They looked up at Joseph. In Joseph and James mine they heard the voice of their grate grandfather Neil. He spoke. *"Ye done well my boys. Your children are strong and brave. Raymond magic is strong for his age. He will do will with his magic. Tom has magic from the wizard and fairy. Ellen will have her magic from Garret and his father. The magic rose will give them more when they need it."*

Then their other grandfather Alex spoke. *"Thank ye for listening to Tom, I couldn't stop Marcos. He thought if he scared Ellen, she would die. I heard Tom talking to her. He told her no one would hurt her or her momma. Tom has strong magic like all of you had seen. When he is older, he will need that magic. There will always be one of the family close to them. We couldn't stop this in our own timeline. Be careful, Marcos will do anything to take the two of them to his master his father. We can hope that Marcos will stop trying to kill Tom and Ellen. We can pray that he finds what he is looking for.*

James knew who was here. In his mine, he heard his great-great grandfather who brought the roses to America.

The spirit of Alex spoke, *"James Tom is a brave boy. He's older than he looks, in action and in thought. It was your son, who knew just what to do. He could see what Marcos was up to. His love for Ellen started the day the two of them could talk to each other."*

Then everyone saw the two spirits of Alex and Neil. Neil spoke, *"Are families will watch over all of you. Marcos will be back on earth soon. We will also be here. On the day Ellen turns fifteen, when he will try to kill her. Will be around until Marcos, unable to come back to earth."*

James went over to his wife and children. Ellen still had Tom's and Raymond's finger. The adults smiled at the two boys.

Tom told her brother what she said. He spoke. "Raymond, Ellen is glad you are her brother, she loves you very much."

*   *   *

The years have gone by fast; Tom is seven years old. He was always around Ellen. In June was Ellen's birthday she was turning five years old. One of her gifts from her mother and father was ballet lessons. Tom watched her as her eyes lit up the moment she saw her ballet outfit. She ran to put the outfit on. He smiled as she tried to dance in her tutu.

He called Ellen in his mind. *"Angel, you look so pretty in your tutu. Do a spin for me."*

Ellen gave Tom a big smile. *"Mick, will you dance with me?"*

Tom had heard that ballet lessons can help his legs to be stronger. *"Angel yes, I'll dance with you."*

*   *   *

On Monday, Ellen had her first lesson. Tom took karate lessons also that day. An hour after Ellen's ballet class. He had asked if he could watch her dance. From then on, the mothers would take turns bringing their children to their classes.

The next day she would show Tom the movements she had learned. He had shown Ellen all that he had learned in karate. The two of them were enjoying teaching each other what they had learned. A month later Tom noticed how strong Ellen's legs were getting. Her teacher was impressed that she had learned all the lessons perfick. She had moved Ellen up to another group. It also moved her to a different day.

When his father was home, he brought them to their classes. Tom's teacher told his father that he was doing well. They want to move him up to a more advanced group. He had stepped into a new level of karate.

Tom watched Ellen in her new ballet class; he noticed that this class had older boys dancing. He remembered seeing two of the boys that were playing football.

After class he went over to talk with one of the other boys. Tom spoke. "Hello, are you one of the football players?"

The young man nodded his head. "Yes, I am, why?"

Tom smiled. "You're quite a kicker, to tell the truth those jumps you make are impress of. I would like to know is that why you take ballet lessons?"

The young man looked at Tom. "You come to all her classes. I've seen you in tournaments for karate. You're quite good at what you do. You like that new girl, she is a beautiful dancer. Are you thinking about joining the class?"

Tom smiled at him. Then spoke, "They call me Tom, thank you. Yes, I've been thinking about it. Ellen's been teaching me what she learned. I teach her what I have learned in karate. She has gotten quite good with the moves."

The young man looked at Tom. "I've been watching you when I'm not dancing. You have it bad for her. I enjoy the movement when I'm dancing with my girlfriend. For football, it helped improve my balance and movement I'm more precise. I can jump hire over the guys with the football. It helps me to run faster. My legs are stronger than just running." These boys were older than Tom. "Beside football. I enjoy dancing with the girls. When you dance there is a special bond with your partner. Are you hoping to dance with that young woman?"

The boys were extremely helpful. "Ellen shows me everything she has learned, yes, I like to join the group. When the two of us dance it's like dancing on a cloud with her? I enjoy karate, I like teaching Ellen what I learned. I notice my legs and balance are much better. I want to do this with her."

The older boy spoke. "You two seem to have that special bond right now. We saw the look she gives you. How long have you known her?

He smiled at the older boy. "From the day she was born, we live near each other I like being with her. The other girls are too flighty for me. Being younger, she doesn't act like it."

The boy smiled at Tom. "Yes, I understand what you mean special. When the group are together, Ellen shows us how she does the dance movements. One of the guys asked her how she does it. She told him in different words, and she breaks it down for us. I can see she would be a good teacher for ballet."

Tom made up his mind to join. "I think I will try out, there are things in motion. Both of our fathers are Navy Seals. Her brother went to the academy. Now he is trying out to be a Navy Seal."

One of the boys spoke. "That something, her brother must be older than his sister. I like the idea of you dancing with her. I know one thing; she has helped the girls who were having trouble with the moves. It helped them to become better dancers. The way she teaches it is a lot different than are teacher. Good luck, hope to see you here with her."

The young man was pleased with what his friend had said. He spoke. "I think it would be good for the two of you. I'm looking forward to seeing you dance with her. If you have feelings for her, put it in your dancing. It gives you more power in your jumps. Good luck, I hope to see you our next lessen."

The Fight Begins

TOM ENJOYED DANCING with Ellen. "It would mean more time with her. He just hoped his dad won't think it's to sissy for him to dance."

While his father was home, he got to see what Tom and Ellen had learned. James had seen how strong his son had become. Out of the back of the apartment he had a rose garden for his mother. The night Ellen was born. He saw his son take Marcos on. This dancing was good in what he did. The two fathers were ready to catch Ellen. He lifted her with no trouble. His karate was right on top. Tom knew how to throw a knife, or dirk. His magic was right on.

He thought he would ask his parents if he could take lessons with Ellen. It had helped with his balance; his legs are stronger it had improved his karate.

That night he asked his parents if he could take lessons. "Dad, you have seen what I can do. I want to take dancing lessons with Ellen. The young men who dance with the girls there. Two of them are football players, he told me that he can jump higher and when he kicks the ball it goes farther. When he must jump over teammates, it's longer and higher. I've been dancing with Ellen here at home. We run every day after school. You can see my Karate is much better. Please can I do this?"

His parents had noticed he was doing well; Ellen's next lesson Tom joined the class. He had to show what he could do, the teacher told him to warm up. She had watched him do his warmups. It was time to show her what he could do. She told him to dance for us, show us what you can do. Ellen told him to do high kicks and leap in the air. Do also spins for her. Then I will ask her to let us do one of the lessons. Tom had done all what Ellen had shown him. His legs were straight when he leaped into the air. He could hold a spin quite long; his kicks were high. All the guys went over to him; the young men gave him a pat on the back.

Ellen had advanced two years in her class. She went over to talk to her teacher. "Ms. Macule, Tom has been dancing with me. He helped me with the couple's parts. Could we show you what we can do? I've shown him all the steps. May I dance with him for you?"

The teacher saw that he was the right size for her. "Will see Ellen… Hello Tom… Ellen has told me you can lift her over your head."

Tom nodded yes. "Ms. Macule yes, I can lift her. Her brother made me lift weights, before he even trussed me to pick her up. I had to build up my arms, he wouldn't let me lift her until I was strong enough. He was always near me until I could lift her with no trouble."

Ms. Macule went and set up a mat so Tom could show her. "First show me how high you can lift Ellen."

Tom took a stand then he lifted her over his head. Then he straightens his arm out. "Well done, I see you don't shake when you lift her. All right, you can show me what you two could do. Be careful doing your dance."

Ellen went over to him. "Tom we will do all the dances that we worked on together."

In Ellen's mine she called him. *"It's just you and me here. Tom, take me to the clouds, so we can dance in the heavens together. We can do this."*

In Tom's mind he answered her. *"Angel, I always love dancing with you. Your brother made me stronger. I could pick you up and put you over my head. You may have two years of dancing. I also have two years in dancing and in karate. I move quicker and jump higher. I love dancing with you. Come on and let's show her what we can do. Let us dance in the heavens today."*

Tom was so happy to just be with Ellen. His love was getting even stronger for her. "Tom it's been fun, I love teaching you the move, it got me thinking. This will help me to teach others later. You could teach also. You have been showing me how to do karate. My brother was impressed with my movements."

In the back of his mind, he thought what if she was right. Then he had to think what he was doing. They moved together as one. Ellen's teacher couldn't believe what she was seeing. When Tom and Ellen finished their dance, everyone clapped their hands. Ms. Macule then asked him a question. "That was beautiful. Tom, have you dance before?"

He smiled at Ellen and spoke. "I have danced only with Ellen. She showed me what she had learned that day. I watched every class she took, only Ellen taught me ballet. Sense I been dancing with her. I find that my balance and movement has been much better. I'm stronger and it helps me with karate. I like dancing with Ellen; do you think that we could dance together?

Ms. Macule spoke. "Yes..., How long have you been dancing with Ellen?"

Tom smiled at her. "From the age of seven, I'm now fifteen. She always showed me the steps, where to put my hands and feet. When we started to dance it was from her first lesson. Ellen and I would work on what she had learned. She had told me it would help me with karate. I been watching her; I saw that she was too tall for the younger boys. All the other girls had partners. I like having better control over my arms and legs. I can run faster, and my karate is much better. I've moved up in the class."

The teacher asked Tom. "Were you always able to lift Ellen?"

Tom shook his head. "No…, the first time. Her brother Raymond stayed near us; he caught his sister. Now, I have no trouble lifting her. Thanks to her brother, my friend. I'm much stronger than I was."

Tim came over to Tom. "Man, you two are good together. Do you think the four of us could get together? That one part you two have mastered it."

Tom called over Ellen. "Would you like to help them out. We can teach them what we do."

Ellen smiled and nodded her head. "Yes… I told you we could become teachers in dancing."

After that they enjoyed dancing and instructing their group. The teacher noticed that they were helping their classmates. It was eight wonderful years, until everything changed.

*　*　*

It was a cold rainy day; Joseph and James had just finished training. Tired and wet, they made their way to the showers. The C'O aid, came over to them. He had a message from the commanding officer of the base. The message read, come to my office after your shower.

After the man was gone, James spoke. "Damn it…, I can hear the hot tub and a bottle of beer calling me. Haven't we worked out enough for one day."

Joseph was under the hot water. "I don't like it anymore then you do. I love my job; training is harder than doing the job. Come on James let's get this over with."

They went quickly to the car. James spoke. "What do you think the C O wants with us?

A soldier came out of the C O office. He carried a listening device. An officer was sitting in the C O chair; he was looking over two sets of records. When Joseph and James step into the room. The officer looked up, and he dismissed the C O.

The C O had stopped to speak with the men. "I don't know what's going to happen too you men. Whatever it is good luck. From this point on you are in his hands. Don't worry about your teammates. All of them will be going with you."

When the door closed the officer stood up. He looked as if he had been one of the Navy Seals. The Officer held himself with pride. He had brown hair with blond streaks.

Could he have served with their Uncle Emile? "Good afternoon, men, you are wondering why you're here. I've been looking over your records. Very impressive skills. You men have been a Navy Seal for eighteen years. During this time. There hasn't been a man killed or come up missing under your command. Your last mission something happened to one of your men. You always knew where the other team was. If that is so. What happened to your teammate? Why is he missing?"

"Joseph you were inside the building. The plan was to place the explosives, get pictures of any plans and machines. James, you took the upstairs doing the same thing. The man that was missing, he went to the basement by himself. Why was that?

"The missing man was Jackson Chamber. Their men called him Lightning Jack. One moment he was there and then he was gone. Did you know Jackson studied you, and your family? That his twin worked at your son's school?

"I see that you had spoken to the C O about him. The day Jackson asked you if you know anything about psychic abilities. The C O replaced him; you didn't trust him. You had sent a man with him, but he took him out. The skills I'm talking about, it's your ability to talk to each other and not aloud."

The officer then looked at Joseph and spoke. "Joseph why isn't this in your records? Your great-grandfather Garret Heart, he was a wizard, his wife was a human fairy. They had given their magic to the roses. Do you… have this ability to do magic?"

Joseph heard James's yelling *"What the hell is going on. How does he know about all of this?"*

Joseph yelled back. *"Shut up, before you confirm that it's true."*

He looked at the officer. "Sir…, I don't know who you are. Our C O said that we are now under your command. May we see the orders?… Sir!"

The officer just shook his head and spoke. "No! Not yet."

The officer was telling them the story of their family. "James didn't Eleanor Heart, mark Marcos? She's had to put rose petals on her nails; she is your great-grandmother. She was able to talk to Thomas. Did you know she had psychic abilities?"

Joseph couldn't show any emotion; he didn't want the officer to know he hit a nerve. He spoke. "Sir…, that information came from Marcos. He wrote a journal the way he wanted the story to go. This information is wrong. Tell me if you have that book… Sir!"

He knew he wasn't a demon. The two of us would know about it."

The Officer looked at the men. "There are two books, I just knew of one. The other one goes back to the 17th century. A man called Marcos was able to steal Eleanor's spirit. She had floated near Thomas. Marcos Huascaran had a vendetta against your family. Is that right James."

James could feel the anger building up. He heard Joseph *"Chill out don't blow it."*

James called back. *"I won't."*

Then he spoke. "Sir… I don't know who you are, or what this has to do with us under your command. What I do know is your information comes from Marcos. Sir… do you know he is a demon. Now could you tell us what you want with us and are team? You need to find Thomas's journal… Sir."

The officer then walked closer to them. He spoke. "Is this part right. That he tried to wipe out all the MacGregor men.

Joseph then spoke. "Sir… Stop right there. He didn't make a deal with Satan. When he is the son of Satan himself. Yes, Marcos tries to kill all the MacGregor men. No, he didn't take Eleanor spirit. She had marked his face, with the magic roses on her fingernails. Also, Marcos was part Fairy.

Then James spoke. "My great grandfather was a twin to the King of the Fairy's. Their father was a Wizard and mother was a Fairy; she was the Queen. To become the next queen a man must get her with child. This was to show knew life in the kingdom. The two twins fought Marcos in the valley of the dead."

Joseph knew that James wanted to go home. He wanted to do the same, what does this man want with us? Then Joseph and James saw Eleanor. She spoke. *"My boys this is one of my cousins. He doesn't have the update of Thomas Journal. He has Marcos book that he put out."*

When the officer herd Eleanor's voice he turned around ready to fight. The officer spoke. "You are my cousin? Eleanor, I didn't think you would come here."

Eleanor looked amused. She spoke. *"I didn't like what I heard. I wasn't scared of Marcos. Be aware these two men have strong magic. Don't mess with their children. You think you know everything about Marcos. What you don't know is something happening with him. He will be letting four other people go after Tom and Ellen. This school you want*

Tom and Ellen to go to will have three of them already there. I don't like the idea that our children's minds must change.

"You have brought James and Joseph here to tell them to try to find Marcos. He will be coming to earth very soon. Right now, he will be trying to have a son with this Fairy he found. When he does come to earth, he will bring two women with him. They will be taking over the man's wife's bodies."

James looked at Eleanor, he spoke. "Granny, their still children. I know my son would give his life to Ellen. He is a strong young man, as he gets older his magic will get stronger. I don't know if she has magic yet, she never had to try."

Joseph then spoke. "Eleanor off and on I burned a rose stem. To see Marcos in the fire, I have seen him try two more times in the spirit world to kill Tom. Ones before he goes to this school. Somehow, he will get into their dream world. I don't know how he will do it. We can't help them, what I saw was Ellen called for her magic and the magic of both Wizards. Marcos will make Tom forget he has magic. He didn't think Ellen would be able to do anything to help Tom. My daughter loves Tom she would give her life to save him.

Then Eleanor looked at the officer and spoke. *"You know the history that Marcos wrote. As James told you, he's half Fairy and Demon. His father is Satan himself; he has just this time to bring his father more souls. Right now, he can try to kill Tom in his sleep. There is time until Marcos goes after them. Ones he is on earth he will give them too a girl and a boy. He will forget about them; his gold is to concentrate on getting his father more souls. His plan is to bring down these buildings that will hold people from all over the world. You do know that you're playing into his hand. Now let these men go home."*

Then the officer wanted to know about the babies Marcos killed. He spoke. "Eleanor what about the babies."

She looked at this man closely, she spoke. *"You wonder about the blood line; the babies are in heaven with the Lord. All those women went into the baby's body just before they were born. The women were able to live again. Everything you need to know is in Thomas Journal. Not the one Marcos wrote, you never knew that Garret changes the young women with the babies. The women got to live the babies died in the mother's body; Satan got nothing. This time around the roses have four people's magic. The Queen of the Fairy's the Wizard who was a MacGregor. Garret's magic and his father's magic."*

Joseph spoke. "Sir…, what does this have to do with you putting us under your command? You're from the MacGregor family; the ability to know who a demon. The MacGregor's family are right down to cousins. We have a right to know when it pertains to our families. You must be out of the loop to not know your truth is part right."

The officer smile at the men. "These ability's you have, can find out that I'm not a demon. It's nice to meet Eleanor. My name is Murdock McKinnon. My family calls me Jim. I'm the cousin of Eleanor's mother."

Joseph spoke. "All right you're a distant cousin, I saw you had this room swipe for listening devices. Where does Marcos fit into all of this?… Sir."

Jim looked at his cousin. He spoke. "Always a soldier, not when it comes to your children. Joseph, with the magic you have. I can imagine I wouldn't have my head for long."

Joseph looked at the officer. He spoke. "Sir… now that you know about our magic, are you a Navy Seal? If you are. You better be stronger and quicker than both of us."

Jim smiled and spoke. "Well said. Yes, I am! Take a seat. I was going to ask you if you believe in a ghost or spirit. But I don't have to do that when Eleanor is here."

Then Joseph waved his hand, he spoke. "Then you don't mind if I look at our records?"

Jim laughed and spoke. "Can I stop you from doing so, maybe if I gave you an order. I'm not going to do that. Cousin Eleanor, do you know if Peter McKinnon came to see me? Right before I left the Highlands?"

Eleanor nodded her head yes. *"Aye… I do know that he sent me to Ye. Now my boys and cousin. Work together be careful. He will mess with the children's minds if he can, or it will be that girl who likes Tom. The first two books Marcos had messed up with. I will let ye tell your story about when ye were fourteen. Be careful Jim these men are the best. Their group is everything ye need to find Marcos."*

Jim smiled at his cousin. He spoke. "Good day my lady. Thank you for coming to see us. Until we meet again. That was one way to break the ice between us. This is what happened to me, the spirit of our cousin Peter McKinnon came to me. I was fourteen at the time. You would say I was a hot head, I thought I knew everything. My father told me a story about the Hearts and MacGregor family. I didn't believe a word of it. Until Peter came to me. He told me to be careful. The demons are looking for people to help take down Tom and Ellen. He said acting tuff will get me a demon to pay me a visit. Peter told me that my father was going to send me to America. I will be eighteen when my father enrolled me in the Navy Academy. Before Peter left me, he placed a cross and rose on my chest; the cross came from Father Sinclair. It has a magic rose on it. But I don't have magic.

"Time past, on my eighteenth birthday. I was placed on a ship to America. My father made me work on that ship. He didn't pay for my way to America. What my father couldn't teach me, the skipper did. Before we left Scotland, I had a visit from a man called Marcuse. He told me; a young man like me could go far. I found out why Peter placed that cross on my chest. The story about that cross my father spoke of. I knew Marcuse was a demon. I felt the cross go hot quickly, then it was gone.

"Marcuse said. Once the country develops the parts. He will build a machine that can control someone's mind. Other countries are working on it as we speak. I've been looking for Marcuse."

Both men looked at him. James spoke. "How could you find Marcuse? It's not yet his time. Do you work for him even under the spell of the magic roses? Or are you talking about when he comes to earth? Then again, you're talking about the man who Marcos will take over his body. This man is in the mountains in Libya."

Jim smiled at them and spoke. Exceptionally good, this man I'm speaking about is in a movement to bring the world down, so he thought. Now we have another man that Marcos is looking at. Eleanor spoke of what he wants to do to two buildings in the USA. The intelligent tells me that this movement of this country will get people coming here. What better way to take a great country down? By sending their people into the country. These people will change things in each state a little bit at a time. There will be other countries working on these things. They will introduced drugs to children to make them weak; it will kill children and teenagers. This will also make it easy to control people. Marcos will have things happen in the 20th century. Right now, we must fine this man and take him down.

"There are people working on ways to control the minds of the weak. What if technology makes machines that children won't have to think about much? They could play games on it and don't have to do work, because they will be paid money. That is what Marcuse said, it's a way to get souls for his master, they can put things in these machine's. The man that Marcuse will take over his body when he is close to death. Then he will come after the USA, there will be phones you can take with you. Marcuse showed me everything. Business will go under because there will be games to win money. Why work when you can get money by playing games?

"That assignment you two was on. Your men were to take pictures of blueprints, files, and machines. When you went to blow up the building. Jack was nowhere to be found; you had a job to do. There were soldiers coming down the road, you did what you had to do. You blew the building up and got your men out. Did you use your magic to find out if Jack was inside the building?"

James spoke. "Yes… Sir. He wasn't in the building… Sir."

Jim then spoke. "Did you find him before the building went up?"

Then Joseph spoke. "No… Sir. One of are men thought they saw someone running into the woods. He looked to be Jack… Sir."

Jim spoke. "Who was the man that saw him?"

Then James spoke. "Bill Colman, he took the place of our teammate who retired. He is Joseph's cousin. It seems to me that the two families are joining forces."

Then the officer then spoke. "James, your son wants to become an engineer. His dream is to build a machine to help people with their nightmares. Tom is like you, James; he has information on building a machine. Your son is a strong young man. He is an engineer; he can build anything. A young man like your son. They would love to get a hold of him."

Jim watched James's face change slightly. James spoke. "Sir… where did you get this information from?"

The officer smiled and then spoke. "The information came from Bill. I had placed Bill on your team to get to know Tom. My men have been watching over your two families. At the school that your son goes to. A strange man was asking questions, to the children. My man said a teacher came over to that man. She made the children wait inside for the bus to come. James, one of the children, was your son. With that said, do you trust Bill Colman?"

James looked at Joseph and he nodded also. "Yes… sir we do. There is something familiar about Bill. We thought he was going to take a while to get up to speed. He knew just what we were about. Bill is one of the family, we found out he is one of Garret's grate-grandsons. Bill's mother comes from Garret's oldest daughter."

Then Jim spoke. "I'm glad to hear that. I'm putting Bill to watch over Tom when he gets out of school. He will be on your team until then. Marcos will be coming to earth soon when we talk. He said there were big plans for the late 19th century. He's been planning this for a long time; he will have money and power. It looks like he will take over someone's body to get this started.

"Peter has been talking to me. What he been watching over is the base deep in one of the mountains. There are tunnels all over the nearby towns. There is a big movement to fine people with psychic abilities. The machine you destroyed; they were using it to enhance these people's abilities. These psychics could do it without help from the machine. They could control weaker mines in their sleep or even kill them. There are new drugs being develop, there using these drugs to soften of the young adults. Did you know that Jack Chamber, was a Scientist and of disguises? There are plans after the two buildings taken down."

Joseph heard James swear. *"Damn it! Jack used us."*

Jim notice that the two men were talking, he went on speaking. "Joseph did you say that his nickname is Lightning Jack. Marcuse gave me a code word; it was Lightning Jack. I need to send you two back to Russia. There is a mountain that people have sent to. These people have disappeared as if they were in a cloud to have psychic abilities. The name of the mountain, was place under cover. We will discuss which men will go with you."

James and Joseph looked at each other. "Sir… we will choose our own men. Bill, Joseph, and me. We can get out without anyone knowing."

Jim looked at the two men. He spoke. "Right now, I need to talk to you about Tom and Ellen. We need to get your children to a safe school. I know of two schools that the two of them can go to. I know that Tom can manage himself, Ellen can also do the thinks he can. To hide that he has psychic abilities he must not remember his name. In this school they have nicknames. They're using teenagers to spy on the other's children."

The two men watched Jim then he asked a question. Joseph, do you think Ellen will have magic soon?"

Joseph answered. "It's hard to tell… Sir. It may happen when she turns twenty-one. I don't know what kind of magic she will have. What I do know, Tom is not going to like being away from Ellen. You don't want to see him angry. Tom has been protective of Ellen since she was born. He took on a demon when he was going on two years old."

Jim looked at the men. "I know of all this. We need Tom in that school; we must keep him safe. Ellen can't go to her new school. Not yet, she's too young. The good news is with her IQ; she can go next year. I don't need Tom out of school yet. I know the school he is in now; they want to skip a grade or two. I need him safe."

James took a breath. He spoke. "Didn't you say that these children work for Marcos? You're putting them into the fire. Eleanor said there is a girl who likes Tom.

Jim nodded his head and spoke. "Yes… what I understand, these children are not as smart as Tom or Ellen. One good thing about this school is Tom can take college courses at this school. I found out from Peter that Marcos can use different bodies. It's said Marcos will be going after Ellen when she is fourteen years old. She will be in Junior High her last year, school will be out soon. Send them to your grandparents for the summer. I have place men at both ranches. They will help keep an eye on them, until school starts."

James spoke. "Why do we have to send them to these schools?"

Jim looked at the two of them. "It's because of what had happened in Tom's classroom. They had people come to talk to the children. Tom's class was giving talks on psychic abilities. This man had given a test to the children. He wanted to see who had the abilities. Tom's teacher got scared, this man was focusing just on Tom.

"I've been placing your men in the Government. Arthur was one of your teammates. When he got out of the service. He took over the line of ships that his family runs, Arthur has Government jobs. He has a ship picked out, with the best team around. Bill will be getting out around that time. He has four years left. Until he reaches twenty years." Then his attention went to Joseph. He spoke. "Joseph your son Raymond had taken ROTC in High School. I wish all the children did that. He then went to the Navy academy and became a Navy Seal. This report has told me he's able to get out of anywhere. I have a place already picked out for him. Does he have any magic?"

Joseph staired at Jim. He spoke. "Sir..., you would have to ask my son yourself. That is for him to answer."

Jim notice answers don't come quickly from the two of them. "All right I will do that if there comes a need to know."

*   *   *

James knew the questions weren't over with. "James, I see that Raymond had married your daughter. This school that will send Tom to. They will hide the identity of the child."

James was at the end of his patience. "This is too much for any family to deal with. My son needs his family. You're pushing on him a name that changes and family being taken away. You're sending him to a school that looks like a jail."

The officer knew the two were at the end of their patience. "A school that will keep them safe. It has two sides, boys, and girls. The name of the school for boys is Deilondotay. The girls Deilondolay. Raymond will watch over his sister on the weekends and holidays. During the summer also. James, your brother Brandon is in Scotland. I like him to watch over your son on the weekends and holidays. During the summer also, I know this is too much to take in. In this school Tom and Ellen will not know each other. They will not know any family members."

Joseph knew that the office chose today to tell us about this. He thought we wouldn't fight this. "Sir, I know that our family didn't come with are sea bag. You are putting the children with family. However, throw them in a school with different children. Are they all under a protection order, Sir?"

The officer didn't think his mind would be that clear. "No there are children with behavior problems."

James was fighting to keep it together. "Sir, you're telling us that there are children that Marcos could turn them into demons."

The officer tried to go on with what he had to tell them. "The family, will not remember that Tom and Ellen are family. Raymond and Alicia will take care of Ellen. The same with Brandon, his family can play the part of uncle and aunt." Raymond, he will be with her family for four years, you all have a strong mind. No pictures with the family, that's one of the school rules. With your children, their mines will not take to hypnosis. To keep them safe, it will have to be magic."

James didn't like any of this. "Sir… I will take care of my son's mind myself. No… hypnosis on my boy, you forget quickly about my magic. Would you like me to send you to the North Pole? I would be very happy to do so… Sir. You sure you're not working for Marcos. If Joseph did what you said. Marcos will be able to get closer to Ellen, this Marcuse is he Marcos?"

Joseph then remembered what the fairies called him. "When Marcos was young his name was Marcuse. The answer is yes.

Jim knew he was pushing his luck. "What I understand. Marcos can use any evil body. He can make them do whatever he wants. Is Marcos also Marcuse? Yes. Remember, he had a hundred years to pick who he wanted to be. We are an undercover group. I need more members to help us. Marcuse must die; I need you on my team.

"Joseph, your parents have a ranch like James. Do you think they can keep Ellen safe for a while?"

Joseph knew how James felt. "Yes. In this school, Deilondolay. Why would our daughter not know her family?"

Jim knew he must end this soon. "The two schools will take their names from them. The children can pick the nickname they like. What name would Tom pick for himself?"

James smiled at the memory of the two children. He spoke. "It would have to be Mick. That is what Ellen calls him when they were little."

Jim looked at James. "Why the name Mick?"

James laughed. "It's for Mickey mouse. The show that the two of them watch together when they were little."

Jim wasn't up to date on things. "All right, what name for Ellen?"

Joseph smiled at the name Tom, called Ellen. "It would have to be Angel. Before she was born, he called her his little Angel... Sir."

Jim knew these names would come easy to the children. "Joseph, I'm aware you're not happy with me. I know these children are special, those magic roses need them. I don't think they will let Ellen use Angel at this school. It's part of her last name, this man that Marcuse is going to take over his body. He had gassed his own people; there women are nothing to this man. In the gas there were children and their mothers. Do you think Marcos care if Tom had died?"

Joseph was at the end of his rope. No… James didn't send him to the North pole. Not yet but he would if he doesn't let them be in control of their children. "I had enough, with everything. Damn it… why should we even truss you? You haven't shown us our orders when it comes to our children. With our wives we will make plans for them. We haven't said if we were going to be part of your team. There is more to this story, what else haven't you told us? … Sir."

Jim took a breath and spoke. "I told you about the mountain in Russia. What do you think will happen? If Tom doesn't go to this school. Marcuse could get his grubby hands on him. He would take him to that mountain. The strongest man hasn't been able to withstand the torture. They had taken one of my men, they sent him back to us. That strong man was nothing but a vegetable. They will break Tom; he will do everything they want him to do. With Tom out of the way, Marcos will get what he wants from Ellen."

James was also at the end of his rope. He didn't let Jim know that he was fighting with himself. Jim was close to sending him to the North pole. "Sir… no dishonor to the uniform. You can order us but not are children, Ellen's name will be Angel. Tom's name will be Mick, you will make it happen, or I promise you will find yourself. Where no man has gone before, you better be a strong Navy Seal… Sir…!!

Joseph didn't like anything he said. He spoke. "Sir… no dishonor to the uniform. Let me get this straight, you're going to send us to this place where your strongest man failed. You make me think you're on Marcos side. How were you able to get hold of us and are team? This mission we only need Bill and are two selves."

What Joseph did next, he waved his hand and sent Jim to the coldest spot at the North Pole. Five minutes went by then he waved his hand and Jim was back. Jim had snow on him he didn't say anything to the men.

Joseph was looking at Jim. "We had enough of this if you forget our two families has magic. My daughter will know her family. In America we change are last name, from Heart to Angel-Heart. You don't have the right to tell us how to keep are children safe… Sir!

"Now with my daughter. She is still young, and my wife won't like not seeing her every day. If you think I will let you send them without their nick names. I'm with James on this. When it comes to are children it will be our way, not your way. This job will take us away from are family. Our wives will have too much time on their hands. Could you find them job's so they can be close to us… Sir…!!"

CHAPTER ELEVEN

Last Summer together

AFTER SAYING GOODBYE to their mother's all their things went to their new room. Angela and Bill will stay with them for one day. Tom and Ellen knew they were going to join there group.

Bill looked at Tom. This boy is more of a man, then I was at his age. I know he's afraid for her, would they take the chance to mate? He knew that both were strong body wisdom, could Ellen be on something so she wouldn't get with the child. Angela thinks Ellen is older than her age.

If Ellen had mated, with Tom then she would have his mark. Then the two could come to their side if they were in danger. "Tom, I want you to know that your dad did everything to try to stop this. They have a man to take you to your new home and school. He was going to have your memory adjusted to not be able to remember anyone here. Both fathers fought for you two. They said no… if there is no other way Raymond will do it to both his sister and friend. We will see Tom off. Jim told him that can't happen, he must go through customs his passport must be stamp."

Angela then gave Ellen a hug. "It will be all right you'll see."

Ellen had an idea to save them both. But right now, they will play the game. "Are you two are staying the night?"

Angela and Bill looked at each other. "Bill, we do have this day off, what do you have in mind."

Ellen thought he went to Tom. "How about we go swimming, he agreed."

Then Ellen whispered to Tom. "We have to talk alone tonight."

Tom smiled and spoke. "How about we go swimming, we can talk later."

Angela nodded her head yes. Bill told them. "That sound like a plan."

At the waterfall they got to see each other in bathing suits. Angela had a bikini on and so did Ellen. It was nice to see Bill react to Angela's bikini. Tom laughed. "Haven't the two of you seen each other in bathing suits."

The four rand to the waterfall. Once there, Bill felt a feeling of being calm, Angela felt it also. Tom and Ellen went right in; they swam to the rocks. Then they clime the rocks and dove into the water. "The two then kissed. They're going to the bottom of the waterfall."

Ellen wondered how deep it was. "Tom, do you think they could teach us scuba diving."

Tom thought she always had clever ideas. "I know they can, we just must put it into their mind."

Bill and Angela went right in, they swam halfway. "Angela, would you like to see what is at the bottom of the waterfall."

The two of them swam down halfway. Something came over them, Bill took hold of Angela. Then he kissed her because there was a need to touch each other. The moment they touched Bill wanted to have her. They had to come up for air. "What the hell happen down there."

Angela didn't understand but wanted him. "I don't know, yes I'm safe."

Bill wanted this but he had to ask if she was dating anyone. "Angela, are you seeing anyone."

She smiled and felt the need to be one with him. "No… if we start dating, we can't tell anyone until we are taking care of Tom and Ellen. Bill, Ellen told me that our aura is brighter together. She said that the two families have married before but at distant years. If we mate, she said for you to give me the cross and rose. That little test they had us do. Ellen said with are hands together, were stronger. She believes we might need it very soon."

Ellen yelled at them. "Hay you two, why don't you try the rocks and go behind the big boulder."

Bill wondered, what do they know? He yelled back. "Did one of you do something to the water?"

Tom answered. "No but the once before us could have. This water can read any kind of feelings. If there are feelings between the two of you. It makes those feelings stronger.

Bill looked at Angela. "Tell me, I can't think any other way to say this. Do you want me to fuck you. I don't have any protection on me."

Angela smiled; she laughed. "I'm on something, so I'm safe. Hell yes, I haven't been with anyone."

When Bill turned to talk to them. They were heading to the grassy spot by the waterfall. "Come on before we lose this feeling for each other."

On top they couldn't see the kids. "Where are they."

He thought for a moment. He heard. "Were safe." Bill took her hand and went behind the boulder. "I haven't had sex for a while. Damn it woman… I haven't been this hot for anyone."

Angela smiled and pushed him against the rock. She went for his lips; her hand touched his heat. She looked at him and licked her lips. That did it, Bill waved his hand and put a bubble around them. This way no one could see them. Another wave and he had no swimsuit on. "Do you like what you see."

She answered him with a wave of her hand. She had no clothes on, and he went for her breast and mouth. As he kissed her, he got her nipple hard. He knew this would get her hot. As he sucked her nipple his hand went for her pussy. One thing came to mind, so he made his finger long and big. As he tried to push in her she was too small. That had answered his question, so he changed plans and just put his finger in her. Bill went and sucked on her nipple; he then felt her nails on his back. Each time she came he made his finger bigger. Now inside her his finger was the size of his heat. Waving his hand they wore on the grass, he was ready to take her. "Tell me now, do you want to do this."

She looked at him, and at his heat. She thought he knows I'm a virgin. She tried to sound that this wasn't her first time. "Bill, I want you to fuck me. Do it, let me be one with you."

He thought for a long time he never felt this way. He spread her legs farther apart. He knew he wouldn't hurt her pussy; she could take his heat without hurting her. Smiling, he guided his heat inside her. He joined with her; he felt the resistance and push through. He kissed her lips and neck. It didn't take her long to grab him, doing that made him realize she was for him. "I have you, are you going to fuck me."

No words came from him; he just started to move. Bill knew this was her first time. He fought not to cum yet, he wanted to give her some more pleasure. Bill had lifted himself up to watch her come, he was right on that spot and she came again. This time her hands held him up, but she was fighting to cum. She had to move her hands to his back. It just kept building until her body was able to have that strong climax. When she came, he came. He took a kiss and deepened it.

Bill turned her over. "You were a virgin, thank you for that right to mate with you. Raise up just a bit, Ellen was right. You are my mate; here is my mark of cross and rose. At the same time, she gave her cross and rose to him. We will now know if the other will need help. You didn't tell me to put a rubber on him. You wanted to feel me cum inside you. You knew I would take care of you. Your my mate and when we can, I will marry you."

She didn't tell him what she wanted. But he heard her thoughts. Angela had heard that if she sat up, he went deeper in her. She revealed how deep he went. Bill came up to her and to her mouth. He laid her back and took her nipple to suck on it.

She pushed and wiggled, "Damn its woman you want more. If you do this time you have to work at it. He lay back and she went right to work. When she came, she sat up straight and felt the power of his climax. "Why have I waited so long."

Bill smiled, "Because it wasn't our time. Tonight, I'll come to your room if you want me to."

She lay on top of him. "I like the way you fuck me. We got to get out of here to check on the kids. Thank you for being my mate. I've been looking for you for a long time."

Bill kissed her and waved his hand; he held on to her as they hit the water naked. She waved her hand to put their clothes back on.

Tom and Ellen also enjoyed each other. She didn't know how long it would be before they found each other. Ellen spoke. "I think it's time to go eat, we have to change."

Tom and Bill wave their hands; they had on what they started with. Tom spoke. "The two of you look more relax now."

Bill smiled at them. "Did you put a spell in the water."

Tom laughed. "No… we didn't have too. When you touch hands, the magic was leading you to now."

*　*　*

The four of them walked to the house holding hands. After they ate the four of them took a walk. "Be careful out there, Marcos will have men with magic."

It's time to go in, you can have the attic, there are two beds. The two of them said goodnights to Tom's grandparents. Together they went upstairs. There were two rooms on each side of the bathroom. Ellen's room was the one on the left side facing the bathroom. Tom had his hand on the door.

He bent down and kissed Ellen one last time. "Let us try the dream world. Call me when you get to the waterfall. I'll wait for you on the rocks."

It was a good test, he thought. But something was coming, he couldn't get it out of his mind. When Ellen appeared, the feeling was gone. Whatever it was it went away when Ellen showed up.

*　　*　　*

The next day Bill and Angela head out. They took the vortex to the base. They met up with Joesph and James. "Are the kids all right."

Bill smiled, "Yes sir, there doing will."

Joesph knew there was something different about them. "You two look rested."

Angela, she had to smile. "Sir... what is in that water, you couldn't help to relax."

Both James and Joesph had to laugh. "Thomas had said. If there was two people who should be together, the water would make it happen."

Bill and Angela looked at each other. "Let me tell you about James and me, we had to put a spell on us. We were fighting not to fall in love with each other's sister. Long story short. Our wife brook that spell, everything's we felt for them came back to us. We couldn't keep are hands off them. You see Marcos sent a demon to our mothers. They killed are sisters. There were two girls that was raped, demons took over the boy's body. Thay got the girls pregnant, these girls came to America. At the time a demon killed your sisters. An angel switch are sisters with the other women. When they were in labor the young girl's baby were dead. An angel came down and switched the babies. If these things didn't happen Tom and Ellen couldn't be together."

*   *   *

Bill had an idea. "Sir… Taking and jumping out of the airplane they will fine us. Same with the ship. We can take the vortex, and no one will no."

Joesph nodded. "It would work, that's if we had a place we already been to before."

Bill looked at them. "I've been to Russia and to the bottom of that mountain. We found that man who we lost. He fought as hard as he could. Doing so he busts a blood vessel to his brain. They didn't brake him he stopped himself from them getting information from him."

Joesph looked at James. "It sounds good, place us aways from that spot. It's getting dark over there we can camp where you did."

*   *   *

Tom and Ellen enjoy their time together. They gave the horses running time. They helped around the place and went swimming and running.

That night Ellen was going to meet Tom at the waterfall. He kissed her as if it was his last kiss. "Tom what's going on, why does that feel like my last kiss."

He had to reflect on what made him feel like this. "The other night when we went to the waterfall. It felt eerie, like something was trying to get into the dream world. But when you came it went away. It could be knowing the days are going too fast for me. I love you, Ellen."

She didn't know what to think about their dream world. "I love you too. If it happens again call me. I'll see you in our dream world."

*　　*　　*

Ellen was having trouble falling asleep. She had a bad feeling, ones before Tom had said Marcos was up to something. She got up and went to his room, but the door couldn't open. There was something green coming out of the bottom of his door. Now she was scared for Tom, she went to check on his grandparents. The door wouldn't open, "What the hell is going on, granny wake up papa wake up please."

She looked at the bottom of their door there was green smoke. With a wave of her hands, she was on their back porch. She saw a small machine pumping in that stuff. Quickly she broke that machine, she had to put on a fan to pull out that green stuff. Ellen had to put a mass on; it was making her sleepy.

Then she went to Tom's window. That same machine was at his window; she tried to break it wouldn't break. She through it down and a fan replaced it. The green smoke was coming out. Ellen found out it was cutting their air off. There was a lot more that was wrong with Tom. Ellen must get to the dream world; she had a bad feeling that Marcos was there.

Tom fell into Marcos's trap

Tom went and closed his door; it was a beautiful night out. He had opened the window for the cool air to come in. He always loved the sound of the waterfall. It always puts him to sleep, but tonight something was wrong.

Tom remembered when he got to go to Vermont to stay with his grandparents for the summer. The waterfall was where he loved to lay in the sun. That big rock and boulder became his place where he felt safe. Tonight, as he stood on the edge of the rock he couldn't see the other side of the waterfall. In his dream world the sun always shined. Tonight, one minute it was sunny, the next minute something was blocking the sun. He found when the sun went out this black stuff appeared, when he touched it, it felt like tar. It was dropping down in front of him. There was a box around him and the tar was on all four sides of him. He couldn't move; something wouldn't let him wake up. His dream world was becoming a nightmare. If he couldn't wake up and the tar was going around him, he would die.

Then he heard a man laughing, the sound was deep. Tom knew that voice, how many times he had come after Ellen and me. *"Marcos how in hell did you get into my dream world. What devious plan do you have for the two of us."*

Marcos snapped his fingers and Mick turned around. Now he tried to call Angel. *"My love you must wake-up, don't come to the waterfall it's a trap. Marcos found a way to get into are dream world."*

Now he was worried that Angel was also in trouble. Is this the end for the two of us?

*   *   *

In Ellen's room she lay down and went to sleep. She heard Mick trying to wake her up then his voice was gone. She couldn't open her window because the green smoke would come in. The machine that Marcos's placed in his window. Ellen replaced it with a fan that was pulling the green stuff out of his room. She had dropped it on the ground under her window where it sat. With a wave of her hand, she was on the path running to get to Mick.

She tried to call him. "Mick …" But her voice hit a wall and bounced back at her.

On the shoreline she couldn't see him or the rocks, there was nothing but darkness. With the wave of her hand, she tried to clear the darkness.

*　　*　　*

Angel was feeling helpless, this was only the second time they were together in the dream world. Last time they were together, they were older. Twenty-one for her and twenty-three for Mick. This time she was desperate, raising her hands to the heavens. She called their great grandfather's; they were the once that had magic. *I call to be twenty-one, and my mate* Mick *to be twenty-three. Strengthen his magic to brake Marcos's hold. Evil has come to do harm to us. Marcos brings the darkness of death. He has the power to enter the dream world. Help us to close the portal to our dream world.*"

Angel pictured herself… as a woman, Mick as a man. She felt a wind starting to blow around her. Her hair felt longer. As the wind pushed her hair across her face. Angel, was even taller than before. Her breast felt bigger, her arms and legs were stronger. She had the build of a dancer.

Angel thought. "What could cut through the darkness, but white fire. With her finger she started to cut around the box. The black tar started to melt away; it wasn't quick enough it was draining her energy. She wasn't used to having so much power flowing through her body. "Mick … *hear me, my power is yours. Through my cross and rose, to yours we are one. I call to the light of goodness. Come to me. Fill my body with the brightest light of all. From me... into* Mick *and through his fingers. Together, we will take evil from our dream world's, forever."*

* * *

The demon was happy he thought he was going to get rid of Mick at last. Marcos laughed, then he had made two big hands go towards him. "Foolish boy… she's not going to come here, how do you think she could help you. She's only a woman, there only good to fuck. Where is your mate, I thought she was going to save you. Silly boy, didn't you know girls are weak? Last chance to say goodbye to her. I'm going to have so much fun with her… after your gone."

* * *

Right under Marcos nose, the demon didn't see that Mick was changing to a man. His arms and legs got bigger; he was now stronger. The hands wrapped around his neck couldn't close any more. Mick felt his body getting stronger, now he was opening those big hands. Once his strength was back, Mick bent Marcos hands backwards, the demon how old. Mick stood in front of Marcos. *"You were saying that women are useless. Think again Marcos, my mate is smart. She is not weak as you made her to be."*

Marcos looked at him. *"How did you turn into a man. No…! she is just a useless woman."*

Mick shook his head. *"Keep telling yourself that. The women now are not weak; we don't hold them back anymore. She is strong and smart; with this light I throw you out of our dream world. Thanks for the talk. It's time for you to leave, don't come back. I place a strong spell to keep you out."*

* * *

Angel had focused on her magic, the powers flowing through her body. It flowed like a bright light, building within her. Until she started to glow, like a star in the heavens. With a flick of her wrist. The light exploded from her fingertips. It bursts into a magical beam that cuts through the darkness. The magic beam went into Mick, their cross and rose was one. He was now twenty-three. Mick focused on his mate. He felt Angel's powers. The more he held back the brighter his body became. Marcos big hands were gone. The light was pushing him back. Mick knew the moment he had all Angel's magic.

With his arms out straight, Mick flicked his wrist. The magical bean lit up both of their dream worlds. It cut through the tar leaving the color of black ink… cutting Marcos hands off. Mick cried out in a loud voice. *"Be gone Satan…! You have no power over us here anymore. Feel Angel's and my powers, with her help we send you back to hell."*

*   *   *

There was a loud scream. The blackness turned into ink; it bubbled up until there was no more. The sun came out and it shined through the darkness. With the power spent Mick fell to his knees. He drew in the air as if he came from the bottom of the pond. It took all his willpower and strength to stand. He had to get to Angel if he was that weak. Mick knew Angel had to be weaker than him. For the two of them never had this much power before. He had to find Angel, then he saw her. She was near the edge of the water. He couldn't see her face, was she in the water or out of it. Not thinking he dove in just missing the rocks. With his powerful arms Mick moved quickly through the water. He was by Angel's side in minutes. *"Angel… my love."*

He quickly checked to see if she was breathing. *"Thank heavens. She must have passed out from exhaustion."*

Mick's hand brushed the sand and hair away from her face. With her in his arms, he held her. He had his bent arms rested on his legs holding him up. Mick found that he had to rest for a bit himself. Afterward, he took Angel to the top of the waterfall. There he laid with her on the patch of grass. He had her head laying on his arm. Angel's body was close to him. A bit of time went by, slowly she woke up. At first, she didn't remember what had happened. Her hand was lying on top of a man's chest. She knew it was a man for his chest was bigger, quickly Angel sat up. *"Who is this man."*

As she went to touch him, Angel noticed her hair got into her face. What is going on as she brought her hair forward? Someone being cute, then she yanked on the long hair. *"Ow....! That's my hair."* Then she started to check out her body. *"Wow....! these breasts are mine."*

She looked over this handsome man's body. He had black hair, like James. He looked like him, but he was younger. Oh..., this is my Mick. He must be twenty-three, that would make me twenty-one. Angel then remembered what had happen. Marcos, had tried to kill Mick in his sleep. I know I like what I see, I hope Mick will like what he sees. She had remembered what her mother had told her.

It was the time when her father had put a spell on him and uncle. Mommy came up the hill with aunty the two men was asleep. Her mother was bolt and went to kiss him. Angel thought, now how did she do that. Oh yes... she laid on her side then left herself over him. Now she was on all four's then she came down and kissed her man.

All in one motion Mick pulled her down to him, his lips asked to deepen the kiss. Then he was on top of her. She enjoyed his hands and mouth. Angel realizes his little friend liked it also. When she pushed against his heat his eyes flu open. *"Mick it's all right."*

*   *   *

He had looked around and remembered Marcos. Everything was all the same as it was before. He then looked at her, her hair was longer and spread out over the grass. Her breast was bigger her arms and legs were of a dancer. *"Do you like what you see."*

Mick nodded his head. *"Good how about we take these bodies for a test drive."*

It was Angel who waved her hand. Mick didn't waste any time; he went after his toys. She had to suck in air as he took her nipple and sucked. The butterflies were strong as he tried another one of his toys. When she came that was all he needed to join her. At times he watched her cum, then when she got to that strong climax he joined with her. Mick then turned her over. *"Are you all right."*

Angel had her head on his shoulder; he felt her nod yes. All she could think of was wow what a man. Then she sucked on his earlobe, Mick heat racist up. *"Are you telling me you like that."*

Mick pulled her down to him, his mouth took her lips and made love to her mouth. *"Do you want me to show you how much I liked it."*

Angel took hold of him. *"You could go twice back then."*

Then it hit her she almost lost him. The tears came and she couldn't stop them. Mick had just let her cry. *"We beat Marcos, I couldn't figure it out this time. We always have clues; this time you were the one to figure it out."*

Angel sat up and waved her hand. *"I seek the letter of Leslie. Come to me. We need some answers. Come out of your hiding place."*

The letter came to her. When Angel opened it, she found there was a message already there.

Trying to kill their fathers

NGEL WENT OVER to the letter. Marcos sent demons to penetrate your father's and Angela dreams. Bill took the first watch; he has no clue of what is going on in their dreams. Good luck Angel.

With a wave of her hand. She spoke. "Leslie's letter, go back to your hiding place."

She turned to look at her man. "My love we must stop those demons before they kill our father's and Bill and Angela."

Mick wished he could have time with Angel. "I understand what you're saying but how will we do this?"

Angel tried to think of a way to get to their fathers. "We have all the family's magic, the magic fairy rose gives us one or more than one magic we may need. Tonight, we will help our fathers and Bill and Angela. They don't know that there in the dream world."

Mick eyes were enjoying looking at her body. "I don't think we should go there with nothing on. It might scare are fathers. Then again, I wish I could make love to you again."

Angel giggled and wrapped her arms around his neck. She kissed him with a promise to make love to him again. "When we get there, we will help each other's father. I wonder if we can make everyone dream the same dream."

Tom smiled he loved the way she could simplify the problem. Ellen turned toward him and put her arms around him. "After the ordeal we had with Marcos, I wished we could stay here together. But we can't. One more kiss before we leave."

Angel waved her hand, and they had on their street clothes. Mick looked at his mate, I have made love to her in the real world. It's hard enough having bad dream, it's too much when demons can kill you while you sleep. He wished they could fix everyone's dream. "I guess this will have to do for now. Take my hand and think of our fathers with Bill and Angela in their dreams. We must make just one dream with all of them in it, before the demons can kill them."

*   *   *

The two of them closed their eyes. They thought of their fathers and Bill and Angela. When they popped into their father's dreams, they saw Joseph was fighting with his knife. He had taken down a few of the demons.

Mick yelled at him. "Joseph, use your magic your dreaming, there trying to kill you in your sleep. If you die in the dream world, you will die in your sleep."

He waved his hand then flicked his wrist. There was a bright light coming out of his fingertips. Joseph couldn't believe what he was seeing. Now he knew that he was dreaming. Mick was a man, and he saved him from dyeing in his sleep. Joseph used bright light to kill all the demons that came after him.

He was so busy he didn't see James and his daughter. Mick and he were able to wipe out the demons that came at them. He saw Angela fight for her life; he yelled at her. Use your magic, this is a dream. She had her dirk and used it as white fire poured out from the point of her dirk. The demons didn't know what hit them. Magic filled the sky. Joseph saw his daughter fighting with James. She was a beautiful woman. The way she fought with her magic, was like a dance. When the demons surrounded her, she did a spin with her fingers pointed at all the demons. She was able to take them all out at one spin. James had taken out the ones that came after him.

The only ones left were Mick, Angel, Joseph, and James and Angela. Bill had gone over to Angela and took her hand. He saw what was happening to them in the dream world.

Bill had come over to them. Mick and Angel smiled at him. Mick spoke. *"Hello Bill. So, you and Angela is on our father's team."*

Bill nodded his head yes. *"Wow, this is how you're going to look when you're older. I didn't know you two knew how to use a dirk. Mick, you're a strong fighter. Angel, that was quite a move, using your dance. That spin was awesome to take down the demons. How did you two know they were going to do this?"*

Right then Angel instinct kicked in. She looked up and saw a group of demons coming toward them. In her mind she called out to Mick. *"Honey demons coming after us. Catch me, put me on your shoulders, while I take these demons out."*

Mick knew what she was going to do. The men and Angela watched her run to him. In one motion he lifted her up and she was standing on his shoulders. Her arms were strait out; she called for a bright light. A light to take the demons out and close the portal, to all who were with them. Ones again the light flowed from her fingertips. Slowly he turned as the light hit the demons. When she was done, he through her up as she landed in his arms. Angel wrapped her arms around his neck and kissed him.

When it was over. Mick told them that Marcos had taken his name back from when he was a fairy. That is now Marcuse; he is showing the demons how to take people out in their sleep. He spoke. "Marcuse wants me out of the way. He laughed at me when I told him that Angel would save me. His replied that she was just a woman. I wish I could have seen his face. He just came at me with big black hands. He knows you and my father are trying to take him down. Be careful Marcuse is taking it to the next level."

Joseph was looking at his daughter. She is on her way to becoming Mick's wife. "Angel tells me have you and Mick been at the roses?"

She gave her father a big smile. She spoke. Are you asking if I have all my gifts from the magic roses?"

Joseph had a feeling that the two of them had been together. He knew to get into their dream world they had to become lovers. He didn't like to have to take their names from them. It's going to get hard for them; to do the things they have to do to them.

Angel looked at her father. "Dad when are you going to take Mick's name from him?"

James and Joseph looked at her. James thought he would play dumb. "Angel what are you talking about?"

Joseph rolled his eyes. Did he think he would get away with that? Angel looked at him then her father. "So, you're not going to take his memory of his family and mind. If that's not true, then it's not true that he is going to Scotland?

Also, there are two schools on a hundred fifty acres. It looks just like a jail, and don't tell me that it doesn't look like that. James, it's not Mick who is asking for this information. Now that you're acting tongue-tied, then I will give you what is going to happen. I will get right to the point. You or my father will not take are names from us. Your magic is not strong enough to push back our names. The two of us have done it for you two. Marcos has two demons involved in this. The one who will be taking him is not. He is a demon, and the doctor is also a demon. We made our doubles to take the ride to Scotland. If he goes his dream world will be messed up. He will be sick, dehydrated, and hungry. I won't let this happen to my mate. Marcos tried to kill him tonight, along with your mother and father. Something inside me knew trouble was going to happen. I couldn't sleep; I also didn't open my window tonight. It was his cross and rose that kept me on edge. It was the only way we would know if trouble was at hand.

*　*　*

After you're done here, when you go back to the base. Put the cross and rose on the back of your men's head. It will help to keep demons out of their minds. Don't forget our mothers. We will take care of our grandparents. Dad, you take care of Bill, I will take care of you. Bill takes care of Angela, and you can that care of James and he can take care of Mick.

Angel saw that Mick took care of his father. She also knew he was having words with him. She looked at Bill and spoke. "Bill you're the one who's going to keep Mick safe. I should say, the three of you. Tell that officer dad that Bill must be working at that school. Marcuse knows that you're coming after him with train soldiers. He has children there; at our new schools they are demons. If you think we're going to be safe." Angel laughed. "That is a go joke; I have to friends they will have my back."

Then Angel waved her hand to the four of them. She spoke. "You will remember everything I told you. You will not remember us helping you in their dreams. When you get back to base you will take care of your men. On each of your men head place the cross and rose. Make sure you put it on the officer's head, and on anyone who will be keeping us safe."

Tom came over to Ellen, he put his arms around her. "It's time to go my love."

He looked at his father. "Dad, and Joseph Ellen is my mate, she has my cross and rose on her.

"My love has the same magic as I do. I married her and did the ribbon ceremony, when she is nineteen, we will marry again. Yes, the rose has dropped in my hand. The Fairy roses give us our magic. Marcuse doesn't need Ellen anymore. He has a Fairy who will give him a son. Besides, he didn't have to rape this Fairy, she wanted him."

With a wave of his hand the two of them were back at the ranch. Tom had thought of something, in are dreams would you marry me tomorrow night? I have the license with me; we can go to Scotland to get married. You can be nineteen to get married there. The two of them had to clean up everything in the house. Tom saw what Ellen had to do to save him and his grandparents. "This dream wasn't what I was hoping for."

The next day they had breakfast with Tom's grandparents. He told them they were going hiking, that they would be home for supper. Ellen made them lunch to take with them. Before they left, they had placed a cross and rose on the back of his grandparent's head. They had said that demons have been taking people down while they sleep.

It was time to visit Scotland. The two of them made themselves look different. Tom made the path under the waterfall. Inside a cave they saw the vortex. Ellen spoke. "We must hold hands then think of the basement of the castle in Scotland."

The two of them waved their hands, they spoke. "Take me to Scotland in the bottom of the family castle."

They came through the vortex, at the end was a door that opened. It was dark in the dungeon; with a wave of their hands there were two flashlights. Tom took Ellen's hand, and they made their way down the hall. At the end there were stairs to climb. On the top he looked to see if anyone was around. They made their way down the hall, to the door to go outside. He looked out to see if anyone was outside. They were out the door running to the road.

The two of them were enjoying the day together. Here in Scotland if anyone wanted to ask who they were, the would say Mick and Angel. "Witch way would you like to go?"

She was looking around. "I like to see my families land."

Mick knew the story, he was hoping Angel was right, that she would be in Scotland next year. He spoke. "Would you like to run or use a bike."

She was enjoying all the sites. Anything they need will use their magic. She spoke. "We can run for a while then use a bike to go back. I like to take pictures of different things. I know one thing, any picture of Scotland we will take with our magic. This school the rules, are over the top. Like no pictures of any kind. I will be drawing different things. I already know honey; you don't have to tell me. I will make sure no one will see the pictures."

The two of them started to run together. Every place that had a beautiful view, they had to stop. The mountains could take her breath away; one spot had a waterfall. Mick was by her side to enjoy the view, the valley had horses and sometimes sheep. The pictures she had pretended to take, were a magic camera. She spoke. "Wow, Scotland is as beautiful as home."

Angel was thinking of the history of both families. Back in history the castle was the home of MacGregor's. Now it was a school for young children. There was so much to see here, they had started to run again. At last, they came to the land of the Heart's. The land had rich green grass, there were two buildings going up. She looked at it closely, her brother was using magic to build these buildings. There were magical men, working on Raymond's house and barn.

Angel looked at Mick. "This will be my home for four years, when I'm not in school. I know that it is early for me to know if I'm going to be here."

The two of them started to walk away. She thought that a Heart has been by a MacGregor side for a long time. "I think it's time to see the school that was in my dream."

Angel took Mick's hand, she spoke. "Ones we get there we will have to stay invisible."

Holding hands, it was Ellen who did the magic. She closed her eyes and pictured the school from her dream. This was the boy's side she thought, the name on the sign was Deilondotay. Tom saw what Ellen meant when she said it looked like a jail. They went through the open gate. The fence had closed in all the buildings. The schools were set up for boys and girls. There were signs that told what each building was. The two of them noticed there were two older boys; they were coming out of one of the buildings. Right then their chest went hot. One of the boys spoke. "I don't like going to school in the summer."

The blond hair boy spoke. "Stop whining you're the one that through all our homework away. This year you're going to get another roommate. I've already talked to the principal; there is a new boy coming to this school. The principal said his name is Mick."

In Angel's mind she spoke. *"Mick, do you think he will be your roommate."*

Mick looked at her. *"I just hope he's not the demon that we felt."*

Angel smiled and prayed he wasn't the demon. *"We will see. Let's put the cross and rose on the back of their head. I would like to see if one could be freed. If it does, then we will put just a cross on his chest. Mick, we were meant to meet up with these boys."*

When they did so, they went up to the sky and floated there and watched. The blond hair boy fell to his knees. The boy with black hair started to rub his neck. He waved his hand and had brought fire up and burned what was on his neck.

He was coming closer to the blond hair boy. Quickly Mick got him on his feet. The boy spoke. "What are you going to do with that fire. Why isn't it burning your hand? Who are you? Get the hell away from me."

Then Angel places a cross on his chest. They saw it had gone hot on him. The blond hair boy heard a car horn blowing. "I'm glad I don't have you for my roommate this year. Fire are you crazy, how did you do that. Never mind, that's my father, I got to go."

He ran to the car that was waiting for him. She went up to Mick. *"Will now, that blond hair boy was starting to become a demon. He must not be under the spell for very long."*

She had taken a picture of the demon. *"Mick, he looks like he might be the brother to that girl I saw. I think I will burn a stem tonight to see if he is."*

They found the building where they had their food. Then there was another fence with a gate. The building was for dancing, there was one for swimming, and a track to run on. They also saw they had horses on the property. Wow, she thought. They tried to go into one of the buildings they were all locked up. The two of them ran for a bit until they came to another gate. This had to be the girl's side, they had everything that the boys had. In the middle was all the activity. This must be where the boys and girls can work on the activity. They went through the girl's side, which was a mirror image of the boys. There was a man in a small building who opens the gate. The sign said Deilondolay.

*   *   *

This time Mick took Angel's hand. He knew where the castle was. "All right let's head back. I like to see the horses on my uncle's land. They didn't run or ride a bike. They use their magic and land at the castle. Angel and Mick Walk down to where the horses were. Off to the side of the barn, she saw a man trying to get the horse to let him ride him.

The two of them were watching him try to get on that horse. When he threw him, the horse came over to them. She took his bridle and looked into the horse's eyes.

Mick saw his uncle, he spoke. "That horse doesn't like to do what he is told."

Angel got on the horse from the fence. Before, the horse could do anything. She squeezes her legs tight, before he tried to throw her off. She had him running up hills and downhills, pushing him as fast as she could. She didn't let him rest ones. Then Angel stopped the horse and got off. She led him around then got back on him. The horse thought he could buck her off. Ones again she squeezed her legs tight around his ribs. Then she got him to run up and down the hill. That horse was ready to go home.

In Angel's mind she told Mick to let his uncle know to get on the fence. That way he could get on the horse easier. He spoke. "Sir come over here. Now get on the fence so you can take over. Don't let that horse rest, use your legs to control him. Good luck."

She was off the saddle and on the horse's back. She had to use her legs to hold the horse in place. Mick's uncle got on the saddle. Angel spoke. "Use your legs with this horse, the tighter the better. Good luck Sir.

His uncle had made that horse run back and forth. At the same time, they popped into the castle. Angel spoke. "Mick, do you think there is something about Marcos in the Library?"

He was thinking, were would any book be about Marcos. "The only place would be in the valley of the Fairy's. As you know he is half Fairy."

She looked at her man. There was that sweet smile she had when she wanted to do something. He knew that she wanted to go to the land of the Fairy's. He spoke. "How about tomorrow after breakfast?"

Angel through her arms around his neck. "That would be lovely, we can find out what he is up to next. I saw what he had done to one of the Fairies. This fairy knew what kind of man he was. She knew about Marcos he was the kind of man this young fairy wanted. Now there is a female demon who also wants to be with Marcos. I heard that she wants to go back to earth. The place he is going he can have more than one wife."

The two of them made their way down to the basement. Mick waved his hand, and the door opened. Together they asked to go to Vermont were the magic rose lived. They were back at the ranch, just in time to have supper.

*　*　*

The two of them walked back. Tom spoke. "Honey, I know that we want to get married, how about we ask the King to married us? I have a feeling that you have plans for tonight."

Ellen was so happy she got to see Scotland a bit. She was rattling on and didn't hear him. The schools were big; they had activities they could do. She spoke. "Will we have found two demons; one we turned the other we couldn't. The magic rose showed me three demons. One of them was a girl, she looked like that one boy with dark hair. She had a voice of a man, its looks like two more year she has left. Honey, do you think we should ask to go to the land of the Fairy's?"

Tom looked around to see if someone was listening to what they were saying. He had to laugh because she was so excited, she didn't hear him. He spoke. "She had a good idea, honey, you got to take it slow; did you even hear what I had said."

Ellen stopped and looked at Tom. She took her hand and hit her forehead. She spoke. "I think so, you want to have the King marry us. Honey, I do have plans to make doubles. You can rest until I find out what I may need. Would you like to help me?"

Tom smiled, he had already had it planned out. He spoke. "All you must do is think of what kind of dress you want to ware."

She thought about it. "I could have a Traditional Scottish wedding dress. So will you help me after I get everything set up?"

Tom nodded his head yes. "After were done I'll make love to you."

*   *   *

At the supper table Tom mentioned the idea of going to the land of the Fairy's. He spoke. "Ellen like to know more about Marcos. She knew what he had done to all those women."

She had been watching grandpa. She spoke. "Please don't be mad at Tom, I wanted to go there to learn about Marcos. After that one time in our dreams got me thinking. I had burned a rose stick to see what he was up to. It took me to the land of the dead, what I saw was his father calling him. Marcos was all black, his father told him. "You have your magic back, clean yourself up. That was all I saw; his father wasn't pleased with Marcos. There was no son from him, even his daughters with to the Lord, the women lived. Today I burned another rose stick and saw where Tom school was. Why so far away from me?"

Then in her mind she heard Tom. *"Stop don't let on that you have magic. I don't want anyone to know. Please honey that's enough."*

Then his grandfather spoke. "Ellen, I wish I had the answers for you. So, you want to go to the Valley of the Fairies. I can tell you this after Eleanor's sons were older. Along with the Heart Boys. They went to the Valley of the Fairies. The Heart boys married one of the Fairy women. You were part Fairy like Tom. Tell you what you can do tomorrow. We won't tell your fathers about this. I would like you two clean their roses there. Check what they are feeding the roses. If the magic roses go down, it may affect our roses here and Scotland."

After supper they did the dishes. "Tom what should I bring?"

He had put the last dish away. He spoke. "The plant food, to make sure you have it if they forgot how to make it. Would you like to set on the porch the full moon is out?

Tom saw Ellen nod yes. He went over to his granddad. "Grandpa could Ellen and I go on the porch upstairs? You know are time is running out. She is my mate, the magic roses showed me the other night. It's in her room she wanted me to put it in something to keep it safe.

Ellen went upstairs to get her rose. She brought it downstairs to show them. "Here is my rose, I know I can't take it with me. Grandpa when we go to the Valley of the Fairies. Tom and I thought we should see if the rose would drop in his hand. We know of three places that have the magics roses."

His grandfather smiled at them. "Tom, you know she is young, but her mind and body are much older. You have everything to keep her safe. Your grandmother and I know you two have your dream world. I know that Marcos came after you, we know that Ellen has her magic. She saved us when Marcos tried to kill you and us. Don't worry the two of you have saved your father's and their men. Be careful at the Valley of the Fairies tomorrow. Remember Marcos can go to the valley of the dead. He also can get into the valley of the fairy's."

Ellen smiled at his grandfather. "Grandpa I've been having visions. When are fathers come here, they will have two men with them? The one called Bill, is the one to keep Tom safe. I see the other man, will take Tom to a doctor who will put him under hypnosis. It will mess are dream world up. The doctor works for Marcos, and he will use black magic on him. This man that took him there didn't know, the school told him to make sure he wouldn't remember his name. He has a new name, it's Mick. The officer told our father they must get Tom to a safe place. There is an officer who is going after Marcos, it has something to do with the two buildings. This will be more in the 20th century. Please don't let your son aloud that man to take Tom to that doctor.

His grandfather looked at Ellen. He knew she was also the one to protect Tom. As far back to the first Thomas there has been a Heart with a MacGregor. He had a feeling that she had a plan to keep Tom safe. All his grandfather did was nod his head. "Ellen my son doesn't listen to me. If you have a plan, then talk to Bill. He is the one that will be with him."

*   *   *

Ellen shook her head no. "Grandpa that is the problem, Bill wasn't with him. He wasn't even on the plane that took Tom over to Scotland. That's fine, I will see if I can contact my brother. Thank you, grandpa, for at least listening to what I had to say."

Ellen didn't know that Tom had stepped out of the room. Then he came back, he was talking to granny. Now the two of them were upstairs. Ellen had to put her rose back in her room. Ones the rose was safe, Tom put her up against the door. His lips and tongue made love to her. "I want to be one with you at the rock."

CHAPTER THIRTEEN:

Building their Doubles

ELLEN LOVED KISSING him, she had a plan to keep them both safe. She would ask Lesley letter how to make two more of us. "Tom, I like the idea of having the king marry us. I can come to the waterfall after I make my double."

He was looking into her eyes; Tom didn't like seeing all that stress. She was too young to deal with it all by herself."

Ellen touched his face. "My love that would be wonderful. But I'm not old enough to get married."

He smiled. "I found out that you can marry at fifteen. We will marry when you're eighteen, in Scotland just after I get out of school.

Ellen looked at him. "All right that sounds like a plan. Tom, you know that a Heart has been by a MacGregor side from the 1600th century. Thank you for coming to help me in making us. I thought I could do it for you. But Lesley told me not to do you everything is about your body."

He knew that something like that should be made by me. "Just call to me and I will be right there. After were done I like to make love to you."

* * *

Tom noticed that Ellen was thinking about something. "What did you and grandpa talk about?"

Ellen smiled, that meant another trip. "Did you know that there is another set of roses in Ireland. We're going to have to clean the roses there also."

He looked at her. "You're not going to stop until everything has been taken care of. Honey your pushing yourself too hard."

She touched his face. "You are my mate, for a long time a Heart kept a MacGregor safe. I will keep my man safe."

Tom went and kissed her again. "I'll give you a bit of time to see what you will need. I love you, see you in a bit."

*　　*　　*

Ellen called for Lesley come out of your hiding place. The letter appeared to her, she heard her say.

Ellen, the only ones that can push back your name are only you two. Thomas and Eleanor could also do it. If you decide to do this, you can set the time when to start. Ellen, Raymond magic is not like yours. There will be a time when he will receive more magic. The time for you to go to the Highlands will be in August. You can start now, push his name back into his memory. Tom must do it to you, now the family will know you as Mick and Angel. You both will have the feeling that the people who are your family will make you feel safe. They will call you Mick and Angel. This spell that you will make you look like someone else. So that no one will see Thomas and Eleanor in the two of you.

*　　*　　*

Ellen had gone to the water and waved her hand. She had called Bill and Raymond. When he saw her the memory came back to him.

He just staired at her. "Before we start there is something that I'm trying to remember. Wait, that wasn't a dream, I took Angela's hand. She was restless and calling for me to help them. Damn it… that was you and Tom, they came after us in our dreams. Ellen you and Tom were grate. That last move, the way Tom caught you and put you on his shoulder, was out of this world. Raymond, she shot bright lights from her fingertips. She killed all the demons. It was as if her and Tom was one."

Raymond felt another strong magic. Tom was trying to break her spell. "Sis you two was in the dream world together. That mean's as a young woman of eighteen and Tom was a young man of twenty. You two have been together as one, Sis what were you thinking? You're not at the age to have a child. Damn it, tell me what the plan is. I hope you use something?"

Ellen staired at her brother. Then she looked over at the house. "Mamma took care of me; my monthly was too much. Now listen to me, I will meet you at the bottom of the castle with Tom. His double will be taking a ride to the doctor who will use black magic on him. When he gets to you, wave your hand over his face to clean that spell out of him. He will get extremely sick.

"For my Tom after I kiss him goodbye, I will say goodbye Mick I love you. When I turn to go. You must wave your hand over his face and say activate spell. Then say it's time to go Mick. Mick will say, "I love you too, Angel. The one-year timer will start for me.

"You and Bill will take him to your place until his double will come to the ranch. The cross and rose will have every bit of magic. He will remember me in the dream world and the name Angel. If at any time I need him or he needs me, we will have our magic. We will be able to go to that place if we need to.

"That man, no I mean that demon. He will only have a copy of Tom; he will act just like him. Everything he will do will make the copy sick. This man is not who they think he is. A demon took his place two weeks ago; I don't know what happen to the other man. Raymond Tom is my mate; I'm not like other women. Don't worry about that part. Tom and I our save to make love. When it's over with and I'm out of school I hope we can start are life together. Please Raymond and Bill help me out with this. Before you go turn around."

He looked at his sister, she was determent to help her man. Raymond turned around and he felt a warm hand on the back of his head. Then he heard her say, "I give you the cross and rose. This is to keep out demons from taking over your mind. I do this in Jesus's name Amen. Please, you two don't tell anyone that I have magic. Even though grandpa knows he had seen the rose. The two of us has hair from each other, Tom made me this neckless."

Raymond looked at his sister. He spoke. "I have a feeling you would do it yourself. All right sis. When it's your time to join him, I will get you myself. So, the two of you have been to Scotland. You saw my ranch and the schools that day. All right sends us back to Scotland, Tom is through."

It was time to make their doubles. "Thank you for helping me."

She had sent them back to Scotland. Then she asked Lesley how to make their doubles. Lesley showed her the recipe on how to do it. First you must have magic fiber clay to start. If you are make a double of yourself, you must work the clay. Take the magic rose petals and dry them so you can grind them into the clay. For each piece one petals, then four drops of your blood. That will mean four rose petals, then four of your hair and four rose petals. Two hairs from your eyebrows then two marbles the color of your eyes. Place four rose petals afterward. On your heel scrape off the dry skin then a rose petal. A piece for each fingernail, then ten pieces of your toenails. Then you put twenty rose petals, then saliva. Take some of the clay and flatten it as big as your face. Then place it over your face, breathe your air into the clay. All your thoughts will go into the clay as you work with it. Touch your eyelid, nose, lips, and ears then your chin. For the last place eight rose petals. Place all in a ball, your fingerprints will also be there. Place the clay in a big bowl then hit it with white fire. Speak the spell. After that is done place the clay in the basement.

Behind her was Tom, without summoning him. He watched her make herself and did everything she did. "I make this double of myself for later she will be my twin. I seal this in Jesus's name Amen."

Ellen turned and saw his clay; she went over to him and kissed him. "You been doing everything I had said."

Tom smiled then said the spell and put white fire to it. He had sent the two clays to the basement where he placed a bubble around the clay. The bubble will grow with the clay.

Then Lesley letter change. She had told them there will be a time that the two of you will want to leave the school. You will want your doubles to take your place. Bill and Angela will also need to make their doubles. For the four of you will step out of the picture for a long time.

She went and kissed him again. He was also scared for them. "You been that scared for me and yourself. I also check to see if Marcos will also do it to you. Honey, he wants me out of the way. I heard Lesley say if he kills me, he is hoping you would die from a broken heart. Marcos was thinking if we were gone then our fathers would give up. They don't know our fathers, they will never give up."

Ellen looked at him, she kissed him. "I think when the time comes, we must take them into us as we make love to each other. They will have our, cross and rose to know when demons are around them. I haven't checked this part. The dream showed me; they are our real twins. What is inside us, had stayed dormant. When we take them inside us, the part that had stayed dormant will make our twins. Once we are out of school the officer will keep us apart. We're not in school; but still, he won't let us be together. After you leave school, I can't see you anymore. That will be too much to handle."

Tom thought about their twins. "Angel so you're going to make them go through it."

It hit her hard, she didn't think about that. "Mick why did that officer put us in this predicament. It's not right for either of us to go through this."

He took her hand and led her to the grass. "Come on I know just what we need. Honey you are a strong woman. Some of the older woman can't handle what you are handling. I love you so much."

When she laid down next to him, she never thought sex could help with stress. Her body moved over his heat. His little friend had woken up and she then took him inside her. His eyes were fix on her lips; she took his mouth in a hungry kiss. "Don't think about anything but me. I need you; all of this has caught up to me. I can't deal with anything else but you. Please wash this stress away for just a little while."

He looked at her, she was quite a woman. He was lucky to have her. Tom had everything put away then the two of them were in the attic. Were he made love to her, he said a spell. Ones they fell asleep they went back to their bed at 5:00 in the morning.

Marcos gives a dream about, their twins

That morning, he slept tell 6:00, he had woken up to his love crying. She was dreaming of him leaving school. It had finally gotten to her; the sex wasn't enough to take care of the stress. He got up and went over to her door. The door wouldn't open, the doorknob turned but nothing happened. Then his cross went hot. His mate was being tortured, he could see in his mind want she was going through. This dream was not them but their twins, Angela was at school it was Mick last day. Their class for ballet was there.

The two of them when to another classroom to exchange gifts. Her gift was a Dale Earnhardt wallet. She had placed a picture of the two of them inside.

His gift was a locket with red roses painted on it. Inside he placed a picture of the two of them. *"Mick why is it we can talk to each other in our mind. When I want to tell you my name we can't."*

He loved to hold her in his arms. *"Angela, I believe it must be magic."*

She was fighting with herself. What she was about to do scared her. *"Mick it's not fair, school is where a boy and girl find the one, they love."*

She remembered trying not to let him see her cry. Mick didn't like it; he had told her he didn't know what to do for her. Mick led her to the middle of the floor. She always loved to be in his arms. He had so much power in them. Now he lifted her high in the air. Angel didn't want this to be their last dance.

Once again, Mick said the same words he had said there first dance. *"Angela spread your wings so we can fly to the heavens."*

It was on that day her heart broke. As their last song came slowly to an end. Angela knew she couldn't say goodbye. To her those words meant she would never see Mick again. He had told her they better say goodbye to the other seniors. Then he could say his goodbyes to the underclassmen. Together they wished them luck, and good fortune. Angela smiled and told Mick she had to go to the restroom. While she was gone, he could say his goodbyes to the others. She gave him her last hug and kiss. Angela looked deeply into his eyes and every detail of his face. She turned around and headed to the restroom. She had grabbed Bunny on her way.

In the restroom Angela quickly changed her shoes. "You're going to run from Mick. Angela there must be another way."

She looked up quickly. "Bunny if there is, tell me the way so I can stop my heart from hurting. No, I didn't think so, give Mick this note. Stay with him to the end, I know you don't agree Bunny. I don't like this way what can I do. My heart is breaking; Mick is my soulmate. I can't tell you how I know this. You're just going to have to take my word for it."

Bunny looked at Angel, she knew her friend. The only way she could handle her emotions. This time that little run will lead her to their dorm. "Angela you're not coming back. The run you are taking has nothing to do with clearing your mind. What do you think it's going to do to Mick? Your running from him."

Angela turned to her friend and shot back. "Then tell me how to deal with this pain in my heart. Saying goodbye to Mick means forever. I can't do it, I'm not strong enough."

Bunny went over to her and put her arms around her. "Angela, you know he will come after you. He's also hurting inside."

Bunny was hurting inside for them. She thought how many students had gone through this. Bunny had helped Angela slip out from the back door. "She, wait for a little while. Give me some time before you give him the note."

That wasn't what Bunny was going to do, as soon as the door closed, she went to find Mick. "Angela told me to wait before I gave you this note. You're both my friends; I don't want to say goodbye to you either. I know your hurting as much as she is."

At that moment; when Mick took the note. He already knew what Angela was doing. He should have foreseen this. She was scared to say goodbye.

*   *   *

The note had said. Mick, I'm sorry. I'm not strong enough to say those words. I can't even write them; in my mind I hear your voice, if only we could tell each other our names. I could deal with being apart for a little while. I can't deal with not hearing from you forever. I made the biggest mistake; they told me to stay away from the upperclassmen. If you fall in love. You may never find them. I didn't listen to a word they said. I had fell in love with you. I can't say those words to you. Don't forget me, Mick. I'll try to find you in New York, forgive me for not being strong enough to say those words.

With all my love Angela

*　　*　　*

Angela knew the moment when Mick found out she was gone. She was not even halfway to her dorm.

In her mind she heard him cry out. "Angela not like this we don't have to say goodbye."

Right then she could feel all her strength slowly drained out of her. She knew she had to keep going. For she knew Mick was closing in on her.

In Angel's mind she cried out. *"Mick let me go. Please don't make me say those words to you. Go back Mick, I will always love you."*

She had made it to the dorm's steps when she heard Mick yelling her name. "Angela please stop, don't end are school year like this. Please, I'm hurting just like you. We don't have to say those words. Please Angela not like this."

In her mine she heard him say. *"I love you, Angela."*

Angela answered him back. *"I love you too. I'm sorry, Mick please forgive me."*

By then the two principals pulled up to the building. Quickly the two of them went to their students.

Mick had yelled. "No… let me talk to her, Angela please don't end it like this…Please Angela. Let me go, I must talk to her. Please Angela don't end it like this."

The two of them were crying, he was pulling his arm away from the principal. "I'm sorry Mic, why can we write to each other. Please don't hurt him, he did nothing wrong."

Angela watched his principal trying to get him into the car. She saw him break away from him and run to her. He took her hand and kissed it. Their eyes met; in his mind he told her *to meet him on Empire State Building on your birthday."*

Angela nodded her head, she turned to Principal Tensaw, "Please! Don't let him get in trouble. I'll take his punishment. This wasn't none of his doing. I couldn't say those words to him. I ran like a scared little girl. Please help me. I'm sorry Mick that I hurt you. Why can we have something to fine each other."

As the principal took her into her arms and led her into the building. Through her tears she heard Mick say. *"It doesn't have to be like this Angela. I love you too, I know it hurts I'm hurting also."*

Mick quickly got the door open. Then he went over to her, was that a dream from Marcos? He thought his cross went hot did it. Then he realizes it could have been the twin they would have our thoughts and feeling a long with our desire for each other.

Tom thought about what was in that dream. That dream there are a lot of holes in it. I don't think our fathers would go along with that the same with Bill and Angela. Also, you will be living near the ranch in Scotland.

Angel opened her eyes and went into his arms. "Honey it's going to be all right. That dream was about our twins. It had triggered the dream of what they may feel. It's when I asked you, want about our twins. They will have to deal with it when they take are place."

Mick brushed her hair. "Angel, I'm not mad at you, yes last night I was a little mad I knew you were keeping something from me. I know you talked to your brother and Bill. I can also see what you are up to. My magic is a bet stronger than yours. My grandfather had all those men magic. When the time comes, we will find an island to live on for a while.

"I know you're not a child you show me repeatedly as my friend makes you come. I'm scared of losing you. Tomorrow is your birthday, you will be fifteen, but your body is more my age. Your mind at times is older than my own brain. I know a woman matures faster than a man. What I'm trying to tell you stopped treating me as a child. Let me help you."

She kissed him again. "I know you're not a child; you have been helping me right along. I have set in motion when your mind, will forget your birth name. You have placed a time when my name will be pushed back. I will forget my birth name, I will become Angel, and you will be Mick."

Mick knew all of this, it seems that we used our nicknames. "Honey, we must get the things for our trip to the land of the fairies. Granddad wants us to check the roses there. He had a feeling that Marcos will try to get to the roses again."

Angel had stop before she went on. "Angel what else did granddad say, that you didn't want me to know yet."

She started to cry. He took her into his arms, he knew it had to be bad. "Honey want are you handling by yourself. We can deal with this together."

She held on to him trying not to cry. "I've been having these dreams. What we did last night, is make a double of our self. There is a man coming here who is a demon. The other man was taken, two weeks ago. Bill was going to be with this man. He was called yesterday, by this demon that he wasn't needed."

Tom looked at her. "How do you know that?"

She looked at him. "I went to the water and brought them here. I'm going to take you to Scotland. My brother and Bill will activate the spell I put on you. Soon Raymond will get more magic. Our doubles will take are place. I will not let any demon get his hands, on my man."

Tom saw the fire in her eyes. He had to see something for himself. With a wave of his hand, he saw that she had all the family's magic. Then he realized he could have hurt her the way he drove his friend inside her. "Angel I'm sorry your only fourteen and I went after you like an animal."

She touched his face; she knew that was going to happen. "Honey it's all right, you didn't hurt me. If you remember when you push inside me. You let me get used to that way. I know when a man is worried or fear something that he knows will happen. The stress gets too much for him to deal with. Sex is what he uses, then he can deal with it. You made sure that I came enough, until I felt relaxed. Besides, you saw my magic if I didn't want you to do what you did…"

*　　*　　*

That morning, they went down to the basement to see their doubles. Tom realized it was going to be bad at that school. He slowly understood why she was doing all of this. Mick waved his hand, and they saw their doubles were just like them. Once they got back, he wanted to sleep with his wife. He liked the idea of her being his wife. "I saw in the water that your brother knows about us being one together."

She had a feeling he saw us talking. "Your right he didn't like it, but he understood why."

That is all she was able to get out. His mouth made love to her. He just wanted to hold her. Mick mentioned their doubles so he could sleep with her. She said a spell at any time the two of them wanted each other. Mick gently ran his hand over her body. He tried not to have her again. The fear of never being able to have her, was too much.

At breakfast grandpa gave them everything they needed for the roses. The two of them made their way to the waterfall. They made the ramp to get to the other side. Ellen stopped and placed her hand on the ramp. She spoke. "In time of need only the two of us can use this ramp this way. I'm called Ellen or Angel."

It was Tom's turn. He touched the ramp. He spoke. "I'm called Tom or Mick."

Together they spoke their own names we will use. No one will be able to use these portals. You have our handprint and voices. This will stay this way only the ones with are magic have the right to use this portal."

The two of them asked to go to the Land of the Fairy's. The door opened and the two of them stepped out. Tom waved his hand, and he was in a kilt with his family colors, there was a long sash. Ellen waved her hand, she was wearing her family colors and a long kilt, the long sash had Tom's colors with hers. They walked up the stairs when a young woman saw them. She knew no one used the vortex. They got their faces closer, she knew. Running down the hall she called out. Thomas MacGregor is here, and Eleanor Heart is with him."

One of the older Fairy's, spoke. "Lass Thomas has passed away. In less it is the next Thomas."

Ellen held his hand as the two of them walked into the room. The King and Queen heard the young lass calling out.

Tom and Ellen walked up to him. He bowed to the King as Ellen curtsy to him. "Hello sire. My name is Tom MacGregor. This is my mate by the Magic Rose, Ellen Angel Heart. We have come to check on the roses. Then ask you if there is any book on Marcos."

Then Ellen saw in her mine's eyes, a man was going to try to kill the roses. "Tom Marcos is going after the roses; I can't let him do that."

With a wave of her hand, she left. Tom went to stop her, but she was gone. The King saw that Tom was worried about her. He spoke. "Are you the next Thomas and Eleanor?"

Tom nodded his head. "Yes, sire my love she has the visions of what is to come. Ellen and I have strong magic. We have the powers of all who came before us."

Then someone came running in. "Sire a woman who looks like Eleanor. She is fighting with Marcos; he had something he was going to pour over the roses."

That is all it took for Tom to go to his mate's side. Ellen had destroyed what he had in his hand. Now Marcos was in the sky. He had large wings, as he tried to hit her with lightning. Ellen had placed a shield over the roses and herself. She had grabbed all the fairies that were in danger and placed a shield around them.

Marcos saw Tom, he knew his powers match Ellen's. They are young but they know how to use their powers. Together the two of them push him back to the valley of the dead. This time they ceiled the doorway. Quickly Tom checked over Ellen. "You scared me to high heaven."

Then he kissed her and held her close to him. Ellen looked at him. "I'm fine honey, we must check the roses now."

She brought down the shield. Another wave of her hand and she was in work clothes. Everything she needed was in a bucket. Marcos couldn't damage the roses. Now Tom was also in his work clothes. He started to clean the roses with her. Ones they were done Ellen took the pale and filled it with water. She poured in what she had brought with her.

That's when all the rose's colors, came back brighter. Tom when over to the rose that he knew was the magic rose. There he thought of Ellen and the rose dropped into his hand. She had seen him breathe in the sweet scent of the rose. Ellen went over to Tom quickly; this rose was the start of the magic roses. Here the magic was stronger than the others. With her magic she put his legs straight. Tom was out longer this time then the first. When he woke, he kissed her and got to his feet, pulling her with him. Now she took the rose and breathed in the sweet scent. Tom was ready to catch her; he picked her up to bring her to the bench. Where he held her in his arms, as his hand brushed over her face.

When she woke up, he kissed her again? "We were out longer this time. Come on we will see if the King will marry us. Before they went inside, Ellen made someone out of the petal. This Fairy will take care of the roses she has everything she needs. The barrel would have water in it, every month the plant food would drop into the barrel. She put a shield over the roses; this fairy would keep the roses safe. For it was made from one of the magic rose petals. Ellen gave her a spell. If she needs help, she could make other fairies to help her or fight with her.

The two of them went to the King, they asked him if he would marry them. It was a magical wedding, now he was kissing his wife. They had a feast, in their honor.

After dancing, Tom asked were the waterfall in Scotland was. The King spoke. "Close to the roses. Tell me, Ellen, are the roses safe from magic from a demon or Fairy."

Ellen had Tom's hand. She spoke. "I use strong magic sire; there is a shield around them. From the magic roses, I took a rose petal and made a rose fairy. She will water the roses and clean them. The formula will drop every month, and the water will fill the barrel up at the same time. If someone or thing tries to kill the roses. This rose fairy will use the magic to protect these roses."

*   *   *

They said their goodbyes. They went through the vortex that led to the Lowlands of Scotland. The two of them walked pass the waterfall. There was the pond and over there was the tree, that the wizard laid in the sun naked. Where a young Fairy coming from the land of the Fairy's. She needed a man to give her a child. She had no idea he was a strong hansom man, who was a wizard. Ellen was watching as if what had happened played out. Tom walked over to that spot and lay down on the green grass. Ellen found she was in the water making her way to this handsome man. She felt the hunger to mate with a man like this one.

She came from the water; this young man is just what she needed. There wasn't a fairy that could hold a candle to him. What she didn't know was he needed a wife and a son to carry his name on. She thought of putting him under a spell to keep him asleep. But he had better ideas, the moment she was out of the water he grabbed her. Pulling her under him. He spoke, "So ye need a child, so do I. But I need a wife and mother to my children. I will give ye my seed, but ye will marry me and take my name. For when I give ye my seed it may be twins. Marry me stay with me until ye conceive my child.

Tom's grate grandfather made a place underwater long ago. They were the first to see where it had started. They dove into the water without their clothes on. The two of them move through the water into a tunnel and come out into a cave. Now they heard the voice of the wizard. This was when they married.

They made themselves older, this was their time together. They played in the water touching each other.

He took her mouth as a finger slipped inside her. "Honey today as we become one, with my seed I will consummate our marriage. They played and kissed; she took him inside her again. The last time she wrapped her legs around him. His mouth made love to her, he couldn't keep them afloat as she took hold of his heat. When he got the message that she wanted him. He went and placed her on the rock. She was on a soft bed, and her body was dry.

They were covered, that is when they heard the voice of their grate grandfather. "Hello, my grandson who has come from one of my children. This time around you have all the magic from who had come from me. Ellen you are the one from Garret, when he added his magic with his father's magic. It made the roses stronger; I'm pleased with the two of ye. When ye leave this place and ye make love to her. There will be hard times, for ye won't remember each other. But the magic rose will remember. As ye start to fall for each other again, hunger will grow as the years start to pass. Once again ye will take her as your wife. The next time ye will have a paper to say you're married. My grandson let your mate do what she must. Marcos will send other people after Ye. What happens here today will come to Ye again in your dreams. Enjoy your time for this is the last time you will be able to be together."

The two of them made their way to the surface, it was time to go home.

CHAPTER FOURTEEN

Four places have The Magic Rose

WHEN THEY GOT back from the valley of the Fairies. The two of them told what had happened, that granddad dream was right. She told them there is a bubble over the roses and a petal fairy takes care of them. They had a feast for them; the king told us about Marcos. We had locked the valley of the dead up.

Ellen then told him that all three places that the roses grow are now protected.

His grandfather smiled at them. "You only know of three places. There is a fourth place, the roses are in Ireland, I haven't heard much about these roses. All I know is one of our distant cousins. He believes that it was Meghalaya son who took the roses there. His brother had moved over to Ireland. There is another valley of fairies. One of the Hearts had moved there, after Tom's grandfather had married one of the fairies.

It said the men couldn't get their female with a child. When a MacGregor was able to get the future queen with child the word went out to all the fairies. Ireland is the place were fairies magic is strong. They have a portal that takes them to their Kingdom. It is said that mortals have been trick, to come to their world. Once there time go slow if a man were about to get away, he found that one day there, was a year on earth.

Tom grandfather was please to talk about the roses. "I do know that the magic roses, have other beautiful roses to be with. Deep pinks and yellows, the fairies don't let many humans, to take care of any of the roses. If you go there to take care of the magic roses, be aware you will be watched. They are still leery of the magic roses could do for them. They know Thomas and Eleanor, it would be nice if they knew you two. If you go someone may ask about these roses. Don't go into the woods, we would like you to come back to us. We will not talk of this with your fathers.

Ellen loved all the stories of the fairies. "Granddad there are so many stories of fairies. Not any about the human fairy, it seems that in Ireland here are human fairies in the magic realm. On Hollow Eve the realm is more open you could find yourself being pulled there. They have magical creatures like banshee and goblins leprechauns, and dragons, and pixies."

"I would like to go see those roses. Tom had gone to all of them. To see if it would drop in his hand. I now have three roses, each time the magic was strong. May we go tomorrow, it was nice to see other places. The fairy loved the little pixies I made from the rose petal. She took grate care of the roses."

Tom was watching his love. He had a pad of paper and was drawing the two of them. Why did that officer talk are fathers to put us so far from the ones he loves. It's going to be hard being so far away from Ellen.

Then his grandfather told them yes you can go. Tom was surprised that he was letting us go. "If we are going tomorrow, we better get some sleep." In his mind he spoke. *I'm hoping Marcos doesn't pay us a visit there."*

Ellen thought about it. "I'm glad we didn't say anything about Marcos. Oh no, I did say he was there by telling him your dream was right."

Tom smiled, he knew his grandfather was watching them. He knew that I wanted to marry her. The two of them got ready for bed, Tom was remembering last night.

He had watch her brother, Raymond didn't like his sister making love at this age. He knew that I was there, listening to them talking.

*   *   *

Raymond looked at his sister. "I had a feeling you would do the spell yourself. All right sis. When it's your time to join him, I will get you myself. The two of you have been to Scotland. You saw my ranch and the schools that day. All right sends us back to Scotland."

Before she did Ellen whisper. "Don't worry, mamma took care of that part herself. I have his cross and rose, he has mine. Tom did the ribbon ceremony I'm his wife."

Raymond had swallow hard. "I don't like this sis, I do know it was your idea. Your body is more than young, don't forget your pill. Tom, be good to my sister. The same for you sis, be good to him. I love you both, bye for now."

Bill was watching Tom. "He had a feeling, if Raymond gave her to much grief, he would have step in."

Ellen eyes went wide; when she had felt Tom was there. She had sent them back to Scotland. Slowly she turned and saw Tom behind her. This time he broke that spell, he's getting stronger.

She kissed her brother on the cheek and sent them back to Scotland. Tom took them to the rock. "You can scold me now. I'm sorry, I lock you in your bedroom."

Tom saw her hands shaking, he wondered if she feared him. "Angel, are you scared of me?"

She grabbed her hands, and mentally she tried to lower the stress. It was too much for her to deal with. He saw she wanted to cry but couldn't. Now her body was shaking. "Angel what are you doing to yourself."

Her eyes rolled back, and she collapsed in his arms. He thought there would be three more weeks left to hold her, but not like this. When she wakes up, I want to make love to her. "Ellen why didn't you tell me about the demons. Honey, you're too young to deal with so much stress. Even my own self, stress can kill. He pulled her into him as the tears came rolling down her cheeks. When she was relaxed, they enjoyed making love. She couldn't get enough of him. After they came, all the feeling she had held back came out. Tom held her, she had thought she was done crying. He kissed her neck and went back to her mouth. "So how is are doubles doing."

Ellen had wiped her eyes. "There doing good in that bubble you put around them. You brought your brother and Bill here. You and I had to do that spell ourselves. Come hell and high waters you will not let me go with that man."

She was on him taking him inside her. She took his mouth in her mind she spoke *Your right my love, I will keep you safe as long as I can.*

She knew it would be sometime before she felt him inside her again. "I know it will be some time before we could be together again. Come on, come so I can fill you with my seed. One day we will let my little friend. He will be happy to send his boys to give to you, our child. Stay there I'm going to clean you. Damn it, why did you lock me in my bedroom?"

Ellen bit her lip. "I could only deal with one person scolding me at a time."

He knew her brother would try to understand her part in all of this. She was up against the rock he slipped inside her. I like being this way with you. I like using sex to get rid of all the pressure. But you had to get things set in place before the family gets here. I don't like you dealing with all of this by yourself."

That night he was thinking about what had happen. He couldn't get to sleep because of it. Every part of his being knew she was crying. When he came to the waterfall, he saw her making something. Then he saw the clay, he had an idea what she was doing. She had been crying the pressure been getting to her. Tom put a table for the clay. She was trying not to cry but couldn't stop. "Mick, I need you."

He had taken her to the grass and put a bubble around them. She waved her hand, and they were naked. Tom was inside her getting her to come. How he will miss her like this. Her last time had built to a strong climax. When she came, he came. "I love you so much."

She had been going over everything. "The spells we did will work, we have our doubles now. Your brother and Bill already know about everything. We have two weeks left; your spell will work. I will watch out for Misty. I will have to play the game, I have asked Lesley what she looked like. That girl's hair was unbelievable she was too heavy to be a dancer. He had shown her a picture of her.

Ellen held on to him trying not to cry. "I've been having these dreams, that's why I thought to make our doubles. The man who's taking you to a demon, is also a demon. This way it won't make you sick. My brother knows everything along with Bill. He will be at the house were you are staying. Your father is not strong enough; our doubles will take are place. I will not let any demons get his hands, on my man."

Ellen touched his face; she knew that was going to happen. She spoke. "Honey we been under too much stress. From here out the two of us will enjoy ourselves. We will go to Ireland and see what they have there. We will clean their roses and replenish the plant food. Also, we will make a petal fairy who will takes care of the roses. I knew you were stressed out worrying about me. I was worrying about you, that is why I took the lead on how we were going to get there. Sex is what we need, after sex we can manage what we must do. Any time we made love; you made sure that I came enough. I know you wouldn't hurt me, honey doing so you wouldn't have sex for a while. I know you saw my magic; with the strength I have. I could stop you; from giving me that pain. No more talking about that okay."

This young woman is no child; she was always right up there in schoolwork. Her IQ is just as high as mine. "All right I give in, honey I'm glad you're my mate. I'm going to miss being with you."

*　*　*

The next day after breakfast granddad gave them everything they needed for the roses. Like the day before, the two of them made their way to the waterfall. They made the ramp to get to the other side. Ellen and Tom stopped and placed their hands on the ramp.

Together they spoke their names at the same time. I place a rose petal on both sides. Only the once who is of our family, has the cross and rose on their chest. No one will be able to use this portal. You have our handprint and voices."

The two of them asked to go to Ireland where the magic roses live. The door opened and the two of them stepped out. Tom waved his hand, and he was in a kilt with his family colors, there was a long sash. Ellen waved her hand, she was wearing her family colors and a long kilt, the long sash had Tom's colors with hers. The dungeon was clean, even going up stares. It seems they use it also. Then they heard voices. The two of them could feel the magic that filled the halls and stairways. They stopped when they saw a pixie that flew down to them. She was a pretty lass she smiled and went up to Tom. Ellen saw she was flirting with him; she knew what she wanted. Now she had to show the pixie girl. She also had magic; she made her a pixie boy from the magic rose petal. The boy kind of looked like Tom. She spoke. "Sorry my little friend but he is my mate. You can have this one but not my man."

The pixie girl looked the boy over and liked what she saw. He also liked her to; she took his hand and the two flew off. Tom laughed "That's knew, I guess she liked what she saw in me."

Ellen looked at him. "My dear she would have made you smaller. You would be her lover."

Tom pulled her into him, he kissed her. "No. I have the woman that I want."

At the top of the stare there was a young man and woman. Over on one of the walls there was a picture of Thomas and Eleanor. They went up on top and looked around. "Hello there, my name is Tom MacGregor. This is my mate Ellen Angel Heart. We came here to clean the magic roses; this is our last stop. I see you have pictures of Thomas and Eleanor. They are our grate grandparents; would it be possible to clean the magic roses?"

The man and woman looked at the pixie. "We don't take care of the roses. There are fairies and pixies that take care of them."

The pixie was with her man; she had nodded her head yes. "I see you met Rosely; she been trying to find a mate of her own. She stays here and cleans the roses."

They walked and looked around a bit of the castle. "Is this a bed and breakfast place?"

The man and woman smile she spoke. "Welcome to Ballynahinch Castle, it set on 700-acres. The grounds surrounded by mature woodland."

Ellen looked at Tom. "After we are done cleaning the roses can we look around a bit?"

The young woman then said. "Your welcome to do so. We have the mountains called Connemara, with the Atlantic Ocean just a few miles away. You might like to look at that, this castle is 18th century Irish castle hotel. It is positioned by the salmon-rich Overnmore River.

Tom saw Ellen's eyes; this was another place to come again one day. "Honey, they have a mix of outdoors activities and a delectable seasonal menu. Can we eat here, at least try the food? What a beautiful place for a honeymoon. This hotel is elegant with breathtaking views, yes, I can see this place goes out of its way. Ireland does has magic, it invites you to enjoy the most of this generous estate.

The two of them went to clean the roses. Ellen had set up the barrel of water she had poured in the formula into the barrel. Then she started to water the roses, the colors were brighter. The pixie watched them closely. Then she made a little house for them in the center of the roses. Next, she made a petal fairy, she gave her some magic to take care of the magic roses. Ellen spoke. "The magic roses are special; they give us are magic. We wear the cross and rose to tell us when evil is around. Right now, my man is checking if the magic roses will give him one rose."

Tom was at the magic roses; there he thought of Ellen. The rose dropped into his hands, he wonders how strong these roses were. He found out how strong it was, Ellen went over to him quickly. She had to straighten his legs, these roses had pixie magic in them. When

Tom woke, he felt drunk. "With this magic rose make you feel off balance."

Then he had the hiccups she laughed. "It made you feel drunk."

He smiled and handed her the rose. When she breathes in the sense, it hit her hard she was out. When she woke, she was dizzy, she laid her head on his shoulder. "Wow can we go eat; I need food please."

It was a beautiful end to their school vacation. They had asked the pixie if she liked her home. She came and kissed them goodbye. Before they left, they put a bubble around the roses. The pixie could come and go as she sees fit. Ellen told her the bubble is to keep out evil. There is a man called Marcos, he would like to see all the roses dead. She made her and him a little cross and rose. "This will tell you if evil is around. The barrel will have the formula; it will drop into the barrel once a month and fill up with water. The fairy is to help keep the roses safe from Marcos. Her magic is to call for help if he comes here. I made a little house for her and her man. She is over the roses; do you like where you're home is."

The pixie nodded yes, she has magic to move her home if she likes. The pixie man kissed his mate and took her home.

It was time to go; they left the same way they came. Back at home, they made it in time to eat.

They told their grandparents about that place and met a pixie who would love to have Tom for her own. She told them she made her a boy pixie; she takes care of the roses and lives there. Now she has her own home in the middle of the roses. Ellen told them how the magic roses made them feel. It made us feel drunk. That night Tom made love to Ellen in the attic. The doubles sleep in their room.

CHAPTER FIFTEEN

The day Tom's name was changed

WHAT A BEAUTIFUL day, the two of them had just made love. It was time to get up, Tom went to the bathroom to get cleaned up. He had sent his double to the attic for now. Ellen also came to her bedroom she had sent her double to the attic. When she came down to her bedroom she had a bad feeling. She then conjured up a bowl of water. "Show me my mother and father."

Tears came rolling down her cheeks, their time had ran out. "Show me Tom's parents."

Tom's parents were riding with her mother and father. Then she waved her hand again over the water, she called to see her brother. "Hay sis what's up. No, it's already that time. They haven't even call me, I wish this weren't happening to you two."

She tried to smile but couldn't yet. "Our parents on their way. It seems time went by too fast for my liking. I will be bringing Mick to Scotland. His double is ready for that man. I don't see how he will pass as Arthur, which is a demon. We must clean the roses and put a bubble over them. I know that the demon will try to kill the roses."

Raymond could feel how hard it must be to let her man go. "It will be all right sis try not to think about it right now. Bill and I will be waiting for you two. Sis he's lucky to have you as his mate."

Then she felt her man. "Thank you, Raymond, see you soon, I love you."

Mick went over to Angel. She got rid of the bowl and went into Mick's arms. "We knew this day would come. A year will go by fast, now what do we have to do first."

Angel didn't want this day to come. "Have breakfast then get the roses ready. Marcos going to have that man pour something over those roses. You will have to say goodbye to your grandparents. I must make a petal fairy. She will have magic to zap that demon. Only granddad and granny could work on the roses with the fairy.

Ellen nodded her head. She spoke. "Before I do anything, I must put this rose with the other three."

She had to put a shield over all the garden roses. She felt Marcos would send someone to take these roses down, this person would try to poison them. Ellen knew if the roses are killed, everyone that has the mark of the cross and rose will lose their magic. Ellen did what she had done to the roses in the land of the Fairy's. Only granny and grandpa could work on the roses.

But as their year's have passed, Tom's grandparents when they're gone from this earth. He will be the one to take care of the roses. The petal fairy will know Tom, put the rose will not remember him. A drop of his blood must be taken, even his mate must give the rose a drop of her blood.

Inside the house, Granny came over to Tom. She took him into her arms. "Stay safe my boy, I will miss you so."

Then his grandfather brought down his things. Tom went over to him and gave him a big hug. "I will remember everything you taught me. You have always been there for me; Angel has put a shield over the roses. She has made a rose fairy; she will clean and water the roses for you. But you both will be able to work on them. She has a bad feeling about this man; Raymond will be at his home waiting for us. Bill is now living at my uncle's place. He is to help with the horses when he is there.

"If my father, ask you who done all of this for the roses. Tell him Angel had a dream, and she told me what to do. I was the one to set the bubble up for the roses. Granddad, they can't know Ellen's has magic. I just want you two and Raymond to know that she has magic. They're going to come after her enough without magic."

Ellen and the two doubles came in with her. Granny went over to her; she knew which one was her. "You're his wife now." She nodded her head yes.

Granny wrapped her arms around her; she was the one to teach her things. She spoke, "I'm glad we went, each time Mick came to clean the roses. He thought of me, I didn't think it could happen again to us. Granny, when the rose dropped in his hand, the power was stronger. I have four roses; Mick had made me a necklace that no one could see. The two of us enjoyed the time at all these places, I made friends with a pixie.

The valley was so beautiful, and the King and Queen were wonderful to us. When I went out to see what the roses needed. Marcos was going over with something in his hand. Then I knew he was trying to kill the roses. I knew it was him because of his marks on his face. When we fought with him, he was in someone else's body. He was testing are powers. When Mick came out with the King, we sent him back to the Valley of the Dead.

"We had cleaned the roses when we were there in Scotland. There is a bubble around the roses, we have a petal fairy to clean them, she has magic to stop anyone who would tries to kill them. I will be back after my father and them are gone, are doubles will act as we would. Granny was it this hard for Eleanor?"

She smiled at Angel. Granny spoke. "She had written it was hard to pretend she wasn't married. Eleanor was older then you two. The feelings are stronger in you for Mick, you both needed to be as one with each other. I believe there will be time for Mick to come a save you. When the two of you came here, you started to act differently. This will give you time to catch up to your body. It's time to leave, you two have done something good here for the roses. Thank you for giving me a rose fairy to clean the roses for me. Sometimes I don't feel good to do so."

Granddad came over to them. He spoke. "The two of you have done well for all the roses. I see that your spell has started. You may have it easier then Eleanor had, that spell will push it back into the back of your mind that you're married. I have seen the two of you act older now. When you made love, you made your bodies older. Ask your brother to push that memory back in your mind. This way you can act closer to your age."

Angel gave him a big hug. She knew that it would have to be Mick to do that. She spoke. "All right grandad, I'll see you when I get back."

At the waterfall, Angel asked Mick to push her memory of them making love together. We can remember their time in the land of the Fairy's in our dream world, right now it must be farther back in her mind. She had done it at the same time for Mick. We will remember that we were married when I turned nineteen. Then the two of them touched each other in the back of their heads.

Their two doubles came over to them. "Ellen, you gave us magic, what do you want me to do."

She thought about that. "This man who is coming here is a demon. What I want you to do, is not use your magic. Let Tom do that for you,

you two have what we have in magic. Tell the man that you believe he is a demon, Tom brings up the cross and holy water. Then you can have him put out his hand and prove that he is not a demon. Watch him for he may have something to kill all the roses. I would have him hang from a tree by his ankles and see what falls out of his pocket. Marcos wants the roses gone one day, soon you will have some of the burden.

She had grabbed her arm. "Ellen what do you mean some of the burden?"

She just looked at her. "You are a part of me; you have everything I know. Think about it and take care of your man."

*　　*　　*

It was time to go to Scotland; they stepped into the vortex together. When the door opened, they were now in Scotland. The two of them made their way to one of the back doors. They headed to her brother's place, being here in Scotland her mind wasn't as stressful. They ran together as one, at times Mick stopped and kissed her.

Angel knocked at her brother's door. When the door opened, Bill had open it. "Come in, we have lunch for the two of you."

Things were getting kind of fuzzy, after lunch they made their way back to the castle. There her brother will activate the spell she had done on him.

Ellen had lost her name for a bit; she was now Angel. She looked over at his face, as Mick had done the same. He pulled her into him, then he kissed her. She was having a hard time letting go of him, she kept kissing his lips.

It was time to say goodbye to him. Raymond spoke. "Angel its time you must go now."

In her mind she knew she had to leave him here. "Mick, I will see you in our dream world. Close your eyes my love. I will always be with you."

Mick couldn't fight them he had to let her go. "I love you, Angel."

She tried not to cry yet. "I love you to Mick see you in the dream world. Close your eyes my love."

He watched her go down the stairs. Raymond and Bill took hold of his arms. That is when he closed his eyes. Raymond waved his hand over Mick's eyes. That had activate Ellen's spell and it also turned on the clock for Tom's.

She stepped off the vortex, now she was Ellen but there was a clock ticking down. She walked to the roses by the waterfall and lay down in the grass and started to cry. When she stopped crying, she saw what had happened here at the ranch.

*　　*　　*

The doubles of Tom and Ellen were on the porch when they saw a car pulling up. The first car was her mother and father; Tom's parents were in the back. She ran to her mother and felt the love pour from her. She went to her father and felt his love. But there was sadness because he was the one to take Tom's name from him. Joesph knew that his little girl was deeply in love with him.

Tom watched her father; he saw that Joseph was worried about what he had to do. Tom spoke. "Uncle Joseph I understand of what you must do. It's all right, do what you must."

Then he saw another car, this was the man Ellen didn't like. The man got out of his car and came right over to Tom. "Hello Tom. It's nice to finally meet you. I heard good things about you, are you ready to leave? We have a long flight ahead of us. Before we can leave, we have a stop to make."

Tom was sizing him up; this man wasn't a Navy Seal. He didn't have the body for being one. "No Sir! …I am not ready. I haven't seen my mother and father for a while. It will be four years since I will get to see them again. I don't care if we do have a long flight ahead. I'm going to have time with my parents."

Ellen then felt her cross and rose. "You're not Arther, he's not a demon but you are. Ellen's father also felt his cross and rose go hot."

Joseph had come right over to him. "I don't know what you're up to. You're not to be here until 8:00 at night. I hope for your sake that you don't take Tom to a doctor. We talked about that; you don't need to be here. We are going to take care of his name. His father told you no hypnoses."

The demon was playing it cool. "I was told what to do, what you say don't count."

Ellen went over to the man. "You don't talk to my father that way. You are not Arthur; he's a Navy Seal you're not. You're a demon."

He looked into her eyes, as he tried to put her into his power. It didn't work on her. "Your just a child."

Her father came over to him. "My daughter is martyr then you, with an IQ over 150. The same with my son you better prove that you're not a demon. Put out your hand, and whole this cross."

The man backed up, he was ready to run to his car. Tom waved his hand, and the man was upside down. A glass bottle fell from his pocket. It broke and what was inside was a chemical that burned the grass. Joesph took his hand and put the cross in it. The demon Howell as a cross appeared on his hand. Ellen then spoke. "Tell me where is Arthur? If you don't tell me I will pour this holy water over, you. You're not a man anymore you are a demon who wants to hurt my boyfriend. You work for Marcos, tell me where's Arthur."

The demon laughed at her; he didn't think she would do it. Without saying anything she poured the holy water over his neck. He screamed. "Stop, he's at the airport in his private jet."

Tom then made a big whole that led to hell. "Tell Marcos he lost to two teenagers again."

He cut the rope, and the demon fell into a pit of fire. The whole was covered, and he smiled at Ellen.

Granddad had wave his hand and Arthur lay on the ground tied up. Granddad then spoke "Marcos want Tom out of the way. He's not going to like seeing his man."

Ellen laughed and so did Tom, then the earth shook. Then all of them laughed, another for the team. Arthur was coming around. "How in Sam hell did I get here."

Then James and Malaya went over to Tom. He went into his mother's arms. He spoke. "I've missed you, mamma, why do you look so tired? Have there been a lot of things you had to do? I love you anyway."

His mother shook her head. She spoke. "I love you to. You could have left out how tired I look. I knew you would pick that out right off. I wished all of this didn't have to happen."

Then Ellen's double came over to give her a hug. There was the innocent in her action. Ellen spoke. "We missed you all so much."

James was with Joseph talking with that Arthur. Then there was yelling. James spoke. "You're not taking my son; we will be dealing with his memory ourselves. Arthur snaps out of it; he will not be taken to a doctor that does hypnoses. He will not mess with his mind, if you do there will be hell to pay. Remember this is no threat, this is a promise. You will not mess with his mind do you understand."

The women had brought the things that the two of them had given each other. Ellen was brought over her angel with ballet slippers. Tom's mother had brought his stuff animal of Mickey Mouse to him."

Arthur came over and he spoke. "They can't have anything like that. Those things can't be at school."

Then granddad came over to him. "Give me their things." Then he waved his hand, the angel with ballet slippers was at her brother's place. Then he took the stuff animal of Mickey to his son's ranch.

Arthur watched Tom and Ellen, he saw them holding hands. He spoke. "You better get used to not seeing her. Beside there are many other girls at that school. Who is closer to your own age?"

Tom was going to send him back to the jet. Ellen looked into his eyes; she put a cross on his forehead and ears lips and the back of his head. "There now can Arthur come out, before our family sends you some where you don't want to be."

Ellen was so glad she made her double. If she were there, she would have had him hanging from a tree upside down. Then her father spoke up. "That is enough from you. You will not speak that way in front of my daughter. My daughter is smarter than you are. Be careful what you say about my daughter. Tom is very protective of Ellen, as I am."

Ellen saw Tom hand was balled up, she heard her say. "Thank you, dad, for saying that. Arthur's mind was mess with. It was just in case his demon fails them."

Ellen's double went over to Tom; she kissed him right on the lips. Tom spoke. "It's all right, a part of me will always remember you." In his mind he spoke. *"Don't cry my Angel, I will always be with you. The rose will tell me if you need me. I will come to you were ever you are."*

Joseph and Malaya knew this was going to be hard on them. He had to take the young man away from his daughter. Then he had to push back Tom's name in his memory.

James's magic wasn't that strong because he didn't believe in the magic. He told his wife he would be right back. Joseph needed help with the spell, he had to run to the waterfall.

He had to ask Leslie the best way to take Tom's name from him. At the waterfall he called Leslie. Come to me quickly, I need your help. The letter appeared in his hands. "You know my heart; how can I keep them safe?"

* * *

Hello Joseph.

The spell you are looking for will take two people. James's magic is not strong enough to even help you; you can ask his father for his help. When James was young, he fell asleep at the roses. A demon took a lot of his magic and told him he has little magic.

James's mother can help by rolling back time, then you can take down the demon. Before he takes James magic from him.

Ellen heard what Leslie said. Quickly she turns back time and sees the demon. She took care of everything then she put back time to now. "Dad you and Uncle James can do that spell. Don't take his memory push it back leave our dream world. Don't ask you may not like what you hear. Now put a protection spell around them before you start the spell. Do not do the spell without it.

Marcuse will do anything to keep us apart, to the point of killing him. Tom's name will be block from him and anyone who knows Tom. When he steps into the plane the spell will start. Joseph, what you do to this double won't matter. Your daughter has taken Tom to Scotland. The two of them has done the spell, this young man is his double as for Ellen also. As you found out that the other man wasn't Arthur. He hasn't even got off the plane. A demon made a double of him; you found out that he was a demon. The one who makes the person of himself must do it himself.

Don't worry about them. Their love is strong enough to find each other in that school. Remember, the spell is to block the name Tom's MacGregor, Ellen's magic is strong enough to break your spell with a kiss. Good luck Joseph.

*　*　*

Ellen knew that Leslie would tell her father that she had magic. Also, Tom is in Scotland. That's why she had to take some of the message from his memory. Joseph knew what to do now. He joined his wife and said hello to James's father and mother. James's father saw the pain in Joseph's eyes. He went and gave Malaya a hug. "Hello Sir."

Joseph went over to James's father. He spoke. "Sir, I just found out that a demon told James the roses had no magic."

He had pat him on the back. He spoke. "The magic is strong in him; your daughter had found out that a demon pushed back his magic."

Inside the house he saw James as a young man sleeping. He saw that a demon told him the roses have little magic.

Now Ellen was acting up. She had a small cross and rose in her hand. She spoke. "You are his father; Tom has magic, and you should also have magic." She went boldly up to James and placed a cross on his chest. She looked into his eyes, with two rose petals in her hands heated up. She placed the petals on his temples, why don't you believe in the magic?" Then she saw in her mind, a demon was telling him the roses have no magic. It was hypnosis when he was a boy, a demon came to him when he was alone. With her magic she took what the man had said from James, those words were wash away from his mind the hypnotic was gone.

Tom came over to his father, in his hand he had a cross and rose. What they had gave them in the spirit world. He will have to give his father another one. Tom had shown him that he could do magic. He spoke. "Dad, you need your magic, why don't you believe in it. I came from you and momma; your family has strong magic. Why don't you believe."

His father looked at his hands. James spoke. "I don't know son."

Tom looked into his father's eyes. He spoke. "Yes, you do know what happened. You got mad at your dog; you hit him with your magic. It had killed him; you buried him by that tree. Dad, you're older now. You have control over your temper. It takes two people to do that spell. Your magic is strong."

Tom then waved his hand in front of his father. He saw the power that his father had. Joseph walked over to them. James was hugging his son. Ellen had given the double some magic. She had felt that it would be needed. Now when they go to that mountain, both men will have a chance to come back to his wife.

Then James remembered that Tom and Ellen saved them in the dream world. James started to say, "The dream world is for lovers, you two are too young,"

*　　*　　*

Tom looked at his father. He spoke. "Dad just leaves it as that. What happened when Ellen saved me from Marcus? That is for us, right now let me say goodbye to my soulmate she is my life."

Ellen walked over to Tom and placed her arms around his neck. She kissed him deeply, her double had tears in her eyes as she walked away from them. This time it was her father, and his father pushed back his name. James and Desirae took Tom's double to the airport with Arthur. They thought it was their son.

Arthur was quiet all the way to the airport. "James, I don't know what to say."

He told him to turn around. "This will not happen again. Marcos is pulling out all the stop, he will try to take both kids. His father wants them. I want you to put a cross and rose on the back of your men's head."

*　　*　　*

They said goodbye to their son. Mick's double didn't eat much before he left the ranch, they went through some turbulence, it made Mick's stomach do flip flops. Before he got sick, Arthur gave him something to let him sleep. His double didn't remember much about the trip to Scotland.

He thought they left in the afternoon. He spoke. "What did you give me Arthur? It made my mind feel like I'm in a dace."

He remembered being place in a seat. There was a man buckling him in. Once again Mick fell asleep. He didn't remember how long he was sleeping. When he was able to stay awake. He found himself on a private jet. Mick didn't understand what was happening to him. He felt he needed to be on guard. How would he do that when he couldn't keep his eyes open? The closer they got to Scotland, everything Mick's double saw he was seeing. He wasn't to remember his love brought him to Scotland.

When Mick slept, he couldn't understand his dream. He heard this girl's voice. She kept saying. *"Mick meet me at the waterfall."*

Could it been his double answer or the real Mick? Ellen thought his double wasn't there yet. She thought, *"Mick, can we just talk?"*

When he didn't answer her, he could hear her crying. He spoke. *"Don't cry I don't like anyone to cry. What can I call you?"*

In the dream he thought he sat on a rock. Everywhere he looked he saw darkness. Even in his thoughts he felt like he was losing his mind. It didn't help when he woke up. Mick would look out the window of the jet. All he could see was pitch black.

He heard a man ask the pilot. "How far are we from Scotland?"

The pilot answered. "Were about two hours out Mr. Stanley."

After a long flight to Scotland, Mick then was place in a car. He was handed a glass of something to drink. "You should be waking up with this Mick, drink it all down."

Mick looked around; he had never seen this place before. He spoke. "Where am I? I don't remember anything."

Ellen was at the waterfall; she was watching the car the double was in. "Raymond there getting closer, don't let anyone see Mick and his double come together."

Raymond looked at his sister. He spoke. "Ellen it's all most over. You had said that there was a demon in Arthur."

She looked at her brother. Ellen spoke. "No, it was a copy the demon made. If it were a double, that would mean it was part of Arthur. We felt like the demon because he made Arther. The demon should have had Arthur make his double.

Tom's dad has his magic. When the three of them go to that mountain they will have strong magic together.

*   *   *

Back in the car Arthur spoke. "Were in the Highlands and driving through a town."

Slowly his double was able to stay awake. He spoke. "Where are you taking me."

Arthur then spoke. "To the family that will look after you. I will go and set up everything at the school. Your new family will bring you there when it's time to go back to school."

Mick looked around. He saw a school that was called Rose Hill elementary. The school was a castle. Then the car turned into a driveway that led to a ranch. "Were here. Be nice to these people."

*   *   *

Mick got out of the car and walked with Mr. Stanley. The two Mick's was face to face. Raymond had the other's frozen in time.

He made the double and Mick Walk toured each other. Slowly they came together as one. He ran over to catch Mick; he got him back on his feet. Before he woken Mick up, he made sure that his dream world was part of Ellen's world. Then he unfrozen the others, with a snap he was back at home.

Raymond was now looking into water. He saw his sister. "Sis, it's done, Mick is here and the double and him is as one. Your dream world is back with Mick."

She smiled at her brother. "Raymond, I feel so lost without him. We haven't been away from each other for very long.

Raymond didn't like what he had done. "It will get better sis, do some teaching of the younger dancers. It will help the time go by faster. I love you, sis. A year will go bye fast, then I will come and get you."

*　　*　　*

Arthur felt something had happen, but he had to get this part of his job done. He spoke. *"Mr. & Mrs. MacGregor. I would like you to meet Mick T.M."*

All Mick could do was stair at Mr. MacGregor. There was a picture that was trying to forum in his mine. It was Mr. MacGregor, who spoke to Mick first.

Brandon had a feeling that he saw something familiar with him. "Hello Mick. If you like you can call me Uncle Brandon. This is my wife, Kimberley. You may call her Aunt Kimberley. We take care of our granddaughter. It will be easier for her to understand that your family. Did you have a nice flight here to Scotland? You came to us on a beautiful day. The sun is out and it's very warm."

Mick looked around; this place had horses. What a beautiful place to be staying at. "I'm sorry sir, I was enjoying the beauty of the land you have. I shouldn't have looked around that quickly. Why do I feel sick to my stomach? I know that it's a hot day. If that is so, why am I so cold?"

Then Arthur was telling them that Mick may get sick to his stomach. "The boy went through a lot; I will leave you with him. My job is not over with; I will go and take care of the paperwork at school. Mick, these people are very nice to take you in. This will be for the weekends and holidays also for summertime for four years."

Mick didn't feel like himself, he felt scared and dizzy. His mind was telling him he knew this man. He couldn't put his finger on who he looked like. It must have shown in his face. Kimberley went quickly to his side. She then put her arms around him. Mick felt safe in her arms, this was a familiar touch.

He had buried his face into her shoulder. She spoke, "Thank you Arthur for bringing this young man here to us. Dear make sure we get all of Mick's things. I'm taking the boy in. Good day Mr. Stanley."

Mick then got very hot; his stomach was turning. He spoke. "Aunty I feel like I'm going to throw up."

Kimberley took him into the house and quickly went down to their bathroom, where he got sick in the toilet. Afterwards he started feeling better. He laid his head on the cool tub and closed his eyes to rest. When he heard the voice of that girl.

Ellen had been out by the waterfall. She felt so lost, then she felt her man was sick. She spoke. *"Mick, I miss you. Are you feeling a little better? I'm sorry you don't remember me. You called me Angel when I was younger, you gave me an angel with ballet slippers. I called you Mick for Mickey mouse. I gave you a stuff animal of Mickey mouse, in hope that you would remember me. I don't like this Mick. They took your name from you. They made me forget my first name; It's the start of me using only Angel. I can't tell you my real name. We can only say are nick names, you call me Angel. Mick, I know we are six hours different from each other. I don't know if we can talk to each other much."*

He stayed on the floor with his head on the tub. He spoke. *"I heard you say come to are dream world by the waterfall. Can you tell me about this waterfall?"*

Angel was please that he had heard her. She spoke. *"I'm so happy you can hear me. Yes, we use to go to your grandparents' ranch. There is a path we go on to get to the waterfall. We must swim across to lay on a big rock. A lot of times you wait for me there, when my grandparents bring me over and drop me off. I'm scared Mick, I feel so lost without you. The two of us has been together all my life."*

Mick felt scared also, was it because she wasn't with him? He spoke. *"Angel what do you look like? I would like to draw you.*

Ellen knew he couldn't have a picture of her. She spoke. *"Mick you can't do that, but you can picture me in your mind."*

He wondered if he would see her again. He spoke. *"Angel will we ever see each other again?"*

She smiled she could picture him in Scotland. She spoke. *"Yes, I will see you next year. Right now, I need to tell you about yourself before my double catches up to me. Mick, this is importin, you're not like other boys. Why I say that is because you and I have magic, you can think of something and wave your hand, it will be there. No one can know about are magic. My brother Raymond along with Bill, are the only people that should know we have magic. Also don't tell anyone that you hear me."*

Mick picked up his head, it had stop spinning. He spoke. *"Angel I won't tell anyone about this. I think they would think I'm crazy in the head. I'll try tonight to see if I can go there. I don't know if we can see each other, we can talk at least. You're making it a little easier for me. I would like to see what you look like."* Mick thought he could use the air to make her face. With a wave of his hand his finger became the pencil. *"Please tell me what you look like."*

Ellen wondered if she should. She spoke. *"I'm just a little shorter than you are. You're two years older than I am. The two of us have a very high IQ. They want me to stay in the last year of junior high school. I'm going to try to skip high school all together. I want to be a freshman in college when I get there. I have bluest green eyes, with long golden-brown hair, I also have a tiny waist. You always told me my lips are a heart shape, that they are the color of the magic rose. We took classes to dance together. You were my partner in ballet. This may sound funny to you. But I'm your soulmate from the magic roses. These roses help us if one day you feel your chest goes hot. That means there is a demon around. Please don't ignore this if it happens.*

"The two of us has a long history together. There is a castle down the road from the ranch. It's a school now, there are roses there. When you feel better go look. Next year before school starts, I won't remember my name. I believe it has started; I think I'm going to go by the name Angel. What I mean, is my name will be taken from my memory. Mick at the ranch there is a pond that a stream flows through the pond. There two rocks in between the rocks they have magic roses. These roses are under a tablet it has magic. Take a nap there and listen to the stream. It will give you peace."

He was done drawing her face. It was her eyes that came through. "You, say that you're my soulmate. Angel, have I kissed those beautiful heart shaped lips? *When it is your turn, I will be there for you. Until tonight, my Angel."*

Mick waved his hand; he had taken her face in both hands. He laid his lips on hers and felt her lips kiss him back.

*   *   *

For a while Angel was staying away from her double. She didn't know what they had done to her. She was so tired that she took a nap over the magic roses. Ellen didn't realize her mother was following her double. Now her double came over to her, slowly she became one with Angel. When her mother came up the hill, she heard her daughter crying.

Desiree knew how she felt. When Angel's father went to become a Navy Seal. She would do anything to go with him. Now they took her daughters man away from her. Granny told her that she knew Arthur was a demon. The demon made a copy of Arthur, that way he couldn't slip by them. It didn't work because Arthur needed to make his own double. The demon was using his own parts, that's why they felt the cross and roses go hot. He didn't get by Angel; it was her dream and the knowledge of how to make a double. Ellen was slowly losing her name. What was her name before Angel?

Desiree knew that the two of them would become one together. When she came to her about her period being all over the place. That was the way to not get with a child. This has been hard on her. Her body and mind have grown a lot this summer. Poor Mick must be scared, now the two of them are scared. Her daughter is a strong woman. She may be my little girl, but now she is a woman a very smart young woman. Mick's been with her from the day she was born. She felt lost without him. She can imagine how Mick feels. Granny had said the roses had dropped into Mick's hand four time. Ellen had told granny that the man who was Arthur, was a demon that he had made a copy of Arthur.

*　*　*

Mick came out of the bathroom. As he looked around. Right off he found his things in one of the bedrooms. He felt like he's been here before. Then he found the stuff animal of Mickey mouse. He wasn't hearing things, what she told him was true. Part of him thought he knew this place. He had to get out of these clothes. Then he saw a kilt in the closet. There is time to learn about this kilt. He put all his things that were staying here at the ranch away.

The next day he was told they were going to the Highland games. Kimberley started to show Mick how to dance. He notices that they weren't surprised that he could do it. The three of them had fun doing the dance. Kimberley told Mick to get his kilt on. Everything you need is in the closet.

At the Highland games, Mick got up and danced with his aunt. He also fought with the sword with his uncle. He was good with that sword. Mick through the dirk and hit the target every time. A man came up to him and asked if he was a MacGregor?

Mick felt his chest go hot. The MacGregor name felt right to him. What did Angel tell him, to be on guard that meant there was a demon after him. "No sir, I'm not from around here. There are a lot of things I can do. Is there any trouble with knowing these things?"

The man was persistent about this. "How about the sword. You can fight like you been doing it all your life."

Then Brandon came over to them. "Mick go over to Kimberley; it's time to eat."

Mick saw Brandon put a hand on his shoulder. There was pain in the demon's eyes, he felt his chest go hot again, he thought about it. That demon was trying to see if he would get scared. It felt good not to be afraid. "Yes sir, I'll go and help her with Emily."

*   *   *

At the end of the week Uncle Brandon took him to his new school. The school was somewhere in the low land of Scotland. He helped him fine his room, this part of the commune was just for boys. Mick was told there was a hundred and fifty acres. What he didn't like was that large gate and the fence. What could be on the other end of this fencing? A feeling came over him, he thought he knew what was on the other side. This place felt as if it was a jail, not a school. He thought a lot of guys could get really scared.

After he said good-bye to his uncle. Mick went back to his room; he left things that people would make fun of him at the ranch. Everything was so different to him, first not knowing his name. But Angel helps him through that part. She had told him Mickey mouse was given to him back when they were young. She also said she was going to the same school. But at the other end of the hundred and fifty acres, it was the girl's side.

Another boy came down to the hall. "Hello, my name is Don. They said if there is another one called Don. To use initial mine is D.C. are you, my roommate?"

Mick looked at him, the young man seemed to be lost. "Yes, Call me Mick. It's nice to meet you, Don."

Mick was trying to get some of his things out of his bag. "This place is big, the things that had to be done just to go to this school."

The young man who he thought was lost, wasn't. "Mick I just found out there's another school on campus for girls. On the other side of the gate, we can do activities. That's where we get to meet the girls. They say you must try out some of the sports. Are you any good in any sports?"

Mick liked the idea to join some of the sports. He thought to go fine the list so he could join. "I can hold my own, did you happen to see what kind of sports?"

Don was ready to go look around. "I haven't seen the list. I heard if you want to meet any of the girls. You must go for the competitions. They pick only the best, there's an upper-class man a cross from us. His name is Cal; he said that there is a girl named

Misty. Cal told us, Misty shouldn't have been her name. Bossy's fit her better them Misty."

Like magic Cal came to their door. "Hay Don don't scare him off. He looks to be a strong athlete. Until we get some girls with some backbones. Misty will have her friends in the competitions. Hi, my name is Cal."

The young man looked to be bit older than him. Mick spoke. "Hello Cal… don't worry about that, they call me Mick.

Cal seemed to be sizing him up. He spoke. "Did you say Mick, what is your initials? Because my roommate is Mick T.M. Also have you had time to eat?"

He thought that food would be good right now. "No, I just haven't felt like eating. I better go and get some food. Cal, that is my initials. I guess that I'm not your roommate after all Don, Sorry about that."

Cal smiled at Mick. He spoke. "Come along with me. Deilondotay does have some really good food. I'll tell you all about are school, and the other side were the girls stay. What kind of sports do you like?"

Mick smiled it his chance to get to know everyone quickly. "Back home I did a lot of running about five miles a day. There is weightlifting; I was a dancer in ballet, and I did a lot of karate. I've horseback riding and I'm a strong swimmer."

Cal was hanging on each other's words. He spoke. "Will now Mick. One other thing, are you in High school or College?"

Mick was telling him a lot about himself. He spoke. "They, say high school with a lot of college mix in. I must take some tests to see were they like to put me. Why do you ask?"

Cal watched Mick down his food. He had shaken his head. He spoke. "Grate because Misty is going to be after you. How about you and I being roommates? I'm in college also. You and I should do some running together. Eat-up I'll show you around."

A teacher came over to Mick. "Oh, good you two already met. Mick have you unpack yet?"

Mick looked up when a teacher came over to the table. "No mam, Cal had been looking for me. I was just a cross from him."

The teacher marked him off his list. "That's good, because you're going to be roommates with Cal."

He was glad he had the right Mick. He spoke. "Grate… I have a lot to tell you. This girl is bad news. Everything you like to do she will go after you. Sometimes she is an evil person if you're a weak young man watch out. Misty seemed to have this power over some of the boys. She has a twin brother. They call him Hawkeye; he used to be my roommate. I had it with him and his sister."

Hawkeye has another sister, because of Misty she is going to another school for the arts. Those two bump heads a lot, I have a sister here. She is called Sunshine my sister likes Hawkeye. For me I like Hawkeye's other sister. He told Mick to be careful around them. There is one rule to follow, that rule is not to fall in love with a girl that is an under-classmate. You may never see her again.

∗   ∗   ∗

Today was Angel's first day at school. She had two friends that live near the ranch. MaryAnn Colman and Stephen O'Connell were in the hall with her. When she felt her chest get hot. She looked around and saw a boy staring at her. He had blond hair; this boy was a small young man. His age didn't match his height. When he smiled. It made him look like a devil, with his hair sticking up.

Angel looked at this little person. She had a bad feeling this was the person who was going to take her down. She thought it wasn't going to happen. She spoke. "Stephen who is that boy? The one with the devilish smile."

Stephen looked at where she was talking about. He spoke. "That boy is Francis. He's living with his uncle in town. His mother sent him here because he was always getting in trouble. I guess I would if I had that name."

Marianne shook her head. She didn't like him at all. She spoke. "I can see why. The first time I heard his name, I thought he had to be one of those guys. But I could be wrong, the way he is looking at you. I would call him a wolf out to do no good."

Angel was getting disgusted with Francis; she couldn't get away from him. He looks at women like they should do what he wants them to do. It's making me feel cheap. She spoke. "Marianne why is he so hung up on me, the way he's looking at me makes me feel cheap."

Right then Stephen Walk to the spot that block Franci's view of Angel. She spoke. "Thank you that is much better. He's not acting evil, Francis is evil. He is using his size to get some power."

Angel knew he was sent to kill her. She wasn't going to be alone with him if she could help it. School was going by fast. Everyone found out that she had a high IQ. Many asked her for help in their schoolwork. Marianne and Stephen were always asking her for help. The two of them wanted to go into law. They had a hard time studying; Angel came up with a way to make studying easier. She had a lot on her plate but that was all right with her. Schoolwork wasn't that hard; she just had to find time to do the work.

Angel was assistant to her ballet teacher, not only to help her but she had to handle older girls and younger ones. Her teacher spoke. "There is always someone knows the form and the steps of ballet. They think their better than the teacher."

At school Francis tried to get Angel alone. She was always one step ahead of him. One day she heard him talking to someone. "Master I've been trying she is always one step ahead of me."

Angel had felt her chest hotter than before. There was a demon in there with Francis, it could be Marcus. She heard him say. "Then outsmart her, she's just a woman. But then again, she could have the magic rose petal on her."

Stephen had run into Angel. She had put a finger over her lips. Then over her ear. "Master her IQ is higher than mine."

Then Stephen walked away from that room. He spoke. "Angel how do you keep ahead of him. You always knew when Francis was nearby."

Angel thought, did he hear what they had say about the magic rose. She spoke. "Stephen, I really can't tell you. Do you believe in magic?"

He just laughed at what she said. He spoke. "Angel when you're an Irishmen. You learn to believe in things that happen and no way to explain it. Both of my parents are Irish, that's why I have red hair. Now tell me how you know."

Angel took a breath, she spoke. "Have you ever heard about the magic fairy roses?"

Stephen thought for a minute. He spoke. "Aye, I mean yes, I have. It was in the 17th century that a young man brought over these magic roses. He said they came from the Lowland of Scotland. These roses had strong magic. They said that the roses came from the land of the Fairy's. I'm not talking about pixies; these were people like us. I've heard that these roses need a man and woman to take care of them. A man from the Highlands of Scotland he was a wizard he married a Fairy. It was said a family member brought the roses to the Highlands. Are you talking about those roses?"

Then Angel felt Francis. She spoke. "I can't get away from him. I will have to tell you a bit about what I know of these roses. Right now, I'm out of here."

Stephen walked with her to get on the bus. They were the last ones; she waved her hand and the door lock. Francis couldn't get out, when they were away from him, she unlocked the door.

They never talked about that subject again. The school year was just about over; Angel had come into the kitchen. On the table was paperwork from Scotland, it was from the school she was going too. It had said that she would be place under a protection order.

It then talked about everyone's ID, that it was place in a vault underground. These schools are named Deilondotay for boys and Deilondolay for girls. There are ten miles that's fence off. This is where the boys and girls can work together on dancing and competitions. That was the only place where a boy could meet some girls. This place you could be involved in the competition. The girls and boys each have twenty acres away from each other. They sleep, eat, work, and play on their own acres. The last ten acres were left for competitions. You would start off with riding horses then get into jumping those horses. Then there is riding bicycles over hills. After you got to the track it was the test of running. You had to pass the batons and finish the race as fast as you could. After that, the last test was swimming.

There was something she couldn't remember. Her brother been coming to the ranch off and on. Angel was trying to remember something about Scotland; it was what she and Mick had done together last summer. Then she remembered seeing a large gate. Was she flying over the land? Her mind was getting a little fuzzy. Little by little Raymond pushed her memory back in her mind using the magic rose. Mick and she had gone to Scotland to see what the school was like. They saw the name Deilondotay, those gates looked scary to them.

Angel thought I knew how to do all those activities. Raymond was doing her spell slower with her. She knew Mick was at Deilondotay. She been having a hard time getting Mick to talk to her. As she tried to go to sleep, she couldn't. What was happening to her? Has Marcos found a way to stop them from going into the dream world? But how did he do it?

Then Angel remembered. She hasn't been able to reach ren sleep. She has too much on her mind. This has been blocking her from the dream world. She has a demon that keeps her on her toes. Angel wondered if there a demon working on Mick. Something is going to happen.

Each night when Angel woke up. She found her pillow was wet again. *"Why do I have to cry every night?"* Closing her eyes, she cried out in her thoughts. A tear fell on her pillow; I can't take this anymore. *"Mick, I need to hear your voice again. How much longer will it be until we meet?"*

Angel got up; she went to the bathroom; she filled the sink with water. She said a spell and waved her hand over the water. "Raymond I can't get to ren sleep, I'm unable to see Mick in the dream world. I have a demon that keeps me busy, he is waiting for me to mess up. I heard his master voice telling him to take me down. He must outthink me, what am I to do? I can't keep this up, very much longer. Please, Raymond you got to help me."

In Scotland, her brother heard his sister crying for help. He went to the bathroom and filled the sink with water. Then he said a spell over it. He saw his sister crying softly. He swore. Damn it, what was going on? "Angel I'm here. Sis, can you hear me, damn it she can't hear me."

Then Raymond's wife came into the bathroom. Alicia spoke. "Honey what's going on." She saw Angel in the water.

Raymond ran his hand through his hair. He spoke. "I need your help; my magic is not as strong as my sister's. I must pull her here to us. She can't get to ren sleep, which means Mick is having the same trouble. The two of them have a demon after them. Their getting them to the point there going to mess up. I can bring her back through the vortex. Bill won't be back until summer.

"Somehow, we must fix what is happening to them. Then he had an idea. He spoke. "Honey takes my hand we must leave her double there. Her double will be able to know everything she needs to know. She can go to school and the dancing classes."

Raymond and Alicia held hands and the two of them spoke the spell. Together they were able to pull his sister to them. It's been a long time since he saw her this week. He picked her up and brought her to the room he had for her. He laid her in bed; he went back to the sink. Raymond looked to see where her double was. That's good she's in bed he thought.

It was time to find out how Mick was doing. In his room he saw that Mick couldn't sleep. His roommate was asleep. He called Mick, go to the bathroom. He saw that Mick did what he said. In the bathroom he created his double. Ones that were done made him go back to bed. Now to get Mick here to the house. He called him. "Mick come to me, I'm Angel's brother, she needs you Mick. Use your magic and come to my home. Angel needs you now."

*   *   *

It was all month; Mick had a hard time to get to ren sleep. He would think of Angel, even try to call her. He been cut off from his Angel, what was happening? Without a good night's sleep, he found he was jumpy. He didn't like what was happening to him. Cal was right about Misty; she does act as if she has the power over men. She was place here for behavior problems. She was bossy and didn't care about anyone but herself. Next year will be her last year here. She didn't go into any college courses. When Misty found out about him, she wouldn't leave Mick alone. Everywhere he went Misty was there. The only place she couldn't go was the boy's side. She would always say, Mick, could you help me with my homework?

Mick opened his eyes and saw Raymond. He spoke. "Do you know where Angel is. Tell me where she is so I can be with her. There is something wrong with our dream world. Where is she I need my Angel. I haven't been able to sleep because I can't get to ren sleep."

Raymond had to get him to come to his home. He showed her in bed; her body couldn't relax. Then the two of them were in the same room. Angel was laying on his shoulder. It was done, now he had to see if they would go to the dream world. He waves his hand over the two of them. Raymond saw them kissing in their world of love.

*　　*　　*

Alicia came over to him. Come on the three of us need is sleep. Before Raymond went to sleep, he placed a spell to shield them from anyone knowing there here. He took his wife to bed, knowing the two are safe.

As they went through their bedroom door, Raymond remembered what she said. "Honey, are you asking me for us to try for a baby?"

Alicia giggled a bit. "No. That is not what I said."

She, giggled again, she turned and looked at her man. She spoke. "I've been trying to tell you, but you been so worried about your sister and Mick. You didn't hear me, that was all right. Honey, you, and I are going to have a baby."

Raymond took his wife into his arms. "We are going to have a baby. I've been wanting to have a little one. With everything going on, I didn't know if you wanted to. I'm glad you took the leap. Honey, I love you so much."

∗   ∗   ∗

At the waterfall Mick pulled Angel into him. He spoke. "Honey, I thought I lost you, I was trying to call you. I even yelled in my mind nothing worked. Then I heard Raymond calling me, I'm glad that he could help us."

Angel couldn't let him go she buried her face in his neck. "That demon won't leave me alone; I get myself all worked up. When I do that, I can't get to ren sleep."

Mick shook his head, he was holding on to Angel, he picked her up and brought her to the grass. He laid on top of her and started to kiss her face, his tongue made love to her mouth. With a wave of his hand, he made themselves older, next were their clothes were gone. He was about to join her when he remembered they were in bed together. He spoke. *"Angel, were in bed with each other. You're still on the pill? Should I put something over him?"*

She smiled at him. *"When we are in the dream world, we are safe. In less you want me their also."*

He looked shy then smiled. *"The way I'm feeling I would have to say yes. I been so uptight when she is around."*

Angel knew how he felt. *"It's been hard for me also. Every time I had a little breathing room my cross and rose go off. He's a little man and use that to get his way. I had to lock the door so he would miss the bus. I couldn't get any sleep, so I called Raymond. He's using are doubles, it's so easy to call them out of us.*

"Honey, I'm not on the pill to have sex with you. I'm on the pill because my monthly was too much. I was ever week. I'm safe and not on any medicine that would compromise those pills."

Then Mick remembered what he had overhead. *"Angel, I think you're going to be and aunt, she had told Raymond the three of us have to get some sleep."*

She smiled. *"I'm going to be aunt, and you are an uncle. How wonderful, Marcuse has us busy both up tight. When we are I can't dream, what is he up two."*

Mick knew what they needed. He slipped inside her and started to make love to her. Her eyes open as he brought them up were they came. "You feel so good I've missed having you this way."

He waved his hand and the two were clean. "Now we can sleep in less you need more."

She looked at her man. "I know one thing Raymond needs more magic. It took Alicia to help him to bring me to him. On the news I heard that there are camps for men to do a job on American Soil. Raymond been looking into this. Arthur been looking into all the guns that been popping up. There been a lot of killing on the streets of New York City. Gandpa said that my father just got back from that mountain."

Mick was yawning. "We can talk tomorrow, I think I can finely go to sleep."

Angels were also yawning. "I will see you in the morning."

*   *   *

Back in school Bill was on duty and he had to cover the building for dancing. He didn't know that this was Mick double. When he was inside Mick, he knew just what was going on. Misty was at it again. She knew nothing about ballet. He knew Mick had it, but he was too tired to do anything about it. Not this Mick, that morning he asked Bill to make a tape on what was to happen that day.

He walked into the classroom with a scale. "Starting today we are going by the rules of ballet. One the young men, must be able to pick up the girls. He had the weights in the room. Now the girls had to be weighed in. Then the boy had to pick up that weighed, the first two failed. The next pair also failed, all of Misty girls had failed. Even though the girl's hair had failed, it was time for Misty to weigh in. Mick went to pick up what she had weighted and couldn't get it over his head. She was ten pounds over his limit; the guys had to help him with the weights.

"We are coming to the parts of dancing; my guys are unable to pick up any of you girls. The girl's hair is unable to go into a tight bun. To all of us, you girls are too heavy for us to lift. There will be a bad accident. Mick had asked Bill to fine a girl that can dance. He had called one of the schools and got a girl to come and dance with him. Lindsey had come over and she was happy to show how much she weighted.

Mick smiled at her. She had asked what he knew how to do. First, he had to show her that he could lift her. With that done, she agreed to run toward him and jump into his arms. Then flip her to put her on his shoulders. She then dropped into his arms. They had done a routine he knew. "Thank you, Lindsey, you're a beautiful dancer. It was a pleasure to dance with you."

Once Lindsey was gone Misty had a fit. The way she was talking and acting the principal had come over. All the boys and girls got out of the room. Mick then yelled. "Enough I had it with you. I will not take any more of you and your mouth. You're not a dancer; I'm not going to dance with anyone this year. I will help my boys with weightlifting. I can teach dance; this year I'm not dancing. I don't want to have anything to do with you." Mick then laughed at her.

"Your eyes are a joke to me. I'm not week that you can get me under your power."

The principal walked into the room, she heard what Mick had told Misty. "Mick, could you leave this room and dismiss your group for today. There will be a new listing to go up, if the boys like to try other girls. That will be just fine, Mick, could you help any of the other new girls that will try out?"

Mick looked at the principal. "I would be happy to help. If I don't have to be around her. I will not help her with her homework. She too lazy to do her own homework, she puts on this act that she's helpless to do the work.

Then the Principal told Mick. "Mick she will not be a loud to come to this side the rest of the year."

*   *   *

At lunch Cal was sitting with Mick. Hawkeye came over to them. Mick had frozen everyone; he had place a cross and rose on the back of Hawkeye's head and chest. He watched a demon come out of him, Mick through his knife that had a small crass on it. Then he went and sat back down. "Hello, Mick Cal, can I set with you."

Mick nodded. "Get your food first then come over."

Cal shook his head. "I heard that she went off on her brother. He had it with her and some of the guys were forced to dance. They have drop out."

Mick took a bit of food. "I thought so, they like lifting weights. They all told me that they were having nightmares on lifting those girls."

Hawkeye came back to the table. "Mick, I'm sorry that you had to put up with her. Be careful some of the guys are under her control. The principal has her in one of the buildings away from everyone.

She must get her grades up on her own when you stop helping her. She stops doing the work if she can't handle it Misty can drop out of school.

* * *

Angel 2 was at her grandfather's ranch. She was five miles from Mick's grandparents. The weekend was over, and it was time to go back to school. This Angel is not going to put up with Francis, when she felt him, she went invisible. Then she touched his head with the cross and rose. It burned the back of his neck, when he turned, she burned his chest. Then she went to her classroom, Francis saw her talking with the teacher. She had told the teacher about Francis stocking her. The teacher made a note she told her to tell all her teachers. Will see how many times he does this. In her study hall she let the teacher know. Right after she came into the classroom Francis was right behind her, the teacher made a note the day and time he was right behind her. She told Francis you're not in this study hall. Go before you're late for class. Steven and Marianne were in her study hall, Angel showed them a different way to study. It was working, this gave her time to do all her own work. She had a test coming up. She had passed the last year of junior high school. The next month will be for the first year of high school. As a sophomore she will be going over all the work for that month. Every part of the book she had a test. Angel kept a 95 to 100 average. At the end of the month, she had the big test. If she passed the test she went on to junior high school. Francis was seen every time the teacher then turned in their papers on Francis. When she was by herself, she went invisible. When it was clear she would come back and walk into class. Teacher would she him looking for her. They made him go to his class.

Mick and Angel met up with their double and they found out that they took care of everything for them. The time spent at her brother's place for two weeks had helped them a lot. At the end of two weeks, they had to say goodbye to each other. Their doubles had fix things for them, they were able to get to their dream world from then on.

*   *   *

At art class Mick was having daydreams. He was seeing a young girl taking care of roses with a young boy. He couldn't see their faces and that was how he drew them. The girl had long hair, it looked to be a golden brown. She always had her back to him, her body looked to have a nice shape. With long legs to top it off, this girl could be a dancer. He had a feeling he knew who they were, then another picture of a baby. She had blond hair her eyes were deep blue. There was a boy, who looked to be a toddler? The baby was holding the boy's finger, the next girl had golden-brown hair. As he drawn them, they had no face. She was dancing with this boy that had no face. As the teacher walked through the rows.

She had noticed Mick's drawing. "Mick this is very different. Why isn't there a face on the older girls? You're making them have a ghostly image. I like the way the baby's hand is holding on to the little boy's finger.

"Mick you should put this in the art show. The toddler dancing is so sweet. Even the little boy can't see his face. Now the young lady with her back to you. You made her as if she had wings, I hope you will put it in the art show. If you win. It will be put in the art gallery for four years."

Mick went to his study room; he was finish with his homework. He had an idea for a poem. He wondered if he should put it in with the painting.

The Magic Fairy Rose from Scotland to America then Vermont

My Little angel

Evil tried to hurt my little angel, I'm little myself.
I took on a demon and won. No one will hurt my angel.
I touched her hand with my finger. My angel took it and didn't let go.
She is a toddler and so am I. A ballerina in her tutu.
My angel and I dance together; we are as one.
My memory of this girl is failing me. Why can't I see her face?
Who am I? Why do I feel lost?
Time has passed since I saw this young lady. She dances like an angel.
Her hair is golden brown; it was shining in the sunlight.
This angel wore a halo around her head.
That's when I first saw her, with my music on I danced for her.
I felt the magic dancing between us. I used
that magic; my leaps were higher.
Angel, will you dance with me? Will you spread
your wings and take us to heaven?
Where we can dance on the clouds together.
Angel, when I'm holding you, I feel whole inside when you're with me.
No please, don't take Angel from me. She is my…
angel, don't take her away from me.

A dream of angel

The baby's hand is little in mine. She has my finger.
I'm a little bigger than her. Who is this little angel?
She's a toddler now and so am I.
This angel is dancing for me. A ballerina in her tutu.
Who is this little girl? Why can't I see her face?
Could this be the same girl? I feel lost.
I'm sitting on a rock. Here I'm older, the sun is shining.

When I turn around, I see and hear the waterfall.
I watch the sun as it dances over the water.
There's water drop's twinkling, could the water be made of diamonds?
A cross is a path of green grass. I would love to lay in that grass.
Am I dreaming? Why do I come here? I can see a young lady.
She's laying on the grass. Her back is to me, Lady who are you?
She has long golden-brown hair when the wind blows.
The sun dances over her hair, could her hair be her wings? No!
The sun and wind make it look to be wings.
Young Lady, I wish you were an angel.
Why can't I see your face? Can you hear me?
Are you the one to set me free?
Oh!... It's just a dream. No! This can't be just
a dream. Please, lady. Set me free.

*   *   *

Mick had taken an engineering class. His teacher asked them to come up with an idea. He thought of a dream machine. It's been on his mine for some time. Mick had been working on his blueprint. Nightmares and just dreams would be a good subject.

When he told Bill about it. "He told him don't do it, that's what Marcuse wants. The machine will help to teach people how to get into their minds. Then they can do it anywhere if they are sleeping. Where do you think the three of us went."

Mick looked at him. "Bill, I don't know what you're talking about. Does it have something to do with this school."

Bill nodded yes, he took the blueprints and locked them up. "I have an idea for a machine to map out the bottom of the ocean. Sense I'm the new teacher for the engineering class we can work on it at home. Think about how big you think it should be. Make a list of what you may need for it.

*   *   *

It was Christmas time. School would be close for one week. The class was told when they came back to school. They were going to build a model of their blueprint. It was good to be back on the ranch. Uncle Brandon had asked Mick to clean the last stall for him. He had done quick work with the stall. Now to place fresh hay. With that done he went inside the house to clean up. There was a note saying. Gone to the store be back in an hour. When the phone rang.

Mick picked up the phone. "Hello, MacGregor resident. Mick speaking."

There was a long pause. He repeated. "Hello, MacGregor resident."

James thought about it and decided to talk with his son. "Hello Mick. This is James, I'm Brandon's brother, is my brother around?

Mick felt calm speaking to this man. "No sir, I just came in. I was in the barn cleaning out one of the stalls. Your brother and his wife went to the store. I could let him know you had called."

James notes that Mick liked talking to him. "No, I will call him back, how are you doing in school Mick? My brother speaks of you every time we get to talk."

Mick thought uncle was talking about him. "I'm doing fine. Since I don't have to dance with Misty. This year is almost done. My grades are A and sometimes A+. I'm helping others with their homework. It helps to make time go faster. Hold on, the truck just pulled in. Please hold."

Mick went to the door and called Uncle Brandon. "Telephone, it's your brother James."

He went back to the phone. "Sir your brother will be right in. It was nice talking with you. I'm sorry. I seem to have dump my frustrations out on you."

He smiled, it made him feel better. "Mick that was quite all right. I enjoyed talking with you. You have a good day."

Mick didn't want to stop talking to him. "I will, where are you calling from?"

Something about him, he found he could talk about anything. "I'm in England, my daughter is here with her husband."

James thought he would see if he would talk about this subject. "Before you past the phone. My brothers said you are having trouble sleeping?"

Wow he thought uncle would talked about this also. "He talked to you about me?"

He was so happy that he liked talking with me. "Yes. We talk about things that mean a lot to us. I'm the oldest. We try to take care of each other when we can. You're now part of this family. We like to take care of you. My son in law has duty so his wife came down to being with her husband. He has a home not too far from my brother's place."

Mick just kept talking, it felt right to do so. "While back I was having trouble sleeping because of Misty. That's not the problem anymore. I'm sleeping fine. It's just when I dream. I can't see any faces. It's the same girl repeatedly. Thank you for listening to me. Your brother just came in. I'm going to help bring in the bags of groceries. It was nice talking to you, Merry Christmas. Before I say goodbye if you call again what may I call you?"

James felt as if he was holding his breath. "What would you like to call me?"

Mick thought about it. He smiled when he came up with it. "If I'm going to be part of this family. How about dad? You don't have another brother, do you?"

This was the best Christmas gift that his son gave him. "No, I don't have another brother."

James was able to talk to his son. He must know deep down I was his father. "All right I'll see you dad take care of mom give her my love."

He felt as a big burden was lifted off his shoulders. "Goodbye, Mick. I'll let mom know that you said hi. It was good talking with you."

When Brandon took the phone from Mick, he saw a big smile on his face. "Hello James. It's good to hear from you, I'm sorry about that. I forgot that Mick was going to be here."

James was so happy that he got to talk to his son. "Brandon that was the best gift I have gotten in a long time. I thought I would find out how Mick was doing. It's been hard on Malaya; she's missing her children. That's why we're here visiting Caroline."

Brandon had an idea to make this the best Christmas yet. "Are you going to be there for Christmas James?"

He smiled it may work, he thought. "Yes, that was the plan."

Now what does his brother have up his sleeve? "James then comes up here, it sounds like Mick needs has family. He called me uncle, and it sounds like your dad and mom. Bring Caroline and Raymond with you. Then Mick can meet you all."

James would love to see his family together. "I'll give Arthur a call and see what he thinks. Raymond has duty before Christmas Eve. Bill and Angela are also here. I will talk with them and see what their plans are. I will let you know later."

He was remembering what Joseph had said. "Brandon, I told Raymond about Mick's dream. I found out that the two of them did their own spell. He doesn't understand why this was happening. Ellen will be in school there in September. Raymond is wondering if it's the spell. He told them to forget what they look like. He believes once she meets Mick it may change their dreams. Ellen said that they talked a little. She must plan it just right when she goes to sleep. There is five hours different for each other."

James just laughed about that. "When Mick came here, Arthur told me that he brought Mick to a doctor. He said that he didn't think we knew what we were doing. Mick is under a spell and hypnoses, you should let Raymond know. Last weekend he was fine, he got to be with Angel. This week he doesn't know which way to go. He can see her but not her face, let Raymond know about this. James why are you laughing?"

James had to tell him what had happened to Mick. "Brandon Mick hasn't seen any doctor like that. Arthur had seen that doctor to program him to think that way. Ellen had a dream that a demon was going to take Mick to a doctor who was also a demon. That demon she had Mick, to put him through hell. Raymond said something that Misty tried to spell with her eyes. He had burned a cross on his hand. I got to go now; I'll call you what I find out."

Brandon smiled about that. "Mick was told that Misty can't be around him. She's where the bad kids go."

Raymond had sent the family to the Highlands. Brandon picked them up on Raymond's land. After his watch he went over to Bill's place. Bill had gone to England to be with Angela. She was working with Raymond until Ellen was ready to go to school in Scotland. In the summer Bill and Mick will work on Arthur science ship, for a week. Mick will be starting to dive in deeper water.

The night before his shift, Raymond called on his grate-grandfather Garret. He found out that Bill was one of Garrets sister's children. One day Raymond thought he saw the mark like his. This mark was given to all of Garrets and his sister's children. Garret's sister had just a daughter by Marcos. Through the years, there were many boys born. Only a hand full had power like Raymond. He found out that Bill didn't know about any powers. Angela was also family on Eleanor side of the family. This was the time for the family to get stronger for what is to come.

CHAPTER SIXTEEN

Misty hair won

FOR THE MONTH Mick couldn't get to ren sleep, he would think of Angel. Even trying to call her, what was happening? Without a good night's sleep, he's been very jumpy. Everything was getting to him, Cal was right about Misty. She didn't act if she was on a protection order. She was place here for behaver problems. This girl was bossy and didn't care about anyone, but herself. Next year will be her last year here, she hasn't gone on any college courses. When Misty found out about him, she wouldn't leave Mick alone. Everywhere he went Misty was there. The only place she couldn't go was the boy's side.

She would always say. "Mick, could you help me with my homework?"

He had tried out of the sports, even dancing. Misty quickly got him as her partner, every time he was around her. His chest got hot he remembered that ment she was evil. To lift a girl that heavy was hard enough. Even though her hair got in the way, the ballet movements made it hard to lift her. Mick wasn't weak, the reason he had Misty as his partner. He was the strongest in the group. It's funny, she said she liked him.

If she fell for him, it's too bad for her. She knows the rules, never falls in love with under-classmen. Mick did his best not to be mean to her. However, the day came when she wouldn't put up her hair. Misty's hair was black. It was very thick and long. Too long for a dancer, hers went down to her bottom. When the girl's dance, their hair was to be in a tight bun. It must be on top of their head. The girls must be slim to do the moves; Misty wasn't slim but heavy. She was heading for a fall, what Mick was afraid would happen, did. She had half her hair down. He had told her to put it all the way up. "No Mick, it's too thick. I can't keep it all up."

He thought if I had scissors. "Misty you're working on my nerves. I don't care how you do it. You can thin out your hair, so you could put it up."

Misty was trying to get him to look into her eyes. "No… Mick I won't do it. I like it this way."

His patience was about to be gone. "Misty, don't you understand. Your hair is getting in my way; it's like a spider web. If you get your hand in it, you can't get out. If you won't cut your hair. Then quit. I don't care if I don't dance this year. Misty if your hurt, then the two of us are out of the competition."

He thought then I would quit. "No… Mick I'm not going to quit. You're not quitting either."

When Misty wasn't looking, he motioned to the camera to watch her. "Misty if we keep going this way, you're going to get hurt."

When she swore at him that did it. "Then fuck off Mick. This is the best I can do. We need to practice."

Mick noticed Misty was doing something with her eyes. Then he laughed. "This is a joke with your eyes. I know your evil, I'm not weak it won't work on me. I have a high IQ, and I don't love you. Back off with your eyes."

They started again. When they came to the part where Mick had to lift her to his shoulders. Misty's hair found its way between his fingers. He couldn't free himself from the hair. She couldn't stand on his shoulders; it looked funny her bent in half. Not for Misty, one foot on his shoulder. The other, wrapped in her own hair. She was high enough to land on her elbow breaking it. "Mick, I hate you. You did this on purpose; you'll pay for what you did to me."

He thought she wouldn't omit it was her fault. "Misty, I told you this would happen. You're so thick headed, just like your hair. It's always going to be your way. Let me help you up."

He thought I wished Angel were here. "Don't touch me."

He had something for her arm. "Misty stop moving, I can see your arm is not right. I have something to mobile lies your arm. Then I can take you to the doctor. Before you start swearing at me. Don't! I've taken all I can from you. I have never worked with someone who only thinks of herself. This will be the last time I have to deal with you. I won't work with someone like you."

Mick went over to his bag and got something to mobilize her arm. He knew there was a teacher in the other room. Mick had asked if someone could watch them. He had a bad feeling that something was going to happen. "Misty… Are you going to let me help you?"

Mick went to change his shoes. "No… you can go to hell Mick. This is not over with. You're going to pay for what you did to me."

He shook his head and thought up his arms. "Misty it's over for me; I will never help you in anything again. Fine someone else to help you with homework. I'm done with you."

It was a good thing that Mick had gone to one of the teachers in the building. She had been watching them. Mick had changed his shoes and picked up his things. He looked out the window and placed the rap on the chair. "Misty good luck with your life. One thing I like you to do."

He knew what she was going to say. "Go to hell… I'm not going to do anything for you."

He picked up his things and went were the teacher was. "All right Misty. Then I will do it myself. I'm not your boyfriend. I never was and never will be your boyfriend. You're not what I would call a girlfriend. Come to think about it' You never were."

Mick had crossed out his name, he was upset. Then he went to the teacher. "Misty had gotten hurt; she doesn't want me to help her. I know this is my first year here. I love dancing, but not with a girl who is overweight, her hair is too long, and she doesn't want to put it up. A ballerina is thin; her hair is in a tight bun on top of her head. Rules for ballet, strong legs, small waist. I have been dancing sense I was seven. My partner, back home was the best. Misty is a joke; her hair had entwined with my fingers. Then she got her foot into her own hair. She said it's my fault, that she fell. I will not dance with her, and she wasn't my girlfriend.

"I wish that there were rules that girls must be at the weight for dancing ballet. They must have their hair up. I have dance with the best; Misty is not ballet material to be a ballerina. One to heavy her hair to thick and long. If you want me to dance next year, go by those rules. Thank you for listening to me. I'm sorry if I was so gruff talking, all she did was swear at me. It got me upset for what she had been doing."

*   *   *

It was over. Misty and Mick were out of any competition. He can now do things he likes to do. Thank heavens he didn't have to work with her anymore. There was always next year for him. He wouldn't dance with Misty again.

Before bed Mick wondered where he learned how to dance. Who did he dance with? I hope I can get to ren sleep. With Misty off his mine. He could ask Angel if she knew.

Mick was hoping she would be there, in his dream. Then he was dancing with Angel, they were dancing on stage together. My Angel is back; Mick took her in his arms. He lifted Angel high over his head. When he brought her down Mick pulled her into his arms. The two of them were now older. They were on the patch of green grass by the waterfall. Their clothes were gone. He was kissing his Angel and making love to her. "I thought I would never see you again. Angel, I need you."

She had missed him as she touched his face. "I need you also Mick. Please let me feel you inside me again."

He took her mouth in a hungry kiss. "I thought you never ask."

The two of them were together again. Mick was moving inside her. The more he gave. The more she took. Until they came together.

Mick had turned around, bringing her on top of him. *"Angel, I needed you so much. I couldn't get to ren sleep. There is this girl with whom I was working. Her name is Misty. I know she is evil. She is working with Marcos. Next year school starts. I think you're coming to the school in Scotland. If Misty is there, she will fight to get me to work with her."*

How he loved this young woman. *"Mick will be all right. I will be there on the girl's side. I saw the paperwork on it. I too haven't been able to get to ren sleep. Marcos has Francis after me. He works for the school paper. Francis has been trying everything to get me alone with him. Mick, we got to be careful. I believe that Misty will get back at you. It may happen when you're not on guard. If I can get out of school without and accident with him. I'll be very happy. I'll tell you this. They were doing a good job keeping us away from each other. Tonight, we are together. We still have some time left. Before you and I must get up, make love to me again."*

She took hold of Mick and heard him grown. He felt her bringing him higher. His hands took hold of her waste. She drove him into her until he cried out. *"Angel, I love you. It's been hard to be away from you."*

To feel Mick cum inside her it was wonderful. Angel said a prayer. In her mine she prayed that they could enjoy each other when they became this age. Until then she will make love to Mick in her dreams. This was hope that one day she would have his children. *"Time to get wet. Come on get up."*

Angel shook her head. *"Oh, Mick do I have too? I like to stay like this."*

He wished it also but soon they will come to wake him up. *"All right, will do it the easy way."*

With a wave of his hand. They were under the water. They had parted and went to the surface. The two of them went to lay on the sand. Mick pulled her on top of him. *"Angel one last time before we part."*

She took him inside her when they both came. She lay down on top of Mick. As she was coming down from her climax. Angel's face changed. She had remembered what happened when he went to school in Scotland. Does this mean they couldn't come here again? *"Mick I'm scared."* She sat up.

He looked at her face, she feared something he thought. *"Scared of what Angel."*

Mick saw her biting her lips. *"When you left to go to Scotland. We couldn't see each other for a very long time. Is this what's going to happen to me? That I'm not going to know you."*

He pulled her down to him. *"Angel, we got through it. Will get through it with you. This time we will be able to see each other. I will find you there. Don't worry about my love."*

In the morning. He felt rested after being with Angel. She might be right. Thinking about what she said. This could be their last night together for a while.

At art class Mick was having daydreams. He was seeing a young girl taking care of roses with a young boy. He couldn't see their faces. He draws them how he saw them. The girl had long hair. It looked like golden brown. She always had her back to him. Her body looked to have a nice shape with long legs to top it off. This girl could be a dancer. He had a feeling he knew who they were. Then another picture of a baby. She had blond hair her eyes were deep blue. There was a boy. Who looked like a toddler? The baby was holding the boy's finger.

The next girl had golden-brown hair. As he drew them. Mick had no faces on them. She was dancing with this boy that had no face. As the teacher walked through the rows. She had noticed Mick's drawing. "Mick this is very different. Why isn't there a face on the older girls? You're making them have a ghostly image. I like the way the baby's hand is holding on to the little boy's finger.

"Mick, you should put this in the art show. The toddler dancing is so sweet. Even the little boy can't see his face. Now the young lady with her back to you. You made her as if she had wings. I hope you will put it in the art show. If you win. It will be put in the art gallery for four years."

Mick went to his study room. He finished his homework, now he had an idea for a story. As he wrote it sounded like a poem. Then he changes the way the lines were at. He wondered if he should put it in with the painting.

Little girls

"Who are these little girls? There's a little boy with her.
Are they a part of me? Am I that little boy? Did we grow up together?
Here is a baby. Whose finger is she holding?
Do I know this baby girl? She is holding that little boy's finger.

Why can't I see their faces? I feel, she is an Angel.
This Angel is bigger now. They are toddlers.
He's always with her trying to keep her safe.
An Angel who dances. A ballerina in her tutu.
Who is this little Angel? Why can't I see her face?
The passing of time they are older.
He's dancing with his Angel.
Will he ever see her face? Where is his Angel?
She's nowhere to be found.
There're mountains in the background.
Am I dreaming here on this rock? The sun is shining.
Where is his Angel?
He can hear water and turns around.
He sees the waterfall.
Here he watches the sun dance over the water.
The water is twinkling like diamonds. Is he dreaming?
This place is made of magic. Will he see his Angel here?
A tree with a patch of green grass. A place to lay with an Angel.
He's a man in this place. Does he come here to be with an Angel?
There she is. With her long golden-brown hair.
The wind blows as the sun dances over her hair.
This place has strong magic.
Between us is water. Can you hear me, Angel?
Here we are older and in love. We can dance together.
We are free here to dream. To play and to make love.
My beautiful Angel. I can see my Angel's face finely.
November 20, 2017

Mick had taken an engineering class. Their teacher told them to come up with an idea. He thought of a dream machine. It's been on his mine for some time. He had been working on his blueprint.

Nightmares and just dreams would be a good subject. The building where he sleeps. Across the hall from them. One of the boys had bad nightmares. After the blueprint was mapped out. He would look for someone to program his machine. Mick never thought a dream machine could be dangers. He would find out when it was in the wrong hands.

It was Christmas time. School would be closed for one week. The class was told when they came back to school. They were going to build a model of their blueprint.

*   *   *

It was good to be back on the ranch. Uncle Brandon had asked Mick to clean the last stall for him. He had done quick work with the stall. Now to place fresh hay. With that done he went inside the house to clean up. There was a note saying. Gone to the store be back in an hour. When the phone rang.

He picked up the phone. *"Hello, MacGregor resident. Mick speaking."*

There was a long pause. So, he repeated. "Hello, MacGregor resident."

James was so happy to hear his son's voice. "Hello Mick. This is James. I'm Brandon's brother. Is my brother around?"

Mick felt as if he could talk to him. "No sir. I just came in. I was in the barn cleaning out one of the stalls. Your brother and his wife went to the store. I could let him know you had called."

James saw an opportunity to talk with his son. "No, I will call him back. How are you doing in school Mick? My brother speaks of you every time we get to talk."

Mick felt good telling him that. "I'm doing much better; I don't have to dance with Misty. She made my life a living hell. This year is almost done. My grades are A and sometimes A+. I'm helping others with their homework. It helps to make time go faster. Hold on, the truck just pulled in. Please hold."

Mick went to the door and called Uncle Brandon. "Telephone, it's your brother James."

He went back to the phone. "Sir your brother will be right in. It was nice talking with you. I'm sorry. I seem to have dump my frustrations out on you."

James remembered that girl's name. She's the one that Marcos sent after him. "Mick that was quite all right. I enjoyed the talk with you. You have a good day."

Mick wondered where he was. "I will. Where are you calling from?"

He must be missing us. "I'm in England. My daughter is here with her husband."

Mick felt he wanted to know about him, wow. "Before you past the phone, my brothers said you are having trouble sleeping?"

James was pleased that he talked about him. "He talked to you about me?"

Mick felt save talking with him. "Yes. We talk about things that mean a lot to us. I am the oldest. We try to take care of each other when we can. You're now part of this family; we like to take care of you."

He loved this family; it was good to be loved. "Awhile back, I was having trouble sleeping because of Misty. She's not the problem anymore. I'm sleeping fine. It's just when I dream, I can't see any faces. It's the same girl repeatedly. Thank you for listening to me. Your brother just came in. "I'm going to help bring in the bags of groceries. It was nice talking to you. Merry Christmas. Before I said goodbye. If you call again. What may I call you?"

James's wondered would he feel like calling me dad. "What would you like to call me?"

In his mind he heard a voice saying dad. "If I'm going to be part of this family. How about dad? It feels right to me. You don't have another brother, do you?"

James felt so good inside, his son somehow knows he was his father. "No, I don't have another brother."

James was doing the Scotch dance. "All right I'll call you dad. I'll see you later dad. Take care of mom."

He was getting choked up. "Goodbye, Mick. I'll let mom know that you said hi. It was good talking with you."

Brandon was worried that his brother would be upset hearing his son's voice. "Hello James. It's good to hear from you. I'm sorry about that. I forgot that Mick was going to be here."

James was happy to hear his son's voice. "It's all right. I thought I would find out how Mick was doing. It's been hard on Desiree; she's missing her children. You can see why we're here visiting Emily."

Brandon had an idea. "Are you going to be there for Christmas James?"

James was wondering why he asked. "Yes, that was the plan."

He feels safe with you. "You got to come up here. The spell is letting him know he's safe with us and you. It sounds like Mick needs a family. He called me uncle, and it sounds like your dad and mom. Bring Emily and Raymond with you. Then Mick can meet you all."

James had a big smile on his face. "I'll give Arthur a call and see what he thinks. Raymond has duty before Christmas Eve. Bill came down here to be with Angela. Soon she will be taking care of Angel. I will talk with them and see what their plans are. I will let you know later."

He thought his brother was worried about his son. "Brandon, I told Raymond about Mick's dream. He doesn't understand why this was happening. What he's thinking what if Marcuse is stepping in and helping Misty. Ellen will be in school there in September. If he is then we had better kept an eye on Ellen. I was told that the two of them did their spell on each other. He believes once she meets Mick it may change their dreams. Ellen said that they talked a little. When she goes to sleep. She must plan her night, so she gets enough sleep. There is five hours different for each other."

How can we fix something when the once who did the spell can't know about them? "When Mick came here Arthur told me that he had taken Mick to a doctor. He said that he didn't think we knew what we were doing. Mick is under a spell and hypnoses. You should let Joseph know. Last weekend he was fine. He got to be with Angel; this week he doesn't know which way to go. He can see her but not her face, let Joseph know about this."

James had to tell him. "Brandon, Raymond planned for you not to see Mick. Your wife did her job, yelling at the demon. That was his double that Ellen had made with Tom. She knew about the two demons. Raymond told me as her time gets closer things will start changing for them.

He thought about it. "Before you hang up James. I have been having a bad feeling about this Misty. She threatened Mick if he's right about her being evil. Marcos might be behind this; you may tell Arthur about this. Just don't say anything about the doctor, he doesn't remember he was kidnap."

Then he remembered about her eyes. "I believe I will call Arthur. Brandon, don't worry. I won't say anything about what we talked about. I will tell him about Mick; she upset my son. He never talks to anyone that he doesn't know. In less he knew it would be safe to talk to me about anything. Deep down he knows I'm his father. That was Ellen's plan to make them feel save when we are around them. He would like to call me dad."

James was going to tell Raymond that Misty threatened Mick. "You have it right; Mick took us quickly. Call me when you find out anything. We have enough food for all of you. My wife had a feeling she would need more food. She called it a woman's intuition."

Raymond then called the officer to get Bill into the school now. He was told everything is going well. Then Raymond talked to Bill, about them getting a job there. I remember Angel said Misty is from Marcos.

James quickly called Arthur, and it was okay with him.

Arthur said "If he doesn't remember you, it means it's holding. Just be careful that no one will follow you to Mick."

CHAPTER SEVENTEEN

Mick went to save Ellen

ILL WAS DRIVING to rose hill; it was a beautiful day. School was out and Mick wanted to teach him how to ride. The sky was clear with no clouds in sight; you could see the peaks of the mountains. The trees were showing new life. Some of the trees had flowers on them.

He was to meet Mick and learn how to ride a horse. He bought some snacks for them to eat on the trail. Bill was too the barn when his birthmark went red hot. He knew Mick was in trouble, his training took over. He pulled into the yard quickly; he had his door open. He shoved his vehicle into park and jumped out of the vehicle slamming the door. He ran full out the rest of the way.

Bill was ready for anything, as he moved in closer to the tac-room. He heard fighting as he looked between the door and the wall. There was a flash back, inside he saw Angel was there and two others. How did the others get here? He saw Mick with a metal handle; he had stepped in front of Angel. A small boy with a mass on, there was a demon inside the boy. They took a swing at Angel. If Mick didn't have a metal handle.

The swing would have killed Angel; Mick had to use all his strength to not go down. Bill knew Mick wasn't in Scotland, he thought a time-warp. He is fighting in the spirit world with Angel. They have their powers, the cross that Mick wears. What did Raymond tell him? This cross was made from Angel's hair. It was put together with magic and the magic rose petals, Raymond had it blessed for Mick so he could give it to Angel. Bill heard Mick call the demon Marcos. As the two of them sent him back to hell. He felt there was someone else nearby, another boy was watching Mick and Angel.

* * *

He saw Mick looking quickly at her. "Angel, I knew someone was in danger. I couldn't see the girl's face, my heart knew it was you. I will always come to you when you're in danger, I don't care where you are. I will find you; I love you with all my heart."

Angel knew him and she was glad he was here. "Mick I will always find you also, I love you to."

Mick felt that a close friend was watching them. "My love, you have good friends here with you today. I don't think you will remember this. The boy on the other side of the boards will know what to do. I don't want to leave you, Angel being away from you has been hard on me. They had done something to my mind; I didn't know the girl with no face. I'm glad my heart knew, the love I have for you brought me right to you."

Now Mick looked at the boy. "Angel who is this boy."

She had taken off the mass the boy wore. "This is Francis, why did he try to kill me?"

Then the two of them heard a deep voice, before them was Marcos. "Will now he's a big disappointment. I told him if he killed you, he could have you after you were dead. I thought, with me inside him, he could kill you. Mick you couldn't stay in Scotland."

Mick laughed. "You can't get over the magic of the roses. Why can't you leave us alone."

Marcos laughed about it. "My father wants your souls. I have no need to mate with her. I have my son, why do you have to be where I'm at."

The two shrugged their shoulders. "Will now Marcos you always are a thorn in our side. Now you get to tell your father we won again. Thank you for bringing me to my Angel, it's time for you to go."

They held hands together; they pointed there finger at Marcos. A bright light shot from their fingertips. Marcos exploded and disappeared. "Angel I will leave this pipe with you. Let your friend tell what happened. I have a feeling Frances will tell them about the demon."

Mick turn to speak to this young man, "Please watch over her she is my life."

Then he pulled Angel into him. He took his last kiss, knowing he had to go back. This young man had seen everything that Mick and Angel had done. Bill and Mick knew that the young man wasn't evil. When Marcos was gone the cross went cool. The young man knew that Francis try to kill Ellen. Mick also knew he was there. Bill heard the young man voice calling Max.

He found out the young man was standing right where he was. They watched Mick and Angel give their last kiss; the vortex didn't care. If they we're trying to hold on to each other. The time-warp was pulling Mick back. The last words to each other were "I love you."

Bill then heard the voice of Max. He was calling for the young man, his name was Stephen.

Stephen felt bad for the two of them. He saw it was pulling on them to let go of each other. Seeing them older, was wonderful. He will remember this man who works out, he smiled at the two of them. When Mick took one last kiss. Stephen knew he was sent back to Scotland and the two of them were safe.

Bill heard Stephen say. "Fairy magic is very strong. Yes, there is magic in Scotland. Could that be where Mick came from? Ellen said she was going to school in Scotland."

Bill understood that Stephen knew he was there also. When the two of them are back in America Stephen will watch over Ellen.

He saw Stephen go into the tac-room. "Ellen are you, all right? Don't say anything, just listen to me. You heard something in the tac-room. You went to grab the pipe. Ellen you were the one to stop him. Let Francis tell his story. If I'm right he's going to be locked up."

On the floor was the metal pipe, Stephen called for Max. "Max where in the barn, call my father. Francis try to kill Ellen."

Max came running. Marianne ran to the house she was calling Stephen's dad. Max had checked Ellen to see if she was all right. Stephen kept Ellen close to him, Max had left Francis where he was. Until the police came, once all the statements were taken. Then Francis's uncle had the ambulance to take him to the psychiatric place in Vermont.

Stephen said. "I saw Francis swing a heavy log at Ellen. He just missed her head. If he hit Ellen, he would have killed her. I believe he would have had his way with her. He didn't care if she was dead. He's been that crazy to get her alone with him. She told me that she picked the pipe up before she went into the tac-room. She blocked the blow, before he tried to hit her again. Ellen hit the log out of his hands. Then she kicked him in the stomach. He hit his head on the boards and went down. Ellen checked him to make sure he was breathing. Then she tied him up and she took off the mass he had over his face.

The ones that did come was Stephen father, and Francis's uncle. An ambulance showed up for Francis. Stephen never told Max of the bright light or the two other men.

"Max, was the one watching over Ellen at the ranch. I wonder if Mick would remember what happened here with Angel. This magic the two of them have, it must call to the other when the one is in danger. The magic rose can bring Mick or Angel to wherever the other maybe. Stephen must know about Ellen having magic. He just saved her by telling a different story."

In the vision, Bill saw and heard what everyone said and did. He had a photograph memory. What had happened to her made everyone scramble. How did Francis cut the fence and scare the horses? No one had seen him, Bill knew what happened. It was Marcos that did everything. Stephen never said anything about what he had seen. Francis was sent away to try to control his demons. The story he told got him placed in a hospital.

Bill talked to Mick and found out he couldn't remember anything that had happened. He didn't know if he should tell their parents what he knew. Soon Ellen will be coming here to Scotland. Would it be better just to let it go for now? One thing Bill knew, Mick would go anywhere to save Angel.

He wondered who would be with Angel after this. He knew of one woman. Angela McKinnon, the daughter of Murdock McKinnon. Murdock had pulled Bill after most of his training for the Navy Seal. This is what happen to Raymond also, could Murdock pull his daughter for this job? Angela was the best woman to protect Ellen. After the Christmas vocation, Misty was sent to the building were all the troublemakers go. They eat, sleep, and do homework. They show them how to cook; they eat the food they make. No calls in or out, there was a tall fence around the building. That was a jail, they had guards watching over the building. They stayed there over summer break or until all homework was passing grades.

*   *   *

Mick seemed happy, maybe he had some idea that he saw Angel. Bill went along with it and had his riding lesson. Raymond will be back here in the Highlands, and Angela will be going to Vermont to watch over Ellen.

When Mick was in school, Bill asked if he could live here on the ranch. The Macgregor's like that idea. In the barn there was a small apartment. With heat and a place to cook and sleep. They haven't heard yet what happened to Angel. When Mick is at the ranch there is someone keeping an eye on him. Today Bill needed to speak to Raymond. He knew that Raymond was in the Highlands. He was claiming the family land. Raymond had to pay the back taxes on the land first. He told the town he would like to raise horses. The MacGregor family was helping Raymond to get started. They gave him the paperwork on a few of their horses. This was to be shown to the town.

It was time Bill talked with Raymond. The incident was too much for one person to handle by himself. Bill had to tell someone what he saw. The incident at the ranch had brought Angela. She will stay with Ellen intel she safe at the school in Scotland. The two of them had to do; a spell on each other. She had told her brother that your magic is not strong enough to push our names back in are memories.

*   *   *

Now she has become Angel. It was set up that Ellen only remembered the name Angel. Anyone that knows the legend of the MacGregor or saw the painting. The spell also made sure that the people of the Highlands. Wouldn't they think they were the next Thomas and Eleanor MacGregor. Bill and Angela could take them diving and camping in the summer. "Hello Raymond, thanks for coming over so quickly."

Raymond looked at Bill, he was worried about Mick. "That's okay, anything about my sister, my wife, and her brother. This is very important to me, tell me what you know. Did you see what had happen on that day?"

Bill told him what he saw. "To save Angel, Mick went all the way to Vermont. Marcos was there in the tac-room. The two of them have their own magic. Mick told Marcos that he has the magic from his great grandfather who was a Wizard and his wife she was a human Fairy. I think it's in the dream world and any kind of time-warp.

After he told him what happened Raymond produced. "Ellen used a spell that their cross and rose knows how they feel it's part of them. They look the same, but to someone else here in the Highland. Eleanor and Thomas, their story goes wave back. My sister and Mick had mated; she wore his mark. As he has her mark, in the past it was a locket. That had the magic back then, she had her cross and rose changes their appearance to one that has seen a picture of Thomas and Eleanor. As you remember when she came here with Mick the words we said started a clock for Ellen. The two of them were married, the King of the Fairies did the ceremony."

"My father investigated Stephen O'Connell. Ellen thinks of him as a true friend. My father and him talked; he had asked her how she knew when Francis was around. He knew the hold family had magic. My father was going to strangle Francis; Stephen had stop him from doing so. What really happened will be kept by him. He was happy to see Francis go away for a while.

"As you know I'm taking riding lessons from Mick. When my mark went red hot. I was driving down to the ranch. I knew Mick was in trouble. I ran to the barn and there I heard fighting. I heard everything when Max came into the barn. Stephen telling what Francis tried to do to Ellen. He keeps saying the devil made me do it. Then he said he told me I could have her sexually after she was dead.

"Marcos is trying everything to kill Mick and Angel. The first time he tried to kill Mick in his sleep. Angel called her Great-grandfather Garret. She knew if she were older, she would have her magic. This time round both will need magic. Marcos tried to kill Angel because his father wants their souls. Mick had me make something for them. Both have a piece of each other's hair with them. There is strong fairy magic with the rose. Now tell me how they were standing. When they let their magic flow. Angel was to his right. When he took her hand. They lifted their hands together. Mick said the words Satan begone. Bright light bored into Marcos's chest. It cut Marcos in pieces; he exploded."

A big smile was on Raymond face. "Wow, I would have loved to have seen that. I knew those two would have magic this time around. Mick had two crosses made from their hair; he had asked me to have them blessed. They wear the cross around their neck. One night Mick asked Angel if he could kiss her. What I understand is she kissed him first. She told him that she wanted his cross and rose. Then she told him she was safe to be made love to. He even asked Lesley if this was all true. I understand that the stress has been ruff on them. The two made love often, when they are together.

*　　*　　*

The two men had walked to Raymond's land. He was doing what his grandfather had told him to do. Raymond had told the family. He had to claim the land, so Angel and Angela had a place to stay. Each time, Raymond's blood touches the land it boiled. When all four corners were done. Raymond cleared the meadow where the house was to go. He also put a drop of blood there and waved his hands over the land.

"Bill what you saw happen with Mick and Angel will stay between us for now. Angela McKinnon will stay here with my wife and sister. I will come back to start my new home. James gave me money to do all this with the help of Garret's magic.

"What Mick had done wasn't the first time. He would do anything to save his Angel. When he was two years old. He had a fight with Marcos the day Angel was to be born. In the eighth month mamma was baby setting Mick. At that time, he could talk with Ellen. She had told him something was scaring her. The two could talk to each other in their mind. That was the only way mamma could rest. Mick told my father that the beautiful lady Eleanor. She told me to tell you, to put a protection spell around there place.

"At the hospital dad was reminded to put a protection spell around the delivery room. Marcos was trying to scare Angel, enough that he thought she would die. Mick kept talking to her. He told her that her daddy wouldn't let that happen. Our grate grandfathers had come to help us. They yelled to get the boy away from that window. Thay saved Mick from a tree limb that Marcos was jumping on. It was Mick who stop Marcos, there was a piece of glass that could have kill Mick. He used that glass and through it like a knife, it went into Marcos we saw the blood. Then the two of us used our magic to push; the glass in deeper. I was only thirteen at the time. Marcos tries to kill my sister and my little brother, now Mick is my friend and brother-in-law. The two of us believe the same way, no one will hurt Angel or Mick.

This is how my sister feels, he is her love of her life. "Soon Angel will be going to school here in the lowlands. I must have the house ready for them. Angel will stay here in the Highlands on weekends and holidays."

The two men were back at the piece of land that Raymond now owns. It was good to see the grass growing. With a wave, of his hand a house appeared.

Bill hit the panic button. "Raymond, isn't this taking a chance? Don't you think they will know you have magic?"

He had a big smile on his face. "Bill, I have already thought of this. If anyone comes here, they will see a part of a building. Every day will show a little more. If anyone stay here all they will see is men building. When the sun goes down. There will be no-one working. When the sun comes up. The men will start working on my home."

Raymond looked at him. "Bill, do you know Angela McKinnon?"

He smiled at him. "Yes, I do. We went on missions together with your father. We also brought Mick and Angel to their grandparents. Do you know if one of the family puts a spell on the waterfall?

Raymond looked at him. "Don't tell me you two hit it off. Mick and Angel got you two to go swimming with them."

Now Bill was turning red. "Yes, and Yes. I know she is the best diver and fighter. I believe the school will ask her to help teach the girl's diving. I work with the boys when the girls heard that the boys were learning to dive. They wanted to learn, she is also a computer expert. I know the school will have her teaching.

"Raymond while we were at the ranch. Angel had a vision that three boys were going to beat Mick up. She saw Misty giving them the orders. They had brass knuckles; Marcos wants him dead. Angela called me and told me that there were two jobs that she and I could do. She will also be the den mother for Angel. I will be den father on Micks floor."

Raymond went seriously. "That will be good. Angel will be diving with the other girls. Bill, I don't know how you could see what Mick and Angel were able to do. When Marcos made his move with Francis, he thought Francis could kill Ellen. We have a little breathing room. We made are move and brought Angela to the ranch. She can go any where's Angel may go. All her things that were going to Scotland I now have. Come on, Bill, we have got other things to do. Angel will be here before we know it."

*　　*　　*

After she had her last dance recital. Ellen had for gotten her birth name. Her name now became Angel. Angela was teaching her everything she needed to know about diving. There was a lot of classroom homework to do. Her two friends also did the homework. They liked the idea of knowing how to dive. The three of them got through all the classrooms work together. The pond out front was just what Angela needed. She had to get Angel used to the tanks, mask, and her fins. Angel's grandfather gave her friends each a mask and fins. This pond had a deep spot to dive in. Angel worked hard. She knew a lot about diving when she left her grandparents' ranch.

At the end of the month Angel and Angela were taken to Arthur's private jet. He learned not to go overboard with Angel. Her past port, Arthur also had. Anything she needs the school will take care of it. Angel found herself looking out a small window. The sun was out. She could see the land below. Then she was up in the clouds. From here out. She won't be able to see much.

Angela gave her some books to read on diving. She also did some drawing and work on her story. After a while she started to get sleepy. They had just flown over the World Clock time zone. Then they landed in Scotland. Arthur had two rooms for them. Angela and Angel were going to share a room.

The next day they went to her new school. Angel will take another test for college. She didn't remember much of the landing. Nor did she remember being help to her room. The next morning

Angel remembered the smell of coffee and something sweet. When she opened her eyes, she was in a big room.

Angela was sitting at a table drinking coffee. "Good morning, Angel. I have some food and a hot chocolate with a little coffee in it. You will need it to take a test today."

At first, she didn't know where she was. "Angela, could you tell me where we are?"

She knew the jet lag was getting to her. "Where in Scotland, I will be taking you to your new school. I want you to get up and get something to eat."

Angel got out of a soft bed. "Okay where is this hot chocolate with coffee in it?"

She took a sip. Angel was remembering her dream. "Angela, I had a dream of a castle."

As she took a bit of food. She was drawing what she remembered. Angel had seen different ages of children. On one side of the castle there were many colors of rose bushes. However, there was one rose bush that was redder than any other color red there. Every time she dreamt, it meant something. Angel had this dream once before. She draws the castle with the deepest red roses. Next, she drawn a man sitting on a Clydesdale. The man had a white baseball hat on.

Angela came over to stand behind Angel. "That's beautiful Angel. Did you see anything in front of the man?"

Angel thought about it. She started to draw the pond. What did she see near that pond? A path leading down to it. Then Angel remembered there were two people walking with tanks. From that moment she felt a present of two men. Those feelings came from her drawing. How can that be she thought? In her mind eye she was on that path with him. Whatever had happened. He knew she was there with him. Angel stopped drawing and quickly closed the book. She moved fast to stand up. Angela was watching Angel draw. She had to move quickly to get out of the way of her chair.

Angela thought something spooked her. She knew it had to be something with her drawing. "Angel, are you okay?"

At first, she couldn't remember Angela that good. Could she trust her? "I'm fine, I thought it was getting late. Don't we have that meeting?"

She knew the spell she was under, took a lot from her. "Your right Angel, we better get dress. Ware something comfortable."

The two of them got in the car rental, they headed toward her new school. Angel was thinking about what she had felt. It didn't take them long to get to the school. Angela pulled into a driveway to a check station. The man told them to park outside the gate.

In Angel's mind she was screaming. *"No... no...no! I'm not a bad girl. Please don't lock me up."*

In the Highland's, a teenage boy was learning more about diving. Mick stood up fast, he had just swallowed a lot of water. Quickly, he went on land, in his mind he heard a girl screaming.

All he could do was scream back. *"Stop...! It's not that bad. The school is not a jail. You'll be just fine at Deilondolay for girls. I'm at Deilondotay for boys."*

When she heard his voice, there was a calming feeling that came over her. *"I'm sorry I screamed; you can hear me. Who are you? How do you know I'm at Deilondolay?"*

After he was able to breathe, he answered her. *"Because I felt the same way when I saw the big gates."*

Once the car came to a stop. Angela turned to look at Angel. "Angel, I hope this fence is not scaring you. One minute you looked scared. You came out of it very quickly. I thought I was the only one that could do that. I think you can take the prize this time. Now that they have stopped, you're okay with it. What changed your mind?"

Angel was biting her bottom lip. She was wondering how much she should tell her. When she didn't understand it herself. He felt like she knew him, he acted as if he knew her. "Angela there is a lot of things happening to me. Give me some time to figure it out."

Here they were, she thought the two of them were getting along quite nicely. Then the spell took hold. "All right I understand, you don't trust me yet."

Angel didn't know what to say. "Angela what would you do if your memory had been mess with. Would you have the answers?"

Right then she knew how to get to her. "At your age maybe not. Angel, you, and I have been thrown into this together. There are things you have been doing that scare me, why I say that you been blocking me out. I was told to protect you at all costs. This is not a jail, you can come and go. The grounds are like a city. Yes, it has a big fence around both schools. The schools are on 150 acres. The information that I gave you didn't tell you much. This school takes up all kinds of children. Some are kids that keep running away from home. Others are troublemakers. They all have their memories taken from them. Now there are children like yourself. Your father is looking for a bad man. You're a very talented young woman.

"Someone would love to use your abilities. That's where I came into the picture. I had tried it out for the Navy Seal; I almost made it. You could say my body told me. No way in hell, are you going to make it? I'm a strong woman. Not that strong to fight all kinds of weather. I tried… It almost took my life. I'm part of this team. You don't remember your family and I don't know them. I was told to protect you at all costs. Do you know what that means?"

She thought I should give her a chance. "I do know what it means, why would you do that? To give your life to save mine."

Angela thought about it. "I'm here because these are my orders. It's like the president he has men that would take a bullet for him. I'm here so your father can go after a man that is evil. Angel, we can talk more about this later. I want to be your friend. I hope you can come to trust me. Right now, we got to get inside. You have a test to take. Think about what I said."

Angel grabbed one of her bags. While Angela grabbed the other one. At the gate, she took a deep breath. With her eyes only on the opening she walked through the gate. Happy with herself she called to her mystery man. *"I went through that gate, I hope I can meet you. Thank you for helping me with this."*

In the Highlands, a young man was walking with his friend. A big smile came over his face. Mick looked at Bill and smiled. *"Maybe, do you like riding, they have some nice horses to ride. We could meet at the stables. I will be heading back to school after freshman. I'm a sophomore this year, may I ask which freshman are you?"*

Angel, was smiling from ear to ear. *"I would like that; I do like horses. I'm a pretty good rider. Hope to see you soon. I'm a freshman in college."*

Mick thought she had a nice voice when she wasn't screaming. He smiled at that. "Okay Bill, let's get the horses, it's time for your lesson. I like to see how fast you can ride to the castle. As the two worked together Mick had a vision of a young girl with which he was dancing. She had ran to him and he caught her. Could that be her?"

*   *   *

Angela placed a hand on Angel shoulder. The two of them went through the office door. After, Angel took her test. They asked her what she liked to take for activities. They were very happy with what she chose to take. Mrs. McPike smiled at Angel. She took Angel to the building where she was going to sleep. Mrs. McPike was the freshman house mother. "Your roommate is called Bunny. She will be here next week. This is when you must be back here."

*   *   *

Raymond and Emily took Angela and Angel to see some of the sights. They stop at the Fair. They saw men fighting with heavy swords. Many things were going on. They heard the bagpipes and saw the girl dancing. "Oh yes, I like to learn those dances. Can I get a kilt? Please Angela could you buy me a kilt."

She was happy to see her relaxing. "All right I'll get you a kilt."

Raymond knew she would want one. "You have no need to do that. Here look in the bag."

Angel squeal with delight. She through her arms around his neck. "Think you, I just love it." She went to put the kilt on.

She thought everything felt right. "How do I look?"

Raymond was feeling she was important to him. "Like a true Scottish woman. Which you are a Scottish woman; it was Arthur who told me this."

There were young men going around looking for girls to dance with. A tall young man came over to them. Raymond knew this young man. It was Mick from the school Deilondotay. Bill was with him making sure he stayed safe. "Hello young lassie. Would you like to dance with me?"

She was happy that someone picked her. "I would love it. I don't know any of those moves."

When Mick saw her, he made a beeline too her. He had ran to get to her first. "I would love to show you. If it's all right with your family?"

Out of all the girls around them. Mick found Angel. Angela looked at Raymond for help. He nodded his head for okay.

They had to play the game. "All right Angel, you can go and dance. Young man what is your name?"

He was looking at Angel while answering her. "They call me Mick; this is my cousin Bill Colman."

Raymond was watching the two men. As they couldn't take their eyes off the girls. "Hello, there they call me Angela. This is my cousin Angel McKinnon."

Before Mick took Angel up on stage. He showed her all the moves they were going to use. Angel was enjoying dancing with Mick. She caught on quickly.

Bill came over to Raymond. "I had nothing to do with this. When Mick saw her, he made a beeline right to her? It was as if he knew she was in the Highlands. Come to think of it, I was showing him more of Scuba diving. When he came up quickly, swallowing water."

Angela listened to Bill, as he told them what happened to Mick. "No that couldn't happen, could it. When we were at the gate to the school Angel got scared. As I looked at her, she looked like she was yelling in her mind. Then she stops, everything was all right with her."

Raymond smiled. "The two of them have this strong bond between them. They may not know each other given name. I think there heart will always know each other."

Bill looked at them. "Now that is just what Mick had said to Angel, when he came to save her."

Alicia watched them as they ran to get on stage to dance. "I had a feeling this was going to happen. He will always know where his love will be. Come on let's get closer to them. There are a lot of people here today. I see a place near to the stage. Let's get that table before someone else gets it."

Sitting at the table. Angela was amaze how the two of them danced together. "Wow, they looked good together, they are so much in sync the two of them."

Then the four felt there cross and rose go hot. Evil was around, they saw a man looking at the two of them. Then they saw the man was a woman. She was smoking a thin cigar; her hair was cut like a man. Could she be Misty? The crowd love everyone up there. Raymond and Bill were on high alert. They went over to Mick and Angel. "Hay you two would you like something to eat and drink."

They follow them back to the table. "That was fun, thank you Mick."

He smiled as he watched her do the dance. Then he felt his mark go hot, "I love this dance."

Angel also stopped dancing when she felt her mark. She had looked around and saw a man. But that wasn't a man but a woman. "How can anyone smoke those nasty cigars. No…, he's not a man, but a girl."

Mick had watched where Angel was looking. "Grate she cut her hair like a boy. Way to go Misty."

Angel looked at him. "Mick, do you know her."

Mick then looked at Angel. "I would have to say yes, she had long hair and was trying to be my ballet partner. If she thinks I'm going to dance with her. It's not going to happen; I don't care if she cut her hair. It was a nightmare with her. Her hair was too thick and long; besides, she was too heavy to lift. She is overweight to be a ballerina."

Then Bill and Raymond came with the food. They saw she was watching Mick and Angel. Raymond came close to her and bumped into her. "I'm sorry sir, I miss judge how close I was to you."

Misty head turned and looked at him. "I'm a woman not a man."

He smiles at her. "I'm sorry, but you look just like and older man, with that cigar in your mouth."

Now Misty was trying to get him to do something for her. "What are you trying to do with your eyes?"

That had done it for Misty, she stormed out not even looking back. Bill was happy to see her go. "You do know who she is."

Raymond nodded his head yes. "I know all about Misty. She's a lot of trouble in my book."

Mick was telling the women about her. "That was Misty she's trouble. Be careful around her if your IQ is low. She can make you do anything for her. What grade are you in, may I ask."

Angel smiled at him. "I'm a freshman in college."

Mick started to laugh. "Oh boy, she is not going to like this. I know that you can dance superbly. Your IQ must be very high."

She smiled at him. "Yes, I've skipped High school. I had a test today to see if I could go into college. I must take a class for English; I will have another test to see if I need to take more classes. Mick, you know how to do ballet. I've sign up for ballet, I also used to teach as an assistant aid to my classmates."

Mick had a worried look. "Angel be careful, she can make trouble for you. Your everything she wanted to be."

After lunch Raymond told her it was time to head home. She wanted to stay and talk with Mick. But she was sleepy. "I need a nap the jetlag caught up to me."

Mick kissed her on the back of her hand. "I've had a good time with you Angel. I hope we can meet again. When you go back to school sign up for the activities. We might meet up with each other."

In school

The week was up she came in at the end, for the freshmen had to be back. Angel had to get back to school. All freshmen had to be back, even the college group. She had to meet Bunny she was a freshman in high school. They thought it would be easier for me to be with someone my own age. But the reason she thought, is too get young girls for the activities. Angel went out running, after her shower she was going for breakfast. When she got to her room Bunny was there. She stood in the doorway watching her jump to one thing then another.

Now she knew how she got her name. "Hello Bunny. I can see how you got your name."

Bunny stopped and looked at her. "You must be Angel; I do hop around a lot. They told me you were a freshman in college. Is there anything you need? I was just putting my things away."

*　　*　　*

Angel thought she is going to be fun to have for a roommate. "I'm going out to find all the buildings and sign up for the things I like to do. She had seen were the boy's side was. Angel had asked when the buildings were to be open. She found out after lunch, but you can look at the horses.

As she walked, her thoughts were about Mick. How she enjoyed dancing with him. When he came over to her, she thought she knew him. Could he be the one she had felt? He said he went to the school for boys. It was on the other side of her school. She hoped to meet him again. She thought Bunny looked to be a dancer. If not, she would love to teach her.

When she went through the gate, it wasn't as bad this time around. At the gate she was going to say goodbye to her. But Angela came in with her, she was heading to the office. I heard that there was a class for computer expert and diving lessons.

Angela was thinking of seeing if they needed a computer expert. "Are you reading my thoughts."

Angel smiled. "I heard you and Bill talking about Misty. There are teachers leaving this year. Two of them are computers and engineers. I knew Bill was upset that Misty was there. He told us there are boys that were simple minded at the school. With them she could have Mick beaten up."

She thought Mick told her; he took karate. The class he was up to a black belt. When did he tell her that?

Angela was please she was opening herself up to her. "That's good but if they get him off guard and put a hood over his head. It would take three people to immobilize him. They even could use those knockout drops."

Angel didn't like what she said. "Then you two should get a job here. Mick is a nice boy; I don't want him hurt. Pick up two applications and fill it out. Give Bill one also, I saw you looking at him."

Angela looked at her, the woman had come out. "Wow, does this mean you are trusting me."

Angel gave her a hug. "I'm trying to Angela. This is all new to me, I'll tell you what happened that day. Not right now is that okay. You know part of it; Bill has the other part."

Angela remembers something that her grandmother had said. If Angel tells you something that is going to happen. Take it to heart. Angela got out of the car and went into the office. "Could I have two applications.

*　　*　　*

Angel ran off to look around the campus. She thought about the handsome young man. She loved dancing with him. Why would it feel so right being with him? What was it about his name Mick?

"Mic..., Micky..., Micky Mouse."

Angel stopped running. The name Micky Mouse was from her childhood. She used to sit with a boy watching the show Micky Mouse. He is a part of my life. It felt right when Mick took her hand. Is Mick from her pass? He made me feel good inside when he kissed my hand.

*   *   *

This must be where they would do there dancing. She when over to the steps, as she climbed. This time Angel was able to open the door to the building. "Angel was wondering about Mick. Since she has been here in Scotland. A young man has been helping her. I can hear his thoughts, I know he hears mine. If Mick is a part of my past. He may like to do a lot of things that I like to do. If he comes to this building I will be here."

She went up some stairs, and she tried the doorknob. The building was open to the students. In the corridor was a bulletin board. There were papers to sign up for dancing. Another one for becoming a team leader. This was only for the senior's and upper-class men. Down one of the halls came a teacher. "Hello. Welcome to the building of arts. Here we have three things. Dancing, painting, photography. We will work with you on what you pick."

She had a big smile on her face. "I know just what I want to do. Can I pick all of them?"

The teacher was glad to have new blood. "If you like, are you and upper classman."

Angel smiled at the teacher. "I'm a freshman in college. I've been a dancer; sense I was five years old. Before I left the state, I was teacher assistant. My teacher liked the way I could explain it to some of the older once. I would like to apply for team leader."

She was hoping someone knew how to dance. "Angel, could you show me something you had done just before you came here. We have new ballet slippers, what size are you."

Angel thought wow there trying to get knew people in. She had on shorts; she told her a size five. The teacher even had a hair bam for her to put her hair. Then she told her to do some leaps and spin. She asked what weight she was at. "I'm at a hundred, a ballerina must have strong legs. A small waist, if she is overweight it will be hard for the man to pick her up. They put their hair up so nothing will get in the way."

Then the teacher watched how she put her hair up. "Tell me Angel is that how all ballerinas must wear their hair."

Angel nodded yes and went over to warm up. Without her knowing she recorded everything she said and did. Angel was now ready to dance. She had dance her last recital, the shoes were grate. It had given her support on her feet. She had a vision of a young boy; she was ten years old. Then she heard *"Focus on your dancing."*

Now she was coming out of a spin. She had walked on her toes then leaped high with her legs in a straight line. Her dance was flawless when she ended. The teacher came out. "That was beautiful. I don't think anyone of the girls could dance like you. What you told me lines up with what one of our boys said. We would like you to meet him. His dancing is like the way you dance. He should be here tomorrow."

After that the teacher came over with rules for anyone who like to try out to become a ballerina. "Angel your name for team leader has been taken by you, leave out dancing. When Mick's come back to school, we will ask him if he like to dance with you."

The teacher looked at her. "Tell me who would like to know. I would, for I met this young man at the Highland games. He was doing the Scottish dance and was looking for someone to dance with.

He said he was from Deilondotay; I enjoyed dancing with him. He told me about a girl called Misty; I saw her. She looked like a man. I was shocked that he had to lift her, he said her hair was thick and she got hurt."

The teacher watched her print her name. Angel E.H. "If it's too much for me. I will drop one. I have my camera with me. I can always show the teacher my pictures. It will be photography."

After she signed her name. The teacher also places her name next to Angel. "You're the one Principal Tensaw was talking about. I hope you can help this school win this year. My initials must go next to your name. Make sure that each teacher does the same. You have these papers in your dorm. Sign up there too. Last year some of the papers got lost. I'm going to make a copy and send it to Principal Tensaw. Good luck."

*　*　*

Outside she called him. *"Thank you, are you the same boy I dance with."*

Mick watched her as she walked to the next building. *"Do you want me to be him?"*

She found out he liked her; he kissed her quickly. She wondered how he did that. *"Angel did you dream last night?"*

She remembered the young man. She giggled *"Why do you ask, tell me did you have a sexy dream."*

Mick thought she was playing with me. *"Because, I remember a beautiful woman, that I had made love to."*

Angel giggled again, she enjoyed that dream. When she woke up it felt real. "I saw your face, you were older, but it was you. How did you know I had receive a vision while I was dancing? Are you able to see what I'm do and thinking."

Mick felt she was getting worried. *"Angel, I had come to the water, I don't know how I did it. I saw you in the water. I was watching you dance when you made that face. Somehow, I knew what it ment. I know things about you; all I can say. It had to be before are names were taken. Just that I know of you. That's how we could dream of each other."*

She liked being with him. *"I'm not afraid of you knowing about my body. You must be right it had to be before they took are name. It seems the school likes what we know about ballet. The teacher checked everything you had said, against what I had told her. Before I left, she put out rules for ballet. She told me the principal told her that I was going to be team leader. She had said that the boy who is a sophomore, if he signs up, he will be team leader.*

Tara

Mick had thought she had to check out the horses. Angel went to the stables she went inside the fence in area. She checked over every horse they had. Two of the horses she thought, one horse wanted to do his thing. The other horse wanted to just eat and relax. A man came outside. "Lass what are ye doing with the horses. I need to check ye out first, before ye get into that fence in area.

Angel looked over all the horses. "I'm sorry about that, a young man that I met today. We got talking about school and the endurance race. There is one horse that needs a new home. I know a family, they work with a lot of horses. They would take this horse and give another in its place. A lot of the horses here like to run. This girl just wants to walk.

She smiled at him. "I'm sorry about that. I met someone before I came here. He told me that Buttercup should only be used to teach the children how to ride. Is this horse used to race with?"

The man looked at her. "Ye are pretty and smart, I've been trying to get this horse a better home. We keep her for one girl to ride. This lass is trouble; the horse can't jump anymore."

Angel ran her hand over the horse's hip. She found it was swollen and hot. "I believe this horse could have rheumatism in her hip."

He watched her closely. "You are right, she has rheumatism in that hip. The school can't give her medicine just so she can jump."

Angel asked Mick if they could take this horse. *"I'm afraid if she tries to make the jump and misses, she could break her hip and hurt the rider."*

Mick ran to ask if they could help them. "I just remember that I give Angel the number here. I told her about the horse Misty rides. Angel could talk to them; maybe they would give the horse to you. That would be a good horse to teach children how to ride. If she can't ride any other horse, she will be out of the competition."

His uncle had a feeling Mick knows Angel. Their abilities to talk to each other came out. "If they call me, we will get that horse. I'm register as a rescue for horses. If they need a horse, I have one in mind."

Mick then told Angel to go ahead and give that number to him.

Hamish was smiling. "Ye know you way around a horse. Can ye ride as well, as your knowledge for horses is.

This time Angel said "Aye…, that I can do. My grandfather showed me everything, he said I was a horse whisper. This horse can tell how people feel. My friend I met gave me this number that you could call."

Angel had gave him the number. "He went into the building and called."

When he came back, he said. "You met Mick, the family he is living with, is bringing a new horse here today. They will take him to their ranch. This horse will be used to teach people how to ride."

Angel smiled at him. "Can you tell me which horse do the boys ride."

He had to laugh. "This one is called Tara; the other one is Lightning he is fast. Mick can ride both horses. But he must work hard to get him to do what he wants. I noticed Tara likes girls; they make over him. When it comes to jumping, he won't go near the jump."

She asked him for a bridle and saddle. "This horse and I are going to get to know each other. I want to race him; he will be the girl's horse to race. Now to see if he is a good boy."

She got on and he didn't want her on his back. He tried to buck her off. She had to tighten her legs. Tara found out that Angel knew ways to get him to do what she wanted. He turned and looked at her.

Hamish laughed and could see that Tara met his match. "Open the gate, he's going to learn who's boss."

She ran him and made him turn fast and then the other way. She got him running and held on if he just stopped. Witch he did. "I'm not going to take this."

She turned him left and got him running again. This time he jumped, she gave him a bee sting. He went over; he knew that she was in control. Again, she ran him and made him jump from start to finish. From the corner of her eye, she saw Hamish through up his arm. They did good. He came over to them, he was smiling. "Lass ye matched Micks time. He wanted to do the race, but this lass wanted to use Buttercup."

She smiled back at him. "Then use that number I give you. He is also a rescue ranch for horses. He will take that horse. If you need another horse, he could help you with that."

She went over and signed up for the competition. Hamish put his initials next to hers. "Thank you, Angel. There coming today to get Buttercup. I have sent a copy to the principal. Lass you're going to help this school. Ye and Mick be careful with Misty, I notice she likes

Mick. She can get some of the boys to do things for her. Not Mick, at times she uses her eyes on him. He would say do you have something in your eyes. That kind of power she shouldn't have it. She can make a person do bad thing."

Angel was glad she could help. "I know about Misty, I met Mick at the Highland games. Thank you, Hamish. I will be team leader. I will pick my team, we will see if they know anything about horses. To do the competition they have to know how to ride a horse and be able to jump over the gates."

He went over to her. "Angel that building over there. You can have lunch. They are coming to get Buttercup today. There bringing us another horse, I'll take care of Tara."

She smiled at him. "Thank you but for him to start trusting me. He must have the good and bad to know if I'm pleased with him."

Hamish was pleased with her. "If you instruct the girls make sure they take care of their horse. Misty didn't know how to saddle the horse. Mick was so happy that he didn't have to work with her anymore. Angel if she finds out that you two were involved with getting rid of Buttercup. If she finds that she can't dance with Mick. Please be on guard she is an evil girl; I'm scared for Mick."

Angel took a breath. "Hamish, Mick had started this. She can't dance ballet, yes, she cut all her hair to look more as a man. I got to see her; she had tried to use her eyes on Raymond. He is the one I'm living with when I'm not in school. Don't worry, we got this. We both have someone that watch over us."

*   *   *

After she was done, she headed to get lunch. *"Mick thank you for helping me. You must be right about knowing me. I feel the same way. That vision was of a young boy. He looked like you."*

Mick was getting a horse ready to go. *"You know that I was the one that yelled at you."*

Angel got a salad to eat. *"You wanted to be a mystery man. With you here I'm going to like this school. Mick Hamish is worried about us. He doesn't like Misty. He said that she can get some of the boys to do things for her."*

He was having lunch. *"The one that looks after me is going to stay at school. The one who watches over you will be there also. How's the signup sheet doing?"*

She had taken a bit of her food. *"Tell me did Misty take down the signup sheets last year?"*

Mick was cleaning his dish. *"I want to say yes, but they never caught her. Why do you ask."*

Angel went over and through her plastic bowl away. *"I thought so, Misty going to have a hard time here. Now the teacher must put their initial on the paper and send a copy to the principal."*

She was walking by the horse stables. *"Oh, good they came here to get Buttercup. That horse they brought here is a looker."*

Bunny gets the girls to watch Angel dance

It was time to go to her dorm. There were papers she had to sign there also. Angel went in the building at the back door. She could hear girls laughing. *"Wow If it stays this loud, she will have to study at the library."*

Then she saw the house mother talking with the girls. "Hello Angel. I heard you been going all around. They said you signed up for things you like to take. Here, I will place my name next to yours. Then you can go meet the girls."

She wanted to do some dancing first. "All right, but first I like to do some dancing. Mrs. McPike. Thank you for your help."

It was time to talk to her roommate. On the way down the hall, one of the girls called out. Angel signed up to be team leader. Bunny wasn't in the room; she had to grab her gym bag. The gym was in the basement where she went downstairs to get to it. To unwind she like to do some dancing. What she didn't know Bunny had asked the girls who liked to dance ballet. She had found out from the den mother Angel was a superb dancer. They had given Angel time to get set up down there. Ten girls follow Bunny downstairs. There was a place to sit and watch her dance. The den mother had follow Angel down.

After she had done her warmups. She went and turned on her music. There she did her routine first she did her leaps and turns once she was done. The girls run upstairs to sign up for dancing. Angel would find out that all ten had taken class for ballet. They had ran back downstairs, to see if she done more dancing. After she had drank her water. She started her next song; this movement was slow and graceful. The teacher had let the principle watch her routine. Everyone had grab her ballet slippers, they were at the doorway putting them on.

Bunny was first to be done. "Angel, will you teach us how to dance like you can."

She was overwhelmed. "Wow, all of you want me to teach you. But you haven't seen me dance.

Bunny smiled at her. "We watched you just now. Please will you teach us what you know."

Angel then gave a little laugh. She smiled at her. "All right, this is how we will do it. I run in the morning; this keeps your legs strong. It helps with your weight also. Make sure you sign up for the Activities. I have signed up for all three, you don't have to.

*　*　*

Bunny had all the questions to ask her. "Could you tell us how long you been dancing?"

Angel smiled at them. "Since I was four, I had to wait until I was five years old to have lessons. I love to dance. When I went on stage for the first time. I did my spins just right. My leaps were higher than before. I knew then dancing would always be a part of me. I became the youngest ballet teacher aid. I showed girls and boys of all ages. They learn how to do better spins and leaps. Does anyone know what classical means?"

No one could answer her. "It is a standards style of ballet. A force that is influence by a teacher. The words I'm going to tell you. This is the history what the judges of the competition could ask us.

"Classical Ballet: a traditional style of ballet. Which stresses the academic technique. This has developed through the centuries. For the existence of ballet.

"Ballerina: a female dancer in a ballet company. This is what we will be.

Danseur: a male dancer in a ballet company. We will be dancing with the boys. You must learn these words and much more. The judges may ask us these words. We are going up against other schools.

"I've been told, Deilondolay and Deilondotay haven't won the ballet competition for three years. Now, how many of you have done ballet?"

Six hands went up. "How many like to learn how to dance?"

Four hands went up. "If you want me to be your team leader. You must sign up on more than one sheet. Tell the others about this. We have a little time before we eat. The ones that have their ballet shoes, if you have shorts on that will be find if there not real tight. You will have to get something that is not tight."

A teacher came from out back. She had ballet shoes for the others. "I have ballet slippers you can have, take care of them. If

Angel would like to have a class to instruct other students. After competition that will be after the endurance competition."

"If you don't make the cut. There are classes you can take. There is next year you will be able to try again. Remember only four will make the cut. Another four will be their understudy. I've heard that Mick will be a teacher for the boys. He told one of the teachers that ballet needs rules. The principal liked that idea. If he didn't sign up, she would ask him herself. She has seen him dance, Misty was too heavy for him to lift."

All the girls were able to get a pair for today. The teacher took their names after they signed up. She told them to do their warmup. The once that hadn't done this before, had to set and watch.

Angel went over to look at each of the six girls positioned. She was pleased to see two of them had it. "Bunny, you did the first position exceptional."

The next girl, her name was Daisy. "You almost have it. Put your heels closer together. Like this." Angel went and showed her. "Yes, that's right. They must touch. It will make your toes turn out. Better!"

The last girl did the movement skillfully; her name was Kitty. Angel went over and looked at the other three girls. She saw that their feet needed work. "Keep trying you'll get it, it's hard to get your body to do what you want. Now you four I would like you to try this. You can watch the others work on their feet positions. I like for you three to hold your arms in front of you in an oval shape. Then we will put it all together. This is all we are going to do for today. Do it again."

Angel did it with them. "It will take time. Work on how you place your feet. Now rest and watch me as I go through the positions.

"1st Position: Your heels should be touching with your toes turned out. Hold your arms in front of you in an oval shape, like this.

"Second Position: Move your feet apart. Open your arms wide but don't stretch them back. They should be slightly rounded and slightly in front of you.

"3rd Position: Cross one foot in front of the other. Bring one arm, curved in towards you, and the other arm out to the side.

"4th Position: Put one foot in front of the other with a space between. Raise your arm and curve it above your head. The other arm out to the side.

"5th Position: Finally, have one foot exactly in front of the other. This time close together. Raise both arms up in a beautiful ballerina oval."

"Before we leave here is three more words to know. Pointes Shoes: The satin ballet shoes used by dancers. When dancing on their points of their toes. Pointes shoes used are reinforced with a box. It is constructed of many layers of strong glue in between layers of material. These shoes are not made of cement or wood.

"Tutu: the short classical ballet skirt made of many layers of net. A romantic tutu: is a long net skirt reaching below the calf.

CHAPTER EIGHTEEN

Nightmare was saved

ANGEL THOUGHT TO have lunch with the girls. It would be good if she could find out how many could ride. She wanted to check out the horses to see what kind they had. Mick had said there was one horse called Buttercup, which was too old to be in the competition. That was the horse Misty rides, no wonder the teacher hoped she could help them to win this year.

The girls here were nice; Bunny got right down to business. She found out in their class there were four girls that knew how to ride. If they come down to sign up for the competition, she can work with them. It would be nice to have one from each grade. She was told that Hamish and Laron oversaw the stables. She had to walk down going pass the building were they would be swimming at. She saw the track and the trail for bikes.

Angel was scoping out the horses a lot closer then yesterday. Buttercup was taken to a better home. There was another horse she wanted to check him out more. She had notice him walking funny.

Off in the distance she heard a horse that was upset. She turned quickly, to see men trying to get that horse into a trailer. When the horse broke away from the men. Laron hollered for me to get out of the way; Angel wasn't scared of the horse. This must be the horse that one of the girls tormented. She knew his name, it was Nightmare. He was coming very close to her. Angel knew how to get on a horse that was scared, she grabbed his mane and swung her leg over his back. She had to get closer to his head, he had to hear her voice. "Nightmare it's just you and me, let's see what you can do."

He had to know she wouldn't hurt him. Nightmare, liked when she kept him away from that trailer.

Angel kept him running full out, she brought him around and took him over the jump's then down the home stretch. As she slowed Nightmare down, she saw men coming torte her. She knew Hamish he was a good man and at lease listen to what she had to say. But she didn't know Laron. He didn't look happy with her. Angel knew she must be in big trouble. Nightmare was hesitant to go over to them. She rubbed his neck. She told him he would be all right.

She brought Nightmare to a stop and quickly spoke. "Hello Hamish, I guess I'm in trouble. You must be Mr. Laron? I'm sorry sir, I know I'm in trouble, you see I've done this many times. I know when a horse is scared. My grandfather showed me how to get onto a horse when I was ten."

It was Laron who spoke. "Tell me lass who are ye?"

She walked, Nightmare around as she spoke to Laron. "They call me Angel; my family has worked with horses for a long time. This horse, someone had tormented him. I don't know how she or he did it. Not yet."

Laron was watching her with him. "Aye, ye are right about that. This is the first time he has acted out with her. The lass didn't want to give him a second chance. She wanted him to be put down before she gets back to school."

Angel knew right where they were taking him. "This horse is a sweetheart; may I ask what girl. I will ask you is it, Misty."

Hamish looked at her, watched her go to work. The principle heard we will sue the school. She wanted him to be put down. How do ye know Misty?"

She had to find why he was acting out. "I met her at the Highland games. No, let me check him out first. Tell me why he is limping, has he been like this always?"

Hamish went over slowly to Nightmare. "Easy boy, let us find out why your limping. We are going to save ye if we can."

Laron had the phone. "Aye, she is here with Nightmare. Hamish is with Angel now. The lass seems to know her stuff around horses. Aye I will call ye back after she checks him out."

The principle was looking up her chart. "Her family said she is a horse whisperer. Stay on the phone until she had looked him over."

Angel was checking his legs. He went over those jumps find. "Nightmare is a fine horse, I know someone who will take him. Give me a bit of time, just don't kill him. Have you seen him limping this bad."

The two men looked at each other. "Let us think. No. I never thought of his hoofs. Do ye think this is what making him act crazy?"

Angel looked at Hamish. "Can I have something to clean his hoofs. He's not walking right. I'll let you know in a minute."

Angel knew there must be something in Nightmare's hoofs. All four of his legs, were given him trouble.

Then Hamish thought for a minute. "With him acting up all the time. I never thought to check his hoofs. A man was called in to put new shoes on Nightmare. It was someone that Misty's father called."

When Angel bent Nightmares leg. There was something between the shoe and hoof. She had to dig it out. She handed it to Hamish and preceded to check all four hoofs. Whatever it was, they had a feeling Misty had something to do with it. Angel looked at the last one, to her it was a device that could shock him.

Bunny was coming toward them. Angel saw her and made the sign for her to slow down. "Is there anything wrong Angel?"

She smiled at her. "You had said that you knew how to ride."

Bunny came over to Nightmare and started to give him love in. "Yes, I have, I came down here to sign up for the competition. He is beautiful, may I ride him?"

Laron and Hamish stepped away from them. This young lass knows what she is doing. They told the principal that, "Angel rode him. Now Bunny is going to ride him."

She looked him over. The last thing she did was look into his eyes. Nightmare was a happy horse. "Bunny, he had a hard time. Show him that you're not like Misty. Look into his eyes show him your happy."

Proving Nightmare was good

Bunny spoke softly. "You're a beautiful boy Nightmare. Can I get on you?"

She got on Nightmare. "Okay Bunny, take him for a little walk. Now turn around and bring him back to me."

There were no limps. Angel looked into Nightmares' eyes. She could see he was a lot happier. Laron watched as the girls did magic on Nightmare. Hamish told the principal about the device that was in his hoof. Bunny looked good on him. "Now take him through the course, Laron had his stopwatch on him. Stop, okay, get ready, set go. Bunny did good riding him bareback. Angel told her to pore it on. Laron showed Hamish her time. "That was good, she just a bit under ye Angel."

Bunny gave him a big hug. She slid off him and came around and gave him a kiss on his nose. Coming toward them was Daisy, she waved at them. "Hello Angel, Bunny, you beat me here. Oh, he's beautiful, what is his name."

Angel didn't tell her anything. She let her do her thing, Nightmare notice they didn't want to hurt him. "May I ride him, if he was mine, I would call him Sugarfoot."

It was as if he wanted them to call him that. "He like the new name."

The principal heard him, whinny. She asked if that was him. Hamish laugh aye; we have a new name for him."

The principal thought about it. She told him to kill the name Nightmare. From here out he will be called Sugarfoot.

Angel looked at him. "Daisy, can you ride bareback."

She smiled at them. "Yes, I'll sign up first."

Angel looked over Sugarfoot. "Are you up to another run boy."

He whinnied and was ready to go. "Daisy went over and asked if he let her ride him."

Sugarfoot whinnied again. "Now take him for a walk, bring him back. Take the course when you come back then we will time you.

Daisy swung her leg over and got on Sugarfoot. She told her to walk him first. Then slowly pick up speed. Laron was pleased with what Angel, and the girls had done for him. He knew that Sugarfoot wasn't a bad horse. He needed more than one person to ride him with no trouble. Off in the distance Laron saw another girl coming toward them.

Angel put her hand up to stop Rose. "All right, are you ready."

She had her hand up. "Get set go."

The men were so happy they didn't have to put him down. "Hamish know about this place where Buttercup is now living. If you're not happy with Sugarfoot, the one who has Buttercup will take him. He rescues horses; these horses after they are well, they need a home. Here is the number."

She went over to the signup sheet. Now Laron had four girls that signed up for the competition. He wonders if Angel will have Rose to ride him.

Laron had called that number. "Angel ye know Mick."

She smiled and nodded her head yes. "We could use another horse, they said they will be bringing us another one. He said that Thunder was born on the night we had a bad storm. When he came out it had thundered, so they called him Thunder.

Rose came over to them. "Oh, what a beautiful horse, he looks to be a sweetheart. Have all of you ridden him."

They nodded yes, after lunch I'm going to check another horse out. If you like to try it out with him, he should be ready to ride. He had a bad time so all of you give him a lot of love. They brought him over to brush him down."

Angel had Rose come over to them. She had to see if Sugarfoot would react to her. Rose walked slowly to him. She had let him smell her before she touched him. Sugarfoot was in seventh heaven with the girls making over him.

Laron and Hamish were looking at those devices when they went off. The men were swearing in Gaelic.

Being zapped

Angel had turned around to see who was late. She saw that he had a box of some kind in his hand. Tyler was pointing at Sugarfoot. He's trying to get him to act up. Laron and Hamish also saw it and felt it.

Each time Tyler kept pushing the button. Laron and Hamish were getting madder; they were extremely angry. They had felt the jolts, on each of their sides. They were going after Tyler. The two men didn't like to be shocked. Laron called the principal and told her to get the guards to come down to the stables right away.

Hamish had the men to surround Tyler and close in on him.

Angel knew which way Tyler was heading. She ran ahead of them and picked up a stick that had fallen. When Tyler came running up, she swung as hard as she could. Tyler went down hard; Laron got to him and placed a foot on his back. "No Tyler, you're not going any where's."

Hamish had the box; Laron put two devices in one of Tylers pockets. "Who put ye up to this? Ye went along with having this horse killed. Life is not to be mess with."

Tyler didn't say anything. "We have the shock devices. I know you were the one pushing that button. I saw you and felt the devices. Boys pick him up."

Hamish put two more devices in the other pocket. Then he pushed the buttons. Principal Tensaw and the guards showed up.

Tyler cried out. "Misty said her father would pay me to get rid of Nightmare. Stop shocking me Laron, Hamish then took the box."

He was angry with him. "I see ye don't like being shocked, ye were making us put that sweet horse down. I want ye to feel what he felt."

Principal Tensaw took the box. "So ye don't care about life. What you did to this horse was not right. The men were easy with you. You're an evil man, just like Misty is an evil girl."

She had seen want Nightmare was doing. To her this device was held down for a long time. The man was swearing and dancing around. The four girls went to get some food. They didn't see what was happening. Angel told Rose she will ride Sugarfoot after we eat.

Checking out the horses

The four girls were coming back to the stables. They saw a new horse in the fence in area. Then she heard Mick. *"Angel, are you back at the stables?"*

She smiled because she liked hearing his voice. *"We just got back; there are four girls signed up. What is this new horse name."*

Mick was happy to hear her voice. *"You're going to love this name, it's Nosy. This horse is always right there to see what the other horses was doing."*

She had to check out Snowflake, the men told her that she doesn't want to jump. The people who had her spoiled her. Snowflake was to fat, and she didn't want to do anything but eat. Angel looked her over and she had to lose a little more. "She could lose a little more weight, by the time training is done she should be at a good weight."

The next morning

Angel was out for her run. She had just got to the fence that was on the boy's side. She could see cars pulling up and the boys getting out of the cars. When she turned the corner, she felt a presence. The same presence she felt at the fairgrounds. Could it be Mick? Should she say something? No, she would want to go and meet him. Is this the person that talks to her when she is scared? Even though her dreams were mixed up, she keeps getting little things. His name Mick, then she saw a flash back. Angel saw a stuff animal, Mickey Mouse. What does it mean to me? She had to get back to the dorm.

After her five-mile run. She went down the hallway of her dorm. Angel could see a few of the sophomores were already here. Bunny and Mary were near her room. Some of the sophomores were also waiting for Angel. "Good morning, Angel. We have some more girls for the two competitions. They heard that we be running in the first competition. They like to run with you in the morning. This is Eva and Joy they have the rooms across from us."

Angel was looking over the girls. They were trouble about something, she could guess what it was about. "Hello girls, you're in early. You must be glad to be back at school."

The two girls gave a little laugh. "No, not really. I'm called Eva. We needed to warn the freshman about Misty. Bunny told us that you are going to be a team leader for ballet and for the competition. How could this be when you're younger than us."

Bunny was upset with the girls; she had her hands on her hips. "Angel, they didn't believe me that you're a freshman in college. They said Misty will get it changed."

She had to think of a way to convince them she was. Right then Angela came down the hall. "I been getting that a lot. Thank you, Bunny, for trying. Things have changed this year. If you would like to be part of my group. Go and sign-up, on every paper you can fine. The teacher will sign next to your name; she will take copies of the sign-up sheets.

Ballet weight

"Listen to the new rules, we are going by what a ballerina must weigh. If you're tall and weigh 130 that is a good weight for you. If you're short, and weigh 130, that is not good. A ballerina is between eighty-five pounds and 130. What I heard Misty was short and weighed over 130. I heard that Mick had asked for rules. When I went to sign up the teacher had me dance for her. She asked me about my hair and how it was put up for dancing. I was told what Mick had asked for rules. He also asked for more control over the papers. If the papers come missing; If Misty's girls are the only ones who sign up. Principal Tensaw is going to have a fit. She was the one who told me to sign up as a leader. Ask your new den mother. "Okay Angel what are you getting me into?"

Angel gave a little laugh. "Thay don't believe me that I'm in college."

They looked at the woman standing next to Angel. "It's true she worked very hard to get to where she is now."

Then she had an idea. "First of all, the horse Misty rode is now at a better place in the Highlands. The horse she had tried to get put down, didn't work. His name is Sugarfoot now; she had a man put devices on his feet. I will be happy to show you what I can do. I like doing some dancing before lunch. If you would like to dance with me. Come down and see what I can do. I run five miles in the morning. You can run with me if you like. It will help if you make it in the competition. Eva and Joy thank you for telling me about Misty. I've heard a lot about her and her father. I'm not going to play games with her; I love dancing and teaching girls much older than me. I have a Hi IQ. If anyone needs help with homework you must let me know. The judges for the ballet competition will be professional ballet dancers. We will make them think of us as professional dancers. We will work hard; I will make you do the dances repeatedly. I won't have you do anything that I haven't already done. Many times, I will be doing it with you. If this is not what you want. Don't sign up for my class. You can go into other classes for ballet. We will be doing a Pas de Deux: a dance for two. The boys will be dancing with us. Also, this year. We will have two girls from each grade. After two weeks I will choose one or two girls out of my group. Bunny just because you're my roommate. It doesn't mean you're safe, do you understand?"

Bunny smiled at her. "Angel, I knew that from the start. The way you showed us, then told us to try it. You got right into teaching us. You're a teacher, in dancing and a leader to show us the right way to treat a horse."

This was a start to be able to work and teach ballet to them. "Thank you, Bunny. One thing. I don't yell. However, there is always the first time for everything. Take care of yourself, don't be late for classes. If you are late and you don't have a good answer. Then you could be taken out of the group. I've heard that Misty is evil, I'll let you know if she is or not. I don't want to hear anyone's bad-mouthing anyone."

Angela went to answer the phone. It was the principal. When she was done talking to her. She went back to talk with the girls. "All right girls listen to what I have to say. Angel, the principal, wants you to go to the building for the arts. She had asked Mick to meet you there. Her plan is to show the girls that the two of you can dance together. It will be shown to both schools; it's up to the boys and girls if they want to be teach by them.

She had a feeling that Mick was going to be the next question. "Angel, do you know if Mick is going to teach this year?"

She thought of what to say. "Who is Mick?"

She smiled when one of the girls came into the room. "Angel, you know who she is talking about. You dance with him on stage at the Highland games."

Angel closed her eyes. "Ou…, him the one that swept me off my feet. He's taller than me and strong enough to lift me. The one who has black hair and golden-brown eyes. I guess every girl who has seen him would be smitten with him. I believe his two years older them me."

Candy nodded her head yes. "Angel, you had seen Misty also, someone in your group said she looked like a man. She was watching the two of you. It was sad he had to try to dance with her. Like you, he was in college last year, he would help anyone that needed help. Misty can't go to the library near the boy's side. I'll tell you this, the two of you look good together. Misty didn't like that; she also likes Mick."

Angel bent her head. She wished the two of them didn't have to deal with her. "I know that the principal wants him to teach this year. He wants to see if the guides want him to teach them. Will see what will happen, I like the way he had showed me how to do the Highland dance. This idea to have us dance together, I guess that we will be on TV for the two schools."

Candy knew a lot more about what happened to Misty. "Before rumors go around, I will tell you what happened that day. I had come down from art class when I heard Misty giving Mick a hard time. Her hair was a mess, I didn't know how she let her hair get that way. Mick had asked her many times to put it up. He told her that something was going to happen. I don't know how he could even lift her. I saw her hair got between his fingers; he couldn't let go of her hair. Mick told her stop; I can't lift you this way. But she doesn't like someone telling her what to do. She had got halfway up when her hair pulled her down. She came down hard on her elbow and broke her arm. Mick tried to help her, but she was angry with him. When I saw her again, she was telling her brother a different story. Cal told Hawkeye what had happen before she saw her brother.

"Angel I will love to see you dance, the girls said you been dance since you were four. If I remember right, Mick said he was dancing from the age of six. It seems that you and he have a lot of experience on dancing. One of the girls said you were a horse whisper. Is it true that her father had devices in his hoofs? To me, asking her father to do that for her, in my book she is evil."

Mick back at school

Bill and Mick were heading back to school. "Mick are you, all right? You look like your worried about something."

Mick knew Bill knew more about what was bothering him. "Maybe! I've been thinking of Angel. There was something special about her. You see I've been hearing this girl's voice. It always happens when she's scared. The day when you and I went diving at the lake. She was at the school gate it had scared her. I heard her scream saying. She didn't want to be locked up. Why does it look like a jail?

"Bill, I don't know why I picked Angel to dance with. All I know it felt right when I took her hand. Just now. She was near the boy's gate. She is running, I know she does it a lot like I do. I don't want Angel to be hurt. You know Misty will be here in two days."

Bill had just stop the car, he looked at Mick. Those two have something special between them. Angela and I must keep them safe. "Mick it will be all right. Come on let's get you sign in. I must find out when I'm teaching this year. Also, I must find out if I'm on your floor, like I should be."

The two of them went into the office. Everyone was happy to see them. "Hello Mick, it's good to see you. We have a new girl that's going to be a team leader. She's been holding ballet classes. This is not all. She found out that someone had put shock devices on Nightmares' hoofs. One of the girls gave him a new name its Sugarfoot."

Her friend in the office spoke up. "Anna! That is enough of that. Laron wanted to tell Mick himself, Angel had saved Nightmare."

She laughed; everyone was happy that new girl was here. "Hello Bill. Your class starts next week on Friday. Bill, you will be taking over for one of the teachers. This class is on engineering which will start next Monday. We are adding girls to the diving class this year. Their teacher will be Angela."

Bill was wondering if Mick was on his floor. Anna spoke "You are on Mick floor; you will take care of the boys there."

Anna looked at her friend. "Sally, I didn't tell them what she had done. Angel is quite a young woman."

Talking with Angel

Bill looked at Mick. He saw that it had please Mick to hear that. In Micks thoughts he said. *"Well done, Angel."*

In her room she heard the praise. All she could say was. *"Think you Mick that means a lot to me."*

Outside Bill helped Mick to take in all their clothes. *"Mick, are you going to become a team leader this year?"*

He had looked toward the girl's side. *"That's a good question Angel. I heard that they are happy you're here. The two horses are also happy. I would love to dance with you, Angel. To do the endurance competition with someone who matches me in everything she does. It's as if you were made for me, wow where did that come from?*

She smiled and wondered the same thing about him. *"Mick, are you reading my thoughts? For I feel the same way. I know we can't know are name, but our feelings for each other. Like you said wow, where did that come from."*

After their clothes were in their room Mick sat on his bed. He thought, she feels the same way as I do. He wanted to ask her if she was his mate. No, he thought, time will tell, one thing he must keep her safe from Misty. Bill had come into his room. He saw that he was heavy in thought.

He knocked on his door. "Mick it's too early to thank of who Angel is to you. If your room is done talk to some of the boys who would like to dance."

Then again just sign up and go for it, you know you want to dance with her again. The phone rang and Bill went to answer it. After the call he came back to Mick. That phone call was from the principle, Mick you are going to teach. You need to go to the building for the arts. Angel will meet you there, shorts will be just find if you can move in them."

Mick smiled, he had his clothes for dancing. He ran to the building then he saw Angel and waved to her. Why does he want to kiss her? "Hello Mick, so were going to do this."

Angel was overwhelmed with the sight of his body. She wished she were in his arms so he could kiss her. "Hello Angel, we are going to do this. Are you all right dancing with me."

She smiled and nodded her head yes. Mick was also overwhelmed by the way her body looked. A thought came to him. His toys were bigger now, how he like to suck her nipples. He went up quickly to open the door for her.

In her mind she flicked her finger at his little friend, he heard her say. *"We can't here, but in the Highland if you like we can see about it then."*

Mick grabbed the door. *"You have magic like I do. Don't tease me, my little friend seems to know you."*

Angel looked into his eyes; she touched his hand. *"I believe your right, Mick what did this school do to us?"*

Mick wanted to hold hands with her. But he couldn't this was going to be hard not to make love to her. "What the hell is he thinking about sex. Then he remembered going to one of the buildings and got a hard on. He was talking to this girl she had her hand around his little friend. He remembered running into the bathroom. He took his pants down she had him inside her pussy.

Then he heard her talk to the teacher. "We will go and get our outfits on downstairs. In the bathroom there were no cameras. They went to a stall in the bathroom; he called her. *"Angel, I want to touch you, can I?"*

She had her arms around his neck. Mick put her up against the wall kissing her. A finger went into her pussy as he pumped his finger in her. When she came, he took his hand away and put that finger in his mouth. *"Your sweet, I know this taste, are you on something? I don't want to get you pregnant. I want to come inside you, I know you and I have been together more than ones with you."*

Angel took hold of him and slip him into her. He got her to come then he came. She felt his heat pump inside her. *"You are mine; I've missed you."*

She kissed him again and moved away from him. It wasn't a dream, but they had to get ready to dance. With a wave of their hands, they were dress. Up stares the teacher was wondering what happened to them. "Were sorry tights don't go on when your sweaty. We will do our worm ups first."

Mick had sign up to be team leader, the teacher put her initials next to his name. She took the paper with her. As they did the warmups, the two of them talked about what to show them. "I want the girls to know it's hard what the men do for us. Women can't be overweight; the men can't pick up women that is not the weight of a ballerina. We're not being mean to the women, we must truss the men. There is time that they could drop us if they forget the moves."

Mick went over to Angel. "She will show you the moves. Sometimes it will look as if he wasn't doing anything. For us men we must protect the girls. If the young women are overweight, it will be hard to pick her up. If they do that to much it will hart the men's back overtime.

"Angel will show you basic moves. First my hand will be on her back, she will go on tiptoes then on one leg, she will be bringing the other leg to a point. I will hold her other hand and bring her around in a circle. When she is on tiptoes, she depends on her partner to hold her in place. I will pick her up until my arms are straight. She will have one leg straight the other to the side straight. The men must always be in top form; his arms must be strong. A man that looks weak, will not get a woman to truss him in different moves."

Then Angel went over what she must do. "For the woman to help him, she must have strong stomach muscles. As he flips her over his shoulder; her job is to keep her muscles tightened. This will show him were her balance is. Don't think he can't do moves like the split, or his legs can be in a straight line as he holds his leg.

Mick and Angel did a dance with some of the moves they talked about. He had flipped her over his head she then flipped again, landing her in his arms. "If anyone like to join us, sign up for our groups. Right now, it is the endurance competition, we will pick eight to ride out of the eight we are hoping to have one for each grade. Hope to see you soon."

To the stables

Angel had gone to the horse stables first. She wanted to ride with Mick, she knew him. Did he make love to me, she had to say yes. It had kind of spooked her a bit. Hamish saw her looking over the two horses they were going to ride. "I like the way you don't take for granted, that the horse is ready to ride. I hope you will teach the freshman everything you know."

She smiled at him and told him she would. "Mick is coming over to ride with me. He is going to sign up to be team leader. We just got done with showing all the students how we dance. They're going to put it on TV for all the classes."

Hamish had seen Mick he wanted to also greet him. "Got to go see Mick, I hope the two of you will be good partners."

He went over to talk with Mick. Both men said hello. "Hello Laron and Hamish. I heard that you found out what was wrong with Sugarfoot. Yes, I know is new name."

The two men were happy to see him. "Mick, it's good to see you. Wow, you sure have filled out a lot this year. Have you decided to be a team leader?"

He smiled at them. "Yes, Laron and Hamish. Now to just wait to see if the other guys will sign up also. Tell me about the girl's team leader. Ann started to tell me until Sally came in."

Mick wanted to let them tell the story. "She didn't tell me much."

Laron was a little bit angry. "I told everyone not to tell you anything. So, what do you know?"

He knew Angel was letting out her horse. "Only she found out what was wrong with Nightmare. Laron what did Angel do?"

Mick's mind was on Angel that was wonderful. "First of all, I'm sorry Mick that I didn't believe you last year. You told me there was something wrong with Nightmare. Now we know why he was doing those things."

This story was going slow Mick thought. "Laron how did Angel get to help Nightmare?"

Hamish saw he wanted to be with Angel. "Mick, I was just thinking about that. She is quit a woman, the way that horse took off. She just sidestepped him and grabbed his mane as she swung her leg over him. She overwhelmed us. You see Nightmare was to be put down, Misty had told her father a story. He had called the school to have him put down."

Mick didn't like what he heard. "Say what…! Misty almost got her way, damn that girl. She is a lot of trouble."

That girl was trouble and evil he thought. "Mick settle down! I would like to tell this story to you. Nightmare must have known what we were going to do. He was heading for Angel. She was right in his way. What she did was sidestep him and grab his mane. Then she swung her leg over his bare back. How Angel did it. I don't no. Nightmare was running full out."

Then Mick remembered a time were a young girl stopped a horse that was trying to run away. *"Angel what the hell were you thinking of? That horse could have killed you. You feared that gate. Why not the horse coming at you? I know you have done it before. I can't lose you."*

Angel took a breath, he knew she didn't want to talk about that. *"Mick, I like those pants on you. It makes your butt look hot. At the fair that shirt didn't show me that you have muscles. A part of me don't remember how we looked. We are both older, I think I've missed a year. Mick, at times things scare me, it shows that I'm still young. I don't like to be locked up, I been remembering little things. Like a stuff mouse, it's Mickey Mouse. Mick, does that mean anything to you? I gave you Mickey the day after you kissed me. Will you kiss me again? If only I could remember our names, why does my head hurt?"*

That had done it for him. "I got to go, we will talk leter."

Mick knew she was in trouble. He called her. *"Angel stops trying to remember our damn names. You will lose everything you have remembered."*

He had open the gate and got on the horse quickly. *"Mick, I'm sorry about being scared at the gate. I don't know why your voice makes everything better. I got to get out of here, I'll be back."*

Mick needed to go after her. He knew what she was talking about. He had started to remember things about Angel. When he tried to remember their names, he lost everything. The spell that was put on him, it restarts as if it was the first day. Mick knew she been in his life for a long time. *"No… Angel don't go. Please…! Damn it… stop trying to think of our names. We know that we been together for a long time. Why can't you just take what we remember as it comes along? Stop trying to remember your name. I remember Micky Mouse, don't let our names take you away from me again."*

CHAPTER NINETEEN

Afraid to lose Angel

ANGEL OPENED THE gate and led Sugarfoot out. She called out and said. "Laron, I sign out Sugarfoot, see you in a bit."

Mick thought she would wait for him. He saw her get on Sugarfoot and ride off. "Angel, I have someone I like for you to meet. Don't go."

Mick went to follow her, Hamish thought something had happened. "Laron, that's okay, I know Angel from the Highland Games. I'll go after Angel; I'm signing out Lightning."

Mick ran to get Lightning. He could feel that she was still trying to remember their names. *"Angel, you got to stop thinking who we are. The magic spell is strong; it will start your memory over. Everything you know will be gone. I remember Mickey Mouse and I'm remembering what you ment to me. That first kiss lit me on fire, you knew what you wanted. What you did wasn't from a young girl. You thought of everything right down to the pills. I remember that you wanted my cross and rose. Angel, you're my mate, please don't think of our names. I have you here with me again. Angel, talk to me please, don't take your mind far away from me again."*

Mick opened the gate and closed it behind him. He took off as fast as Lightning could go. Something was wrong, she had stopped talking to him. *"Angel, I would do anything for you. Do you really like my pants? I love everything about you, your breasts are bigger than before. Those pants you have on make you look sexy. Angel talked to me."*

It was scaring him; he thought could that spell take away are ability? Then we can't talk to each other in our minds. "Why did she try to think who we are. I hate this, why do we have to be in this school? I just got her back and now I might lose her again. *"Angel where are you, please tell me where you're at. You're scaring me. Angel…!"*

*   *   *

She was setting on a rock near a stream. He got off Lightning and went over to her. She was crying, now he was panicking.

Did the spell restart on her? "Hello Angel."

She got up and ran right into Mick's arms. He wrapped his arms around her and thought, is she still with him? At least she trusts him. He told himself to relax, maybe it didn't go as far as it did with him. "Angel are you, all right?"

She looked at him, a part of herself knew who he was. "I don't know where I am?"

She looked up at Mick. Her eyes looked lost, but she didn't step away from him. "Angel, do you know me?"

As she held on to this handsome man, she felt safe in his arms. "Yes, you are Mick. I dance with you at the fairgrounds. We had something to eat together. You took me on some rides there."

Angel was still holding on to him. "Is that all you remember?"

She knew he was worried about her. He was so gentle with her, his body felt good. Why does she want to kiss him? "What I remember, I had a headache. It was getting worse, I tried to remember something. Until I heard the voice, I've heard this voice before. The day I saw those big gates, I remember screaming in my mind. He told me then; it wasn't a bad school. Now he told me to stop trying to remember our real names. Mick, why can't we know are names."

Angel laid her head back on his shoulder. His hand brushed over her hair. She had felt when he tried to swallow. *"Mick please kiss me. I feel so last, make it go away."*

Angel looked up at him and closed her eyes. Mick bent his head and laid a soft kiss on her lips. She pulled his head back down to her lips. She opened and he took the kiss deeper. She heard him say, *"I love you, Angel. Right now, our names mean nothing. Just you and me, we must stay here for a while. Angel, I want to be one with you. I can't right now. Your taking my defenses down, my little friend would like to be with your girlfriend."*

She looked at him and remembered feeling something slip inside her pussy. "Angel let go, I have to put some distance between us."

Mick tried not to hurt her, but she wouldn't let go of him. She grabbed his hand and pulled him along with her. "No… you come with me right now."

Behind some bushes she took him. Not letting go of him, she pulled him down when her. He saw her wave her hand and felt a bubble was around them. "Angel, do you know what you're doing to me?"

She waved her hand again; there was a blanket under them. Then there pants were gone and his heat so close to her pussy. "Damn its woman, how can I say no to you. Angel, I want you so bad, all right you said you're on the pill. Thank heaven, I don't want to stop him from doing this with your girlfriend."

He pulled down her blouse and took her nipple. She arched her hips and brought his heat closer to her. His head popped up, her fingers pushed his bottom down to her pussy. The hunger was there as he became one with her. They took what the two of them needed, she knew he was her mate, and she needed to be one with him. This what he needed, as he brought her up until he felt her come. He came right after her. "Angel."

He kissed her lips and neck and turned her over on top of him. She sat up slowly and felt his heat go deeper inside her. Then she heard another horse. "Someone is coming."

They waved their hands together; they were clean and dressed. They were sitting on the rock when Hamish came up to them. "Hay you to is everything all right here."

They got up and walked over to him. "I'm sorry Hamish. The things we must do, just because of Misty. I got a little overwhelmed, the two of us feel like we know each other. I was trying to remember our names. Come to think about it, the more I thought about our names. The more my head hurt, I wanted to know who he was. Our dance moves were flawless, we just knew what we had to show them. Thinking about are names gave me a headache. I know Mick, we been dancing for a long time. I knew him and trusted him with my life. Some of the moves we did, I could have gotten hurt bad. I tried to remember our family, were we lived and who we were. Faces went out the window along with names. I remember dance movements, with this young man. He was tall like Mick. I hope that you won't keep us apart, the two of us didn't ask to be here. But we can help the two schools.

*　　*　　*

Hamish smiled at them. "I thought you knew each other, you can remember something. Like you said, names went out the window, your secret is safe with me. Come on, it's time to go back."

The three of them went back to the stables, Mick and Angel worked together. She had taken the saddles off, and he put them away. *"Mick, do you think he will keep are secret?"*

Mick had just put away the last saddle. *"I believe he will, Hamish watch over all of us. Some time he doesn't catch everything. Like the time he was out when Misty had Sugarfoot have new shoes put on him."*

Angel thought about what he said. *"If you think he will keep are secret, I will forget about him for now."*

That part is done, now to see if she would like to go on a date this weekend. *"Angel, would you like to go on a date with me this weekend?"*

She looked over the horse's back. *"I would love to go somewhere with you. Did you know that Angela like Bill."*

Mick smiled. *"I remember a bit of what happen. I was glad that they brought in Angela to look after you. I heard Bill talking with Raymond. He wanted to see if he should talk with the officer. He told him no that it would cause more trouble than it was worth. I heard him say that was strong magic for me to go to your side."*

She thought that was why she asked him to give her his cross and rose. *"Angel what did you remember?"*

Mick knew she remembered something about the night he gave her his cross and rose. *"You remember the first night we made love."*

Angel had a big smile. *"You caught me thinking about that night. Mick, this is my second day, and I don't want to be here. I would like to be on an island just you and me."*

Then Mick saw Hamish. "Hello you two. Laron wants to know when you like to do the endurance competition."

Angel thought about it. "The juniors are coming back tomorrow. It must be done tomorrow; the next class is seniors. All three horses have been brushed."

Hamish knew they didn't want Misty there. He looked at Angel's face, she looked worried. Even Mick had the same look. They're afraid that someone will tell Misty what the school has been up to.

The two of them went out the gate. "Angel, would you like to eat with me tonight. Then we can go to the library and check on some of the books for ballet.

She was just thinking about food. "How did you know I was hungry?"

Mick wanted to make her smile, he knew she had felt something. "You are always hungry after exercising."

She looked at him and giggled, she knew what he ment. "That sound like a plan, it should be around lunch time."

The principles are putting their foot down

As soon as they left, the boys came down to sign up for the competition. They had seen the two of them dancing. It was on the school's TV. The two principles spoke the list that they will go by on TV. They told them that Mick and Angel will also be team leaders for competition. Both students are in college, and a teacher will put her initials next to your name. I will have a copy of the list. I found out that they were a teacher assistant for three years. Angel is a horse whisper she will teach you how to take care of the horse you will ride.

In the lunchroom, the TV was on, they saw themself dancing together. They had went over to get their food. There wasn't anyone in the lunchroom, it was nice to set together to eat. As they ate Mick then looked at her. "So, when are you going to tell me, about your vision?"

Angel had forgotten Mick knew when she had a vision. "Tomorrow Misty will be here at school. There is a question on whether she passed last year. If she didn't take summer classes, she will repeat the grade."

Mick took a breath, and in his mind he swore. In Angel's mind she said thanks for that. I still had to hear you swear. "Sorry, were will she pop up?"

Angel took some of her food. "It will be at the swimming pool. I don't want you involved; it will be better if I handle this. Girl against girl goes better then boy against girl. Like when you were dancing with her, she said it was your fault. Yes…, I heard about it from Angela. It's a good thing that you had a teacher watching you two."

Mick looked at her, he knew she kept an eye on him. "I hate to see you tangle with evil. Watch out for her eyes. Marcos might give her more magic."

Angel looked at him. "Don't worry about me. Raymond told us that her magic isn't that strong. He was able to brush it away from him. She would think that she will be dealing with you. It will catch her off guard. Come on, let's go look at some of the books on ballet."

Mick took her hand. *"Angel tonight I want you to think of me. I will be at the waterfall sitting on a big boulder across the water. There we can be together; will you try to meet me there?"*

She smiled at him, how she loved this man. *"I will try again if we can't go to the waterfall. I'll have to talk with Raymond on this subject."*

Now what

They walked to the library; on the steps they saw two girls and two boys. *"Mick, do you see the girl that is trying to keep the group from running over to us."*

Mick could see she trying to be a helper to Angel. *"Is she the one that has her arms out trying to stop them from running over to us?"*

When they were close enough to them. The two of them said together. "Sit down we will be there in a minute."

The two of them walk to the building. "Will now we have a group wanting to talk to us."

They watched Angel and Mick. The two of them, walked in sync with each other. One of the boys spoke. "That's Angel, wow she's hot looking."

He saw one of the girls speak. "Micks hot looking, he has a nice bottom.

Angel had to laugh. "It seems we have fans, were both hot looking."

He had to chuckle. "I have a feeling they want to know if we know each other. Are dancing was flawless so we would have to know each other, for us to do what we did."

The group watched them walk very close to each other; Bunny waved at Angel. "Who is that young girl, she seems to know you?"

Angel had waved back at her. "She is my roommate, I believe she was the one to organize this group."

The two of them went over to the group. Mick spoke "I know the young man who is Jim. How he hated Misty and still does."

Jim was going to stand up when Bunny told him. "Jim don't get into their face. Angel won't take it. Can't you see Mick and Angel are on guard? Their body language tells me."

Jim turns to her. "What the hell do you think you are, miss know it all."

Bunny didn't like this boy the way he was acting. "I have six brothers, there all different. I learned their body language to try to keep a head of them. Shut up and set down."

Jim stood up and looked down at her. Mick bellow. "Set down Jim, are you going to start trouble."

He sat down hard, with his hand cross. "Bunny."

That is all Angel said, when she spoke. Bunny sat right down. The other two looked at each other. Angel spoke. "Enough Jim if you want to be in the dancing group or the endurance competition. Keep your mouth close, I will not have any swearing or talking down to anyone. If you don't want to be black ball from the competition you will learn to keep a civil tongue in your mouth.

Then the girl in the back raised her hand. "Yes…, I don't know your name miss."

She stood up. "They call me Lilly. I want you to know that Misty has stayed back. She will be here tomorrow. How I know this, my brother is Cal. He knows Hawkeye they been friends for a long time."

Jim slammed his fist down. "Damn it, we are going to be stuck with her for two more years. Hell no, I don't want to be in the same room as her. I'm not going through that again."

Jim got up and was heading to the boy's side. Angel went over to him; she had the cross and rose in her hand. Then she tapped the back of his head. Jim stopped; he had balled his fist up. He shook his head, as if trying to clear his mind. There was something going on with him. Mick was ready to step in front of Angel. She called him. *"Mick stand down, I got this. Is he one of them that Misty could manipulate."*

Mick looked at him and thought about it. "I think he's, her gofer. He is always listening to people's conversation."

Jim held his head, then spoke. "Get out of my mind Misty. No, I will not be your gofer anymore. They freed me from you. Goodbye."

He had turned to face Angel. "I don't know what happened but thank you. I always tried to fight her but couldn't. On summer camp, one of the counselors talked to me. I started to feel better about myself, I didn't have to be one that was a gofer."

Angel then went over to him. "I'm gladded that had helped, here is something else to let you know when evil is around. It will help you to get away from that evil person."

She had come up with a silver cross. Angel had place a rose on it, but you couldn't see it. "Keep this on you at all times. You're a person that evil liked to manipulate if it goes hot get out of there. You should be all right from here on. You don't have to show the cross, keep it covered."

Angel waved her hand, and the cross went into his skin. Jim smiled, the boy seemed to be lighter then air. He went back to the boy's side. "Angel how did you know he was Misty's gofer."

Lilly was amaze what had happened. "Will you do to me as you did to him. I feel like I'm always around evil."

Mick smiled at her; he went over to her. "We can help you three.

He touched the back of her head. "I have a question for the three of you. Do you believe in magic?"

Lilly looked at him. "I knew it, the two of you have magic."

Mick smiled at her. "A dear friend had given this to us. This is all I can do; he told me that evil is around us more. Evil uses drugs, to control the people. They now know how to get into someone's mind. They found out it was easier to do it when the person was asleep. I have some of the guys who have been helping me, to put a magical cross there is a rose on it.

This rose has magic. "You can take a cross I will give you and place it on the back of their head. It has be blessed, it's a way to save people that don't have a high IQ or are simple minded. They are the ones that evil goes after."

Randy was a freshman, he didn't know what to think of all of this. "This girl Misty she sounds scary. What you done for Jim, would you do that to me?"

Angel went over to him and touched the back of his head. She then gave him a cross on his chest. "This one you don't have to keep it hidden. It's a part of you. Now you're safe from evil, if you need help with homework we will be at this library. Go sign up for what you like to do."

Mick took care of Lilly, then the girls went back to their dormitory. "We're going to our room. Tomorrow you are going to do the race. Misty is going to be here, will keep an eye out for her.

Angel looked at Mick. "I'm going to my room; I want to take a shower and go to bed. I want food and a little time to wake up before we race tomorrow. Us on TV is going to run until everyone is back at school. I'm going to tell Angela we are doing the competition after we eat. I want everyone to keep their eyes open for Misty."

The big race

Angel got everything ready that night. She took her shower and went to bed. In the morning, she was up before anyone got up.

She met Mick for breakfast. "Hello Angel. Did you sleep all right last night?"

Angel felt eerie as she was rubbing her hands over her fingers. "No…! I don't remember if I even dreamed, I'm sorry about that. Maybe I was trying too hard. Mick, I don't know why I'm so upset about things. The TV was on, and the principal had that show on a loop. She will get the word out about us."

Mick knew how she felt. "It's all right, Angel. Come on, wright, get some food. Just remember. It should be a lite breakfast. We're going to be running and swimming."

She looked at him, last night she had told Angela that she was worried. What will Misty do when she finds out everything she has done has been changed. "Mick we can go there after an hour. I just didn't want to be around the juniors. Then she thought, no Misty's friends would be seniors. They will come here, the next day. Can you remember if Misty was mean to the lower classmen?"

Mick thought about it. "Hawkeye told me last year. Misty's grades are not good, she been a royal bitch to the sophomore. When I had cut her off helping her with her homework. If she stays back the seniors won't stay around her. Last year the sophomores will be moving up. They will be the new juniors."

Now she felt so much better. The two of them went to get his riding boots. They came to a group of juniors that were signing up for their classes. "Hay Mick is that, Angel. I want you to know that we appreciate you, Mick. Even though we couldn't do any dancing you still helped us out. We heard you two are going to do the first race. I heard that many of the guys will sign up for your class."

Mick was so happy, many of them had the cross and rose on the back of their head. "Thanks guys, I want you to meet Angel. We don't remember are name, but we been friends for a long time. As children she showed me all the dances she learned. She was my teacher it helped me in karate. Even the football players told me it helped them when they played football."

Angel smiled at Mick. "What he hasn't told you, those guys wanted to know how he lifts me so easy. That's when he started a program of lifting weights and had them running every day. Mick started that a girl can't be overweight. The day I got here and came to sign up, the teacher asked me all these questions. Without knowing, I had backed up what he had requested. We will start with a big group, then we will pick out the best of all of you. Two from each grade, the once that don't make the best will be backups."

Angel then spoke in her mind. *"Mick, get your boots, we got to go."*

Mick nodded his head. *"I will get my boots, go on and get the horses ready for us."*

Mick then said to the guys. "I must get my riding boot. Angel will be getting Sugarfoot and Lightning ready for us. I know Laron is going to set me up. Hamish lets him have his fun."

Then she saw Bunny, Mary, and Rose with a few of the new juniors. "Angel there you are…, Angela told us to go help you. She wanted to make sure Misty didn't interfere with your run."

The girls looked at the boys, she saw some of them liked their looks. "Did any of you sign up for ballet?"

Laron tried to embarrass Mick it backfires

The boys said yes. "Bunny told them they were going to help set up the route for the competition."

Mick got his boots and headed out the back door. Angel was there getting the horses ready to ride.

He had gotten over to the stables there was Laron. He could see Hamish was helping Angel with the horses. He knew Laron was going to embarrass him. The group had found out that the two of them had left. They had gone looking for them.

Mick was hoping to go help Angel. However, Laron wanted to finish his story. "Laron, I know you want to embarrass me. I know you're going to tell me that Angel has a nice package. I know she is beautiful and that she is not bossy. She is nothing like Misty, she is true to her friends. Angel loves animals, yes if a horse was in danger. She wouldn't think twice to help him. She has long strong legs and a big heart. Right now, I want to help them. It's time for are race, not telling stories."

Mick went passed him to put up his shoes. Hamish smiled and bit his lip. But couldn't hold in a laugh. Mick when to help with the horses. Hamish pat Mick on the back. "You got him good, I know it would take someone like you to get him back."

Mick looked at him. "Is that what I did. I just wanted to help Angel with the horses. I'm sorry I did that to him; I just need to help her."

He saw her checking out their feet. "I've gone over their legs, they look good. Shall we get this race on? The bikes are all good, I don't want any trouble. The path is where there could be an ambush from Misty. There are a lot of people here today."

Mick was proud of her. "Angel you're a beautiful woman with a slender body. Her height matches quite nicely with me. Her face is of an Angel, with rosy lips and beautiful eyes. Those eyes, a man could drown in those bluish green eyes. To top her looks off she has long golden-brown hair. I love your ponytail."

The race will begins

Hamish called the principals to send the word out. Mick and Angel were doing the endurance competition. The boys that would like to sign up were there. More of the girls came out, same with the boys. The two riders rode side by side, the girls and boys yelled. "They can beat the other school time."

They were lining up along the trail to watch the race. Everyone knew these two were good at everything they did. They had to beat the other school's time. It was on camera; this was to prove that their time was right. The two schools hid their faces; they could only see the horse or what they were riding.

Then they heard Laron say. "Back up kids, the race is going to start. Angel and Mick, you will end up at the swimming pool. My men will be timing you two.

"Listen up everyone. As soon as they are ready, we will start. From this point on. The teachers are the only ones to talk to them. They will give them water; this is an endurance competition. They are going through to the end."

Angel closed her eyes. The two were focusing their energy between each other, they were as one.

Laron walked over to where they could see him. "Good Luck, are you both ready? Make your schools proud, we need you to take the other schools down."

They looked at each other and nodded. "On your mark, get set. GO…go!"

The horses were off in a flash. Laron watched the two of them go around the court quickly together. When they came to the gates. He never saw two teammates in sync with each other. The horse's hoofs flew over the gates without touching. One after another, they cleared the gates. The horses flew like the wind to the finish line.

The schoolmates yelled. "They did it, Angel and Mick did it."

They had fifteen minutes to rest and got changed. The next run was bicycling. Angel put her hat on. She wore a light-yellow top and a navy-blue pair of shorts. She had her hair in a long braid. It went down the middle of her back. When Mick looked up from putting his shoes on.

He stopped and stared at Angel. *"Wow…! How long has it been? My God she is beautiful. Wow…! What a woman."*

Then he heard. *"Thank you, Mick. Your quit hot yourself."*

There was no time to think when Mick heard. "10, 9, 8, 7, 6, 5, 4, 3, 2, 1."

All the schoolmates chime in. "Get to your bicycles, ready set. GO…go!"

The two of them where off. They were on the path to the racetrack. The next run would be the Relay Race. Mick was in the back of Angel. He just couldn't help himself. In his thoughts all he said was. *"Wow…! My woman has a nice bottom."*

Mick understood why Laron commented about her legs. He was a lucky man to have a woman like her. "I know all about those legs of hers. When there around me I will do anything for her. This weekend I want to have that sweet derriere and my little friend inside her. Then he saw Angel look back at him. She motioned him to come up beside her. Mick knew his thoughts got away from him. *Sorry about that honey, I met what I said.*

He saw that the path was wide enough for the two of them. She also wanted what he wanted. All she said. *"Mick you're on, do you know of a nice place to be together as one."*

Then she heard Mick's voice. *"Yes, I do know a place, Angel. But don't slow down, we have no time to think like that. Just to do what we set out to do."*

Angel looked over at him. *"You started this, I just finish it."*

They made it to the track. The teacher was Scott Friedrich. Once Mick and Angel sat down. Scott handed them both a bottle of water. "You have fifteen minutes. Change your shoes and catch your breath."

The two drink the water down. "Angel how do you want to play this?"

She thought about it. "I want you to go first. You're better with passing things to me. Your arms are longer than mine. When you pass the baton to me. I have a long stride then you do. I'll bring it home."

Mick understood what she meant. He hasn't seen Angel run in over a year. He knew she was fast. I'm remembering things. A nice slim body and long legs. Yes, she was right for him to go first. Both schools were cheering them on. The two school's new Mick was fast. They were hoping that Angel was just as fast, he gave her a smile. "Times up, who goes first?"

Mick stood up. "I will go first."

Then she heard him in her mind. *"Angel when the time comes. I'll get that baton into your hand. I know that you will bring it home for are schools.*

He was ready and nodded his head to go. In Angel's mine she said. *"Good luck Mick."*

The teacher asked him. "Mick, are you ready?"

He nodded his head. "All right get set. GO…go!"

Angel watched Mick take off. He was a tiger running down his prey. She could feel her whole body getting in tune with his. Her mine focused on his hand. All she could see was his hand and the baton. Angel could mentally picture herself taking the baton. She felt the power between them. They were as one, Mick saw her hand. The pass went flawless, as they had yelled for Mick. They all yelled even harder for Angel. "Go Angel go…!"

It was in her hand, and she was running at top speed in seconds. Mick was gasping for air. It didn't matter. He had to watch Angel run. The power in her legs made him think of a cheetah. Angel moved gracefully through the air. In the blink of an eye, she had run past Mick. She turned and walked slowly over to him. Angel dropped to her knees beside him. Scott brought them each a bottle of water. He watched Angel breathing slowly and smiled. The two of them drunk deeply of their water. They had twenty minutes to change their shoes. The two schools were yelling they had seen so far, they were beating the other school.

After drinking their water and changing their shoes again. The two of them didn't have to say anything to each other. It was an easy jog to the swimming pool.

*   *   *

Mick remembered more as the two of them jogged together. Last year was hell for him. He hoped that Misty would stay out of their lives. He knew at the end of school. He had felt the cross get a little hot. No time to think about it. They were at the building.

Miss Rosemary Stover was waiting for them. She ran this building for both schools. A bottle of water was place in their hand. As they ran up the stairs. Angel watched Mick as he took off his shirt. In her thoughts all she could come up with was. *"Wow...! You're stronger now. I felt it when you left me when we dance."*

She had to stop thinking. Angel slipped off her shorts and top. She had on her swimsuit under her clothes. Mick had a hard time when he saw Angel slender body. He couldn't say or do anything with their classmate watching. Only Angel saw his mouth drop open.

She did hear him say. *"Wow...! You have blossomed into a beautiful woman."*

Mick couldn't remember when he saw such a beautiful woman before. Angels knew their bodies had changed, even with they made love they didn't realize the changes. *"Mick, are you going to be all right when I take off my shirt and shorts."*

He shook his head. Angel saw his cheeks turn pink. As he fought with his shoelaces. *"Mick, you and I will have to talk this weekend."*

Mick bit his lip and thought. *"No..., talking at first. I want to play with my toys. When I have touch all your body then we can talk."*

Angel walked over to the edge of the pool. She had to focus on her breathing. She was trying to get herself ready. She dipped her hand into the cool water. Angel wet her neck and under her arms. Mick was doing the same. Each time the two of them could feel the power between them. With her eyes close she felt her body was mentally and fiscally in tune with Mick. There was no time to ask Mick what was happening to them.

Rosemary had called out. "Times up."

The two of them stood up. They walked over to take their positions. The other teachers had their scores and stopwatches. "The rules are as follow. First the two of you will swim underwater. When you push off the wall. You will be swimming on top of the surface. Angel and Mick. Good luck. On your mark. Get set. GO…go!"

Together they dove into the water. Angel was moving the fastest. She was the first to push off the wall. She knew Mick would be coming fast, his power was in his arms. Angel's lead was going fast. She had to hold this small lead. At the last minute. They were neck to neck. It felt like magic. The moment their hand reached out at the same time. Rosemary called out at the time. In swimming they beat the other school's time. Both principals were there at the pool, they had to be a final witness to their swimming time.

All their classmates were yelling "They're the best."

When each teacher called there times out. The classmate found out that Angel and Mick beat all the other schools scores.

Mick had swam over to Angel. He knew that Misty wouldn't be able to take Angel's place now. *"Come on, we need the hot tub. Then you can take a shower to wash up."*

The hot tub felt so good on her sore body. "Mick that was a workout, I run five miles daily. I don't miss a day most of the time. This hot tub feels so good."

Mick loved this woman, he knew she was his mate. When he made love to her and gave her his cross and rose. He knew he would marry her. "Angel come over here, I'll rub your shoulders then send you to the showers. Then you can go back to your room and take a nap."

Angel was so happy to be here with him. "Your turn for a shoulder rub Mick. We pushed ourselves hard. Next time we will have everything down pat. Thank you Angel for being my partner. It's time for you to get to the showers."

Mick got to his feet. He helped Angel out of the tub. "I feel like a rag doll."

She smiled at him. "Angel, thank you for being my partner. We have just two months to get four more teams ready. Do you think we can do this?"

She smiled at him. "I believe we can, but it's time to hit the showers there calling to us. More hot water hear I come."

Mick took her hand. "Be careful Angel, something is going on with Misty. I think evil has taken her over completely. I don't know if she will be given more powers. Now go get in your shower."

Angel was remembering her dream. She had to get in there and out, she didn't want Mick fighting with Misty. She knew she would do something to make it look like he hit her.

Angel faces Misty

The shower felt so good, she had stayed under the water to long. Then her cross started to get hot. With a wave of her hand, she was out of the shower and was dress. She heard yelling from the pool area. The voice sounded like Mick. The other voice sound gruff like a man. Mick wasn't happy with what was going on. Why was a man yelling at Mick? Angel peeked around the corner. There in front of Mick was a big boy. He had a short haircut. The haircut was cut like an old man. Then Angel saw that he was her. An evil woman who talks like a man. Angel saw Mick, he was as tired as she was.

In the bathroom she pictures Mick and sent him outside. Angel heard him swearing. *"You can't take her on like this."*

How she loved him, this was her time to deal with Misty. *"But I can, Mick, don't try to get in here. I'm putting a bubble up; Mick I had taken on Marcus and sent him back to hell. Misty is panicking, I just put the cross and rose on the back of her head.*

Mick's fists pounded the door. *"Angel don't do this she could hurt you."*

Misty goes down

She was walking over to Misty. Her head wasn't facing Angel. In her hand was the cross and rose. She sent it to the back of her head. Misty turned to face her attacker. "Hello Misty, I took Mick out of the picture. I also gave you something, sorry if it's burning your head. You're not going to have him. Why did you do that to yourself, you look like and old man."

Misty had turned around; her hand was rubbing the back of her head. "Who are you, how dare you take my partner from me."

Misty was walking toward Angel. "He never was your partner. Mick is my mate, we been together for a long time. You're not strong enough to be his mate, I will fight for him.

The bubble held Mick out and Misty in. She had it that no one could see them or hear them. "If you think your master will hand him to you, think again. I've sent Marcus back to hell before. She saw that Misty Eyes was trying to get her to do something.

Angel laughed at her. "Misty you better do better than that. Your IQ is very low, I'm tired of this game you play. Things have change, the schools like winning. You're not a ballerina, and the horse you had rode is not any where's you can get to him. Besides the horse you wanted to have killed I had stopped it."

Misty was getting madder by the minute; she could see her blood pressure was going up. "Are we getting mad, your face is very red, you could have a heart attack. There you go with your eyes; I had enough with you. Stop now before I let go on you."

Angel tried to get her to stop before she had to use the mirror. When Misty was at that peek with her eyes. Angel brought up a mirror. What Misty saw was herself, a demon was trying to get back in her. She grabbed her head and screamed again.

Angel had taken down the bubble and put it around herself. Misty kept screaming, then yelled "they're going to kill me. I fail to get Mick's soul."

Angel saw Rosemary come out and she had her phone with her. She didn't see the three demons, but Angel did. The demons took Misty to the edge of the pool. There they push her into the pool. The teacher was telling the principal what was happening. Then she saw the door open, and two guards came into the pool area. Rosemary told them she's in the pool; she never came up. The men dove in; they were having trouble getting Misty to the surface. The ambulance came and the men helped to get her out of the pool. They put her on the gurney and got her into the ambulance. One man was bagging the patient. They had to zap her with the paddles. Now one saw what had happen.

The mystery woman

Rosemary heard the scream; she had seen it was Misty. Quickly she called the principal, in minutes two guards came into the pool area. Rosemary saw there was something pulling her into the pool. The cross and rose had pushed the demon out. Angel saw she held on to her, then two more demons appeared. The first demon hit her she fell into the water; she was under the water for a long time. Two guards dive into the water; they found it hard to pull her up.

The guards told the principal under the water they felt hands trying to break their grip. When they came up with her. Rosemary saw she had a wig on her, her clothes had things to make her look fat. Angel had seen those demons. The woman that came up was not Misty. They took her soul and placed a new person in her body. What Angel saw was a beautiful woman, her hair was still black. The wig had disguise her, there was a new Misty. All the fake clothes were taken off her. They moved quickly to get her into the ambulance she wasn't breathing.

Angel had seen what happened, everything Misty said was true. She had to get out of there; she slipped out of the back door. No one saw her come out of the building. Then she saw Mick and went over to him. She had pulled him into her bubble. "Angel why did you do that; I didn't want you to get involved with her."

Angel thought how to tell him Misty was dead. "Mick don't say anything until I'm done telling you what happen. After I sent you away, I put a bubble up. Misty didn't turn around; I saw an opportunity to send a cross and rose at the back of her head. Misty started to do her thing with her eyes. I heard in my mind that I would kill Mick."

"She got mad when I laughed at her, that made her angry. Her face was red; I thought she could have had a heart attack. She was getting out of control when her eyes were at their peak. I brought up a mirror, she screamed then she said their going to kill me. I didn't get Mick's soul. The demon who held on to her after she came out of her. She had spun Misty around. She got her close to the edge of the pool. Two more demons appeared they manhandled her. The girl hit Misty, she took her into the water with the two demons. The guards told the principal in the water; they felt other hands trying to pull their hands off Misty. When we got her up, they saw a wig on her and the clothes were something to make her fat. The knew Misty had black hair and her face was not gruff looking. With all those wet clothes off her she was thin and pretty.

Mick and Angel heard, in their minds. *"It's too bad that you didn't stay out of its Angel. I knew he wouldn't work with Misty. You both will pay for what the two of you did."*

After they head that Message the bubble was gone. Bill and Angela came over to them. Bill spoke. "I want you two to come with us."

They took them to the lunchroom. "Mick did you hear what I heard, was that Marcus."

Mick nodded his head yes. Bill spoke. "What happen, you two look like you saw a ghost."

Angel then looked at Bill. "I saw the ghost and heard him. It was Marcus, the two of us has taken down the people that came after us. Francis was sent to a sanitarium. Misty was brought down to hell. She was replace with a girl prettier then Misty."

Marcus has planned to get us back. The dream I had was three boys going after Mick. I was trying to keep him safe by putting a bubble around him. It had drain my energy, for I didn't have magic at the time. I can't tell you when or how."

CHAPTER TWENTY

A Shield Around Mick

THE NEXT DAY Angel woke up to her nightmare. She noticed she wasn't in the room she was assigned to. She saw Angela, she was sleeping on a cot near her. Then she saw a nurse doing something next to her, she was in the hospital. There intravenous fluids, being pumped back into her body. Angel saw a nurse changing the bag. Angela got up. "Can you tell me how she is doing?"

The Nurse took Angel's vitals. "Her temperature is still high; she is going through the fluids as fast as we can replace the bag. We went to a bigger bag."

Angel could feel that Angela was scared for her. She called Mick, she couldn't hear him. Why was she in the hospital? She told herself to think of why she was here. That night Angel tried to dream of Mick. He told her that he sat on a big rock at the waterfall. There will be green grass nearby. She couldn't get any picture of Mick; Angel could only see darkness. There was no sunlight anywhere. Then she felt someone was in trouble, who could be in trouble? How could I see when it's pitch-black?

It kept popping up in her thoughts. She then felt evil through the darkness. She understood why she couldn't dream of him. Mick was in trouble; Angel placed a hand on her chest, which is where Mick's cross and rose was. He had given her it after they made love, she was now his mate. They were trying to stop me from helping him. "Mick…, *show me where you are, danger is coming after you.*

She tried to cry but couldn't, no tears would come. Something was wrong, she felt so week. In her dream Mick was heading to the gym to lift some weights. The hallway he went down had a room to the right. Angel saw three men coming quickly behind him. They had evil inside them, demons that would kill for money. They were using the senior's bodies to kill or main Mick. She woke up quickly, it was when the seniors were coming back.

The time was 6:00. Angel got dressed and ran to the principal's office. She rang the bell then pounded on the door. *"Please open the door I need help."*

Principal Tensaw came to the door. "Who is it?"

Angel felt hot inside her body she dismissed it; she told herself it was a hot day. "It's Angel, Principal Tensaw I need to speak to you. It's very important, it's about Mick."

Her voice sounded as if she was scared. "Angel come on in, tell me why."

When the door opened, she ran into her arms. Principal Tensaw could feel that she was hot to the touch. "Angel, take a breath here drink this water. Now sit and tell me why you're so scared."

Angel drank the water down. "It's about Mick. I had a dream that three seniors were going to beat Mick up this morning. He was going down the hallway to the gym. There is a room off to the right. Two of them grabbed him. The other one punches him in his side. He had something on his knuckles. The third man grabbed him around the neck. He shoved something into Mick's mouth and tied it behind his head; they place a hood over his head. All three men hit him and dragged him into the room. I felt evil was with them, these men were enjoying hurting Mick. Please, it's happening right now. Misty had gone to these three seniors; she gave them the day and time. It was to be today at this time. My dreams are never wrong."

Principal Tensaw remembered when Arthur Stanley signed up for her parents.

He had said. "If Angel ever tells you about something was going to happen. Believe her, it's a gift she has."

Mrs. Tensaw also knew Angel never was in the other School. She was able to describe that hole hallway right down to the room.

She quickly called her husband. "John, take three of the guards and go down the hallway to the gym. The room off the hallway, Mick is in trouble. Please hurry, there is not much time left. Call me when you can."

Angel had placed a magical bubble around Mick. She had to use her own energy to make the bubble, she knew it would cost her. It was Mick's life; he was fighting to stay alive. Mick's magic was blocked just like hers. They had magic but it was off their own energy. The day of the competition, someone made a magical spell that was place into the hot tub. At the time she didn't think that anything was wrong. She could use her magic, however today she couldn't.

Mr. Tensaw's wife found out that someone was in trouble, he grabbed three of the guards. The principal had his secretary call the police. The four men went quickly down the hall. The room off the hallway the door was locked. There was laughter inside. The principal told the men to break the door down. There were three seniors beating another boy up.

Bill had just came back from the hospital when Angela called him. She told him Mick was in danger; they have him down the hallway in a room just before the gym.

Mick's arms were behind him; the biggest boy was holding him. There was a hood over Mick's face. The principal noticed that the two boys were going after his legs and ribs. They were using brass knuckles; Mick was able to keep his legs moving. They notice the men wasn't that smart, they knew they were there but kept beading him. The guards had moved in quickly; they grabbed the three men. The young man had fallen to the floor. The principal went over quickly to him. He took the hood off. They even had a gag over his mouth.

Mr. Tensaw told them. "Have our secretary take the picture from this camera. The camera will activate when the door opens. Send the picture that this camera had taken along with the police. Tell them to book the three for attempted murder. Take the three brass knuckles with you."

Mick started coughing up blood. He said. "Misty paid them she had known that I wouldn't work with her. They said this was the best job Misty had given them. She doesn't want me anymore if she can't have me no one will."

Bill got around the men and went over to Mick. "The ambulance has just got here."

They checked over Mick he was having trouble breathing. He had Bill come closer to him. "Bill check on Angel, they put a spell in the hot tub. I know she is the one that helps me. They were trying to break my ribs and legs. Somehow, they took part of our magic, I couldn't use power just my energy. That is what Angel is using. I should be bleeding internally or dead. I didn't cough much blood up."

After Angela called Bill, she ran to the principal's office. Inside Angela saw Angel on the floor. An ambulance was called when they got there, they had started an intravenous fluid on her. She was dangerously dehydrated, Bill called Brandon and Raymond. He told them that three boys had beaten Mick up. Angel saved him by putting a bubble around him.

There was a spell in the hot tub, it took their magic powers from them. They had to use their energy for their magic.

Before they took the boys out of the room. Mr. Tensaw said. "It's not like you boys to do anything like this, was Misty's brother in on this?"

One of the boys said. "Her brother wouldn't think of anything like this. I don't understand, Mick should be dead. How could he stop us? We were going after every part of his body. A demon had put a spell in the hot tub."

The other boy said. "Shut up you fool! Where going to jail."

The last boy had a deep voice. Then the men laughed. "Were not going to jail, these boys are going to hell. Mick, you won this time. Misty still must kill you; the Master wants you dead. Watch your back when you get out of school."

Then the three boys dropped to the ground; all three were dead and they disappeared.

*   *   *

When they were punching him, Mick didn't feel it as much. The Men from the hospital came to get Mick. As they picked him up, he could feel the pain. Whatever was around him was getting weaker. The pain was getting more intense. Mick closed his eyes. It was Angel who saved him. Yes, he could feel a bubble around him. The bubble was getting thinner; the pain was getting stronger. When he checked on Angel his mind saw her on the floor. She was so weak that she couldn't sit on the chair anymore. *Angel takes down that bubble, before it takes you away from me for good. I need you, Angel. Please do what I ask of you.*

Mick and Angel were taken to the school's hospital. Their bodies had two big bags of IVS, what happen. Mick knew now what was happening. *Angel your dreams have come true. Honey, you got to take that bubble around me away. You're in danger of dying from dehydration.*

Take the bubble down now, let the doctor see what happened to me. Honey, I know I will pass out, take care of yourself now, I love you, Angel.

Mick felt the pain when she took down the bubble, it was so intense that he blacked out. Before the two of them collapsed they heard a voice from be on. It was Marcos and he was talking to Misty, they were laughing. *"Misty, you did good if it works, we will have five souls."*

She just looked at Marcos. Then she heard Angel. *"Misty you're dead, someone is in your body. You drowned I saw three demons who took you under the water. He's lying to you, you're in hell."*

*   *   *

Angel could hear Mick scream. Tears were trying to roll down her cheeks, there wasn't enough water to do so. She was so weak. It took a lot from her to keep that bubble around Mick. Angel was having a hard time staying awake. She had fallen off the chair onto the floor.

*   *   *

The picture had change. "She saw Raymond and Branden in a waiting room. Mick's Uncle and Bill was there; he had a bandage around his head. Mick and Angel are not doing that good.

Someone had chloroform to put Angela asleep, that's why she didn't hear Angel get up. Bill was hit over the head.

Bill then spoke. "Raymond Angel told us about her dream, everything she told us came true."

Angel couldn't do much, she used her mind to see Mick. Her brother was there; she needed to tell him that Mick is, in part of the dream world. He can't get to the sunny part where he gets his power.

Both Mick and Angel were at the hospital. She had a high fever; Angel was dehydrated and delirious. She was calling for Mick. Brandon MacGregors was called to the school hospital. When Angel collapsed.

Raymond we were also called to go to the school hospital. The doctor was with Brandon and Bill. The hospital front desk, told Raymond the doctor will be with you as soon as he can. You can wait for him in the waiting room. When Raymond went in the room, he saw Bill and Brandon. "Bill what happened to you. "I was hit over the head while I sleep. I heard something that's when I got hit over the head. They had used something to put Angela asleep.

*   *   *

Mrs. Tensaw's called her husband. She wanted to know how Mick was. "Hello John. How is Mick? Could he tell you who put them up to this?"

Mr. Tensaw spoke. "The doctor is checking him over right now. If you didn't call me when you did. Those men were trying to break his ribs and legs. Mick was fighting them the best he could. I don't know how Mick was able to stand the pain. I asked the men if Misty's brother had something to do with it. They said No."

Then she heard Mick. "My God is that Mick screaming? Poor Mick. Dear just because Hawkeye is Misty twin doesn't mean he is as evil as her."

He thought about what she said. "Oh, dear whatever had saved him. Just stopped blocking the pain. Mick just blacked out."

Then she heard a thump. "John holds on. I heard something, John, you better get someone over here. Angel just fell off the chair, she is burning up. John, I believe that Angel, is more involved than we thought. She was the one that dreamt Mick was in trouble. She saved him; there is more then we know. I must go, there here to get Angel."

Mr. Tensaw's wondered how they could do what they had done. "How could she do that?"

She thought the same thing. "I don't know. We must keep this quiet for now."

When she hung up, she thought. "I believe, she was the one helping Mick stay alive. I'll try to keep Angel out of this. All I know Scotland is full of Magic."

Raymond knew what was going on. "Mick was attacked that's why you're here; Angel was the one who saved Mick."

That damn officer Raymond thought. The kids were safe at home. "Misty had three seniors trying to kill him. Those boys were demons; they had died after their job was done. The way the doctor spoke Mick should be dead. They worked on his ribs, stomach, and legs. The bruises are there, not the damage."

The doctor came in and talked to Raymond. "Angel has a dangers' high fever. As fast as we get her intravenous fluids into her. Her body is burning the fluids up just as fast. The fever keeps her dehydrated. She's delirious because of the fever. What I don't understand is her calling for Mick. There is something about the two of them. Mick should have been killed; something put a bubble around him. All his bones were saved, his muscles have some damage, Mick skin tells a different story. There're bruises he has; these bruises show me there should be internal bleeding. There weren't any, we don't understand what could have save him.

"Now we have Angel, her body with through a lot. She used up a good part of her fluids in her body. If we don't get the fluids back up, her body will begin to shut down. If I didn't know better. I would say this had to be magic, I've never seen it before. My grandmother had spoken of it."

Raymond waved his hand; the doctor had been paused. "Do not say this to anyone else." He waved his hand again. "Thank you, do what you can for her doctor."

*   *   *

Brandon was making himself a cup of coffee. When Raymond came back in. He waved his hand, and the room became a safe place to talk or do magic. "Angel is not good; Mick is not any better than Angel. If I don't stop this, will lose them both."

Raymond had also made a cup of coffee. "Angel was able to put a bubble around Mick. Something had block their magic. Angela been by my sister's side, she told me that there was something in the hot tub water. It had block there powers, the two of them used up their energy. They didn't have much left after the endurance competition. Without magic you have a piece of it. Mick and Angel have strong magic it flows through the body. Somehow the cross and rose were blocked.

What they have now is just energy, the competition took most of the energy. Their magic is the power that comes from the magic rose. Somehow the cross and rose were blocked. Angel's magic couldn't join her energy with Mick. She had to save him without his help. Mick was using his energy to fight the men off. Right now, Mick is waiting for Angel to come to him. She can't. Somehow her memory of their dream world has been blocked. She scared and couldn't hear Mick. I need your help, Bill and Brandon. I must help Angel get to Mick in the dream world. She's weak and too scared to find Mick, keep me anchored here. I'm going to try to help her find Mick."

Brandon wanted to know who messed with their memory. "Raymond Angela said that there was a spell place in the hot tub.

With the cross and rose blocked, if they were the ones to take away their names it would mess with their spell.

He thought about that. "Brandon that makes a lot of sense. The two of them have strong magic, no one has that much magic. Only Thomas and Eleanor have the same magic. The spell that the two of them had done to each other. If they think too long on that subject, their memory starts over.

After they know more, he would have to tell is brother. "Your right, remember Angel made a double of Mick. It would make sense if Mick were the one to take the spell, and have hypnosis done to him. I wish I knew what spell they put into the hot tub."

Raymond was worried about them. "I must get to my sister and take her to the dream world. Mick always goes to the side were the sun was. She been calling for Mick, the only one who can help them is me. I need you two to keep my body safe. We know evil is in both schools."

Bill knew he was right about that. "I want you to know that the four of us been giving the cross and rose on a lot of the students. Angel had freed one of the students. He was Misty's gofer; the boy was so happy to be free from her."

*　　*　　*

Bill had some magic; if trouble comes there way. Brandon's magic is stronger than mine. The two men could do what Raymond asked him. Raymond had to prepare the room; he sat in a chair.

Then Bill waved his hand. "Sleep my friend, save the ones we love."

In the dream world Raymond called upon the magic of Garret. *"Grandfather, I need your help. Angel and Mick are too weak to call upon their magic. She's scared and doesn't know where to go to find Mick.*

Her energy is very low; she has a very high fever. Mick's energy is also low; I must get her to him. When there together they can heal each other."

He saw a bright light from the heavens. *"Raymond, you know the place. It can only be with the magic roses is. Not the roses here in Scotland. Go to your sister and call for her spirit. Pick her up and take her to Mick. Show her the way there, where she needs to go. Once together they will know what they need to do."*

Raymond knew what he had to do. Angel can't go to Mick because she has no memory of the place. Standing next to his sister he placed a hand on Angel's forehead. *"Sis, hear me. I need to give your memory back to you. You will remember the place where we grew up as children. You will have everything you need. One thing you will not have. If someone asks you who you are. All you will be able to say is Angel. You will remember me as your brother. Sorry about this part, you and I cannot say brother or sister to each other out loud. We can only say it in our minds. When you dream, Mick and you can be together in the dream world.*

He waved his hand and everything he said was done. *"It's time sis to bring you to Mick."*

Raymond placed his hands under her shoulders and legs. He picked her up and pulled her to him. Angel was a strong young woman.

Seeing her and feeling his sister's body this weak scared him. *"Angel, you must tell me where to go. I know how hard this will be to talk to me."*

She opened her eyes and smiled at her brother. Raymond felt a little pulled from his energy. Not much because he was her brother and not her mate. *"Do you feel better sis?"*

She was so happy to see her brother. *"I can tell you to go to America, then to Vermont. We lived on the land of the MacGregors. Take me to the waterfall, where the magic roses are."*

Raymond waved his hand, and they were at the waterfall. He could see Mick laying on the large rock. Angel then said. *"Mick must of swim in the black of the night and climb to the top."*

It was hard to see the ones he loves, this way it pulled at his heart. *"Mick it's Raymond, I have Angel with me. Can you stand by yourself?"*

He had a feeling he used all his energy to get to the rock. *"Angel is here, I'm too weak I can't stand by myself."*

Raymond knew he had to do it the hard way. He placed Angel on her feet. Then he waved his hand to pick Mick up and keep Angel standing. He called his grandfather. *"Grandfather, Angel needs to become twenty-one, Mick needs to become twenty-three. This must be done now, please grandfather we can't lose them."*

Raymond stood holding them up with his magic. This time when Angel turned twenty-one, he got to see what she would look like. Now that she was stronger Angel left her arms and called for her mate to be twenty-three. A golden light came down to his sister, it filled her body with heavenly light. With her arms out stretch she sent the light to filled Mick's body. The two of them turned to Raymond and the golden light filled him. He never felled this much power flowing through him.

A voice came from the heavens. *"Grandson, you have more magic then before. A piece of it went go to Bill."*

Raymond waited until his grandfather said more. What he did was showed him that Bill gave Angela his cross and rose, magic went to her. She could do the things Bill could do now. There will be trouble coming their way. Raymond didn't understand why they wanted Mick dead. One thing was clear; Bill and Angela were on campus but evil still got to them.

All they can do is do their best. *"I understand Grandfather. When Marcos comes to earth his name will be Marcuse. He plans the attack with Mick. Angel can see what Marcuse is doing in her dreams. If he goes after Mick and keeps Angel busy. Angel won't see Marcuse trying to take down our fathers.'*

"*That is right Grandson, that's why he is sending people after Mick. The stakes are too high. Marcuse is trying to find ways to make people who are weak to do his bidding. Not only he has to bring Angel and Mick to his master. He must bring a lot of souls this time around. Angel can see what Marcuse is doing when she is with Mick. The two of them can stop him each time.*"

Raymond looked to his sister. She was beautiful and had only eyes for Mick. He wondered how many times Marcos has come after them. Then he heard. "*He tried to kill Mick while he slept. It was the night their fathers were also fighting in the dream world. Demons where attacking both Mick and their fathers. Also, that night Angel became Mick's mate.*"

He had given his sister the Magic Fairy Rose that night. "*Mick, can you come over here?*'

He felt so much better, he stretched his arms and shoulders. "*I'll be right there Raymond.*"

Mick dove into the water and swam to the other side. When he got to shore Angel ran into Mick's arms. He wrapped his arms around her and kissed her deeply. Raymond watched them. The two of them were glowing with bright light. From a toddler on. Mick fought demons for Angel.

Angel would put her life in danger and many more times to save him. He didn't say anything to them of what his grandfather had shown him. He knew they would have to do it again. These powers will help Bill and Angela. If we do not keep Angel and Mick safe. It will mean the end of the Magic Fairy Rose, and the MacGregors family. Raymond felt he was missing something…, but what could it be.

*   *   *

Then Angel cried out. *"Raymond daddy is in trouble. Marcos knew I would see what he was up to. He could only block one thing at a time from me."*

Raymond had a bad feeling, the reason the two of them were hurt was to keep Angel from finding out about their father and James. *"What are you talking about my love."*

The three of them felt the danger, it wasn't them but their father's. Part of the dream was in darkness. There should have been two dreams. Marcos blocked the dream of daddy and James. There walking into a trap. They will be killed along with their men. In the building there is four Americans. The helicopter just set down, there moving out. *"Damn it! That is what I was missing. When he goes after Mick. Marcuse also goes after our fathers every time. This is what grandfather mint."*

Raymond was trying to think were they were going. *"How much time do we have?"*

Angel tried to see in her mind. *"Wherever they are, they just touch down. The buildings are all in cement. There is sand everywhere. Raymond the building that there going into. When they open the door, it will blow up. Marcuse will not be in that building. He's inside a mountain in another town; Raymond their guide is in on it."*

Angel and Mick looked at Raymond. They hoped that there was enough time left. *"Damn that Marcuse. Join hands we three will be like an antenna for Angel. Sis, you are going to have to tell dad what is going on."*

They held hands and thought of Joseph. *"Daddy stops…, you must hear me you're in danger. The building you're going to go in, is a trap."*

Joseph put up his hand to stop his men. *"Angel is that you."*

She had let out the breath she was holding. *"Hello daddy, I called you because you're in danger."*

Angel felt her father was going to brush her off. *"I can't talk now; I'm on a mission. Talk to me later."*

This had upset her. *"Damn its daddy, I know you're on a mission. Stop right there, don't you dare move. You and your men are in danger. You must listen to me. I never call just to talk, do I?"*

Joseph thought his daughter swore, that's not like her. "Go head and tell me what is going on."

Angel had waved her hand. Then the three of them could see what Joseph and James were doing. The waterfall became a TV with its own antenna. *"Daddy you never question my dreams before."*

James came over to him, he wanted to know what was going on. Then Mick called his father. *"Dad standdown Marcuse set a trap for all of you."*

Mick then waved his hand so the three of them could talk to their father. Raymond then spoke. *"Dad there are three of us here in the dream world. Mick and Raymond are here also."*

Then James heard what Raymond was talking about. *"You're in the dream world, what the hell happen? It's not night there yet why is Raymond there with you? That's yours and Mick's dream world not Raymond's."*

Angel was getting upset with her father. *"Really daddy that is all you can say. No bells are going off in your mind. The words danger is not worrying you.*

James then hit Joseph in the arm, he touched his ear for him to listen. *"You have my attention what's going on. What do you see?"*

Angel took a breath. *"What I saw was Tim opening the door. That building had blown up, taken all of you with it. The four American's are inside the building. Marcuse is in a small town; there is a tunnel leading to that mountain. Your guide is one of Marcuse's men, he has the detonator to a bomb in his pocket. You will die one way or another; dad we have a plan to let us handle this."*

Josephs wanted to know why he was in his sister's dream world. *"Dad before you ask me why I'm here. You two better come home when this is done. You can call but it's a long story."*

Josephs had a thought Marcuse went after the kids like the last time. *"Understood, do you three have a plan."*

Raymond was pleased with Mick coming up with that idea. *"That is affirmative, we're going to start a devil sandstorm. Once the storm is over the building. Mick will get the American's out. Angel and I will keep the storm over that building. When the American's are safe. I will grab the guide and slam him into the door. This should set off the bombs inside the house along with his bomb. Where do you want the American's?"*

Raymond watched his sister and Mick the two was looking in building to place the American's. *"Mick is there any way you can scope out the area for us?"*

He was changing the channels to look inside the building. Then they saw were to put the American's. *"Sir we found a place; it's the fifth building down looks to be empty. I will place them there. Tell your guide you will take your men and circled around to the back. The guide knows there are bombs on the back door also. We're going to start the devil sandstorm."*

James had moved his men out. Their guide didn't seem worried about anything. Once James was cleared, Joseph made sure his men was out of arms-way. Raymond, Mick, and Angel took their hands one on top of the other. With the other hand they made a circle.

They started the storm, one of Joseph men saw a twister and pulled back were there was more cover. Angel shouted. *"Mick you're up, get those four people out."*

Mick use the waterfall to see were the four men where at. Not wasting any time, he grabbed the Americans and place them in the fifth building.

The three watch the sandstorm. They knew when the American's were safe. *"Dad the American's are out, you can move in. Don't bring them back this way."*

Joseph and James were pleased with the three of them. *"Well done you three, you saved us once again."*

One more thing to do was take out Marcuse's man. The three were happy to help their father. anytime. Angel spoke. *"You're up Raymond."*

He made it look as if the guide was sucked up into the twister. There was a big explosion. The whole building went straight up into the sky. The twister took the building away from the other buildings. *"Dad it's done, the Americans are safe. James has them, come home after you get done. Bring James with you. There is trouble at Mick and Angel schools."*

Raymond didn't like Marcuse going after his sister and Mick. He knew when their fathers were coming after him. Marcuse put up a smoke screen so Angel can't see what he is up to. *"All right be there as soon as we can. Will done you three."*

Before he left, his grandfather told him. You have magic that is as strong as Mick and Angel. This way you can't change what they have done. *"Mick I must go, the two of you did grate. I can't have Angel and you, unable to find each other."*

He thought about what he said. How can we stop Marcuse from trying to kill our father's, Mick, and Angel. First take care of the two love birds. Then talk with the family to see what we can do.

Raymond touch Mick's and Angel's forehead. *"From now on, you two will know each other always. If something happens to your memory. You will always have each other in the dream world. No one can change this; I give everything back to you. However, you will not be able to say your full name. You can't tell anyone where the family is from or sign your name on paper. You will be only Mick and Angel. They cannot get your name from you even with a machine. I have done what I could for you two. The two of you have memories all the way back to when you were little. Take care of each other. You only have now to enjoy each other. For hard times will be coming are way again."*

*   *   *

After he left Mick and Angel. Raymond had to stay in the spirit world. Here is where the safe zone must be. Any work that is done to any love once or people he cares about. Raymond had to do it in the spirit world. Grandfather Garret just told him how to do it. Raymond wrote everyone's name down on a magical paper. He even signed his own name. Then he made the bowl out of magic. Tearing the paper at each of the names. He dropped it into the bowl. When that was done. He added one magic fairy rose petals for every person. Then he took a piece of Angel and Mick's hair. He made a cross with their hair. The cross had to be dip in holy water. This was to bine them to Tom and Ellen. Raymond places a drop of his blood to make the spell strong. On another piece of magical paper. He wrote the spell. Then folded the paper and placed another drop of his blood. It was time to light everything in the magic bowl. With his magic he called for white fire. When it was over it had brought Raymond back to his body.

*   *   *

The two men looked at him. *"Raymond how did it go?"*

Raymond got up and stretched. "Mick and Angel are safe, could you get me some water?"

His mouth was dry; the two men went and check on Mick and Angel. "Here I just got word that Mick is out of danger. Before I brought you the water, I checked on Angel. The nurse said she is doing well."

Raymond had drinks the water down. "That's good."

He put down the glass. "Why were you gone so long?"

Raymond thought about it. "Do you remember the time when Marcuse tried to kill Mick in his sleep. At the same time, he sends men to my father, James, and Angela. You had no idea that they needed you in the dream world. Somehow, we must have a way to let us know when they are going after Marcuse. I have a feeling he could care less about Mick and Angel. Marcuse's father is the one that wants them.

Angela came into the waiting room. She looked around, she had just missed what they were talking about. The doctor came right behind her. "I don't know how they did it, but Mick is out of danger. He didn't lose any blood; there was no blood in his kidneys. There was a lot of bruising on his body, but no blood clots. His bones are fine, and he has no damaged blood vessels in his legs. I have no clue on that subject, once he can sit up and walk to the bathroom, I'll let him go home.

"Now for Angel, she had acute dehydration. She was very lucky that her kidneys didn't shut down on her. Whatever happened she used a lot of her body fluids. Somehow her body kept the fluids that we gave her this last time. There is no blood in her kidneys. If Angel doesn't have any more fevers and she has stopped burning up the fluid. She can also go home, the two must rest and keep them home from school for one week. I want to see them for a week from today,

I have heard that the two are in all the competition. At the end of the month the two of them can do the competition."

The small group thanked him. When he was gone Raymond told Bill and Angela to hold hands. "I give Bill and Angela more of their powers. I was told that you will be needing this magic. I'm going to talk with the officer, I'm asking him to let me know when they are going after Marcuse. Angel should have had two dreams. One of Mick and one of our fathers, I don't know if we will catch when Marcuse goes after them again.

*　　*　　*

The two of them were in the Highland's, Mick and Angel couldn't do any running. They could walk two miles. All classes were put on hold for a week. They had to find out what happen to the three young men.

That Saturday everyone was at the MacGregor's ranch. Mick and Angel were on the pull-out couch bed watching TV. When the news came on, the reporter talked about the rescue of the four Americans by the Navy Seals. He reported they were all safe, the only casualty was their guide. He was killed when a devil sandstorm appeared. The man was sucked up into the sandstorm, it was taken away before the building blown up. The reporter commented if the Americans, were in that building it would have been a trap. They were found five buildings down.

Everyone knew what happened, it was disclose to everyone. When Angel went into Micks arms, she saw the other dream that Marcuse had hidden from her.

Raymond went over to the two on the couch bed. I'm glad the three of us were able to save them all. The two of you have good ideas, how about taking a nap before we eat. That took a lot out of the two of you, make sure you can go to the dream world. After supper you can lay in the hammock and watch the stars.

Angel was in Micks arms laying in the hammock. "Mick how much longer will we have to go on like this? I was able to stop are fathers this time."

Mick felt the same way. "You're here with me, will do what we can. I will love you as much as we can. Right now, we will take one day at a time. Until the next time we must fight. One day our fathers will send him back to hell. We have school do get through. I'm looking forward to doing the competition with you, it will be fun teaching again.

*   *   *

A week from Friday Mick and Angel went back to the school's hospital. They had to see the doctor who took care of them. He had to sign off that they could go back to school. "Hello Mick, Angel, I'll see you after. Your color is much better Mick, how's the pain."

He was setting on the examining table. "It's much better, mostly I'm sore. I've been listening to my body; I can't lift to much weight yet. Running I can't do full out, jogging is not bad. My five miles is now down to two. Then I walk, the bruising is getting better, it's not that angry looking."

The doctor then asked him about his kidneys, have you had any trouble going or any blood. "No to both. I've been drinking water a lot more."

He checked his heart and blood pressure then had him pee in a cup. "Mick you look good so far, I like you to come back in a week. I want to make sure there are no blood clots showing up. By the end of this month, you should be ready for anything. Did you use any of those pills I gave you."

Mick told him only one. "They made me take one when I was at home. I didn't like the way it made me feel. If the pain was too bad, I took Tylenol, it helped. I didn't need that much just the first week then off and on."

The doctor signed the papers to go back to school. "Keep doing what you been doing. If anything comes up come back to me. If your kidneys stay clear for the next two weeks you will be good after that."

Mick had to ask about how he felt. "Sir will I stop looking over my shoulders?"

The doctor looked at him. "Mick that will take time you can talk to a psychologist if you like."

Mick shook his head no. "No not at this time, I'll see how it goes."

Then it was Angel's turn, the nurse gave her a cup to pee in. When Mick came out Angel went in. "Hello Angel, how are you doing. Any pain or blood when you pee? Do you have any trouble going?"

She smiled and shook her head no. "I've been staying out of the heat. If I run it's at sundown, I've drink more water. I have a bottle of water with me. I find I must take it easy for a while. Mick and I don't have to do the competition; we had done it the day before those men went after Mick. The two of us must get are teammates ready for their run. This was the first time I felt like that. Sir will that happen again."

The doctor checked her heart and listened to her breathing. "Your lungs sound good, no blood in your kidneys, they are clear. Come back at the same time Mick does. I don't want you to push yourself. If your kidneys stay clear for the rest of the month. You should be good from there out.

Bill had check out no dizziness of headache the doctor asked. "I feel find sir. Then your clear to go." Afterwards Bill drove them back to school.

*   *   *

It was lunch time, Mick and Angel were at the lunchroom near the activity side. Bill had come through the teacher's entrance. When he saw Hawkeye, they hadn't told Mick about Erica yet.

Angel felt fear and anger within Mick. She did know if he was going to run or fight, something had to be done. She waved her hand, and everyone was frozen in place. "Mick, are you going to help me."

At the time there were ten people in the lunchroom. "I'll take the boys, and you can take the girls. Thank you, Angel. I hate to say it, but I've never felt that scared before. This way we will know who was evil."

Then Angel had an idea. "When we go to give them the cross and rose. We will do just what we did here. When there frozen in place if we give them the cross and rose, they will have a glow around their face. Mick Cal has the glow; we had gotten him before school started.

Bill had gotten the cook and his helpers. "Mick, don't worry Misty is gone."

After the last person was done Angel unfroze them. The two of them were setting back down. "How do you feel now?"

He looked at Hawkeye and Erica. "You've been right how I been feeling. I'm not week but they got to me. Now I've been looking over my shoulder a lot. Hawkeye and Erica look more relaxed; you always know how I feel. Once all the two schools are done. Evil will have a hard time getting into the school."

Bill and Angela went into the teacher's lunchroom. When Cal had his arm around Erica's waist. She looked scared to meet Mick and Angel. Hawkeyes came over to the table. "Mick, I know that you went through a lot with Misty. Erica was born after me, Misty is the youngest. Didn't Cal tell you about her?"

Mick nodded his head. "Hello Erica, it's good to meet you. Are you and Cal going for the competition?"

Erica smiled, she felt as if she was lighter then air itself. Mick saw everyone glowing, Hawkeye and Sunshine had a big smile on their face. "That's why we are here, to ask if the four of us could try out for the competition."

Hawkeyes saw that Mick wasn't as nervous, the first time he saw him this morning when he came back to school. "You can try out; the best will be taken. Are the four of you going to dance this year?"

Hawkeye smiled. "That's why we're here, to also get some food. How are you doing, you two?"

Mick closed his eyes and took a deep breath. "Erica and I are in the same boat, wondering if Misty had set more traps for us."

That got a big smile from Erica. "That's just how I feel, right now I feel calm. I saw you two on the TV dancing together, then the competition was on. How will it go this year?"

*　　*　　*

Angel smiled at them. "Go get your food and set with us. Mick, the ones for the endurance competition, I think everyone should go through a physical. It took a lot out of us; I want everyone not to have that trouble. I think we should have horses first, then the bicycles, then the track. We can make the run four miles then they walk one mile, then they can also do the swimming part. That way more of the kids can take part in the competition. How about teams of four, there will be eight in all.

"I have the idea that all the classes will have a chance to dance. Mick, you, and I will have to talk to both principles. I think that way we can have competition in their own grades."

Angel had gotten a notebook out and wrote down everything she came up with. "How about letting the grades have their own sign-up sheet. They must dance for us. If we can get enough, we then can pair them up. I like to have four groups."

Them Mick thought about one thing. "What if a higher grade wanted to dance with a lower grade what then."

She thought about it. "Okay, we will have the girls compete against each other. The same with the boys, we will see how many would like to dance. I think everything we come up with, we will have the book write it down."

*   *   *

After the four got food, they came back to the table. "Mick, I'm sorry for what my sister tried to do to you. I hope you don't think I'm evil like her."

Then Angel took it out of Mick's hands. "Hello everyone, I'm Angel. Mick and I have remembered that we know each other. Don't ask who we are, that part we don't remember. Names and where we live, we don't know. What we do know is we've dance with each other for a long time. I had gotten Mick to dance with me. I showed him all the things I had learn. One thing led to another; ballet helped him in karate. The two of us are very close."

Mick took her hand. "Angel, I think that is enough about us."

Cal had looked at the two of them. "Angel I've heard that you had a dream that Mick was in trouble. You went to the principal's office saying that. I know he was hurt badly, because of what I have seen on his body. One of the guards said what they were using he should have been dead. Something was put around him they thought it was magic."

Erica was watching Angel's eyes. "Then she said enough Cal. If there was magic, would you like to find out if she does. What if both have it? I know about magic my sister had it in her eyes. Misty could get some of the young men to do things for her. It's time to tell things about my sister. The three of us used to be very close. I know about her powers; it only works on the week. Our first year here. The two of us would fight, I always had some boys around me. I tried to get my sister to take care of herself. She acted more of a boy then a girl. Misty never fixed herself up, the next year I saw her talking to this older boy. I didn't get to hear what he told her; all I knew after that day she was different.

"Misty called one of the boys over to her, when he came over. She had asked him to see what was in her eye. After that, the young man would do anything for her.

"One day she tried the same thing with our brother, it made Hawkeye mad. He told her if she tried that again, he would kick her ass. I'm in my third year here, just before school started. We were at the park, the three of us were letting the dogs run around. You see I saw my sister talking to this man with the red eyes.

"I had a bad feeling about him; I got closer to them. He had told Misty if you want to keep your powers. There is a young man called Mick, he's coming to your school. Get him under your power, you have one year to do so. At the end of the year, if he is not under your power kill him. Misty thought that she had power over me, it didn't work on me or our brother.

"She has no willpower to be part of anything. She would do what the kids say, she is weak and easy to control. Misty thinks she is a big deal; now that she has powers. But in the past, people picked on her. We were sent here because of that day in the park. I knew she had made a deal with a demon. I saw him disappear; Misty could make people do bad things. When her eyes went red, it hypnotizes that person. Then she can tell them what to do. They would do anything she told them. Mick, you must have a strong will. When you started telling her what to do, she lost it. My friend told me that she was losing it in dancing. Misty knew her hair was too long and thick. She believed that she could do anything with her powers. When she got hurt, she said it was you that did it. One of the guys had told Hawkeye that you made her fall. This is how the story got to Hawkeye; he then heard it also from Misty. It was not until Cal talked to him. Cal asked the teacher, who saw the two of you trying to dance. She said, "Mick didn't do anything to Misty. It was her own hair that got her hurt."

Hawkeye told the rest of the story. "There is a story going around the two schools. The story was told that our father who had these bad things done."

Angel looked at Hawkeye and she was upset. "Like putting devices on a horse's hoofs and shocking him to act up. Because Misty wanted him to be put down. I know all about that, the guy said that her father would pay him."

Hawkeye wince then went on with the story. "That is what I'm talking about. It was blamed on our father. To tell the truth, he's our uncle not our father. Our father is also a twin; he is a Navy Seal. Who is now missing in action? On top of that, our uncle went missing the day Misty sent those guys after you.

"The day of the fair you went right pass our sister. Mick, she had a weapon on her that day. When you went over to Angel, she went crazy.

"Now the day of the race. Someone saw her go into the pool area, sometime before you two got there. After everything was done, some of the kids heard yelling. Then they said Mick was outside, and Angel was still inside. Now, if it is true that you two have powers. We want to know what happened to our sister. We know she went back into the pool area. Some of the kids said they heard screaming; two guards came in and dove into the pool. They tried to pull her up, the guards said there were hands that were keeping them from grabbing her. The same kids said they didn't see you until a long time afterward. None saw you go into Micks arms. What we don't understand a short wig and a suit to make a person fat. The girl that came out had long straight hair. She looked like Misty, but prettier."

Angel looked at the two of them. "You're not going to like what I tell you. This is how it went; I told Mick that I would handle Misty. Anything he did she could turn it around on him. Yes, I have magic, but you won't be able to tell anyone. No one could hear us; I had sent Mick out. I stayed in the shower too long. I had place a cross on the back of her head. She was scared not of me but of them. She tried to get me under her control; it didn't work on me. I told her to stop before I had to do something. She didn't stop so I put up a mirror, Misty screamed when she saw herself. Then she said their going to kill me. I saw a woman that came out of her. That woman had hanged on to her, she was backing her up. She screamed again, two more demons came, and man handle her into the pool. After the first demon I pulled the bubble around me. I saw the guard's dove into the pool. The teacher she was talking to the principal. The guards came up and said we can't grab her; there are other hands pushing our hands away. She had to be dead to come back up, when the body had come up it wasn't her. But her short hair was gone, even her clothes had gone off her. The woman had long black hair and had a small waist. Your sister was dead for some time. Then she came back and is now in a coma."

Then Mick looked at Hawkeyes. "What do you want from us Hawk?"

Cal spoke softly. "You believe that wasn't their sister. If you two have powers, we know you're not evil. Us four believe that Misty did something to the two of you. Something she done almost got you two killed."

Sunshine then spoke up. "Angel my mother she dabbles is spells; I was out of the house with Hawkeyes. My mom told me Misty as for a spell to put in water. The spell was to block anyone from using magic of any kind. The four of us saw the skills that you two have. We feel different inside. Please tell us what happen that day with Misty."

Mick was holding Angel's hand. Under the table Angel put a bubble around them, no one could hear them or see them. Then she put up a spell that they couldn't speak about what they were going to tell them. Then Mick spoke. "I got out of the shower first; I knew evil was around my cross went hot. Yes, we can tell when evil comes around us. Put it this way on all your chest there is a cross and rose. This will tell you if evil is around, it will go hot on you. On that day I knew Misty was at the pool. I went out there to confront her, my plan was to back her into the pool. Misty was screaming at me; her eyes went red trying to get me under her power. It didn't work, she knew it wouldn't work. She must have set it up that morning with the three boys. Those boys went to hell, they disappeared, they had demons inside them. Misty needed souls she was short two."

Then Angel took over the story. "I was enjoying the hot water. When I heard yelling, I got out quickly. I yelled at Mick and told him enough and sent him out the back door. Misty didn't like that she came around to me. She told me I had no right to send her partner away from her. I chuckled. I told her Mick was never her partner. Mick been my partner for a long time. She didn't like that at all. She came over to me. Then turned on her red eyes, I had it with her. That's when I put up a mirror in front of my face. What she saw was the evil in her, she started to scream. I had sent the cross and rose to the back of her head. She was backing up for a minute when I saw the demon come out of her. But that demon hung on to her then two more demons appeared, and they pushed her into the pool. I found myself in a bubble, I could see what was going on. Then two guard's doves into the pool, and the teacher came out. She told the guards she feared Misty. It took them a long time to get her out. Two days I've been scared, what I saw and felt with Mick. That spell your mother made worked. From being week from that race and not having my powers to help Mick. I use my energy. I kept that bubble around him until I was almost as bad as Mick. I thank they took her to see Satan himself. If she comes back, she will have a new body and more powers. There is something about Mick and me, evil seems to want us. There have been may times evil has come after us. Mick and I are soulmates.

Erica's wanted to be friends with Angel and Mick. "I don't want you to hate us. When Misty received her powers, she turned on me. I tried to help her, the style she came up with. Her and I went around about how she was taking care of herself. She stops washing her hair and body. Sunshine and I decided to get her into the shower. We had brought clean clothing for her. We strip her and wash her all over. She didn't know who had done that to her. That demon told her; she had three boys coming after me. They almost rape me; Hawkeye had me watched. He had found out what Misty was up to. My brother and Cal my boyfriend, they saved me from getting raped. Momma had taken me out of this school now that Misty is gone. I'm able to come back to college. Misty goes after simple mines. Our mines are stronger then hers, Misty couldn't get any girls under her powers. As far as we know of. Her powers are weak; she can only go after simple mines like hers."

Sunshine had something else to tell them. "Angel, we saw the two of you dance; the freshman told us all about the way you teach. You gave them even the history about ballet."

Hawkeyes wanted Mick also to know how everyone feels about him. "Mick you did grate with all of us guys. The weightlifting helps us to pick up the girls. To lift are sister that was unbelievable, but you did it. You brought in rules for ballet, the two of you always help everyone."

Then Erica's add something else. "Angel, you try to help Misty, one of the girls said she scream their going to kill me. If you were here last year, she wouldn't gone evil. You were right to get Mick out of there. Fighting with a girl, a boy would get into big trouble. Two girls don't get into trouble as bad. Angel you're quite a woman to be in college. You're two years younger them Mick, am I right?"

She smiled at them. "When Mick was back home, he was going to be in the second year of college. I had to work hard to get through High school. I had to prove that I could do college. I have some college credits; that I had done back home.

"I have ideas for the two activities; we will have to go through both principles first. Mick and I can't do much yet. At the end of this month if everything goes right, we can dance again.

*　　*　　*

It was the end of the endurance competition. There two schools took over half of the awards. All their hard work paid off. The next competition will start next month. The two schools didn't want to wait. They were working with a big group of all the grades. That went on while the other competition was taking place. Mick and Angel were the only ones that could go the hole way. The two principles had talked with the other school. They told the school that the children's endurance wasn't about to do all of it. Everyone at the other school tries to top Mick and Angel. They couldn't come up with anyone to top them.

*　　*　　*

Now it was time to put on a ballet show. It was going to be a love story not like Romeo and Juliet.

Mick wanted to show a different love story.

Angel has been working with the girls they have broken it down in grades. The same with Mick, he had broken it down to grades. There was a big turnout for both schools. After all the grades were done and they had the best for the love story. Now it was time to come up with the story.

On Monday, the two groups will be dancing at the activity building. There top girls were Erica, Marianne, and Sunshine with Angel. They wanted to get here before the boys did. With there backpack the girls jogged to the activity building. Something was up, the girls were nervous. Angel was hoping the run would help them, it didn't. Why would they be nervous? Angel knew why. The others will judge the boys on their story line. The girls had to react to what the boys said and did.

All the girls had their hair in a braid. They thought that they would get here before the boys.

When they got closer to the building. Angel knew they were being watched. "Girls the boys took the bus."

But the building wasn't lit up. Angel told the girls to go get their showers. At the steps she looked up at the second-floor window. *"Mick you and the guys cheated, you took the bus no fair."*

In the window stood four young men watching them, they had all the rooms dark. When Angel looked toward the window. Three of them jumped back. "Mick how did Angel know you are here?" Randy asked Mick if he told Angel they were going to be here first. Cal told him that she would always know were Mick was. "What the hell! Mick you said she couldn't see us. I don't understand."

Mick gave a little laugh. He knew Angel would have known they were up here. She always knew where he was. Just as he knew she was jogging to the building with her girls.

Something wasn't right, he thought. "What was bothering him? We worked with all of them in the competition. Why is this any different, ballet dances you can tell a story of love. This will be the first time he tells Angel his love story in front of everyone. Last year was a bust for him, Angel had heard him. *"Mick go to the bathroom so you can fuck me, we both need this honey."*

He had gone quickly to the bathroom stall. Then he felt his heat go inside her, it had to be a quickie; just to take off the edge. The two of them felt better, he came out at the same time Angel did. "Angel, have I told you I love you."

She smiled and put her hand in the back of his neck. She had brought him down for a kiss. She could feel there was more to this. "Mick did the doctor tell you something?"

He closed his eyes; it wasn't his health. It was his legs and arms could he be able to lift Angel. She heard him thinking of what was bothering him. "You don't trust your body, have you been babying yourself. I should have known this, go get your ballet slippers on. I want you to go in that room and warm up."

*　　*　　*

Angel went over to the next room. "I have a big favor to ask of you all. Marianne, you have been dancing the longest beside me. I want you to oversee everyone for a little while. Something came up, I must check on something before we started. You can work on the guys' love story, okay."

The girls knew something was wrong, this wasn't like Angel. Cal spoke. "

I know what's up, Mick hasn't been himself. He used to go down and lift weights, he's scared of that hallway. He won't go down without someone there. Angel is making him work it out with her."

She walked into the room and closed the door behind her. With a wave of her hand, a good size padded mat appeared in the middle of the room. She did some of her warmups, then told Mick to get on the mat. "We are going to start out, as if you were trying to become my dance partner. I don't like hospitals, maybe this is going too far. I hope not, I want to dance with you."

He shook his head, he felt like a little boy. Quickly she went over to him. "Stop this, it wasn't your fault, Mick you were attacked. Shake it off and let's make sure you're all right. We are going to do this in steps. First step sees how high you can lift me."

The small group went into the observation room. They watched to see what the two of them were doing. He thought he shook but was able to pick her up and put her down. "I will run to you and jump into your arms. Mick don't think just do it, we done this many times before."

That was the second step, he did just what she said. She had no doubts he could do it. Angel gave him a kiss; the third step. She was to him and jumped into his arms and them he put her on his shoulders. The fourth step she jumps down into his arms. The fifth step, I will go to you, and my body will turn a bit, you will lift my whole body onto your shoulder. I will be on my stomach when it's done.

Then she told him to put on his music. "This is your dry run, to make sure you can dance the way you had plan."

With a wave of her hand the mat was gone. She walked over to the window and drank some of her water. It happened so fast, she felt a strong pull from her energy. Angel's hands started to shake, quickly she placed her bottle on the windowsill. She had to grab the sill to steady herself, with her eyes closed she took deep breaths. She knew Mick was joining with her energy, this way the two could use it between them. Each time they did this, their energy was getting stronger. Will there be a time when this won't overwhelm her body? Angel knew their group was watching them.

She felt the energy slowly increasing. For a moment it overpowered her, she shook a little more. Then she heard music, slowly she opened her eyes. Angel still held the windowsill with one hand. There in the middle of the floor stood Mick. She noticed he was more confident; he stood tall, his body was masculine. Is this the first time she really looked over his body?

He wore a tank top with yellow around the neck. He looked hot in his tights of a darker blue. Mick smiled when their eyes met.

All she could say was *"Mick, do you have something really big planned?"*

He gave her a little nod and started his routine. Angel heard the tempo getting stronger. She could see the power he poured into his dance. Mick leaped higher into the air. His legs and arms were apart in front of him in a V shape. As he turned, he landed with a step and with down on one knee. His arms one in front and the other in the back. The next part was a turn, turn then a leap with his arms and legs behind him. A turn in the air and landing, with a step then down on one knee. His arms were one in back and the other in front. Then Mick did a high leap and spins landing with his feet in a V repeatedly. When the music stopped. Angel watched what Mick would do next. Slowly the tempo of the music softened. This time Mick walked closer to her. The two of them were a few steps away from each other. There before her he stood tall in front of her, he felt whole again.

*   *   *

Mick looked at the woman he loves. "I need to tell you a story about a woman called Angel. For one year he was without her. The two of us have gone through a lot. As far back to the time she was born. At seven months I could hear my lover in her mother's womb. We talked to each other; evil didn't want her born. This young woman is younger then I, her body don't show it. Even her mind is much older. Here I stand looking at a beautiful woman, so many times she would give her life for me. As I would give my life for her.

*   *   *

I hear the music playing, what's happening to me. Strong energy poured through me, as my legs started to dance as a ballerina noble. I can jump higher; as I leap into the air and go farther. My spins are longer, could this be magic? Could this be love that gives me this power? Now I see a sunbeam that came from the heavens. There was a bright light, out of this light came a beautiful woman. Her silhouette was of an hourglass.

Beautiful angel, have you come down to earth to dance with me? Your hair is of sunshine, a golden-brown. Your eyes are the color of the ocean, a sea blue. A man could drown in them and be happy doing so. Your lips are the shape of a heart, they are of a rosy red. Let me steal a kiss to taste your lips of honey. Angel of mine, without you I'm lost. Your wings are the color of a light blue; did you fly down to the earth to dance with this humble man. Angel let us open the window, spread your wings so we can fly to the heavens. Let's dance on the clouds together, please beautiful Angel. Let me dance with you so I could have a taste of heaven."

Mick came closer to her, with her arms up to her side she walked on her toes. He followed her, his arms on her waist when she dropped. He brought her back up then ran his hand over her straight arms. Then with his arms crossed and his hands under her arms he brought her over his back. The two danced together then she went on her toes he spins her. He put his hands on her waist and picked her up over his head. Her legs up in the air his arms were straight with her over his head. She brought her leg straight as he brought her back down. On her toe the other leg brought to her straight leg. Mick spun her a few times, then she danced around to his back, he went down to one knee as she bent over his shoulder. Mick lift her up with her legs straight, she came down then tip toe around him.

As the music went to the next song. Angel did a high leap; her legs were straight in a line. Her head and back were bowed with her arms behind. When she landed, she was on tiptoes and her arms in front of her. Angel walked around Mick on her tiptoes. *"Mick get down on one knee, I'm going to lay over your shoulder when I do pick me up."*

He did what she asked then he stood. Angel turned around on his shoulder. She slid down his body. As she led her head on his shoulder. Angel pushed herself up then touched his face. He had remembered these moves. She was going to do some spins in his arms.

On her tiptoes she did a spin in Mick's arms. She swung her leg out then brought it back to her knee, repeatedly. Her arms were close in front of her as she spun. Angel then dances around Mick on her tiptoes. The last part. The two of them moved as one. Angel ran and leaped into his arms. She was in a sitting position. Mick through her up into the air as she turned. Her arms were on his shoulders. As her legs went into a straight line. Mick held her with one arm, the other arm straight out. Then he turns her to her back. He brought her down. Angel's legs were in a straight line as her arms.

*　　*　　*

This year a lot had happen Marcuse almost won. There were four young students was killed. They found out Marcuse father, Satan wanted their souls. Each time he goes after us, he also goes after their father's group. Raymond had saved Angel and Mick. When she ran to Mick that's when she saw what Marcuse was up to. The three of them took down evil once again.

The competition had change for all the schools. Mick stories that he came up with, was chosen for their love story in the ballet play. They got top awards in ballet; at the other school they would like the two that came up with teaching everyone in large groups.

Angel and Mick were given the teacher award. The other school had asked if two of their students could go and learn Mick and Angel's ways. This way no one would get hurt.

Another year had come, and Mick had two years left. Angel had three years left. See what will happen next.

The End